More ~~praise for Legacy of Kings~~

"Sexy and full of secret plans, *Legacy of Kings* has a lot of elements coming together to make an unputdownable story with many memorable characters. Written for teens, the book will cross over to adults as well. This could easily be the next big saga."
—Jackie Blem, bookseller, Tattered Cover Book Store

"With its intriguing blend of history, political intrigue and mystery, *Legacy of Kings* reminds me of *Outlander*. I can't wait to find out what happens next."
—Anne Allin, bookseller, Lake Forest Book Store

"An intricately woven tale of magic, romance, and deception, *Legacy of Kings* has something for every reader. Once you start it, you won't be able to put it down. Fantasy fans will truly adore this one."
—*Katie's Book Blog*

"*Legacy of Kings* is a stunning, imaginative and spellbinding saga that will send readers back to a time of magic and myth, prophecy and fate, bloodshed and brutality, dishonesty and deceit. It is a tale that will capture readers' interest from the start, will ensnare them as the story unfolds, and won't let go until the very end."
—*Fiktshun* blog

"*Legacy of Kings* is a complex and highly original novel that transports the reader back in time to a beautifully imagined era wrought with action, romance, and realistic characters. It will enchant the reader from the very start and have them begging for more."
—*A Dream Within a Dream* blog

"Action and fantasy lovers will gobble it up."
—*School Library Journal*

"Steeped in sorcery and historical detail."
—*Publishers Weekly*

**Books by Eleanor Herman
available from Harlequin TEEN**

Blood of Gods and Royals series

(in reading order)

Voice of Gods (ebook novella)
Legacy of Kings
Empire of Dust

ELEANOR HERMAN

LEGACY OF KINGS

HARLEQUIN®TEEN

Recycling programs
for this product may
not exist in your area.

ISBN-13: 978-0-373-21193-7

Legacy of Kings

Copyright © 2015 by Paper Lantern Lit LLC and Eleanor Herman

Printed in U.S.A.

To Rachel Dyment, whose brilliance, bravery, and good looks will, as with Alexander himself, propel her to conquer the world.

ACT ONE:

INNOCENCE AND GUILE
340 BC

Excellence is never an accident...
Choice, not chance, determines your destiny.

—Aristotle

CHAPTER ONE

KATERINA RACES ACROSS THE MEADOW, SCAN-ning for any roots or rocks in her way. Her heart thumps wildly in her chest. Her legs ache. The gazelle leaps slightly ahead of her, its hooves barely touching the grass. It is a blur of tan and white, with long, black-ringed horns; a creature not fully of the earth, but also of the sky.

Ahead of them, the forest looms, and far beyond it, she knows, lie all the villages and woods between Erissa and the capital. A sudden breeze rushes through her tangled brown hair. Her lungs burn. Instinctively she knows the gazelle does not fear her; it is challenging her. She can feel its heartbeat, its heat, its *aliveness* radiating in her own chest. It *wants* her to catch up with it.

When Kat was a child, her mother always told her to keep her special understanding of animals' thoughts and feelings a secret—such knowledge was dangerous. But that was before...

Into her mind flows the image of her mother's shining blue eyes, her cream-colored veil slipping from her golden-brown hair. She hears her voice: low, throaty, with just the trace of a Carian accent. Kat is flooded, momentarily, by a sweet, familiar comfort. But then she feels the harsh pang in her throat that always follows, as her memories dissolve into echoing screams.

Kat stumbles and the gazelle leaps ahead, kicking out front and hind legs at the same time. Raw, visceral rage consumes her, forces her to run faster, through a copse of razor-edged grass that rips and shreds her bare legs.

The sun is sliding down toward the horizon. The gazelle casts a brief glance back at her with enormous, moist brown eyes. *It's time. It's time, it's time, it's time.*

The gazelle dashes into the tree line at the edge of the meadow. Kat surges forward, just inches behind the creature now, focused on the horns, perfectly straight like unlit torches beckoning her, even as the animal darts through the trees. As deftly as possible, Kat follows, dodging branches and ducking beneath low-hanging limbs.

In the next few strides she will be able to touch—

She slams into something hard.

Reeling backward toward the ground, she sees blue sky and green branches overhead, grass and mud and blue sky again, and then…blackness. Kat realizes that her left cheek is on the ground. She opens her eyes, and they focus slowly.

"Kat!" It's Jacob's voice. "Are you all right? I'm so sorry. I thought you saw me."

Slowly she sits up, rubbing her head, her breath coming in jagged gasps. A pair of strong, tanned legs stands before her, leading up to the broad, commanding form of her oldest friend. The boy Kat has known longer and better, it sometimes seems, than she has known herself. A boy who, until recently, was equal parts playmate and pest. Now, he has grown taller and handsomer and somehow resists falling into either category the way he used to.

Kat cranes to look around him and can no longer see the gazelle's graceful form. She's lost it.

"Here," Jacob says, offering her a hand.

Kat can't get her breath enough to speak, and her head is still spinning, but she grabs his hand and allows him to pull her to her feet.

Jacob raises an eyebrow, making his broad, tan face look a little goofy. "You're a mess," he points out unhelpfully. "And you've cut your legs, Kat." He shakes his head at her like she's a wayward pony who keeps breaking out of its pen.

She brushes herself off, scoffing. "I'm fine, Jacob. At least, I *was* fine until you got in my way."

"I can't believe you were after that gazelle on *foot*. You're crazy." He shakes his head.

"You're clumsy," she throws back.

He smiles. "That's me."

She can't help but laugh a little, shoving him out of her way. "Well, now that you've ruined my fun, the least you can do is carry my supplies home. Come on," she says, taking the game bag with knives and nets off her back and tossing it at him.

He catches the bag against his chest. "Holy gods, what's in here?"

She shrugs. "Only some trapping gear."

"Kat, hang on a minute. You can't go back like…like that."

She turns to stare at him, still unable to fully take in the *new* Jacob, the Jacob who has existed for several months now, maybe longer—the Jacob who is more than just a hilarious partner in crime…whose broad, muscled shoulders, and lop-sided grin keep causing her pulse to stutter just slightly.

"Like *what*?" she demands, knowing full well she probably looks like a living tumbleweed that's just been dragged across the countryside by a strong wind.

He rolls his eyes. "At least wash off in the pond before we head back for dinner. It's kind of…important."

She cocks her head at him, wondering what he's hiding—she can always tell when he's got a secret. When it's clear he's not going to say anything further, she sighs and follows him to the wide, deep pond at the west end of the meadow, where, she knows, wolves and foxes venture out of the woods at dusk to lap its clean water. On the hottest nights of the summer she has even seen a bear and its baby bathing and floating, two dark lumps that could've been fat fallen tree trunks but for the bubbles drifting from their mouths.

She takes off her leather shoes and belt and sinks into the cool water in just her tunic, all the way up to her waist. Her breath is coming more slowly now; her head has stopped spiraling. She closes her eyes and sighs.

Then she hears a rippling sound. It's Jacob wading in beside her.

"Come on. Why were you after that gazelle?" he asks, laughter in his voice. "I could tell you weren't planning to kill it."

"I was *racing* it, not chasing." She sinks under the water completely, feeling her hair float around her in the murky silence. Though he knows almost every little detail about Kat—the way she likes her goose meat prepared just on the brink of completely charred, the way she nibbles her thumb when she's worried and disappears into the fields when she's sad—this is one thing he doesn't know about, wouldn't understand. This feeling deep in her chest, this *perception* that others don't share. The way the animals whisper to her in their strange language of hunger and need and drive. Their focus. Their wisdom.

And sometimes, their warnings.

She surfaces, takes a deep breath of air, and rubs the water out of her eyes. "For the first time ever, I was going to catch up. And you ruined it." She splashes water at him.

Jacob turns his head away too late, then begins laughing. He charges back at her with an even bigger splash. She screams, then runs toward the grassy edge of the pond, feeling the water's resistance over her tired legs. He follows her, splashing her back as hard as he can. She turns to splash him again and he stops abruptly, his mouth falling open in surprise.

"What? Scared?" she says, before realizing his gaze is directed not at her face but her body. Kat looks down and gasps. Her unbleached tunic is soaking wet...and perfectly transparent. He can see, well, almost *everything*. Feeling heat rise into her cheeks, she quickly covers herself with her arms.

Moving through the heavy, waist-high water, he reaches her and places his hands on her shoulders, even as she starts to back away. His look is so intense, so full of feeling, Kat suddenly can't move.

His chest rises and falls as though he's having trouble breathing. "Kat, I want to tell you... I—" He closes his mouth, clearly unable to say whatever it is he's holding in.

Kat can't remember the last time she and Jacob didn't know what to say to each other. The way he's looking at her now, with his hair dripping pond water down his big, strong, square face and shoulders, it's like they are two strangers.

His lips part again, and she feels her whole body start to shiver just slightly.

And then he is leaning in, so close she can smell the familiar, earthy scent of clay dust in his hair, so close his lips touch hers. Suddenly, he pulls her strongly toward him and her arms drop away from her wet tunic, grabbing his back as he kisses her, his tongue softly parting her mouth.

The kiss is slow and hesitant at first, and then, when she doesn't pull away, it grows deeper, and Kat finds herself clinging to him. She can feel his hard strong body against her wet clothes, sending tingles all across her skin.

How could this be happening? her mind is screaming. Jacob is like her brother—no, not brother. Foster brother. Son of Cleon the potter and Sotiria, the people who'd raised her since she was six after…after…

Her thoughts melt into feelings so strong they overpower her. He is kissing her eyes, her neck, pressing himself tightly against her wet tunic—

"Jacob! Kat!"

They separate so quickly that Kat falls into the water with a hard splash. When she stands, arms crossed over her chest again, she sees Calas, Jacob's little brother, running toward them.

"There you are!" Cal pushes his curls out of his eyes. "Mother wants you both to come home *now* and help with dinner. It's rabbit stew!"

Rabbit stew? That's Jacob's favorite. Now she *knows* something is up.

She and Jacob slosh out of the pond and wring the water from their tunics and hair. From her sack she grabs a spare cloth she usually uses for wrapping game and throws it around her shoulders. They sit on the grass to lace their shoes and put on their belts. Then they start following Calas, who is running and skipping ahead, beating the tall grass with a stick.

The silence between them is thick. Kat still can't completely comprehend what just happened. Jacob's hands. His smell. His lips… It's all an unreal dream, and yet she knows it *was* real. And something, some small voice deep inside her, knows that it has been coming for a long time, even if in the moment it felt like a shock.

But what does it mean? Will everything be different now? She shakes her head, unable to process it, trying to focus instead on what the mysterious dinner could be about. "So? What am I missing? Why the celebration?"

Jacob shakes his head. "It's…well…unexpected," he says slowly, and for the second time that day Kat knows he's hiding something important from her.

"Did Cleon get a big contract?"

"No," Jacob says, smiling sheepishly.

"If you don't tell me right now what it is, I'll—" She raises a playful, faux-threatening hand.

He grabs her wrist. "You'll what?" he whispers.

Suddenly, she's embarrassed, and turns away.

They keep walking. Finally, it seems the silence is too much for Jacob, too.

"I wanted to wait to tell you," he begins. "Doros and Kyknos came from a meeting of the village elders, and believe it or not, *I* was chosen to be Erissa's contestant in the tournament. I'm going to be in the tournament," he repeats, as though he can hardly believe it.

Kat stops dead in her tracks. The Blood Tournament. The name conjures up images of knives flashing, throats slashed, arms and legs hacked off, eyes gouged out. "They chose *you*?"

"You don't have to act quite so surprised." For a second, he looks wounded. He clears his throat. "I'm going to do it. I leave tomorrow."

"You can't go," she says quickly. "They'll kill you. You're only seventeen. Some of the contestants are Olympic athletes, professional wrestlers, and soldiers. Think about Bendis!" When their village had sent Bendis to the tournament four years ago, he never returned. "He was twenty-five," she presses on, "and bigger than you, and—"

"I've trained with the village militia," Jacob cuts in.

Kat can't help but roll her eyes. "With rusty swords and bent arrows. That training is a joke." *You'll get killed.* She can't shake the horrible thought from her head, but she can't say it, either. *I can't lose you, too.*

Jacob plucks a piece of leaf from her wet hair and sighs. "Kat. I'm no good as a potter. It's like Father says—I'm all thumbs. Even Cal can throw a better pot than I can. I need to find my own future, away from here. In case you haven't noticed, I'm a man now, and I need to do something with my life." The words come out hard, determined—it's a side to him she doesn't always see. "It's a great honor," he says, lower now. "The best contestants in the Blood Tournament are chosen to join the king's elite guard, the Hypaspists."

"So you'll leave us," she says. It's the simple truth. Someone may as well say it. Even if her throat aches as she does. "You won't come back."

He runs the back of his hand over her cheek, startling her. "I'll come back," he says softly, "once I have something to offer. Something to offer...you." She can see his tan face blushing. "Just, don't...don't do anything in my absence."

They've stopped walking again; Cal runs down a dirt road ahead of them.

Something to offer you. She knows what he means, suddenly and seriously, and it's as though she's been plunged backward into the pond all over again.

The kiss—everything that happened between them only moments ago—it shocked her. Amazed her. She had no idea something like that could happen, with *him*. She had no idea how much she had wanted it before. She couldn't believe how good it felt, and right. But still, what he's saying now...

It's so much more than that, isn't it? He wants her. Wants to be with her, and have her, only. Not as a sister or friend. As a wife.

And even though her body is still vibrating from his touches, and even though she's tempted to pull him off the side of the road and kiss him again, the idea of *wife* stops her, freezes her. She wants him. She didn't know it before, but it's so clear now.

But she's not ready. She still has something—something terrible and desperate and secret—that she must do. Deep within her, inside her bones and in her blood, she knows she won't ever be happy otherwise.

She swallows. "I won't…do anything in your absence," she says. Because at least that part is true. The village boys who flirt with her mean nothing to her. "But I can't— I don't—" She stops, at a loss for words.

But he obviously hears her hesitation, sees the stricken look in her eyes, because a wave of pain washes over his face. He takes a step back. "Of course. I understand."

Then he turns and strides briskly away from her.

"You don't," she calls after him, but he doesn't turn around. How can she tell him she needs to finish the unfinished? He would say she was crazy, risking her life for the impossible. He would try to stop her, would ruin everything.

Miserably she trudges behind him, passing the young olive trees Cleon and Sotiria planted when she joined the family, a future dowry for a new daughter, then the goat pen, where Hecuba and Aphrodite, brown milk goats, stand staring at them, mouths working diligently on leaves, tails snapping against flies. She could swear Hecuba shakes her head as she bends down for a bite of grass. It's almost as though the animal can sense what Kat has done, sense her mistake. Kat huffs. She can't take the silent judgment of anyone right now—not even a goat.

Jacob swings open the tall wooden gate to the courtyard and stops in his tracks so suddenly that Kat bumps into him.

"If I don't make it out of the arena alive," he says out of nowhere, "I want you to know… I've always loved you. Even when I was six—and how old were you, five?—and we were just rolling marbles behind her loom."

Kat sucks in a breath. She loved to sit behind her mother's loom, watching her delicate hands weave the weft between the long lengths of warp yarn, then batten each new thread tightly down against the others.

But now she feels mute, lost, staring into those bright eyes she has grown to know so well. She wants to tell him she loves him, too, but the words are stopped in her throat. Instead, she removes the long iron pin from her shoulder. At its center is the stone Jacob found two years ago near a stream, smooth and flat and oblong, a gold-flecked olive-green. She remembers the day he found it, his joy at its perfection carved by thousands of years of icy spring water tumbling down mountains and gurgling though forests. He held it up awestruck, as if it were a gleaming gift from the gods. Then he had Phineas the blacksmith make it into a cloak brooch and gave it to her.

She holds it between them. "Take it. To protect you in the games."

She places it in his palm, avoiding his gaze. His hand feels strong and warm, and something stirs inside of her, mouthwatering, like the smell of plums simmering and leaking their juices over a fire.

Jacob. *Her* Jacob.

They go in through the front door and are surrounded by greetings called out over the comforting clatter of pots and pans. The room smells like new bread and simmering rabbit stew. The oil lamps have been lit, giving the small space a cozy glow of gold and brown. Tonight, Kat notices, the altar at the side of the room is piled high with offerings: an *oenochoe* of wine, a garland of flowers, and a jar of honeyed figs.

Her stomach hardens. These are prayers to keep Jacob alive.

Kat is silent during dinner. Afterward, when the family takes turns reading aloud from tattered old scrolls of Homer's works, she goes to the courtyard to draw water from the well to wash the dishes. Night is falling, and the world is quiet except for the squeak of the lever as she hauls up the heavy wooden bucket, and the soft murmuring of the wind.

And then, through the darkness, she feels someone staring at her.

She looks up.

There, waiting just outside the gate, is the gazelle.

Now, its glossy eyes say. *Now*.

She looks up at the blazing half-moon rising above the distant trees and shivers from head to toe. Laertes, the village stargazer, has said that in two weeks' time, when the moon is full, there will be a total eclipse, ending the thousand-year cycle of the Age of Gods and ushering in a new age. It's a time when magic—good and evil—enters the world as if through a door. It seems to Kat as if all of nature—including herself—has a kind of quivering expectancy, a heightened awareness in preparation for the event. Perhaps it is starting already with this gazelle.

She unhooks the sloshing bucket from the rope and places it on the side of the well. Quickly she opens the gate and emerges on the lane. The gazelle waits for her and then, nodding slightly, takes off.

Now. Now.

The two of them fly down the lane through the pewter air, and this time the race seems effortless. Kat isn't competing with the gazelle; she is one with it, part of it. They are not separate entities but one entity in two bodies. She feels no pain, no ragged breathing, just an exquisite lightness and exultation as her feet barely touch the road.

Her stride matches the gazelle's, and together they stream into the gathering night. She wants to keep running forever across meadows and mountains, through forests and valleys, over oceans, even, their feet lightly glancing off the water's glassy surface as the sun rises and sets and rises again. She reaches out to touch the gazelle, feeling for a moment its thick bristly hide. With a grunt of satisfaction, it veers off to the right, into the meadow and toward a band of trees, and the magic goes with it. Kat comes to an awkward, staggering halt and watches the creature disappear.

She bends at the waist, then, hands on her knees, to catch her breath. She is aware of her rapidly beating heart, a crushing cramp in her side, a throbbing pain in her knee. Her legs ache intolerably, and she can hardly imagine having run so hard and so fast only moments ago—it was as though her mind had briefly left her body.

But now it's back, and suddenly she is worried again about Jacob, about the impossible thing she needs to do if she ever hopes to have him. And she does want him. More than anything. But how can she say she'll be his wife? When she can't say for sure that *she'll* survive the task she has both dreaded and dreamed of for years?

She limps back toward the house. A lone kestrel floats past her, borne by the breeze—just a blot in the darkness—back to its home in the branches. She knows that even in its sleep, it dreams of prey, of flesh.

It is cutthroat.

Vengeful.

The rising evening wind blows her hair into her eyes and wraps it around her neck like a scarf. Like the beautiful, diaphanous scarf she still keeps, the remnant of her real mother.

Still looking up at the sky, watching the kestrel disappear into the darkness, she tastes the old, acrid flavor of anger and longing, and realizes exactly what she must do. *Now.*

Now.

CHAPTER TWO

HE IS NOTHING BUT SWEAT AND HEAT AND movement. Sand sprays into his eyes as Hephaestion throws him to the ground, but he catches himself, grit digging into his palms. Alexander quickly flips himself upright. Sitting on bales of hay, their friends Telekles and Phrixos cheer loudly.

As the two boys circle each other in the round, sandy training pit, Alex watches Heph closely, the tightening of his jaw, the set of his shoulders, the slight tilt of his stance. Beyond him is a blur of painted canvas targets for spear-throwing and archery. Heart pounding, Alex takes a few steps toward his right, but now the sun is in his eyes, glinting off the pile of heavy, sweaty armor the boys use for weapons training and long-distance runs. Squinting, he circles back, noticing the tension in Heph's arm, watching for any sudden shift of his position.

Alex and Heph charge at each other head-on. Heph quickly gets the advantage, throwing his arms around Alex's back and squeezing tightly. Then he jerks left, right, trying to throw Alex off balance. Heph, more than anyone, knows Alex's weak spot, his left leg. For years now, Alex has trained his left leg more than his right, hopping on it until it screamed in pain, tying training weights to it and walking for miles.

Alex instinctively dodges to the right and instantly curses himself, realizing this is exactly what Heph wanted. As Heph tosses him onto the sand, he bites his tongue and the coppery taste of blood fills his mouth. *Too fast*, he chides himself. *I react too fast.* Weakness, he has learned, isn't in the leg or arm or back. Weakness is in the mind.

But if Alex is too hasty in a fight, he knows Heph's weakness, too...

Heph grins, obviously basking in his triumph. His dark eyes—almost as black as his thick, wavy hair—are half-closed like a pleased cat who has just caught a mouse.

There it is: Hephaestion's greatest fault. Pride. It almost got him killed last summer when they joined King Philip's campaign against marauding Molossian cattle thieves. Heph, riding out in gilded armor on a fine white horse, assumed that barefoot, filthy men with matted beards couldn't be dangerous. He took on three of them, who almost skewered him alive. Alex had to rescue him.

In a single fluid motion, Alex leaps up, grabs Heph's head, and pulls him into a headlock. They struggle, and Heph finally manages to slip out of his grasp.

"Come on, ladies," growls Diodotus, his crooked nose casting an uneven shadow on his scarred face. "The king wants me to train you in wrestling, not dancing." His hairy shoulders bulge out of his leather breastplate, making him look more like a mountain bear than a grizzled old soldier.

Telekles jumps up and spins while he calls out, "Heph, you'll shame us all in the arena. Stop twirling!"

Phrixos claps a large hand on Telekles's shoulder and yanks him back down.

His face a mask of determination, Heph grips Alex's shoulders. But then he hesitates. "There's a messen—"

Alex takes advantage of Heph's momentary distraction to twist suddenly, throwing all his weight into the move. His arm locks on Heph's left elbow; he wraps his free arm around Heph's opposite shoulder, then lifts him off the ground and swings him in a semicircle, dropping him face forward on the ground. Then he leaps onto his friend's back and pins him there to the loud guffaws of their friends.

"You win," says a voice muffled by sand.

Alex smiles. He slides off Heph, who pushes himself up to sitting position, wipes the sand off his face, and points behind Alex. "I was trying to tell you there's a messenger," he says, spitting a wad of sand and saliva, clearly annoyed by his defeat.

Alex turns, swiping his tousled blond hair out of his eyes— he's got to get it cut—and sees a page boy of about fourteen staring at him, wearing a look of repulsion. No, not staring at *him*, staring at the scar on his left leg—the long purple mark that has wound around Alexander's thigh like a snake since birth. He feels the familiar prickling heat of embarrassment spread over his chest, flooding his face, burning the back of his neck. He yanks down the bottom of his tunic which had become caught up in his belt in the fight. Still coursing with adrenaline, he has half an urge to pummel the boy's narrow face.

But before he can even reprimand him, Alex catches the messenger's eyes—and then all sounds are silenced; all surrounding light and colors fade.

It's happening again. That stirring. That knowing. That power he can't control.

Suddenly he is disembodied, frozen in place, traveling through a tunnel of white light, pulled forward by an unseen force. It's like he has left his body completely. At the other end of the white tunnel, a small room emerges—it's somewhere in the palace. He sees a fire pit and smells the smoke wafting up through a hole in the ceiling. A woman is stirring a pot. The boy's mother. Of course. The father must have died recently—Alex can tell from the sorrowful bend of the woman's body and the wrinkles in her brow.

A baby coos in a cradle: the boy's little sister.

And then, Alex is jolted back from the dark room, returning with violent wrenching speed to the present. He finds himself back in his body with the usual unbearable ringing in his ears. The page boy is watching him strangely.

Alex looks around at Heph, at Diodotus, at handsome Telekles and round-faced Phrixos, at the sunbaked tiled roofs of the outbuildings, as if he has never seen them before. Everything seems small, dark and brittle—an elaborate illusion.

He rubs his forehead, frustrated, then raises his eyes, one dark brown, one gray-blue—the startling combination always serves to make people uncomfortable—and stares hard at the page. "What do you want?" When the boy doesn't immediately respond, he repeats: "What. Are. You. Here. For?"

In a high-pitched voice, the boy says, "A thousand apologies, sir. Your father wishes to speak to you immediately."

Alex nods. "Come on, Heph." His anger has evaporated and with it, his energy. He is suddenly exhausted.

Telekles and Phrixos spring into the pit, eager for a bout. Telekles, who models himself after the Trojan War hero Achilles, keeps his blond hair unfashionably long and his body perfectly sculpted. He dances and wheels around his opponents, confusing them. Phrixos is heavier, stronger, and slower. Usually Alex would stay to watch this amusing match between opponents that remind him of a mongoose attacking an ox, but he needs to hear what his father has to say to him.

On the side of the wrestling pit, Heph picks up his silver

cuff and snaps it around his wrist. He puts his torque of twisted silver carefully around his neck, while Alexander tries to repress his impatience.

As Alex and Heph leave the training ground, they pass the stables, chicken coops, and goat pens. They skirt the barracks, a plain two-story wooden structure with small windows where the palace guards sleep. Black smoke is rising from the smith's forge next door, where the smith is loudly hammering armaments into shape. They walk up a winding staircase, and down the narrow, dimly lit corridors in the service wing, emerging on the ramparts overlooking Macedon, Philip's kingdom—the kingdom that will one day belong to Alex—where they pause, leaning on a low wall.

The sandy town of Pella is spread out at the feet of the palace, a grid of straight roads broken by temple plazas. Thick ramparts and bristling towers encircle the town in a stony embrace. The gray walls, coral roofs, and olive-brown landscape used to be all the world that Alex knew, but now the view seems dry and crumbling compared to the lush grottoes and lakes of Mieza.

Mieza's Temple of Nymphs, where Aristotle trained Alex and Heph in matters of logic and strategy for the past three years, was so different—the landscape there a rich, almost glowing green, the sky deep with purples and blues. About two dozen privileged thirteen-to-sixteen-year-old boys—including Phrixos and Telekles—spent their mornings there learning and their afternoons wrestling, riding and hunting. In the evenings they held lively discussions of poetry, philosophy, and history.

Then two weeks ago, shortly after Alexander's sixteenth birthday, came the messenger from King Philip commanding Alex to return home. Then, as now, demanding that Alex run like a child when the king snapped his fingers.

Down on the street, a man driving an empty cart is cursing bitterly, trying to back up his donkey and cart to make way for another vehicle. *That's how it is*, Alex thinks. Someone always has to give in.

But not for long.

He has other plans, plans his father doesn't know about. And if he succeeds, he'll be the greatest leader this world has ever known.

When Alex reaches his father's office, the guards lower their spears and stand aside, their faces hidden by red-crested helmets with long nose and cheek plates. He knocks.

"Father," he says to the door, "you wanted to see me."

"Come!" thunders a deep voice. Slowly, Alex pushes the door open and enters. Heph stays outside until he hears, "Bring that coxcomb of a friend of yours, if you wish!"

Alex senses rather than sees Heph slip into the room and take his place at Alex's side but a bit behind him. Out of the corner of his eye, Alex notices Heph straightening his tunic and adjusting his belt. Alex smiles inwardly at his friend's fastidiousness. Just knowing that Heph is beside him gives Alex the strength to face his father.

The room is nothing like the rest of the royal apartments, most of them decorated by his mother. There are no tasseled, silken cushions here, no chubby cupids and pretty maidens on frescoed walls, none of the gauzy curtains Queen Olympias prefers blowing in the breeze, no delicate ebony chairs inlaid with ivory and mother-of-pearl.

King Philip's office is as close to a military camp as it can possibly be. He has a cot with a coarse blanket where he usually sleeps. There are a few crude stools and folding camp chairs and tables. War trophies—swords, axes, spears, and bloody flags—hang from unpainted walls.

Wearing an old blue tunic and a scarred leather belt, Philip stands looking down at a table covered with papers as one of his advisors, Euphranor, a small man with a gray beard, stands nearby to read him the words he cannot read himself. Though the letter in front of Philip is upside down to Alex, even from a distance of several feet he can make out the large heading: *From the Aesarian High Lord Mordecai to King Philip II of Macedon, warm greetings. We ride tomorrow to Pella for the games and further discussions on that urgent matter which we hope...*

Alex wrenches his gaze away from the letter as he feels the king's single eye—a glowing, reddish-brown—fix on him. Long ago, before Alex was born, Philip lost the other one on the point of an enemy sword.

A Cyclops, Alex thinks. He looks just like the one-eyed creatures with unnatural strength and brutish intelligence who all disappeared long ago, as so many strange beings had: the flying horses, the women with snakes for hair, the sprites of springs and forests, the bare-breasted sirens who combed their long golden hair on rocks and sang sailors to their death. Olympias insists that Philip wear a black silk eye patch when he is in public, but when he is alone he pushes it off impatiently. Now the empty socket and the lumpy scar that runs through his eyebrow like a lightning bolt are visible.

Philip sits down heavily in a leather folding chair and bangs his favorite mug on the table. It was once the skull of the enemy who speared Philip's eye. A year after the incident, the king went back, killed the man, cut off his head, boiled the skin off, scooped the brains out, and had the sawn-off skull silver-plated. Amethysts glow darkly from the eye sockets.

A young male slave jumps forward with a pitcher of wine and pours it into the skull. The king drinks greedily, slams the mug down again, and wipes his graying beard with the back of his hand. "Though it has been well over a decade since the

Aesarian Lords have visited Pella, they are growing in power. I've invited them here for a demonstration of their might. This is our opportunity to show that we refuse to cower to their arrogant threats and fearmongering about magic." Here, the king snorts in disgust. "Shortly thereafter, I leave with my army to Byzantium. The oligarchs are not keeping the terms of our alliance. They're flirting with Persia. They can't have it both ways. In my absence, you are my regent."

From the corner of his eye, Alex sees Heph nod. This is what they were expecting when the summons came to return from Mieza.

Alex nods. "As you wish."

"It *is* as I wish. But don't worry." Philip waves his large hand as if he's swatting a gnat. "My council will be in control as they always are when I'm at war. The people will feel safe with my son on the throne. But, Alexander," he says, fixing his eye on his son, "don't disappoint me."

Alex feels the irritation rising despite his best efforts to remain calm. It's exactly as he feared. No responsibility. An empty honor. A joke. It's worse than having no honor at all. He completed his three years' training at the academy with the highest praise from his teachers—who were notoriously unbiased, even when it came to the king's son. And yet his father is still treating him like a child. While Philip is off once again botching alliances and having his way with mistresses, Alex will be a puppet on a throne. In that position there isn't anything he *could* do to disappoint his father.

It's because of his weak leg, it has to be. It's one thing for an accomplished soldier to bear scars, and another for a young man, still green when it comes to battle, to have such a blatant imperfection. He's worked so hard to hide it, most people in Macedon don't even know about it. Philip must be worried that people will discover his heir is a cripple, and everyone knows physical deformity is a punishment sent by angry gods. No one wants a regent—or, heaven forbid, a king—despised by the immortals.

He opens his mouth to object but suddenly his mother sweeps into the room on a wave of perfume and rustling purple silks. Alex sees that her slender feet are encased in amethyst-studded sandals of silver leather shaped like meandering snakes.

"My son would never fail at anything," she says sweetly, "although some of the king's *other* children might." Olympias barely tolerates the many children of palace maidservants, cooks, and laundresses who bear a striking resemblance to King Philip.

Philip's philandering always baffled Alexander, given Olympias's beauty. With her silver-blond hair, wide emerald eyes, and perfect white teeth, he understands why his father married her, the dowerless daughter of the shabby king of rocky Epirus. How old must she be now? Thirty-six? Most women that age have run to fat and wrinkles, lost teeth and have gray streaks in their hair.

Reaching up—it seems to Alex she has gotten shorter in his absence—Olympias runs a bejeweled hand over her son's head and says, "Did you know we are having a feast tonight to celebrate your regency? It's a great honor."

Alex is silent. An *honor*? More like an insult. He should probably walk away before he tells them what he really thinks about it.

"We're roasting two cows and three sheep," she says to Philip. "I've arranged to have the magician, the lute player, and the girl acrobats. We'll open up the best amphorae of Chian wine," she finishes.

Alex needs to get out of the room immediately. The walls seem to be closing in on him. "With your permission," he mutters, and turns to go.

"Wait!" Philip commands, and Alex reluctantly turns back around. "I have other news. I've made plans for *you*, my boy." His wide grin reveals his cracked and missing teeth.

Olympias gives her husband a look. "Not yet," she hisses. "Now's not the time."

The king cocks an eyebrow. "Are you contradicting me?"

She bats her long black lashes caked in kohl. "Please, Philip."

Philip pauses, then turns to his son. "Very well. You may go," he booms, making a dismissive movement with his hand.

Alex and Heph walk in silence down black marble hallways to their wing of the palace. Alex can't stop the powerful sense of urgency pulsing through his veins. He and Heph need to act on their plans. Now.

In the corridor outside their bedroom doors, Alex hesitates. He hates his own room, which his mother has enlarged and redecorated in his absence. His gilded bed is so high he could practically pole-vault onto it, and wide enough to sleep an entire family. He particularly hates the life-sized marble statues throughout the room, gaudily painted with pink skin and gold hair and blue robes, staring at him with unseeing eyes.

"*Your* room," he says to Heph. They enter through a small door next to Alex's large double doors. The minute Alex is inside he feels comforted by the coziness, the simplicity. Heph's room is small, with a floor of brown glazed tiles and a single square window. The walls are painted ochre; the low bed in the corner has a plump mattress stuffed with straw. The only luxury is the bronze mirror on the wall.

Heph sits down at the small olive-wood table in front of the window. "So," he says, "regent."

"It's hollow," Alex snaps, joining him at the table. "He made it clear I'll have no power. Plus, there's something worse coming, Heph. This other thing he has planned for me…"

Heph looks at Alex curiously.

"I think he's found me a wife," Alex says.

Heph bursts out laughing.

"Seriously. They are going to throw some ugly princess into my bed as part of a military alliance. And I can see my mother is already distressed at the idea of competition within the palace."

"Do you think they've picked that lady from Crete?" Heph says, trying to keep a straight face and failing.

"Ah, yes, Princess Demetria, shaped like a boulder and sporting such a lovely moustache."

Heph cracks up again. "Or Princess Thetima…"

"Of Corinth, right. The one who smells like a goat and has the worst case of acne I've ever seen." Alex can't help but start to laugh, too.

"But maybe it's *Artemisia*," Heph suggests hopefully, allowing the name to linger on his lips.

Alex recalls the tall blonde princess of Samos, the symmetry of her face, the soft curves of her body. Getting stuck with *that* wouldn't be so bad. But Alex knows what beautiful women are like—dangerous. The rivalry and jealousy with his mother alone would make palace life completely unbearable. He knows there are whole countries that go to war just so the kings and noblemen can get a break from their wives.

He clears his throat. It's funny for Heph—because it's not Heph's life they're joking about. "Whoever it is," he says, leaning forward, "I have no intention of sticking around the palace to be made a fool of, not by the phony regency and not by some ridiculous marriage. We'll go east like we discussed." Even as he says it, he knows that it's what he has to do. "But sooner than we thought. As soon as we can get everything we need for the journey. Where did you put the map?"

Heph immediately gets serious and moves to the bed, kneeling down and counting four tiles from the leg. He removes

the tile, thrusts his hand into the darkness below, and brings
out a fragile scroll, which he carefully unrolls across the table.

Together they lean over the faded brittle document drawn
on ancient animal skin. Alex reaches out a hand to touch it, remembering the first time he saw it a few months earlier, when
he and Heph were exploring a cave near Mieza. It wasn't their
first; they spent much of their free time in the foothills of the
mountains hunting and camping out. They'd found ancient
temples with fallen columns, abandoned villages covered in
vines and brush, and other caves littered with bones, broken
pottery, and charcoal hearths long cold.

This cave, however, had been different. As they'd entered,
torches held high, they saw an altar of sorts at the far end,
and above it a giant painted eye, almond-shaped, kohl-lined,
the iris shockingly blue. On top of the altar was a vase so ancient it bore no bearded warriors or lithe maidens in swirling skirts, just jagged, primitive lines of paint. It was, Alex
could tell right away, a vase from the time when the gods still
walked the earth. He had found the scroll nestled inside the
vase. Bearing it carefully back into the sunshine, he and Heph
unfurled it, frowning at the archaic language. It took some
time, but they finally deciphered it.

Now, Alex puts a finger on the ancient lettering indicat-
ing Macedon's capital, and traces the route. From Pella, they
would take a ship across the sea and land at Apasa. Then it
would be only a few days' walk inland until they reached Sardis, the beginning of the Royal Road. They'd use it until they
got to Cappadocia, where they could veer off the road and
swing up into the Eastern Mountains. His finger stops above
a faded mark: the Fountain.

Alex stares at the description: *Fountain of Youth, Well of
the Gods, providing physical healing and spiritual power to all who
drink of it.*

Heph puts his own finger down on another line of faded writing. "And there, guarding the fountain, are the Spirit Eaters, whoever they are." Heph glances at Alex. "Whatever they are."

"Heph, it's not supposed to be easy," Alex says. "It's a *quest*." Even the word is exciting. "If it was easy it wouldn't be meaningful." He nudges his friend. "Then the poets would never write songs about us."

Heph moves to the window and looks out over orange glazed roof tiles. "Who will be running Macedon if the regent has disappeared?"

"The same people who always do when Father is off mindlessly killing people: the Council of State and Leonidas, with my mother interfering as much as possible."

Heph passes a hand through his black hair, turning back to face Alex. "Two Greeks, in the middle of the Persian Empire."

"We know good conversational Persian," Alex says, thinking about all those years with tutors learning the strange barbarian language.

"With a thick accent," Heph counters. "And how will we get the money for travel? I think I've got two drachmas to my name, and I doubt you have more than twenty."

Alex feels a pang of bitterness. Of course he hasn't forgotten their lack of funds, and he resents that his friend thinks he has. How could he forget Leonidas's tightfisted ruling over the royal treasury? The old man is convinced that gold is one of the greatest corrupters of young minds, and refuses to give the prince—or any of the other young royals at court—access to the coffers.

But it's more than that—Hephaestion simply doesn't *need* this like Alex does. He doesn't need the fountain's healing waters. His body is perfect already. And he doesn't have the pressure on him that Alex has. He doesn't understand.

But still, he has a point. Money, even for the prince regent, is always a problem. "Good thing the tournament is in a few days, and we've been training the past three years."

Heph shakes his head. "You actually expect me to win the prize money?"

"You know I would do it if I could." As a prince, Alex can't fight in the Blood Tournament himself. He's supposed to be impartial, supervising the fighting from the royal balcony. "And yes, I do expect you to win. You're the best fighter I know." Alex closes his left eye and says, imitating his father's booming voice, "But, Hephaestion...*don't disappoint me.*"

Heph laughs. "I won't," he says. But his face becomes serious again as he stares at his burgundy wool cloak, which he always keeps neat and free of wrinkles, hanging from a wooden peg on the wall next to the door. Alex knows he is looking at a day long past when he fought a warrior more than twice his size, a day that cut his life in two pieces: before and after.

Alex stands up and puts a hand on Heph's shoulder. "You did what you had to then," he says quietly, "just as you will at the tournament."

CHAPTER THREE

CYNANE ARRIVES LATE TO THE FEAST, AS SHE always does, and stands in the interior doorway, her onyx eyes narrowing as she takes it all in. Flickering shadows from dozens of torches dance and leap across the walls and columns of her father's throne room. The painted figures on the walls seem to move slightly in the fire's glow: muscular, winged gods; lush, naked goddesses; and legendary beasts.

Her eyes shift to the center of the room, where a large round fire pit lies cold and dark. The night is too hot for it, and already the warmth and smoke of the torches is stifling. Servants carrying heavy platters push their way through the throng to the trestle tables in the courtyard as drunken guests, their banquet wreaths already lopsided, try to pluck off the delicacies. Theopompus, the royal minister of provisions, his blond hair gleaming with gold dust, licks the juice off fat be-jeweled fingers.

A magician in a long dark robe covered with silver crescent moons is making white doves appear and disappear. Beneath the raucous laughter and loud conversation, Cyn can faintly hear a bard's harp. But most of the guests are more concerned with the slave pouring well water into the bathtub-sized *krater* next to the fire pit and using a large wooden paddle to mix the wine. The men whistle and hoot, begging him to keep the wine strong.

She has little intention of staying. She'll make her appearance, get some wine, and hopefully return to her chamber with a soldier—preferably one who will be gone by the time the sun rises tomorrow.

For now, she approaches the *krater*, and the men crowding around it give way, sizing her up hungrily. She smiles while handing her chalice to the slave. It's a work of art she designed herself—dark gold, and engraved with ancient creatures: men with horses' bodies; winged harpies, sprung from the blood of the god Uranus; Euryale, an immortal woman with crystal eyes whose scream could kill; and Cerberus, the hound who guards the gates of Hell, his three heads each bearing ruby eyes.

Cyn's mother, Audata, used to sing lullabies of sorcerers' spells and tell Cyn bedtime stories of magical creatures that once roamed the earth. Of invisible Taulus who possessed a secret power called Smoke Blood and could melt silver with his breath, and the witch Medea who knew how to speak with plants and coax poison from their leaves. Of magic rituals and power born from betrayal. Fantastical stories meant for gullible children. But Audata whispered that such magic still existed in the world—if you knew where to look for it.

And maybe, Cyn thinks, such dangerous knowledge is what got her killed.

When the slave fills Cyn's goblet and hands it back, she drinks deeply. The wine is fragrant and blood-colored, and it fizzles slightly on her tongue, leaving a dark warmth in her throat. Still, it doesn't settle the tight feeling in her chest.

Tonight is Alexander's night.

As she slips through the crowd, she intentionally brushes against different men. She's not sure why she does it—to remind herself of her power over them, perhaps? Or maybe because even through the coarse cloth of her dress, it feels kind of thrilling when they touch—as if anything could happen. But suddenly a man's hand is on her hip and he is pulling her toward him—*too* close. He smells of fish oils and garlic, and he's far too old for her. Instinctively, she grabs his wrist and twists it backward. Startled, the man cries out and releases her. She slides back into the thick of the crowd before he can recover.

Instinctively, her right hand slides to her thigh, where she always keeps her dagger hidden underneath her robe. If any man ever grabs Cyn to do violence to her, she will kill him. While his hands are around her neck, or ripping off her clothes, she will not flail her arms in flapping protest the way so many women do. She will slip her dagger from its sheath and stick it straight into his stomach, twisting it upward until it finds his heart.

She will not die like her mother died. Helpless. Alone. Crying out for assistance that never came.

Touching the dagger, she breathes more deeply.

Someone collides with her, nearly knocking her over. Cyn whips around. "Watch where you're going!"

The face staring back at her is round and childlike, the mouth droops a bit on the left, and the protruding eyes don't entirely focus. It's Arrhidaeus, Philip's half-wit of a son from one of his lesser wives.

"S-sorry, sister," he mumbles. "Where's Heracles?"

His pet rat, which she can't help but find disgusting. "I think I saw him playing with the cats. Better hurry, or you'll find only a whisker." Arri blanches, and Cyn feels a spike of frustration as Arri scrambles back into the crowd. Even Arri receives more respect than she does.

A son with a weak mind is a misfortune. But even the strongest, most intelligent daughter is simply worthless.

While tonight is a celebration for everyone else, to her it's a nauseating reminder that Alexander—with his limp, his hideous scar, and bizarre eyes—will rule Macedon and its conquered territories. She will get nothing—besides, perhaps, marriage to a drunken and idiotic nobleman twice her age, followed by a lifetime of domestic servitude.

She thinks back to all her years of training: spear-throwing, archery, wrestling, weight training, riding, hand-to-hand combat. At first her stepmother tried to prevent it, claiming it was unsuitable and shameful, and no man in his right mind would ever want to marry her. But King Philip, passing a calloused hand over Cyn's disheveled dark hair, finally said, "Her mother is dead. Let her train as it is what she wants to do, and it will do no harm." It was one of the few kindnesses he had ever shown her.

Little did he know he was training her to one day grow strong enough to topple him, to conquer *all* of them.

She eyes the crowd again, looking for the right target— he must be tall, and handsome, of course. But then she spots Olympias. At just the same time, Olympias notices her. She's sitting on her throne on the dais next to Philip, but when her strange green eyes land on Cyn—eyes that could belong to one of the snakes she worships at the altar beneath her bedroom—they light up. Olympias rises slowly, slithers down the steps, and passes through the crowd as guests ebb out of her way like the tide.

Before Olympias can reach her, Cyn ducks behind the fattest man in Pella, the wealthy spice merchant Lykourgos, who rather looks like a magical creature himself, a human head perched on top of an enormous wine barrel of a body. She circles the eternally drunken Lord Claudius, who is angrily poking his thick fingers into another man's chest, and heads for the door to the courtyard. But there she is blocked by four servants carrying an entire roasted boar on a platter, cursing and maneuvering in the crowd as they angle their burden through the door.

"Cynane." Her stepmother's voice is smooth as wet silk.

Caught. Cyn straightens and turns around. The queen is smiling broadly, baring her sharp, white little teeth, with long incisors like fangs. Her hair, carefully crimped with curling tongs, floats down to the thick golden belt at her waist. Gold, emerald-eyed snakes twist around her arms. Cyn notices with some satisfaction that her towering crown is calculated to make the petite queen appear taller than she really is—which is still shorter than Cyn.

"Oh, dear. Look what you're wearing." Olympias pouts at Cyn's simple robe, the color of shadows and smoke. It is her favorite garment for three reasons: it gives her the feeling of being invisible, seeing but unseen. The slight scratch of its rough weave makes her skin tingle. And most important: her stepmother hates it.

Cyn says nothing. Silence irritates her stepmother more than anything.

She can see Olympias struggling to remain polite. Is it a trick of the firelight or have her green eyes constricted into slits?

Just then Alex calls, "Mother!" and pushes his way toward them.

"Ah, here comes my son, the *regent*," Olympias says, obviously knowing those two words—*son* and *regent*—stab Cyn just as cruelly as if they were blows from the dagger strapped to her thigh. Olympias tosses her long white-gold hair like a horse and turns around with her arms outstretched.

Hephaestion hangs back a few feet behind Alex. For the first time since he's been back at the palace, Cyn really *sees* Heph: his prominent cheekbones, his square jaw. His black hair is thick and wavy; she can picture him standing in front of a mirror with a comb and a flask of scented oil, tugging the glossy curls into just the right position. His red tunic is perfectly fitted to his frame. He wears a silver torque, wrist cuff, and ring. She's overcome by the surprising urge to find out how it would feel to touch him. He seems so stiff, so hard. Like a steed that needs a good breaking-in.

Suddenly, there's a white fluttering all around them. The magician has taken his final bow, and all of his doves are flying into his open cloak, where they disappear. He stands up again, flashing something long and bright—a spear. It's as though he has fashioned it out of the birds themselves. People clap as he waves the spear around. And then, as though caught by a spasm of evil, his eyes go wild and he lunges… straight toward Alexander.

An assassin.

Philip immediately rises from his throne, unsteady, his silver ram's-head *rhyton* falling to the marble floor with a clatter and a splatter of wine like blood. Olympias shrieks, her crown toppling over, with its pearls catching in her hair.

The crowd gasps. The music in the background stops, the last notes hanging discordantly in the air. No one moves. Except for Hephaestion. In an instant he has pushed Alex out of the way of harm, so that the magician's spear makes contact with his own chest instead.

But as the spear touches Heph, it turns into a white silk scarf.

The spectators burst out laughing and clapping. The harpist starts playing. Alex pats his friend on the back and says something that makes Heph smile. The merriment has risen to a higher decibel.

But Cyn feels rooted to her spot. Stunned. Shaken. It's not the magic trick that has distressed her. It's Heph. What he was willing to do.

He really was ready to die for Alex.

Soldiers talk of heroism all the time; poets sing about the glory of self-sacrifice. But Cynane has never actually seen a man willing to put someone else's life before his own. True loyalty—it's almost unheard of.

And it's exactly what Cyn has been looking for all these years.

Correction: it's what she has been looking to destroy.

According to Audata, her mother, most magic of the blood was inherited. It came down through generations, like eye or hair color. But not Smoke Blood. Smoke Blood was earned. It allowed a person to triumph over pain—over death, even. That power could be found. Could be *made*—with an act of great betrayal, the blood of someone turned against his child or beloved friend.

Cyn had once overheard her mother desperately sending prayers to the gods to show her an act of true betrayal so that she could become Smoke Blood. Audata seemed to need that power urgently to protect herself against some perilous threat.

The next day, Audata was dead.

While the festivities go on without her—Olympias, now distracted from her mission to make Cyn miserable, is dancing with her son—Cynane is catapulted back to being ten years old. In the two years since her mother's death, Cyn has asked everyone she could if they had ever heard of Smoke Blood, or any magic that could protect a person from death and pain. Ancient Gordias, the minister of religion. Her tutors. Her nurses and governesses. Everyone thought the lonely motherless girl was making up tales and waved her questions away as nonsense.

But Cyn sensed, deep down, that it was her destiny to fulfill her mother's wishes and discover this Smoke Blood: a power, her mother had claimed, that could stop death. A power that was truly invincible. A power that could have saved her mother's life, if she'd found a way to it soon enough.

Desperate for answers, she decided to break into the library's archives that housed scrolls about magic and myth, and which the Aesarian Lords had once tried to confiscate when she was just a baby. But Philip, prickly at anyone telling him what to do, had locked up the documents instead. Maybe— just maybe—there was information in there on Smoke Blood.

The archives were locked in a small room behind the main library reading room, where she and her tutors came to borrow scrolls on drama, history, and philosophy. Fortunately, its sole window faced a little-used palace garden. One night, Cyn propped a small ladder against the wall and, with a chisel, loosened two of the window bars, enough for her to push open the fretted shutters and slide inside. She lit an oil lamp and saw floor-to-ceiling diamond-shaped pigeonholes, with five or six crumbling scrolls thrust into each one.

She read for hours, learning of the nature of magic and how to cast powerful spells for a variety of purposes. More interestingly, she learned of something called Snake Blood, and something called Earth Blood—both rumored types of magic supposedly passed down through lineages descended from the two gods who saved the world from a great evil. But nowhere could she find the reference to Smoke Blood. When her lamp guttered and went out, she reattached the bars and slipped quietly back to her room as dawn glimmered on the horizon.

And so, although she had no guidance, she has spent the

years since then practicing spells memorized from those ancient scrolls, and searching for someone who might offer up the blood of true betrayal. If Heph, whom Alex clearly trusted completely, spilled Alex's blood, it would be the ultimate treachery.

This is her chance.

The flickering figures on the wall are smiling now, bending their heads, shaking their long, dark ringlets, beating their white wings, beckoning to Cynane. *Free us. Bring us back into the world we have forgotten in our long sleep.*

She inhales sharply, rubbing her eyes. Still they seem to move and whisper. She looks around the room. Can no one else see them?

"Lady, you dropped your goblet," says a low voice, pulling her out of her moment of breathlessness. It's a handsome, broad-shouldered warrior with an island accent of soft *r*'s and *l*'s. "It is beautiful," he says, holding the goblet high, admiring the jewel-encrusted engravings. She hadn't even heard it clatter as it fell from her hand in the fluster. "Like its owner."

She takes the chalice from him wordlessly, then begins to swim against the thick tide of people, toward the door that leads to the corridor, all thoughts of finding a male plaything forgotten. She pushes past Cassandra, Olympias's sour-faced handmaiden, and Hagnon, the parsimonious royal minister of finance, who always scowls his way through expensive festivities. She grabs a lit torch from a wall sconce and, holding it high, passes from the throne room and turns right, with each step leaving the laughter and smells of the feast farther behind.

She needs to think. She needs a plan. She needs... Hephaestion.

She crosses a rear courtyard and enters the kitchens, where she grabs a piece of raw meat from a pile about to be spitted. Then she goes down winding staircases, across more courtyards, walled gardens, and through multi-pillared arcades. Finally she reaches it: the royal menagerie.

Smelling her scent on the air long before she appears, the hellion howls a welcome.

The hellion. One of the few left on earth.

Torch held high, she takes in the animal's dark form as it stalks back and forth inside the large cage. A black panther with gleaming, silky fur, the hellion's slanted eyes glow yellow in the darkness. Black bat-like wings stretch lazily from its back as the creature hisses at her approach.

She holds the slab of meat between two bars. "Come and get it," she whispers, and the creature lunges so quickly and gracefully that it almost takes her hand off with it.

The hellion swallows the meat whole. Its forked red tongue licks away drops of blood on its chin. Then it leaps at the bars again, baring fangs. Cyn draws back with a slight inhale. The animal's claws rake against the metal, making a horrible screeching sound, before it lands back on the dirt, staring at her hungrily through the cage. It paws the earth, wanting more. Always more.

"I know," Cyn whispers softly.

The beast adjusts its featherless wings, black against the black night, before turning away with a low murmur, something between a growl and a purr, curling itself into the far corner of the cage.

Cyn stares up at the brilliant night sky and thinks about those whom the gods made into stars: Helen of Troy's twin brothers, Castor and Pollux; Orion, Heracles, and Pegasus, the winged horse who carried Zeus's thunderbolts through the heavens. If only she had the power of the gods. If only the gods hadn't given up thousands of years ago.

Then she looks back at the hellion's cage, its strong iron lock catching the moonlight. And an idea begins to form.

CHAPTER FOUR

JACOB SHIFTS THE PACK ON HIS BACK AS HE trudges down the dirt road toward Pella. Birdsong peppers the silver stillness of the fields with short piping whistles, long shrill tweets and raucous caws. As the sun crests the horizon, burning through dew and turning the world a shimmering rose-gold, the high-pitched buzz of crickets is drowned out by the throaty croaking of frogs from the surrounding marshland. Jacob stops for a moment to close his eyes and savor the sun on his face like a warm hand. But it doesn't still the anxious stirring inside him.

The problem isn't the Blood Tournament, or the very serious chance that he'll be killed in front of thousands of spectators. The problem is Kat. He hasn't seen her since she left the dinner table last night. This morning, while the rest of his family cried and embraced him and wished him luck, she was nowhere to be found.

Jacob turns back to face the road. His legs are heavy. His whole body is torn between moving forward and staying. He can't stop thinking of Kat. His sudden impulse to kiss her and the way she gave in so readily, the heat in her body responding to his. It had seemed almost impossible to resist. His body feels hot again just recalling the way she let him touch her waist, her legs, her jaw, her hair.

But then, when he'd hinted at the future, she'd turned silent and strange. He hadn't even uttered the word *marry*, but she must have understood. She had rejected him, even if she hadn't exactly said so—he could feel it in her hesitation, the twist of her lips, the way she had refused to meet his eyes. He didn't understand. She wanted him. That much was obvious. Why was she holding back?

His jaw tightens. He'll have to risk his life in the tournament without any answers. And that's a dangerous way to enter—without a strategy, with his mind more focused on Kat's rejection than on winning. It's a very good way to end up dead.

Jacob takes a shortcut through the woods, a hunter's track that will eventually spill out into the hill country near Pella and meet the main road. He thwacks away underbrush with a long stick, savoring its rough, harsh sound. *Kat. Kat. Kat.* He channels his frustration into his muscles, working hard to cut through the density of the woods.

The tournament, like Olympia's more famous games, takes place every four years. It is very different, however, from the Olympics, which consist of orderly events such as running, wrestling, and discus throwing. The Blood Tournament is a single free-for-all held in a large arena with a simulated landscape made to increase difficulty, featuring added natural challenges like quicksand or cliffs. It is hot, bloody, and chaotic, with fighting taking place all over the stadium until the crowd—and the king—approve a single victor.

Initially the king of Macedon invited contestants from twenty major cities scattered over the mainland and the islands. But two generations ago, five villages near Pella sent all their men and even some women to the capital to support the troops against brutal invaders from the north. To honor their bravery, the king allowed them to join in the tournament. However, no one from the villages has ever won; few have even survived. Most are killed or wounded in the opening moments because the professional fighters and battle-hardened warriors from the great cities consider the men from the Five Villages easy meat. For this reason, many of the villagers in Erissa have debated whether an invitation to participate in the tournament is an honor or a curse.

Jacob raises his stick to whack a sapling out of his way when he notices a hornet's nest near the top. He inhales sharply. It seems like a sign.

He needs a plan.

Hours go by as he ploughs through the forest, mulling over his options. Sweat drips down his forehead. Coolness and shadows wrap around him now, and the smells of loam and sweet decay rise to his nostrils. There are patches of forest near Erissa, bits of the enormous wood that once covered all Greece before people cut down the trees to make fields for crops. But this one sprawls for many miles in every direction, and its trees are as old as the Titans, the race of giants that ruled the earth before the gods were born. Some say the Titans still live here disguised as enormous trees, ready to reach out with twig-like fingers and devour unsuspecting travelers.

He's crushed by the unfamiliar sensation of being completely and utterly alone. His throat aches, but he wants to save his water. He should have brought a second flask.

He starts hiking again, glancing warily at the thick black trees on either side. For decades bandits have inhabited these woods, robbing and killing travelers. It hasn't happened in recent years, not since Philip became king, captured every last robber in the forest and tortured them to death gruesomely and publicly, first gouging out their left eyes to match his own. But still.

After a time, the loneliness fades into numbness, and the numbness into a prickling awareness, as though he's being watched. He stops again and could swear he feels a pair of un-blinking eyes boring into the back of his neck. A trick of the woods? Taking his knife out of its sheath, he pivots right, left.

The silence of the forest is punctured by a sharp snap some-where to his right. An animal, probably, startled by Jacob's ap-proach and running deeper into the woods. Still, he is cautious now, and veers away from the sound. Periodically he hears more cracking twigs, the rustle of leaves, a flight of fright-ened birds. Are these the normal sounds of the forest, or is there someone else in here, following him? He starts to jog, and the cracking sounds seem to keep pace.

He stops abruptly, and abruptly the sounds stop too. This proves it. Someone must be following him.

He moves forward again, faster now, more alarmed than before. The sound of rushing water taunts him through the trees. Jacob makes his way to the banks of the Astreus River, splashes some water on his sweaty skin, and fills up his flask. Here the river is narrow and deep, fiercely tumbling over jag-ged rocks. Normally he would follow the track downstream for a couple of miles or so to the sandy shallows, where he could easily cross. But Jacob has to be smart if he wants to shake off his pursuer—whoever or whatever it is.

He studies the foaming water splashing over sharp rocks. These rapids could easily shred him to pieces before tossing him downstream. He looks up. Ancient trees lean across this narrow part of the river, their enormous boughs interlacing like roof beams. He walks up and down the riverbank, search-ing for overarching limbs that look sturdy enough to hold him, and selects an oak tree, whose thick boughs intermingle with those of a white poplar leaning in from the other side. The oak must be centuries old, its huge roots like gray snakes slithering toward the water. Adjusting his backpack, he climbs up quickly from one strong branch to another and crawls out on the longest one stretching across the river.

It's easy at first. The branch is thick and strong. But as he goes farther out over the water, he feels it begin to sag with his weight. Up ahead is the thick silver-green branch of the white poplar stretching toward him, but not close enough.

He balances carefully, edging his way toward the poplar. The oak branch groans in protest, sinking farther. He curses, grabbing the outermost twigs of the poplar, pulling himself toward the thicker section. He's almost there when he hears a tremendous crack and starts to fall toward the lethal rocks below. He pitches sideways, managing, just barely, to grip the poplar bough, clinging to it in panic as the branch he was hanging from moments ago plunges into the river. To his horror, his backpack has loosened and drops into the raging water with it. He pulls himself the rest of the way across the river, hand over hand, as sweat drips into his eyes, almost blinding him. Then he swings his legs around the branch and hauls himself up.

He sits there, wiping his eyes and his brow, catching his breath, watching his pack tumble downstream in a torrent of froth and spray. Shaken, he climbs down and finds that his tunic is torn and muddied. Great. Even better, all his food was in his pack. He'll need to trap something for dinner. He checks his belt. Thank the gods he tied his fire pouch and drinking flask onto his belt, instead of stashing them in his pack. And his knife is still in its sheath.

At least, he thinks, as he starts off again, he is leaving his mystery pursuer behind. He sticks to the river's far edge, searching for a good spot to fish. He carves his way a little farther downstream, where the rushing waters and whirling eddies slowly subside. Here the river is wider, quieter. Stepping silently along the shallows, he looks for the shadows of fish feeding in a favorite spot. Finally, he spots them, a dozen or so, large oblong shadows in the olive green water, waving their gossamer fins lazily.

Jacob snaps off a bunch of branches and quickly cuts a spike at one end, then jams them into the soft silt of the river's edge, forming a rough V-shaped trap. A fish can easily swim in, attracted by bait, but will have a hard time swimming back out.

Standing knee-deep in the water, he surveys the woods for any movement. There is a swishing sound behind him. He turns, startled, sweat prickling on his neck and chest, but sees only a hawk plunging into the river and emerging with foam on its powerful wings and a small fish in its talons.

He cuts two pieces of a narrow vine to serve as his bait lines. Then he examines the trees and ground for insects, landing on two fat red-eyed cicadas on a tree trunk. He ties the bait lines around them, wades into the trap, and attaches the lines to the stakes, allowing the bugs to float.

Just then, something out of the corner of his eye catches his attention. On the last trees arching over the river, a dark shadow creeps across the branches, scuttling on its belly like a giant spider.

Jacob's blood turns cold. Every hair on his body stands on end. In an instant he is sloshing out of the water and running into the woods, barreling through bushes and branches that scratch his limbs and tear at his clothes. Who—or *what*—is following him?

When he and Kat used to go hunting as kids, they always had schemes for how to trick bandits and scare them off or catch them before *they* were caught. This should be no different.

Jacob quickly snaps a couple of green-tinged branches and strips off the leaves and twigs to form the springy base of a trap. He ties a vine to it, then, climbing partway up the tree, loops the vine around a high branch until the trap is taut. Anyone stepping on the noose will release the trigger branch from its hook. The sapling will spring upwards, and his pursuer will find himself hanging upside down in a tree. He covers the noose with dead leaves.

Then he takes his knife from its sheath and places it on the muddy track about a foot beyond the hidden noose. It's valuable, with a polished ox-horn hilt and steel blade...and it will be clearly visible to anyone on the path following him.

Decent bait for a robber.

Up ahead is a small clearing where a large tree has fallen, bringing several others down with it. Jacob flings branches into the middle of the clearing to prepare a fire. He knows his pursuer will smell the smoke. Good. For tinder he plucks dried ferns and peels off bark, then squats and strikes his fire steel on the flint. A shower of tiny sparks rains onto the tinder and it bursts into flame.

He steps back from the fire and sits on the fallen tree. He strains to hear the surprised cries of his pursuer and the snap of the sapling springing back into place. Maybe the man is circling the clearing, having missed the trap, and will leap at him from the other side. For a moment Jacob feels helpless; he doesn't even have his knife. He picks up a sturdy fallen branch and sits back down, every muscle in his body ready to jump up at the least sound, the crack of a twig, the shoosh of leafy branches pushed aside, the startled cry of a bird.

But he hears nothing other than normal forest noises. Cicadas. Flies. Occasional birdsong. The late afternoon is warm,

and the fire is making him sweat again. Long shadows are falling across the clearing, and night will be here soon. Night,
and the danger of attack.

Impatient, he walks quietly down the path to check on his
trap and stops in his tracks.

The knife is gone.

The sapling is upright once again.

The trigger branch and empty noose are dangling halfway
down the tree.

Someone has disengaged the trap.

Grabbing his stick tightly, he turns around in a slow circle,
looking up in the highest trees, down in the brush. If his pursuer is human, he will be here, watching him. Then Jacob sees
a hooded figure crouching behind a bush. With the energy
of built-up frustration, he flings himself forward, sending the
pursuer sprawling onto the dirt and leaves. His opponent isn't
large or very strong, but he's scrappy, feisty, as if he thinks that
through sheer force of will he can wriggle from Jacob's grasp
and disappear into the woods. It's only with difficulty that
Jacob finally pins the man on his stomach and sits on his back.

"Who are you?" Jacob demands, his voice coming out
harsh, like a growl. "Why are you following me?"

A grunt rises from the dull brown cloak. A very feminine
grunt. "It's me, you idiot," a muffled voice says.

Shocked, he stands up and the figure flips over. The hood
falls back, revealing a mane of light brown hair streaked with
sunlight.

"Kat," he says, incredulous. And then, he understands. How
she knew to avoid the bent sapling. How she knew to unhook his trap.

How many traps had they made together in the fields and
woods outside Erissa? Hers were usually as good as his, sometimes better.

"What are you doing here?" he demands.

"Oof." She sits up, rubbing her chest and wincing. "Help me up first."

He pulls her to her feet, and she looks at him with those wide, frank green eyes. He quickly turns away.

"That trap was hardly your best work," she says, brushing dirt from her knees. "It couldn't have caught a badger, much less a person."

He shrugs. "I had to improvise. Now, why are you following me?" He still can't look at her. He's surprised at the anger in his own voice. What's she doing here now, after she so obviously rejected him?

Near the fire she throws down her pack, which, Jacob can't help noticing with irritation, *she* managed to cling on to when she climbed over the river.

"Here's your knife," she says, plucking it out of her pack.

"Kat—" he begins again.

"I'm coming with you," she says, her eyes bright and determined. Before he can protest, she barrels on: "If I had asked to come along you would have said no. And if you had spotted me early on you would have sent me back. But now we're so far from home you can't let me walk back alone, can you? So you have to take me with you." She grins, clearly pleased with herself.

But he's not playing. Not anymore. Not after last night.

"You shouldn't have come," he says, his voice cold.

Kat's jaw drops a little, which gives him a small amount of satisfaction. It's his turn to resist, and she obviously doesn't like it.

But she recovers quickly, shrugging. "I guess you don't want any of my supplies, then," she says, turning away to pull a flask of wine and another of water, a loaf of bread and some hard-boiled eggs out of her pack. Jacob notices a flash of something at the bottom of her bag: a shimmering golden gauze with a meandering pattern of dark green snakes. It tickles the lingering suspicion at the back of his mind. It's Kat's mother's scarf—her *real* mother's.

He knows the story, though Kat never likes to talk about it. His own mother told him: how Helen, Kat's mother, stole the scarf and other items of great worth from the queen when she was a lady-in-waiting, and had used the stolen objects to buy her own loom and a place for herself and her daughter. Why would Kat bring the scarf with her to Pella? It's just another layer to her impenetrability. Her secrecy. Whatever it is that's causing her to play cat and mouse with him.

"Because of you I almost got myself killed," he shoots at her as she gobbles down an egg.

"It's not my fault you're clumsy," she says. But when she looks at him, it's with a quiet intensity in her eyes. "Believe me," she says in a different voice, "I know how important this journey is for you. It is for me, too."

"What aren't you telling me?" he asks, softer now, approaching her slowly like she's a deer that might startle.

She bites her lip, stepping closer to him, too. Her eyes seem to go dark, hard. "If I could tell you, I would."

He grabs her arms and feels her sharp intake of breath. He wants to shake her. He wants to kiss her. He wants to do so much more.

Instead he releases her and backs away. "Keep your eggs," he says. "I'll get us something fresher than that."

He returns to the river, letting his hot head start to cool. Golden-orange rays of the setting sun reflect off the water as he wades over to his fishing trap. *This* one rarely fails him. All it requires is a little patience. Sure enough, inside are two fat perch wiggling about, which he easily spears with a stick, staring at them until their squirming ceases.

And that's when it hits him—how he's going to win the tournament.

Because sometimes it doesn't help to chase after the thing you want. No. Sometimes you have to wait, however long it takes, until what you want most *comes to you.*

Jacob feels a smile slowly stretch across his lips. He knows how he will survive the tournament, and not only survive, but win.

An unbearable weight has been taken off his shoulders and Jacob hums an old lullaby as he returns to the campfire and stokes the flames. The world is sinking slowly into deeper gray-blue shadows, and Kat is wrapped up in her traveling cloak, already fallen asleep.

Jacob cooks the fish and eats alone, picking out all of the fine bones. Trying not to look at Kat's curled form, her long bare legs sticking out from under the cloak. Kat, who has grown into such a beautiful girl, who just yesterday pressed herself against him in the pond. He pictures her wet see-through tunic and her taut body beneath it, feels the urgency of their kiss like it's happening all over again, the beating of her heart, her breaths coming in excited little gasps…

He hears her breathing now, but it is the long, regular breaths of sleep, and he is consumed with the desire to wake her, to take up where they left off in the pond. His whole body is screaming for it.

It takes every ounce of his self-control to lie down a safe distance from her. He sighs, listening to the forest sounds. There is a constant low buzz of insects. Somewhere nearby, an owl hoots. A pack of wolves is howling, too, but far off and forlorn. He lies there in the darkness and prays for the tantalizing fantasies of Kat to release him so he can sleep. After all, this journey isn't over yet.

They still have a long way to go.

CHAPTER FIVE

HOLDING A FLICKERING OIL LAMP, ZO PUSHES open the creaking door and enters the storage room. Immediately a faint musty smell, mingled with spices, tickles her nose.

She holds her lamp high, but its tiny flame casts only a small golden halo. She can just make out the bulky shapes around her, blacker than the blackness of the air. Her thick long hair sticks to her back, slick with sweat. The westernmost territory of the Persian Empire is usually cool and breezy, but for the past few days it seems as if the sticky heat of Babylon itself has engulfed it.

She turns around and is relieved to see the dim outline of a torch in a wall sconce next to the door, which she lights, discarding the ineffectual lamp. Holding the torch high, she sees old tables, rolled-up carpets, and traveling trunks. Palace detritus, tucked out of sight.

"Cosmas?" she whispers.

She hears something stirring in the dark and turns. It's just a cat—one of the palace mousers, no doubt, that guard the basement grain rooms against vermin. She calls more loudly this time, "Cosmas?"

Casting her a disapproving glance, the cat winds itself back into the shadows. There is a shuffling noise in the darkness at the far end of the room, and a door opens along the back wall, revealing a figure holding an oil lamp.

It's him. "Zofia," he says, and her heart almost breaks at the sound. It has only been a couple of weeks but it feels like forever. He's so tall and broad-shouldered he fills up the doorway. She first saw him three months ago from the women's viewing room over the throne room. King Shershah was giving out awards for bravery. Cosmas had been one of four soldiers who had raced into an inferno and rescued a family from the flames.

Zo noticed him immediately. He was taller and broader-shouldered than the other three men, and his profile was like that of a god on a coin. Despite his impressive looks, he seemed uncomfortable with the honors and accolades. As soon as the ceremony was over and the feasting started, she saw him sneaking food into a napkin, which he stuffed in his pocket, an action that rather deflated the romantic notions she was already feeling. Was he stealing food for himself? Or did he have poor relatives who would welcome it? When he snuck out a side door, Zo pulled back from the women pressed against the latticed windows and wound her way into the courtyard.

He was on his knees, feeding pieces of chicken to two young calico kittens, their mother nowhere in sight.

He looked up when he heard her and smiled sheepishly.

"But they're honoring you," she said, gesturing to the throne room.

He shrugged and a smile hovered over his lips. "In some ways I would rather be fighting my way through a burning building than receiving an honor like that. I don't like crowds." He looked down at the kittens gulping down the chicken. "I saw them on my way in," he said, "and they seemed hungry."

She walked up to him slowly, tentatively, unsure how to behave around a man who was not a close relative, a servant, or a eunuch. A man who was young and handsome and incredibly sweet.

"Where's their mother?" she asked, looking around. "They are young enough to still be nursing."

"I don't know," he said. His dark eyes were warm and kind, with lashes so thick and long any woman would die to have them. "Perhaps she abandoned them. It happens sometimes. My mother abandoned me, so I know how it feels."

She inhaled sharply, amazed. "My mother abandoned me, too," she said. He looked at her with compassion. "And then something even worse happened," she added, lowering her voice.

"What?" he asked softly, bending toward her, his black eyebrows knit together in sympathy.

"She came back!"

He threw his head back and laughed, and she laughed with him. And they began to talk about life and family, love and bitterness, friendship and rejection and loss.

That was how it started. Stolen meetings, stolen kisses, fantasies, dreams.

And now, after tonight, nothing will be the same.

Zo hadn't thought to be nervous, but now waves of tingly heat rise up her spine, flowing through her chest and flushing her cheeks as she takes in the angles of his face, the high cheekbones, the straight nose, the curve of his jaw.

"I've missed you," she says, unsure of how to start. Every time it's like this between them—a new beginning. "You've been away so long."

Since she's apparently frozen in place, he crosses the room to her.

"Just two weeks," he says with a slow grin, taking the torch from her and setting it back into the wall sconce. He places his clay lamp on a dusty table.

"Each time you go, I'm so worried you won't come back," she says, feeling like she's blabbering, like she's already making a mess of her plan. "Your life is so…dangerous." She doesn't mean to sound like such a young, scared girl.

But part of her knows that that's exactly what she is.

He smiles broader now, and his dark eyes crinkle into half-moons. "Not really that dangerous. The Persian Royal Guard is the best fighting force in the world. And I don't think we'll be storming a city anytime soon."

He grabs her, pulling her to him, and she feels the delirious rush of being in his arms, feeling the hardness of his chest pushing against her. This isn't the first time they've kissed, the first time they've touched. For months now it has escalated, becoming harder and harder for her to break it off before anything actually happens, to stagger back to her room aching and unrequited, her hands and lips hot and sore, dreams of his smile torturing her in her sleep, causing her to wake again a thousand times drenched in sweat and desire.

But now…

Now she won't have to say no.

And then, he won't be able to say no to what she has dreamed.

Them. Together. For the rest of their lives.

She knows he'll make the perfect husband. She knows he wants her just as badly as she wants him.

If she hesitates now, she could lose her nerve altogether. She steps back from him, unties the cloth belt at her waist, and opens her silk robe, her arms shaking a little. The air in this abandoned room, mostly underground, is cool on her skin.

His eyes widen, and he inhales sharply.

"Tonight," she says. "I want to show you how much I love you." It's the line she has rehearsed in her head these past couple of weeks, but it sounds different now. Oddly silly. She hopes he can't tell how nervous she is.

He stands rigidly, as if afraid to move. "But Zofia, you are a princess—"

"No, technically I'm not," she says firmly, feeling cold now, and exposed. "I am only the king's niece. I am of no importance, I promise you. The king has never even mentioned marriage to me." This last part is sort of true. Close enough, anyway. Her uncle certainly hasn't ever mentioned marrying her to anyone appealing.

"But surely the king will be angry. If we're caught…"

"Shh." She steps toward him and puts her finger on his lips, unable to keep standing there like that, her robe open, not knowing what to do with herself. She wills herself to be brave, wills him to give in to her touch.

He does.

"Zofia." His voice is urgent, a ragged whisper in the dark.

Zo opens her eyes. No, it isn't really dark. Through the slatted shutters of the small, eye-shaped windows of the basement storeroom, slivers of gray light fall on boxes and tilting amphorae, and on the old carpet where she and Cosmas are lying now, curled into each other's naked bodies.

Oh, god. It happened. It happened exactly as she had planned. She feels a huge sense of inevitability, like a tight ball of silken thread, starting to unravel itself inside her chest.

She blinks, breathing in Cosmas's musky smell—the leather of his riding gear, mixed with something sweet, too, something she can't quite name, a mixture of dates and oranges and salt.

She blinks again.

Light. The sun has risen. Could it be so late? Panic-stricken, she sits bolt upright. Cosmas, too, jumps up, entirely naked but holding his sword.

A thick, coarse laugh echoes through the room, and Zofia stifles a scream, turning to see her handmaiden, old Mandana, standing there in the doorway with her hands on her broad hips.

Blushing furiously, Cosmas picks up Zo's robe and covers himself with it. Even in such an embarrassing situation, Zofia can't help but smile. He's so handsome. He's so kind and sincere and so passionate… And he's hers.

"Zofia," Mandana says, ignoring Cosmas now, "your uncle wants you to join him for breakfast. Quickly." She snatches the robe from Cosmas and throws it around Zo, causing Cosmas to yelp. He may be a fierce soldier, but he's no match for a burly old nurse who has seen every horror the world has to offer. It's much worse for him than for Zofia—Mandana has seen her naked daily, ever since she was just a baby.

Zofia turns to Cosmas as he fishes around on the floor for his green tunic and red-and-white-checked trousers. "Can I see you tonight?"

He shakes his head. "I have to report back to camp today."

Without any further ado, not even a parting kiss, Zo is pulled away. Mandana spins her around and she screeches a little as she's pushed out the door, down the dark, twisting corridors, and up the winding secret staircase to her room. They emerge through a small door in the painted wall, in between winged, human-headed lions facing each other, and Mandana shoves Zo toward a basin of water.

"A quick wash," she says, and her smile reveals her missing teeth. "It's pretty obvious what you've been doing."

Ten minutes later, Zo wears a freshly pressed emerald-green robe and matching trousers tied at the ankles. Her waist-length reddish-brown hair—the result of frequent henna washes—is pinned under a golden diadem. Mandana hangs golden amphora earrings in her ears, and clips on gold armlets, anklets, and rings. Zo studies herself in the mirror. Here, in Lydia, gold is as common as iron or bronze in other parts of the world.

As rich as Croesus of Lydia. It's the phrase people everywhere use to describe unlimited wealth. Four hundred years ago, when King Midas wanted to be rid of the curse that everything he touched turned to gold, the god told him to wash his hands in the river of Sardis. He did, and gold flowed into the river and surrounding countryside. Then, two hundred years ago, King Croesus noticed that the streams sparkled with gold dust and found the rich mines in the surrounding hills. Croesus minted the world's first coins. Now Zo's own uncle, her mother's brother, King Shershah, controls the gold.

But what does all that gold matter if you can't be with the person you love?

Mandana douses her with lavender perfume. Then she picks up a bell on Zo's cosmetics table and rings it loudly. A moment later, a bald man enters, wearing thick eyeliner and enormous gold earrings, his red robe billowing over his potbelly.

"Frava," Mandana says to the eunuch, "take Zofia to her uncle in the summer sitting room. She mustn't keep the king waiting." She turns to Zo. "Your lady mother, too, will be there."

Zo pulls a face. Better to get this painful breakfast over with. She prefers to eat sitting cross-legged on a carpet with Mandana and some of her ladies-in-waiting: young, unmarried girls from noble families who laugh and gossip with her about men and fashion.

She slides her feet into green leather slippers placed next to the door. The curved toes are so exaggerated that it's hard to walk, but they're the latest fashion at the Persian court. She and Frava scurry as quickly as they can down the brightly painted hall of the women's quarters. When she reaches the king's apartments, the guards nod and open the double doors. Leaving Frava behind, she crosses her uncle's private council chamber and emerges in his summer sitting room.

Zo loves the breeziness of the room, three sides of which can be opened up to the balcony overlooking the courtyard of the palace of Sardis with its long, rectangular green pool and cheerfully sparkling fountains of glazed blue tiles.

King Shershah is seated in a chair next to Zo's mother, Attoosheh. As Zo enters, her uncle smiles at her and gestures for her to take a small chair on the other side of the table, next to her six-year-old half sister, Roxana.

"My dear," he says, "you look lovely, glowing."

Shershah always takes great pains to cultivate his royal image, and today is no different. His iron-gray hair is oiled and curled. His cone-shaped hat, tilted back slightly like a fat goat's horn, is studded with gold and turquoise ornaments. Strands of gold and little gold bells are woven into his still-black beard. His flowing linen robe is dyed with the most expensive color of all, royal purple.

Zo curtseys to her uncle and her mother, then kisses Roxana on the cheek, and obediently takes her seat. Does he know? Can they all tell what she has done? Is "glowing" a euphemism? Mandana said it was obvious, but that was when Zo's hair was tousled and the musty fragrance of Cosmas's body still clung to her like perfume.

"Eat," her uncle says genially, gesturing expansively at the table. She takes some bread and honey on her plate and pretends to nibble at it, though she has no appetite, and her thoughts keep wandering back to Cosmas. The gentle but strong way that he held her. He was so careful not to hurt her, even though she could sense the intensity of his desire in the way he looked at her body and trembled when he touched her and moaned and…

Her mother is studying Zo intently with her large, dark blue eyes—Zo's eyes. Everyone always says the two are almost twins, with the same coloring, the same height, the same long, slender bones. Now, with those eyes fastened on her, Zo wonders if *she* knows. Can mothers, even selfish, mostly absentee mothers, tell if a daughter is no longer a virgin? Zo sniffs, staring at the embroidered napkin in her lap.

"We have excellent news for you," Shershah says, picking up his golden goblet and swigging wine. "We've come to an agreement with King Philip of Macedon that you will marry his son and heir, Prince Alexander."

Zo feels her heart stop beating. She stares at him, her mouth open.

Air. She can't get any air.

He nods and smiles, evidently quite pleased with himself. "Surprised, eh? He's the most eligible bachelor on the royal marriage market. You thought I wasn't going to do anything for you, but I've been negotiating this for months."

Oxygen floods into her lungs at last. "Me?" Zo asks, hating the squeak in her voice. She blinks rapidly. "But—why not one of your own daughters, Uncle? You have so many." More than twenty, isn't it, with how many wives? She only knows a few of them well. Most were sold off and shipped out long ago like so much royal cargo.

He dabs delicately at his mouth and beard with a napkin. "That's exactly the point, Zofia. As a king sworn to serve and obey the Great King Artaxerxes, I must marry all my daughters to Persian kings or princes. But Artaxerxes will not mind if I marry *you* to Macedon."

"But why do you need a connection to Macedon?" she asks, thinking quickly. "You have the might of the entire Persian empire behind you, Uncle. Who is King Philip? A mutilated, illiterate barbarian who supposedly killed his last wife in her bath in a fit of rage."

Shershah barks out a hearty laugh. "True, he is all that. But he is also a brilliant strategist and general who has tripled Macedon's territory in the past twenty years. And the oracles predict that his son, Alexander, will become the greatest king ever, far greater even than Artaxerxes."

He plucks a fat black date out of a golden bowl and holds it between his thumb and forefinger, gesturing with it as he continues. "Mark my words—in the near future, when Philip has consolidated his kingdom in Greece, he will cast his eyes across the sea, and he will march. Right on the coast, Lydia, with its gold mines, will be the jewel for his crown, just as it was for Cyrus the Great, who conquered Croesus. Everyone wants to possess Lydia."

Zo's heart sinks. Because Lydia is *as rich as Croesus.*

"And if Philip marches against Persia," her mother adds, her tones, as always, low, well-modulated, "he will not burn the city of his beloved daughter-in-law. He will not slaughter her relatives. He may even let us stay here, ruling it in his name, handing the taxes we collect to him rather than to Artaxerxes. Our life may remain much the same." She carefully adjusts the sheer, midnight-blue veil hanging in shimmering folds from her diadem.

Shershah genteelly spits out the pit of the date into a priceless amber cup as a servant scurries over and refills his wine goblet. The king's large hand, well-manicured and bejeweled, reaches out and hovers hesitantly over several dishes, finally settling on a bowl of cheese-stuffed olives.

Zo tries to keep the raw panic out of her voice. "But I have no importance to this dynasty. Give me to some valiant soldier of noble family as a reward for bravery. That will encourage your guard to *fight* the Greeks."

"It is good you are modest, my dear," Shershah says, nodding as he spits olive pits into the little cup he has brought once again to his mouth. "A lovely thing for a woman to be." He takes an ivory toothpick from the table and begins cleaning his teeth, digging the toothpick in and out as he covers his mouth with his other hand.

Attoosheh is still staring thoughtfully at Zo. Zo looks away, fighting the urge to scream; her mother has no right to voice any opinion about Zo's future. Zo's father, a royal official, died soon after her birth, and Attoosheh jumped at the chance to marry the king of Bactria, a territory at the far reaches of the Persian Empire, many hundreds of miles east of here, leaving Zo behind to be raised by Mandana and other nursemaids in her uncle's palace in Lydia. Zo grew up hating the mother she could hardly even remember, and told everyone she was an orphan.

The first time Zo ever clearly remembered setting eyes on Attoosheh was when she was twelve and stood in the women's observation room of the main palace gate tower, watching through latticed windows as the former queen of Bactria returned to her native city after her royal husband's death. Zo saw a beautiful woman lying down on the swaying royal litter born by tall Ethiopian slaves, exhausted by the six-month journey from Bactria. Weakly the woman clutched her infant daughter, Roxana, to her breast, a useless girl unwanted by the Bactrian dynasty.

Attoosheh recovered rapidly, and within weeks of her return to her brother's palace, she attempted to play the role of mother as if she hadn't abandoned Zo so many years earlier like a pile of dirty laundry.

Now Attoosheh leans forward and asks quietly, "Are you afraid of leaving your home? You will not be far. Macedon is a two-day sail across the Aegean. You will be able to visit us, and I will be able to visit you with Roxana."

Roxana looks up at Zo, smiling broadly. She has lost her first tooth, and the wavy edges of its replacement are just starting to poke through the gum. Zo ruffles her dark curls. Roxana is the only real gift her mother has ever given her.

"You are right, Mother," Zo says carefully. "I don't want to leave Sardis. I want to stay here. Marry a Lydian, not a barbarian with a foreign language and foreign gods."

Attoosheh smiles. "From all reports, Alexander is young and handsome."

"And crippled," Zo says, scowling as she remembers the rumors, widely disputed but too gruesome to be ignored.

Shershah stands up. "Enough. She will leave in the next month. We must prepare the chariots, litters, horses, and tripods as the dowry. Gold tripods, of course, not bronze. Gold trappings for the horses. The Greeks will expect that from Lydia."

He carefully folds his napkin, sets it on the table, and snaps his fingers. A servant rushes over to clear his plates while another places an empty golden bowl before him. The king extends his fingers over the bowl as the servant pours steaming rose water over them. A third servant offers him a fresh linen napkin on which he dries his scented fingers.

Zo feels as if she is going to vomit. Once she and her friends visited the Greek merchants' temple in Sardis where a great white bull was decked with garlands of flowers, his proud horns gilded. He was led up the marble steps and stood there in blissful ignorance until the hammer knocked him unconscious and the flashing knife slit his throat.

But she is not an animal. She will not stand idly by while they make her a sacrifice for the sake of their ridiculous politics.

As soon as her uncle has left the room, Zo stands up, too, throwing her napkin on the table. "I am in love with someone else," she announces, looking her mother straight in the eye.

Attoosheh's eyes are cold and hard, glittering with rage and something else, too—sadness, maybe. Or pity. "You will marry Alexander, Zofia. You have no choice."

Each word strikes Zo like the blow of an ax on soft flesh. Feeling sick and dizzy, she runs from the room, stepping out of her fashionable slippers and racing ahead barefoot.

Behind her, Frava picks them up and chases after her, his fat feet slapping on the marble floor. "My lady! Slow down!" he begs.

But she doesn't slow down. She speeds up. Back in her own chamber, she tears off her gold ornaments and flings them hard at the wall. Then she throws herself into Mandana's arms. As the sobs come, Mandana shushes her.

"This is just the beginning of your journey," Mandana murmurs, guessing at the source of her distress. "You'll get used to it. Everything will be fine."

The beginning of your journey.

As she hiccups, trying to catch her breath, Zo stares past Mandana's shoulder, through her bedroom. Mandana is exactly right. Zo *is* on the brink of a big journey.

Just not the one everyone else expects her to make.

Her mother was wrong—she *does* have a choice. She will run away. To Cosmas. His camp is only twenty miles from Sardis on the well-maintained Royal Road. They will get married, and she'll live in one of the little cottages the officers' wives have outside the base. No one there will recognize her, not if she disguises herself in middle-class clothing and gets rid of all this disgusting gold, the cause of bloody warfare and hateful marriages.

What reason does she have for staying here, anyway?

Mandana, she thinks with a twinge. She will miss Mandana's hearty cackle and gap-toothed grin.

Roxana, she thinks. How will she live without Roxana? The little sister who has always cheered her, playing around in Zo's room while Mandana did Zo's hair, eagerly helping choose her outfits and jewelry. The one person in her life who is pure and innocent and full of joy. She thinks of her little sister's smile, the way her nose squinches up when she is forced to eat anything pickled.

Zo's chest aches for a moment, and she wonders if she can really see this through.

Then she pushes those feelings out of her mind, squares her shoulders, and focuses on Cosmas. Being with him is worth it. Being with him is worth anything.

ACT TWO:

THE BLOOD OF BETRAYAL

A friend to all is a friend to none.

—Aristotle

Chapter Six

"TRY NOT TO BREAK ANY BONES, BOYS,!" DIODO-
tus cries. "We need everyone in the arena tomorrow."

In the dusty training area, Hephaestion is facing the contestant from Crete, a small dark man with coal-black eyes.
As Heph and the Cretan circle each other, wooden practice
swords outstretched, Heph sizes up his opponent. Speed will
probably be his strength.

As if in direct answer to his thought, the Cretan bolts toward Heph, but Heph parries the blow just in time, twisting
his opponent's sword up and around, sending it flying out of
his hand. Heph could claim victory now, but it would be too
easy. The tournament tomorrow is about showmanship. A
man who kills and wounds numerous contestants could lose
the victory to the fighter who has fewer notches in his belt
but has entertained the crowd more.

Even though this is only practice for the real thing, Heph
throws his sword on the ground and leaps onto his opponent's
back. They tumble, somersaulting, to the dirt. But the Cretan
moves so quickly Heph suddenly finds himself pinned face-

down. He relaxes every muscle in his body completely, as if giving up, and the Cretan, feeling the fight gone out of him, loosens his grip. Then Heph flings the man off his back. An instant later he is sitting on the Cretan's chest, his knees under his chin, pinning his arms by his side.

"Victory for Macedon," Diodotus says with unmistakable pleasure in his rough voice.

Heph smiles. *Victory*: one of his favorite words. He closes his eyes, inhaling the practice-arena smell of sweat and heat, of leather and metal. Here he is, Macedon's victor, living in a palace, with the finest clothing, food, and horses, the best friend of the heir to the throne. At that moment he feels all-powerful, almost a prince himself.

"That's three so far," Diodotus says. "You're doing Pella proud, Heph. Don't stop now."

Heph nods. Proud. He will make them all proud. Then he'll win the purse of gold so he and Alexander will finally have the money to secretly start buying provisions for their trip across the Aegean and deep into Persia—and no one, certainly not Leonidas with his tense watch over the royal coffers, can stop them. In the Eastern Mountains they will seek out—and find—the fabled Fountain of Youth, whose waters can heal any defect and render a warrior invincible.

Heph doesn't recognize the young man who presents himself next for a trial spar. The helmet, with its long nose and cheek protectors, covers most of his face. It's probably the contestant from the island of Chios—tall with long, slender limbs, which look both flexible and strong.

The opponents nod to each other, crouch, and begin to circle, swords drawn, shields raised.

"I know who you are," the Chian says, moving his wooden sword through the air slowly. "You think you're the best friend of the prince regent, don't you?" His voice is smooth and sly, taunting.

Heph frowns but doesn't take his eyes off the man. This is obviously a trick to distract him. "That's none of your concern."

"Isn't it?" Beneath the helmet, the Chian's mouth breaks into a thin white grin. "The prince has told a lot of people in the palace that he's tired of you. He says you're like a weight around his neck."

Heph squints, trying to read the Chian's eyes—hot with passion and cold with calculation. Eyes that are oddly familiar. In that instant of hesitation, his opponent lunges, and stabs Heph's leather breastplate just above his heart.

"You're dead!" the Chian hisses. "Dead in the arena and dead in the prince's heart."

Shock is replaced by rage bubbling up from the pit of Heph's stomach, churning in his chest, burning his face. A red haze almost obscures his vision.

"I'll show you dead," he says between clenched teeth, and with a furious swing of his shield sends the man flying. As the scarlet fog lifts, he sees the Chian sprawled on the ground, unmoving. Instantly, he's flooded with regret. Hundreds of Chians came to see the tournament; it will be a disaster if their warrior can't compete. Heph kneels beside the fallen warrior, and gently removes the helmet. Cascades of long black hair tumble out.

"Cynane!" he cries, trying to ignore Diodotus's cluck of disgust.

She grins. "Fooled you."

"By all the Olympian gods, what are you doing?" he demands.

"It was my only chance to test myself against the competitors. Naturally," she says, making a wry face, "I'm not allowed to participate in the *real* fighting."

She stands up—she's as tall as he is, which makes him uneasy—and dusts off her skirt of leather lappets. He sees now that the long legs are smooth and shapely and feels like a fool for not having recognized her as a girl—a wild, fiercely beautiful girl. She examines the inside of her wrist, which is bleeding.

"I'm sorry," he says, taking a step toward her. "I've hurt you."

She raises her wrist to her mouth, licking off the blood.

Suddenly, Heph can't help but imagine what it would feel like to have that pink tongue on his skin, to have those long, tan arms and legs wrapped around him. *No*, he says to himself, horrified, willing the thoughts away.

"What did you mean when you said Alex wanted to be rid of me?" he asks. "Was that another joke?"

She raises her shining eyes to him and bursts out laughing. "Good luck in the games." She throws down the wooden sword and leather shield, then strides jauntily toward the palace, her tangled black curls swaying, without answering his question.

"Crazy girl," Diodotus says, clapping Heph on the back. "There's no point in making a complaint. I've tried before."

Heph throws down his helmet, shield, and sword. His gaze follows Cyn as she passes the stables. She's always been wild. One time she ordered a bowl of boiled goats' eyeballs for breakfast and sat there sucking and chewing on them until Olympias stormed off in a fury while Philip roared with laughter. Another time she appeared at night in the bedroom of the wine-sodden Athenian ambassador dressed as the warrior goddess Athena, holding a golden bow and arrow. The man ran throughout the palace banging on doors and telling everyone he'd been graced with a divine visitation.

But now, her wildness has taken on a different tone. And the strong, fluid lilt in her step as she strides away from him tugs on his consciousness—though whether its message is one of warning or intrigue, he can't say.

As far as he knows, Alex has never liked his sister. Is it really possible that he could have privately conferred with Cyn in the few days since they've been home and didn't tell Heph about it? No. He and Alex tell each other everything. They have no secrets.

The warm air is split by the sound of wood on wood. Two men—these are so thick, battle-scarred, and ugly, they must be men—pick up his discarded equipment and face off, grunting and cursing, each one maneuvering arms and legs and backs to throw the other, but Heph is no longer paying attention.

As he walks back toward the palace, he replays that day in Pella, five summers ago, a day much like this, when the smell of hot baked earth rose over the marketplace. The merchants' tables were heaped high with roasted meat and fresh bread while hunger gnawed at him, burned in his stomach like hot embers. He looked around, hoping to spot a fallen apple or crust of bread. Then he saw the blond boy standing in the crowd, carrying a fat yellow leather coin purse.

A boy like that wouldn't miss the coins, Heph had thought, eying the gold cuff and fine emerald-green tunic embroidered with gold. But those coins might buy Heph a snug place to stay when it rained. Might allow him to buy a thick cloak and boots to survive the winter, when winds cut across the Macedonian plains like the searing, merciless knives of a northern enemy. So he jostled his way next to the golden-haired boy and easily cut the strings to the purse with his small knife. Then he darted back into the crowd and began to run.

That was his mistake. Running. He might have been smart but he wasn't exactly practiced at thievery. If he had casually examined the fruit vendor's pomegranates, for instance, the boy wouldn't have known he was the thief. But all too soon, the boy caught up and, grabbing Heph's arm, spun him around.

They stood there for what seemed like an eternity as the life of the marketplace surged all around them, and Heph had the uncomfortable feeling that the boy was looking not at him but into him, into his soul and his thoughts and memories. Vendors at their tables unrolled bolts of cloth and Persian carpets, weighed fruit and vegetables, and counted money. Shoppers examined ivory combs and leather hides, smelled perfume, and haggled over painted vases.

"Has this street rat stolen your purse?" thundered a deep voice. Then time sped up again, and Heph turned from the strange mismatched eyes of the blond boy to see King Philip staring at him with his frightening, all-seeing eye. The crowd had pulled back from the king out of respect, or, more likely, fear. "I'll string him up right here and now."

Fear clogged Heph's throat, weighing on his chest, making it impossible to breathe. But the blond boy—Prince Alexander, he realized—took his purse from Heph's hand and said, "No, Father. I dropped it. This boy was just returning it, I'm sure."

Heph's mouth fell open.

The king shook his head, probably disappointed that he couldn't order an execution, and waved away the assembled crowd.

Over the years, Heph has learned that Alexander was wise beyond his years, that he could see things others could not. He never quite understood why or how, but it was clear to him that Alex *saw* him for his true self.

Still… Heph has always wondered. *Why?* Why did the prince lie for him?

Alexander watched his father, who had lost interest in Heph and was pursuing a pretty milkmaid on her way through the market. Then his intense gaze returned to Heph. "Where do you live?" Alex asked.

"Nowhere," Heph replied, shaking his head. "And everywhere." He gestured to the marketplace, to all of Pella.

Alex raised an eyebrow. "Well, since you returned my coin purse, the least I can do is invite you to the palace for a meal, a bath, and a change of clothes," he said.

Heph was embarrassed. He knew he was skinny, filthy, and ragged. And the thought of the palace scared him. It would be teeming with judges and counselors, soldiers and guards, some of whom might be on the lookout for a black-haired, eleven-year-old urchin accused of murder. He didn't entirely trust Alexander. He thought it might be a trick after all, and Alexander meant to punish him.

But he was far too hungry to turn down the possibility of a good meal.

They've been inseparable ever since. It never occurred to Heph that a prince, living in a palace, could be just as lonely, and in some ways as hungry, as he was himself. The other boys at the palace have been pushed in Alex's direction by ambitious fathers, desperate for influence and wealth. Alex has never chosen any of them as his friends. Only Hephaestion does he choose to trust.

Heph has never understood why.

Only that he must do everything to protect that trust. It's what kept him alive. More than that: it's what has given him a reason to live.

Now, passing the animal pens and barracks, through the gardens bursting with color, and up green marble stairs, Heph looks around as if he is seeing it all for the very first time. For years he has considered this palace his home. But now he is intensely aware that it is not his home, not really. Heph has no family, no wealth or position of his own. Everything he has is because Alex gave it to him.

On the rampart overlooking the town, he stops to clear his head. A little voice says, *And he can take it all away.*

CHAPTER SEVEN

FROM HIS POSITION ON THE ROYAL PLATFORM overlooking the arena, Alex takes a deep breath as he watches the gates swing open and musicians sweep in like a jangling, colorful tide, then spread out in ripples. The insistent beat of drums, the lilting notes of flutes, and the tinny sounds of long bronze trumpets fill the huge space. Dancing girls with wreaths on their long hair smile and keep the beat with wooden hand clappers. Flag bearers toss poles and pennants into the air.

The Blood Tournament has arrived.

Alex has only been back in Pella for a little over a week now, but already he feels itchy with anticipation, with the need to *do* something.

Sitting to the right of his father, he scans the arena and its complicated, engineered landscape, trying to judge where Heph will have the best advantage. In the center of the terrain is a deep pond. Some sections of the ground are grassy, others sticky with mud, and yet others pits of quicksand. Piles of boulders represent cliffs. At the far end of the arena stands a forest of tall artificial trees, each bearing hundreds of bright green linen leaves, interspersed with live saplings and thick bushes.

Alex sees that a crowd of bettors has gathered near the spectators' main entrance, the one where the names of athletic cheaters—some of them centuries old—have been engraved on the walls for everyone to spit on. Scribes are writing down bets; money is changing hands; people are arguing over odds.

Around the arena, all the seats are packed. Ever since he was pronounced regent three nights ago, Alex can see a difference in how the public responds to him, how faces turn his way to stare. He pretends not to notice.

To the right side of the royal box sit the thirteen visiting Aesarian Lords in their billowing black capes like so many crows eyeing the field for carrion. Rumors have always swirled around the powerful Lords, but over the past few days Alex has found himself studying them, wondering what they really want in Macedon. To the right of the queen, Olympias's handmaidens whisper to one another behind ostrich-feather fans, except Ariadne, who bats her big blue eyes at Alex and sighs. On Philip's left hand, the five royal ministers discuss the physical dangers of the simulated landscape.

But Alex notices that one seat in the royal box is conspicuously empty: Cyn's. Neither Philip nor Olympias seems concerned about it. Perhaps these past three years when he was in Mieza, they grew used to her disappearing act. And maybe her absence is for the best. Whenever Cyn enters a room, it's as if a gust of wind blows out all the lamps.

Over the cheering of the crowd, the royal herald loudly calls out the names of the contestants from the nine islands: Crete, Aegina, Ithaca, Chios, Skyros, Samos, Naxos, Lemnos, and Andros. They step forward one by one and bow deeply to the royal family. The herald then introduces those from the seven great cities: Athens, Sparta, Corinth, Thebes, Megara, Argos, and Troezen. Next, he announces the men from the three sacred sites: Delphi, Dodona, and Mount Olympus.

Each man wears a red-crested helmet and a leather breastplate strapped on over his tunic. Their ages range from sixteen to thirty-five. Most are muscular, others sinewy, and a couple are obese, as if their sheer weight might protect them from swordplay. Many bear scars from soldiering or tavern fighting. Alex recognizes the man from Athens from the reception the previous night. He is dark, well-spoken, and slippery, like most Athenians. Alex could hardly get more than a grunt from Sparta's candidate, nicknamed the Red Giant, an oak of a man with flaming red hair who, he heard, was receiving the best odds in the wagering.

Finally, the herald announces the men from the five villages: Tyrrhos, Ichnai, Herakleia, Allante, and Erissa. No one from the villages has ever won, and most were shipped back home as cinders in a burial urn. Alex looks at the five contenders wondering if they will all die in the first few minutes of competition. Three of the men are well-built and seem fairly confident, but they are no doubt poorly trained. The Tyrrhian is no bigger than a twelve-year-old girl, stringy and imp-like, with a twinkle in his blue eyes and a smirk on his ugly, monkey-like face. One of the villages—Erissa, was it?—has sent a boy around Heph's age. He's tall and broad but looks completely awkward in a torn-up maroon tunic that's already stained in mud. He will probably be the first to die in the arena.

Then the herald cries, "Hephaestion of Pella!" and the crowd jumps to its feet, cheering and applauding. On the other side of the arena, Alex sees Phrixos, Telekles, and their friends from Mieza wildly waving blue pennants with the sixteen-pointed gold star of Macedon.

Heph, tall and self-assured, waves to the crowd, obviously

in his element as their champion, their favorite. He walks in a wide circle, arms open, acknowledging the love of the spectators. He seems calm—if you didn't know him, you'd have no idea how hard he has worked these past few years, and especially these past few days. Ever since the feast, Heph has done nothing but drill and practice and sweat. And now, here he is, beaming, looking strong, handsome, easy. Perfect.

Alex feels a sudden pang. No matter how hard he has trained, he himself is not perfect, and *cannot* be perfect. Not with the hideous scar and the limp he works so hard to hide.

But no more. Not after Heph wins; that is, if his Achilles heel—his pride—doesn't get in the way of victory. If he doesn't take on five men at once to show off to the crowd. With the prize money, they will plan their quest. Find the Fountain. Heal Alex's leg.

Heph is still basking in the adulation of the crowd. For a moment, Alex sees not Pella's tall champion in a gold-embroidered royal blue tunic, but the skinny boy in filthy brown rags in Pella's marketplace who stole his coin purse years ago. When Alex grabbed Heph, swung him around, and looked into his dark eyes, he seemed as always to travel inside them, down a long dark tunnel. When he emerged, he was in a bright villa. This thief, Alex knew then, wasn't born a beggar. He came from a noble family who owned an exquisite estate in the hills outside Pella.

In his mind, Alex was transported, full of that familiar stirring, that *knowing* he has never been able to explain but had always felt. Inside the young Heph's eyes, Alex saw the unthinkable moment—an act both of honor and horror—that had changed Heph's life forever.

He had seen how Heph was forced to flee for his life as a result.

In a moment, Alex knew this boy could be trusted—that he would do anything for the people he loved.

A trumpet sounds. Its notes still quivering in the air, the herald cries, "Deliver the weapons!" Slaves rush onto the field to give each contestant the two weapons he had chosen the night before. Heph accepts a sword and shield, as do most of the men. The Red Giant takes a horse and a spear, which is risky. Most fighters would love the speed and height provided by a horse, but don't want to give up their shield. If the horse—a large target—is felled, its rider will have no way to defend himself.

The contestant from Mount Olympus, appropriately god-like in his physique, takes a mace and a shield. Alex shudders. One blow from the spiked iron mace would shatter a man's skull to fragments, though it's clumsier to wield than a sword. Oddly, the imp-like Tyrrhian accepts a sword and a slingshot with a pouch of pebbles. Alex has never heard of any competitor using a slingshot. And the village boy in the maroon tunic takes a sword and a large net attached to long ropes. That, too, seems unusual.

Next to him, Philip is grunting and laughing, ridiculing the competitors and their choice of weapons. He nudges Alex with his elbow. "Should make for a quick game."

The trumpet sounds again, and the herald cries, "Let the competitors take their positions!" The twenty-five men lined up in front of the royal box scatter to assigned spots around the arena.

Now all the trumpets blare out a frenzied call to attention. Gordias, the white-robed, white-haired minister of religion, rises unsteadily from his seat and raises both hands in blessing. "May the gods grant victory to the best man!" he cries, his voice surprisingly strong for such an old man, and sits back down.

Radamanthos, the palace chief of protocol, minces up to King Philip in his perfumed robes and hands him the royal handkerchief. Clutching his drinking skull in one hand, the king rises and looks around the stadium, clearly savoring the heightened tension. After what seems like an eternity, he cries out, "Let the tournament begin!" and drops the handkerchief.

Immediately the Red Giant spurs his horse and gallops full force toward the Megaran, who raises his sword and shield. Alex can see that he is planning on slashing the horse as it rides by, but before he can get in close enough, the Giant skewers the man with a spear that goes straight through the leather shield and breastplate. Blood gushes from the hideous wound in the man's chest. The Megaran falls heavily to the ground and the crowd roars its approval.

At the same time, Alex notices the village boy in maroon take off his helmet and disappear into the trees. Obviously he has removed the helmet so no one would see the bright red crest among the leaves and branches. Is he hiding? Many contestants use the forest to catch their breath or regroup before coming out to battle again, but never has Alex heard of anyone racing into the forest as soon as the tournament started. It's disgraceful.

Alex curses himself for losing track of Heph. Where is he? Where is the royal blue tunic? He scans the arena and finds his friend surrounded by three islanders, who evidently have an alliance to rid the contest of the most likely winners at the outset. They are circling him, swords pointed toward him, taunting him.

Three against one.

Alex clenches his fists, forgetting to breathe.

Heph spins around, a whirl of arms and legs and sword so fast it's hard to see what he is doing. But when he has stopped, one man has fallen to his knees, a bloody gash in his armpit, that vulnerable place the breastplate doesn't protect, and a second is bent over trying to staunch a wound in his abdomen. Both throw down their swords in surrender.

Heph now turns to face the third islander, a thickset man with the air of a military veteran. Roaring in anger, the man charges Heph and the two swords clang furiously again and again. The islander is much larger than Heph, but also slower. At first it seems that his sheer size will be enough to roll over Heph as Heph falls backward, giving up ground. The islander is confident now, overconfident, and just as he lunges forward Heph leaps out of his way, his sword pushing deep into the man's thigh. The wounded man cries out in pain, grabs his leg, and falls to the ground writhing.

Before Heph has the time to catch his breath, the contender from Corinth is running at him full force. Heph turns to face his attacker, and it seems to Alex that his friend is not a warrior wielding death in his hands, but some sort of dancer, turning, leaping, and with every move forcing the bigger man to retreat. The Corinthian parries Heph's blows adeptly, but is unable to hold his ground. With each step backward he is closer to the pit of quicksand. Some of the crowd—Corinthians, perhaps, or those who wagered on the man—scream at him to watch out, but he's so intent on avoiding Heph's sword that he doesn't hear them.

He steps back and his right leg sinks deep into the sucking, squelching mud. Horrified, he tries to free himself, but the effort makes him sink in up to his knee. Heph could run him through now but turns to find another contestant to fight as the Corinthian lets his sword drop and falls forward, both hands desperately scrabbling for purchase on the grass.

There is so much action in the arena Alex doesn't know where to look, though he always stays aware of Heph's position. One man—the Cretan, Alex thinks—chases another—

the Samian—up the boulders. At the top, the Samian turns to defend himself and their swords glint in the burning sun.

The Red Giant has thundered across the stadium to spear another opponent in the mud. As the horse, with a whinny of triumph, canters back to the grass, the Giant sets his eyes on the men from Dodona and Argos, who run into the forest to the hoots and howls of the spectators. He turns his horse and spies across the stadium the Mount Olympian, who has just cracked the Troezene's skull with his mace, and gallops toward him. The Skyrian and Athenian have impaled each other through their leather breastplates and fall to the ground, conjoined by death.

Now Heph is near the pond fighting the Tyrrhian. Though Heph is lean and graceful and a foot taller than his opponent, the Tyrrhian is a skilled acrobat, somersaulting and backflipping out of the path of Heph's sword to wild cheering from the crowd. He has no shield to impede his tumbling, just a sword in one hand and his slingshot and bag of pebbles tied to his belt. Alex feels a rush of worry as he notices Heph's mounting frustration.

Stay calm, Heph.

The Tyrrhian makes a show of being afraid, his rubbery face twisting into a fake grimace, waving his hands in panic and running toward the water as the crowd laughs and claps. Heph follows and stands still a moment, his face like thunder. Alex knows he can't bear being made a fool of in front of King Philip and all Pella. Ankle-deep in the pond, with a quick motion, the Tyrrhian pulls out his slingshot and shoots a pebble at Heph, which smacks him on the forehead. His head snaps back and he puts a hand to the bruise as the crowd bursts into laughter. King Philip is slapping his knees and guffawing.

The little man takes a comic bow and plunges into the water, a furious Heph wading behind him.

No, Heph, it's a trick. Alex wills him to turn back. But Heph, up to his waist now, raises his sword to plunge it into his elfin opponent. Except the man is gone, disappeared under the water. Heph stabs the surface repeatedly, to the howls of the crowd, as the Tyrrhian climbs out the far side of the pond, laughing, bowing again.

Still fighting at the top of the heap of boulders, the Samian thrusts his sword into the Cretan's side, and the Cretan cries out in pain, tumbling down the boulders to the grass, where he remains still. Then the Samian clambers down to attack Heph, who is sloshing out of the pond in frustration as the Tyrrhian makes for the forest.

Alex sees with horror that Heph is shaken by the crowd's laughter. He isn't ready for the Samian's attack. On top of that, his clothing is now soaked and no doubt heavy. With a high, ringing blow, the Samian hits Heph's sword so hard it flies out of his hand. Alex gasps.

Heph has no time to pick up the sword. Clearly enraged and mortified, Heph holds his shield grip with both hands and uses it as a weapon, pummeling his opponent, slamming it into him again and again so quickly the man has no time to raise his sword. Finally the man collapses on the ground, his head bloody. Heph picks up the Samian's sword, which he sheathes, and then retrieves his own. Now the fickle crowd is on Heph's side again, standing and clapping, crying, "Pella! Pella! Pella!"

Alex breathes a sigh of relief.

On the other side of the arena, the Red Giant of Sparta has speared two more men. He is the victor on his side of the field, Heph the victor on the other.

Now the Giant is racing toward Heph, spear raised. Alex's heart pounds, but then the Giant's horse snorts in pain. The Tyrrhian jokester has jumped out of the bushes and fired his slingshot repeatedly at its rump. As the Giant roars in rage and tries to control his horse, Heph sprints toward the boulders, scrabbles up into the makeshift cliffs, and throws himself down onto the horse behind the Giant. The Giant tries to twist around to get his hands on Heph, but his horse, already stung by the slingshots, panics and rears up, standing on his back legs and neighing loudly, his nostrils flared. Both Heph and the Giant fall to the ground.

The Giant must have hit his head; he's slow to sit up, shaking his head, as though dazed. Heph, who landed on his side, leaps to his feet, grabs the horse's reins, and steadies him, then in two swift movements slices the reins right off the horse's bridle. Standing behind the bewildered Giant, he uses the reins to truss the larger man like a chicken for roasting. The crowd applauds and hollers. The redheaded beast of a man is coming to his senses now and struggles to break free of his restraints. His roars of protest echo throughout the arena.

"Kill him, kill him, kill him!" the crowd chants.

Alex knows Heph would never kill a disarmed man, helpless and bound. His sense of honor wouldn't permit it.

He bows and thrusts his sword into the ground, a sign that he will not kill him. Many in the crowd, hoping for more bloodshed, are jeering now, booing, though Alex knows that won't upset Heph nearly as much as their laughter did.

Alex looks around the field at the bodies, some of them heaving in pain, others eerily still. Those who survive until a victor is declared will be rescued. The Corinthian who fell into the quicksand has only his head above the muck, having realized that every movement only succeeds in further entrapping him. He, in particular, must be praying to all the gods for a quick victory. Over the course of the tournament, Alex noticed that several men took advantage of the forest's cover, but they'll have to come out sooner or later if they wish to avoid eternal shame. In fact, he's surprised that none has emerged so far.

Only two fighting men remain on the field: Heph and the rascally Tyrrhian. The jokester is no serious threat to Heph, Alex knows. And the men in the woods—cowering at first sign of trouble—won't be either.

Alex feels a surge of triumph. *Heph will win.* Armed with the purse of gold, perhaps they can leave Pella within a few days.

The little Tyrrhian runs out of the bushes, doing cartwheels and laughing, not about to let Heph win without another fight. Heph looks at him with distaste, as if an annoying fly were buzzing around him. Then, surprisingly, the village boy in the maroon tunic emerges from the trees, sword in hand.

"Cowards!" he cries. "Come and get me!"

The Tyrrhian smiles at this turn of events and pulls out his slingshot. Heph walks toward the villager, sword raised. The crowd goes wild in anticipation.

Just then the main gate to the arena opens. For a moment no one enters. Then an unearthly howl echoes across the stadium. The hellion.

The great black beast springs into the arena, opens its huge mouth, and roars again as the crowd goes silent.

Alex's heart plummets even as he rockets to his feet. The hellion wasn't supposed to be unleashed.

Whose idea was this?

The beast races across the arena, trampling the corpses of fallen men, then raises its enormous head, closes its eyes, and sniffs the air, nostrils twitching. Alex knows that look: it's hungry. Which means it's not simply going to fly off into the wild. It's going to stalk.

The yellow-green eyes become incredibly focused and it almost seems to freeze, recognizing living prey. In a swift move, it leaps onto a pile of boulders, wings flapping, and one of the wounded contestants falls from the rocks, screaming.

In the stands, some spectators rise and run frantically from their seats to the safety of the exit tunnels, knowing the hellion could very well fly over to them and bite off their heads. Others sit riveted, waiting breathlessly to see what will unfold. Looking down at his choices, the creature studies the wounded men, all of whom have the sense to lie absolutely still, and the three remaining warriors. It focuses its attention on the little Tyrrhian.

Truly alarmed for the first time in the tournament, the Tyrrhian bolts toward the pond, evidently hoping that this cat, like all others, hates water. The hellion narrows its eyes and decides the water, and the prey it holds, isn't worth the effort. Turning its massive head, it spots Heph, who throws his shield to the ground and unsheathes the extra sword in his belt.

That's right, Alex says silently. The thick leather shield is like paper to the hellion's claws—it will do Heph no good anyway.

Alex turns to his father. "We must stop it," he says. "Call out the guards to corral the hellion. This is not part of the game."

But Philip waves his hand dismissively. "Nonsense," he says, bringing the skull goblet in his other hand up to his mouth and swigging deeply. "This is the best tournament Pella has ever had. I bet the jester in the water will be the victor, and your friend will be a meal." Olympias laughs, a silvery, twinkling little laugh like the fall of water on stone. In that moment, Alex despises his mother. He wants to wrap her long blond hair around her slender neck and strangle her.

The hellion crouches on the rocks, its muscled torso trembling. Just as it's about to spring, the village boy near the forest starts hollering, jumping up and down to attract its attention. The giant cat swivels its head to stare.

Gracefully it leaps from the boulders, wings outstretched, and slinks toward the boy, its luxurious fur gleaming blue-black in the sun. The boy retreats into the forest, continuing to taunt the beast.

Alex frowns. What does the villager think he's doing?

The hellion, low to the ground on fast cat legs, races in between the trees for the kill. Heph follows swiftly, both swords outstretched. Today's victor will have to kill the hellion.

But before Heph can make it into the forest, there is a leafy, rattling sound, and then an animal howl of protest. The crowd leans forward. A large branch snaps. There is a thud followed by another roar of rage. And a moment later the village boy emerges from the trees bent forward diagonally as he drags the hellion in a net, claws and fur sticking at odd angles through the holes. The creature is bucking, thrashing furiously against its restraints.

Heph's mouth drops open in mute shock. Alex can feel Heph's devastation as though it's his own. It *is* his own.

The crowd goes wild. "Victor, Victor, Victor!" everyone shouts, standing, clapping, and stamping their feet. Some have brought drums and pound them, shouting "Victor! Victor!" The crowd has turned to King Philip.

The village boy, instead of standing in front of the royal platform to await the king's decision, puts up his hand as though to ask for patience and returns to the forest. As the audience cheers, one by one he drags out four hogtied contestants who took refuge there. It's obvious that he was using the net, which ultimately conquered the hellion, to ensnare his other opponents first. Very clever.

Laughing, the king stands and nods, and the crowd rises to its feet and cheers loudly. The village boy—Jacob something—is the confirmed winner. Jacob something. Alexander's ears are ringing, and his hands feel numb. A dozen men race onto the field with stretchers to remove the bodies and tend to the wounded. The Corinthian in the quicksand is saved at the last possible moment, when only his nose is up above the sludge.

Heph throws down his sword, acknowledging his loss. Alex can see by his face that he's furious. He walks quickly off the field, head down, then exits through one of the competitors' side doors as the victor is still being crowned with the sacred laurel wreath.

Alex pushes through the crowd out of the arena and spots his freckle-faced groom, Kithos, holding his horse. He swings up onto Bucephalus, savoring the height and power he always feels sitting on top of the great black stallion. He pats the horse's big shoulder and clucks softly to him. No one was ever able to tame him besides Alexander, and now, Alex will ride no other horse but this one.

As he scans the sea of people for a sign of where Hephaestion has gone, he notices a commotion. The crowd has made a small circle around a scrappy girl who appears to be fending off Lord Claudius, a big brute of a man whose two favorite pastimes are wine and gambling. Even as Alex watches, the girl reaches out and punches Lord Claudius directly in the face. Heph is there, ordering his guards to pin the struggling girl down. Suddenly, as if she knows he's watching, she turns toward him, and for a moment their eyes meet. The girl's eyes are dark green like jade, and to his surprise, he learns nothing from them.

He turns Bucephalus toward the fight, and the girl whose eyes he cannot read.

Chapter Eight

SPEARS OF HOT PAIN FLASH DOWN KAT'S ARMS as the two soldiers pinion them tightly behind her back. She fights the urge to cry out because she doesn't want to give the satisfaction to the boy who ordered her arrest. Arms crossed, he is standing in front of her, staring at her coldly. Ignoring her screaming muscles, she stares back at him defiantly.

Just after striking down the drunken, enraged Lord Claudius, just when she was ready to make a run for it, a boy came swaggering over, hand on his sword, and ordered the soldiers to arrest her. Obviously, they all think she swindled the drunk lord out of his money, even though she won it honestly. She recognizes the person who just ordered her arrest, now, as Pella's contestant in the Blood Tournament, though she can't remember his name. He wears no badge of office or military insignia. He's only sixteen or seventeen, and yet he's ordering people around as if he were King Philip himself.

She notes his jewelry, his dark curls, and the heavily embroidered royal blue tunic that is now ripped and stained from the fight. Obviously this boy puts in more time on his appearance than she does herself. But he has a huge purple welt in the middle of his forehead where the midget Tyrrhian hit him with a slingshot pebble. If her arms didn't hurt so much, she would burst out laughing.

As if he can read her mind, he brushes his bangs down over his forehead to cover the lump. Then he walks up to her, examining her closely. His face just inches from her own now, she can see the fine angle of his jaw, the way his wavy hair frames his dark eyes perfectly. She can see why he might think himself handsome. He's probably used to other women cowering before him or fawning over him.

Kat hates men like that, men who are too attractive for their own good—and know it.

"You're a spitfire, aren't you?" he says, then raises a hand to the guards. "There's no need to use such force."

They release her arms. The pain doesn't stop immediately, but the agony softens as she rubs her still-aching shoulders and biceps.

"This girl might be able to deck a drunk but she could hardly harm a trained fighter." He chucks her under the chin, and she knees him solidly in his groin. He doubles over, gasping, as she turns to her left and elbows the one guard in the nose before turning around to kick the other one in the shin. She spins around again, elbowing the first one hard in the jaw and punching the other one in the neck.

The townsfolk gathered around her cheer her on again.

"Look at her fight!"

"*She* should have been Pella's champion in the tournament."

Furious now, the guards throw themselves on her, driving the breath from her chest. Her face is pressed into the hard ground as the men hold her down. At the lightless, airless bottom of a heap of armor and sweaty, hairy flesh, Kat wonders if they will break her bones or, worse, smother her to death in a muggy fog of fermented body odor. But then she hears a voice cutting clear and cool through the soldiers' grunts.

"What's going on here?" It is a young man's voice and, oddly, one that seems both comforting and familiar.

The weighty load on top of her removes itself. Gulping in fresh air, Kat pushes herself to her feet and sees her rescuer on a beautiful black stallion. He's muscular yet slender, dressed all in royal purple. A gold crown sits atop his strikingly light hair. If anything, he's just as handsome as the other man, but his unusual eyes—one brown, one pale blue—make him seem otherworldly.

And yet familiar. She's heard of the boy with such eyes. Everyone has.

It's Prince Alexander.

Kat looks down and sees that her tunic is ripped and bunched up around her belt, revealing way too much of her legs, and hastily pulls it down. "I was defending myself against a man who tried to rob me, when the royal guards…" She trails off, unsure whether it's wise to accuse the guards of mistreatment.

The prince slides off his horse as the crowd respectfully backs up. "Who gave the order to arrest this girl?" he demands.

"I did," the pretty boy says, putting one hand on the hilt of his sword as if grasping for authority. He glares at Kat—no doubt he hasn't forgiven her for the ache between his legs. Good. She hopes he'll still feel it tomorrow.

"Heph." The prince shakes his head, looking exasperated. "Why did you do that?"

"I saw her fleeing the stadium. She's been accused of cheating on the bets. How else did she know a seventeen-year-old named Jacob of Erissa would win?" He holds up her heavy bag of gold and silver coins, his face flushed, obviously furious at having been bested. "Witchcraft, some say. Or she rigged the tournament somehow."

The prince turns to Kat. For a long moment, his strange eyes search hers as if looking for something. Whatever he's hoping for, he doesn't seem to find it.

He frowns. Breaking off his gaze, he says, "She doesn't look like a witch to me."

"My lord," says one of the guards. "She knocked Lord Claudius unconscious."

A few spectators step backward, revealing the red-faced man, eyes firmly shut. His large stomach is rising and falling heavily. At least he isn't dead.

One of the prince's eyebrows shoots up in surprise. "Explain," he says. Kat can't tell what he's thinking.

Kat nods, acutely aware of a sore place on her lower lip. She touches it and sees blood on her finger, which she wipes on her tunic. "He was drunk, my lord, and upset at losing a great deal of money to me. He tried to take my bag of winnings, but I've handled thieves before in my foster father's pottery shop, and dealt with this *lord*—" Kat gestures disdainfully toward the red-faced man "—the same way. I punched him. He fell. Apparently he bet on one of the losers, Hephaestion."

The dark-haired boy winces as if she slapped him. *Of course.* He must be Hephaestion.

The prince bristles. "Hephaestion is a well-trained warrior and athlete who was bested today by the Fates." Then he smiles, a smile that touches her in an oddly unexpected way, and she can't help but smile back despite the fact that every muscle in her body is throbbing. "Though you are right about Lord Claudius who, especially when drunk, is trouble."

He turns to the guards. "We will not arrest her. She won a wager and defended herself against a soused-up brawler. This girl has committed no crime."

The guards stand back.

"Heph, give her back her money," the prince says.

Kat sees that Hephaestion's ears burn red in embarrassment. Reluctantly he holds out the bag. She's tempted to stick her tongue out at him but remembers she's far too old for that now and besides, a prince is watching her. She accepts the coins from him.

"Are you from Pella?" Alex asks her.

"No, my lord. Erissa."

"Same as the champion?"

"Yes, that's why I wagered on him. We are from the same village, and I know he is both clever and brave."

"Where are you staying?" the prince asks.

"Last night I slept on the porch of the temple of Artemis," she replies. With Jacob staying in the contestants' dormitory, the temple was a safe, clean place, administered by matronly priestesses who dispensed clean sleeping pallets and wholesome food in return for any donation at all to the goddess.

Heph makes a disdainful noise.

The prince doesn't seem to notice. He's staring at Kat again. Finally, he says, "Since my friend and my guards did you such offense, the least I can do is invite you to stay in the palace. Do you have a trunk of clothing at the Temple?"

Kat looks down at her tunic, which is now torn in several places and stained by dirt, grass, and blood. "This is my only clothing," she says. Heph snorts. "I also have a pack."

The prince puts a gentle hand on her shoulder. "Come," he says, "we will arrange a room, a bath, some fresh clothing, and a meal." He snaps his fingers and one of the guards picks up her pack and hands it to her. Alex hops up on his horse and pulls her up behind him.

Kat turns to Heph and sees him staring at her, so intently it's as though she can feel his gaze, hot against her bruised skin.

Then he catches her staring back, and to her satisfaction, he stalks off, his gold-trimmed blue cape swinging wildly behind him.

The prince takes the horse's reins and makes a clicking sound, signaling the stallion to move. "You have quite an effect on my friend," Alex says as the crowd parts before them.

"I hope it's the effect of a sharp knife on a blown-up pig bladder," she says.

Alex chuckles.

She puts her arms rather clumsily around his waist so she won't fall off if the horse bolts. A light, warm scent rises from his neck, something sweet, like honeysuckle. His shoulder-length blond hair shines gold in the sun. How can it be, she wonders, that moments ago she faced the loss of every penny she had and imprisonment in a dungeon, and now she has her arms around the handsome young prince, riding a magnificent black stallion?

Because you belong together, she suddenly senses. It's as though the horse has told her this with the very movement of its body, the flick of its ears and snap of its tail. But that's impossible. The heat and excitement of the day have gone to her head.

She leans in toward Alex a little more, trying to clear the dizziness and set her thinking straight. She knows she was supposed to meet Jacob at the competitors' entrance; they should be celebrating his win together. She wants to tell him how proud she is of him. More than that, she wants to press her mouth against his and fall into his body and tell him everything she's been holding inside for so long.

But here is an opportunity she never thought possible: Alexander himself, taking her into the palace.

And, if she's honest with herself, leading her exactly where she wants to go.

She feels a sudden stab of nervousness deep in her gut.

They ride through the marketplace, with its shops and taverns, then past the soaring white columns of the Temple of Ares. Turning right, they go through a residential section of broad courtyard houses with numerous balconies and louvered windows.

As they approach one of the side gates of the palace complex, two guards snap to attention and open them. Inside the gates, Alex hops off first and helps her down, his strong hands on her waist. He gives the horse's reins to a servant and leads her past an athletic training area, stables, goat pens, a barracks, and a smithy.

She looks around in wonder. The palace complex. If her mother were alive, would she recognize it? Did she walk here? Did she ever brush a hand against that wall? See the smoke rise from the blacksmith's fire? Hear the clucks of chickens in that yard?

Alex stops outside a small door of the palace itself and looks at her with those strange eyes. Both Kat and Alex open their mouths at the exact same moment to speak. "It's not often I—" they both begin, then stop.

Alex shakes his head, laughing uncertainly.

Kat can't believe this strange coincidence—it's similar to how she felt running beside the gazelle, and yet it's unlike anything she's ever felt before. Without knowing how, Kat senses an understanding between them, like they're both cut from the same cloth. She's not certain how she can tell all this from one brief interaction, but she can. It's odd that Jacob, the boy she's known almost forever, has become so mysterious to her recently, while this stranger—and a prince, no less—can make her feel as though she belongs.

Perhaps it's just the relief of having been taken in, on top of the weariness of travel.

Perhaps it's just loneliness.

"Come on," Alex says, grinning, and opens the door.

As they walk down hallways, up twisting staircases, and through courtyards, the happiness Kat felt moments ago gives way to tension. What does Alex *want* with her? Will he send a guard to escort her to his room tonight? Isn't that what princes and rich men the world over do with girls like her? Surely Prince Alexander hadn't invited her to the palace just to be *nice*.

Perhaps she can still make a run for it. Or she can bathe, eat, get a change of clothing, and then sneak out before he sends for her.

Just as speedily as she has the idea, she rejects it. Being a guest in the palace is an amazing piece of good luck. She was wondering how she would gain entrance, and here she is, an invited guest of the prince.

It's the perfect way for her to complete her mission.

It's the perfect way for her to get her revenge.

They're on the second story of a wing of residential apartments when they spot a skinny, long-legged boy wandering the hall muttering to himself. He must be about twelve, though his way of moving and talking to himself makes him seem much younger. When he notices Kat, he runs up to her and stares with protruding reddish-brown eyes. She notices a large rat peering out of a fold in his tunic with beady black eyes, and draws backward.

"Y-you d-don't belong here," the boys says.

A chill runs up her spine. Who is he?

Alex grins and ruffles the boy's dark hair. "She's a friend of mine, Arri," he says. Turning to Kat, he adds, "It's my half brother, Arrhidaeus," and taps his forehead while giving her a rueful smile. Kat nods thoughtfully. She heard that a lesser wife of King Philip had borne a son. She's also heard that Queen Olympias had intentionally dropped the baby on his head.

"Arrhidaeus!" cries a cool, slightly accented voice. "Come now, we must return to your quarters."

Kat turns to see a smiling slender girl with her hand extended. Her skin is the color of burnished bronze, and her hip-length black hair so straight and shiny it hangs about her like an expensive cape.

"Yes, Sarina," Arrhidaeus says, taking her hand. As she leads him away, the young boy gazes back at Kat with a haunted look in his eyes. For some reason, it makes Kat sad.

Kat and Alex turn the corner and almost bump into a striking red-haired serving woman carrying a water pitcher. She's tall, perhaps twenty-five, and impeccably dressed. A palace handmaiden, Kat decides, staring at her with wonder and a touch of longing. What must it be like to work here, as her mother once did?

"Ah, Daphne," Alex says, and the elegant woman turns around and curtseys deeply. "Please find a suitable room for..." He turns expectantly to Kat.

"Katerina, my prince," Kat says.

"Katerina," Alex says. Daphne takes one look at Kat—the filthy, ripped tunic, the tangled hair, the smears of blood and dirt on her face—and her disdain is obvious.

"She was assaulted by Lord Claudius and ably defended herself," the prince adds, obviously noting Daphne's expression. Daphne's face at once softens into a look of sympathy.

"Poor thing," she says, putting an arm around Kat's shoulders. "Come with me and you will be fixed up in no time."

Kat turns back to thank Alex but all she sees is his purple cape and pale blond hair turning the corner. Daphne leads her down two corridors and opens a door to an airy room with painted walls, wide windows, and pink marble floors. She has never seen a room half so beautiful. And this is just a guest room. What do the royal apartments look like?

"Rest," Daphne says, "and I will look after the things you need." She slips out, closing the door softly behind her.

Kat looks out the window at a courtyard garden with a statue of blue-bearded Poseidon rising from a fountain, bearing his trident. The roses—fuchsia and red—are in full bloom, and one side of the garden is a riot of purple hyacinth. It reminds her of a story her mother told her when she was tiny. Hyacinth was a vain, ambitious boy, who competed in throwing the discus with the god Apollo, only his discus boomeranged back, hit him on the head, and killed him. In sorrow, Apollo turned him into a flower.

Somehow the myth reminds Kat of Hephaestion, trying to outdo the real prince, Alex. A puffed-up, pretend princeling. If the gods made Hephaestion into a flower it would be the kind that made people sneeze and gave them a bad rash.

The room is abuzz with activity. Servants pour through the door, bearing fresh clothing, food, and wine. Two men carry in a heavy copper tub, and several others empty buckets of hot water into it.

"My lady," says a cheerful voice, and Kat turns from the window to see a woman carrying a basket. She is about forty, short, and plump, with gray-streaked brown hair and snapping dark eyes. "I'm Iris. I'm here to give you a bath."

Give me a bath? Kat thinks. The last person to give her a bath was her mother. She can give *herself* a bath.

Seeing her reluctance, Iris walks to the tub and from her basket plucks a vial of flower essences, which she upends into the water. The rising steam is heady, sweet-scented.

"Come," she says, smiling, "before it cools."

The bath is too tempting to resist. Kat removes her tunic, sandals, and belt, and steps quickly inside the tub so the water can cover her. The hot water on her muscles, so sore from the long journey to Pella and then the bruising fight with Lord Claudius and the guards, relaxes her instantly. She closes her eyes and inhales the scented oils, wondering if she will fall asleep and drown.

Iris takes a pitcher, dips it into the water, and pours it over Kat's hair. Then she starts massaging her head, neck, and shoulders. Kat has never been so relaxed in her entire life. After every inch of Kat's body is scrubbed, Iris bids her to stand and dries her with fine linen towels. Then the hand-maiden rubs oil and perfume on Kat's skin, combs and pins her hair, and helps her put on a peplos, the traditional long women's robe that Kat rarely wears in Erissa. This one is of soft-combed wool, the color of a robin's egg. It's light against Kat's skin, like a gentle caress.

Next Iris hands her a gilded leather belt, and a pair of new leather sandals. When Kat sees herself in the polished bronze mirror, she's surprised to see a woman stare back at her. For a moment, she wishes Jacob were here to see her metamorphosis, but she quickly dismisses the thought. Jacob would probably laugh if he saw her dressed as a fine lady.

"Sit," Iris says, gesturing to the pear-wood table with gilded lion's feet. "You must be hungry."

As Iris removes the covers from various dishes, Kat looks in wonder at the food. Lamb and venison in rich plum sauce, apple-honey cakes and cheese bread, celery and carrots in vinegar, a platter heaped high with dates and pomegranates. Iris pours wine from an ivory *oenochoe* into a chalice, and Kat takes a sip of something so musky and fragrant it is more like perfume.

She realizes that she's starving and digs into the food with abandon, savoring the unusual flavors concocted by expert chefs in the royal kitchens. She practically swoons in her chair at the taste of it. *Jacob will never believe it*, she thinks. *When I go home, no one will believe it.*

And then she remembers that she might never go home.

And that she doesn't even know where Jacob is at this very moment.

Her appetite has disappeared. She pushes her plate away. She will send a message to Jacob. Tonight. Someone, maybe Iris, will be able to help her.

Iris is still watching her, standing with her hands folded primly over her apron, smiling.

"Please sit," Kat says, laying down her knife and looking up at the woman standing beside her, ready to serve. "Please," she says, when Iris appears about to resist. "I can't bear to be gaped at. Besides, I'm an orphan, a potter's adopted daughter from a village no one has ever heard of. There's no need for ceremony with me."

Chuckling, Iris takes the offered seat.

"Does Prince Alexander often invite young women to stay in the palace?" Kat asks, wiping the grease from her fingers on a finely woven linen napkin.

Iris shakes her head. "This is the first time that I know of, though he has only recently returned from school."

That, at least, is good news. At least he doesn't ravish a different girl every night. She studies the pleasant face across from her. "Are you a maid in the palace?" she asks.

Iris raises an eyebrow. "I am one of the queen's handmaidens," she says, with just a hint of superiority in her voice. "But we all must prepare for more duties this week with so many visitors for the tournament."

Kat's heart skips a beat. "My mother was a handmaiden to Queen Olympias many years ago," she says carefully.

"Was she?" Iris smiles. "What was her name?"

"Her name," Kat says, "was… Helen." There it is again,

the same mixture of joy and pain whenever she says the name. No, not just pain. A daily insult that she is gone. An aching emptiness Kat can't fill. A burning thirst for revenge.

"Helen?" Iris frowns. "Tall, brunette, large blue eyes? I knew a Helen originally from Caria who came here with the queen's suite of personal attendants when she married Philip."

"Yes," Kat says with a sharp exhale.

Iris sits back, shaking her head, amazed. "We all wondered what happened. She was such a lovely, laughing girl with so many admirers. One night she simply disappeared. No one could find her." She lowers her voice. "We hoped she had eloped with a lover. So many of the queen's ladies marry well and leave her service. Some marry palace officials or wealthy Pellans. Others marry visiting dignitaries and go to foreign lands." She smiles brightly. "Where did she go?"

Kat looks down. "She went to a village, married, and became a weaver of beautiful cloth. My father died soon after my birth, and my mother when I was six."

Iris crosses her hands in her lap. "I am sorry to hear it," she says, and sounds as though she sincerely means it. "She used to weave the most stunning cloth for the queen's gowns. She was the queen's favorite, most trusted handmaiden. Those two spent so much time together talking, it made the other handmaidens jealous."

Kat's mouth drops open. Favorite? Most trusted? Made the others jealous? How could that be?

Iris doesn't notice Kat's reaction. "We didn't know she was gone at first. She disappeared on the very night that Prince Alexander was born, you see, after helping the midwife deliver him, and the whole palace was in an uproar," Iris explains. "King Philip threw a feast. Everyone drank. There was brawling in the corridors. The next day the entire palace had a headache and a black eye." She laughs. "By the time we all recovered, we realized that Helen was missing. I still wonder why she left without saying goodbye. Or perhaps she tried to tell us, and we were all too drunk to notice."

Kat is growing more perplexed by the moment. Her mother disappeared the night Prince Alexander was born? She helped the midwife? According to Helen's story, Queen Olympias stormed into Helen's room, found the stolen scarf, and threw Helen out. But how could the queen have denounced Helen as a thief and stormed anywhere while she was still weakened from giving birth? And what else did Helen steal? For surely the scarf was only a symbol of some greater betrayal, a betrayal that led to Helen's eventual death.

Kat comes to a sudden decision. If she's ever going to untangle the mysteries of her mother's past, she must risk exposing Helen's crime to Iris. She stands up, opens her leather pack, and brings out the scarf. "Do you recognize this?" she asks.

Iris stretches out her hands to take it and makes a clucking sound. "I haven't seen one of these in many years," she says, holding it up and admiring the glinting gold and intricate pattern. "All of the queen's ladies had them. We wear special scarves so that everyone can distinguish us from the ordinary palace servants. Every few years, the queen gives us a new pattern, woven at her instructions in her homeland of Epirus. See? I'm wearing mine now." She removes the scarf around her neck, blue snakes swallowing their tails on a background of shining silver, and offers it to Kat.

Kat takes it and immediately sees a similarity in the weave of the linen and the design. She feels nauseous with confusion.

"The queen loves her snakes," Iris says, laughing. "She has snake scarves, snake jewelry, and snake sandals. Not to mention *actual* snakes—at least a dozen of them. She calls them her pets, but at night they're also her bodyguards. She lets her snakes out of their pen to guard her. Anyone who comes to her room uninvited will be struck down by their venom."

Kat runs a hand over her forehead and feels dizzy. She sits down heavily. Could what Iris says be true? It doesn't make any sense.

She closes her eyes and journeys back to the day that she has relived every day since. The day when the sound of hooves slamming hard into the road made her mother turn from her loom and look out the window.

"The queen," Helen said, a shocked expression on her face.

Kat joined her mother at the window and saw soldiers on huge black stallions, royal pennants waving in the air, and on a white horse, a small blonde woman, who must have been the queen. They pulled up near the house in a cloud of dust, the woman slipping easily from her horse.

Kat wanted to race outside to greet them, but her mother held her back. Fear cracking her voice, Helen said, "Hide, Katerina! Hide!" Helen pointed to the large wooden box of oily, untreated wool ready to be washed, beaten, and dyed before Helen spun it into thread. "Now," she urged.

But Kat didn't move. Helen ran into the front yard, closing the door behind her, as Kat peered out the window and watched. The queen was questioning Helen, who was trying to calm her, waving her hands in protest. Kat couldn't make out most of what was said.

"Come, I will show you," Helen said, turning toward the house. The door was flung open just as Kat dove into the pile of wool and covered herself with it. Through a crack in the slat, Kat saw Helen kneeling before the fire pit and loosening some bricks as the queen and her soldiers entered. Then Helen pulled out an ivory box set with turquoise. Kat had never seen anything so beautiful in her entire life. It must have come from the palace.

The queen opened it and stared, her lips curling into a smile. Then she looked up at Helen and said, "You should have brought this to me years ago instead of making me search all of Macedon for you, you stupid lying thief." As she snapped the lid shut, she added, "Kill her," and two guards at once ran their swords through Helen, who was still kneeling. Her face wore an expression of surprise, not pain, and she fell backward onto the packed earth floor. Kat was just about to pop out of the wool box—either to throw herself on the soldiers or try to help her mother—when the queen said, "Search the premises." She turned on her heel and marched outside.

One soldier climbed up the ladder to the sleeping loft; another ran outside to search the outbuildings: the dying shed, the woodshed, the smokehouse, and the latrine. A wiry man seemed to enjoy smashing Helen's precious loom to bits. A large soldier marched over to the wool box where Kat was hiding.

Help me, Father Zeus, Kat prayed silently, squeezing her eyes shut. *Help me, Hera and Apollo and all the other gods.*

Taking his sword in both hands, the soldier raised it high. "Are you in there, little girl?" he asked softly.

Suddenly, the air was pierced by the hysterical, whinnying cries of horses.

"What is it?" asked the small soldier who had stopped smashing the loom.

"The horses," another one said, walking toward the window. "They're going crazy. The queen's mount is trying to throw her! Come!"

Kat heard footsteps, men shouting orders, a woman's high-pitched commands, all drowned out by the screams and stamping sounds of horses. She knew, without understanding how or why, that the horses had saved her life...that they had sensed her panic and had panicked as well.

Quickly, Kat emerged from the wool box and climbed upstairs, forcing herself to ignore her mother's body, though pain screamed through her chest. She was filled with the aching desire to throw herself next to her mother, to hold her. The soldiers would be back, she knew. Where could she hide? Looking around, she saw two sleeping pallets, an open chest, and clothing strewn about. She pushed herself out the small back window, stood on the ledge, and, grabbing tufts of the thickly thatched roof, pulled herself toward the top, just as she and Jacob used to do until her mother caught them and told them it was dangerous. The thatch was a sandy brown, as were her tunic, her hair, and her skin. Perhaps like a chameleon she could cling there, blending in.

The horses' violent frenzy had quieted to periodic snorts and the intermittent stamping of hooves. The men returned to the house, crashing around. Finally, they went out front insisting they had found no one else. A deep voice barked orders; a woman's cool voice replied. Still clinging to the thatch, Kat heard them gallop away.

She wasn't sure how long she stayed on the roof, feeling the sun beat against her, too terrified to move. It was as if she became part of the roof itself, melting into it, watching a large bird circle lazily overhead in the turquoise sky. It was almost sunset by the time she at last made her way off the roof and swung her legs over the window ledge.

Their modest bedroom was destroyed. The mattresses had been cut open, wool stuffing strewn about. The wooden chest that had held their clothing was smashed to bits. Even their garments had been ripped and shredded.

All except Helen's scarf.

Kat picked it up from the floor and buried her face in it to inhale her mother's scent.

Cautiously she descended the ladder to the lower level,

shaking uncontrollably. Everything here, too, was smashed, including the wool box she had been hiding in, its contents strewn across the floor. Her beautiful mother, blue eyes open wide in surprise, was slumped near the fire pit where she had fallen. An amphora near her was broken, and the red wine ran into the red blood, mixing with it. Kat knelt beside her mother, calling to her, stroking her face, cradling her head.

At some point, she knew she had to leave. It wasn't safe. The soldiers might come back.

Kat gently laid her mother's head down and removed the leather thong around her neck. Dangling from it was the silver pendant Helen always wore hidden next to her heart. The Flower of Life, as she had called it. A six-petaled flower within a circle. She had told Kat that this symbol was magical…and forbidden.

On the far side of the fire pit Kat pulled up three bricks and removed a leather pouch that Helen always told her to take if something bad happened to her. Inside was a substantial amount of drachmas Helen had earned.

Numbly, Kat stumbled out into the gathering dusk. She walked straight into the forest, clutching the bag and the necklace to her chest, the scarf billowing behind her. She wasn't aware of where she was going, but after a time she saw Cleon in the distance, taking newly fired pots out of his kiln. Jacob ran to greet her and, seeing the blood all over her face and tunic, called to his father.

Later, Cleon and the village elders told her they had buried Helen. They asked Kat who had killed her. But she simply shook her head and said, "Bad men."

Though she never spoke about what happened, she thought about it often. She eventually figured out that the queen must have tracked Helen down to punish her for stealing something, and that Helen had tried to pay for it with money in the box. But what? It couldn't have just been the scarf. It had to be something more valuable, something that even all those drachmas couldn't buy.

Now Kat knows that Helen didn't tell her the entire truth. The scarf had not been stolen at all; that was not the reason she had left the palace and been killed. There has to be more to the story than Kat ever realized.

"My lady, are you all right?" Iris is saying in a concerned voice.

Kat opens her eyes and forces herself to smile. "I'm afraid I'm tired and ate too quickly."

Iris stands up and gently takes her scarf from Kat's lap. "I'll have the dishes removed and the bath emptied," she says, pulling the scarf around her neck. Pointing to Kat's disgusting ripped tunic, she says, "I assume we can burn it?"

Kat nods.

"Good. Any questions?"

Kat starts to shake her head, but stops suddenly. "Actually…is it possible to deliver a message? To the Blood Tournament victor?"

Iris gives Kat a knowing look that makes her cheeks flush and says, "Let me or one of the other handmaidens know, and we will find you a servant to deliver any kind of message you wish." Iris winks at Kat and heads toward the door.

Kat shoots out of her chair and puts a hand on the older woman's shoulder. "Iris," she says, "please don't tell anyone that Helen was my mother. I am afraid she might have done something disgraceful to leave the palace so quickly. I don't want anyone to know."

Iris studies Kat's face a long moment and says, "I was very fond of your mother. For her sake, I won't." She crosses the room and quietly closes the door behind her.

Kat returns to the window, leaning her head against the

glass, her mind still swirling with everything she has learned. The tall trident of the Poseidon fountain casts a long three-pronged shadow over neighboring flower beds and the water makes a calming sound. Helen may have stood at this very window, staring out onto an evening just like this one. Kat breathes in a blend of fragrances so magical that the old rankling burden of her mother's murder is lifted for just a moment.

But then it returns, full-force, and with greater clarity than ever before. The queen is cruel. She killed Helen for no good reason. No amount of contradictions in the story can change that fact. Kat *saw* it.

Besides, everyone in Macedon knows Olympias played a role in the death of Philip's previous wife, too, stabbing her in the bathtub. She dropped poor Arrhidaeus on his head and ruined him for life. How many other people has Olympias killed and hurt? How many more will be her victims if she isn't stopped?

This is Kat's duty. It's her mission. She will never be able to think of anything else—she will never be able to love Jacob or feel free—until she has done what she has come here to do. It's time.

Kat's thoughts jump to Prince Alexander, the kindness he showed her, the connection she feels between them. When she pictures Alex's searching eyes, a dark feeling, thick and watery, wraps its way through her chest tugging at her heart like river reeds. Or snakes.

She hadn't expected that. She hadn't expected *him*.

It troubles her that she is going to kill his mother.

CHAPTER NINE

OLYMPIAS CLENCHES HER TEETH AS HER BED-
room door is thrown open with such force that the brass handle slams into the frescoed wall, adding yet another crack to
the plaster. Seated at her dressing table, she knows immediately
who it is, even before catching his eye in her polished silver
mirror: the only person who *can* push through her guards and
fling open her door. Philip.

Stifling her anger, she refuses to swivel around to face him,
instead flashing him a brilliant smile in her reflection. Thank
the gods her maids haven't removed her makeup yet.

"My lord," she says, softly enough that he is forced to step
closer to her, bringing with him his perpetual stench of old
wine and sweat. Even the perfumed smoke of myrrh and
amber rising from her incense burners can't mask it. But she
doesn't wince. She never winces. Her stepmother in Epirus
used to beat her for showing any emotion and if she grimaced
during the beatings, she beat her even more. "I didn't know
I was to have the pleasure of your company tonight," she replies, subtly daubing jasmine oil on her neck.

Even the word *pleasure* tastes like ashes in her mouth. The long years have worn at her, like the tide against the rocky shores of Epirus, her homeland, which she hasn't seen since she was sixteen. She has never feared her husband—not really—but she is beginning to loathe her own life—her own lie—like one who has become entrapped in a tomb of her own making.

Philip waves a hand. "I just came to tell you we're leaving for Byzantium at first dawn, well before you're up, I imagine. I'll send word when we camp outside the gates."

Olympias feels a wave of relief surging through her. She knows what Byzantium is code for: his mistress in the north, with whom he maintains an unsettling—but conveniently distracting—obsession. The palace walls that seemed to be closing in on her, a bit more each day until she could hardly turn around, suddenly recede and she has space, light, air. And the timing couldn't be better.

She sets down the fluted agate perfume vial and turns slowly toward him. "Oh. I see," she says, casting her eyes down and wondering if she can manage to call up a tear. Like many battle-hardened warriors impervious to suffering and death, Philip crumples at the sight of a beautiful woman's tears. And right now she wants him to appoint her to the Council of State—five royal ministers she despises for never listening to her—who will hold the real power when the king is gone, "advising" Alex, the regent, but actually running the nation.

How to cry? She thinks about the silent scream inside her that has lasted seventeen years, and when she raises her chin, she knows her eyes are glistening. She dabs at them with the long, wide linen sleeve of her night shift, transparent Egyptian linen dyed scarlet with the ground-up shell of the kermes beetle.

"My lord," she begins, her voice cracking with just enough

emotion to be noticeable, but not so much as to be overdone. "I have a request—"

The moment is ruined when the door opens again, and her handmaiden, Daphne, enters carrying a silver tray. On it are plates of dates, figs, and candied rose leaves, the queen's usual bedtime snack, along with a painted *oenochoe* of wine and two cups: one plain clay and the other gold. The handmaiden's eyes dart from Olympias—who feels her face burning red with fury at the untimely interruption—to the king. She curtseys to both, eyes firmly on the figs, and sets the tray down. Philip leers at the statuesque redhead; it's obviously not the first time he's admired her beauty.

Olympias forces a cool smile at Daphne and nods. The young woman nervously pulls a date out of the silver bowl and, with evident reluctance, pops it in her mouth. She swallows with difficulty, then tries a fig and some rose leaves. She pours a splash of wine into the small clay cup and swigs it quickly, her eyes wide.

"You're using a taster now?" Philip asks in surprise.

"It's the Aesarian Lords. Yesterday I heard that they are resorting to poison since you won't hand me over to them. Are they leaving tomorrow as well?" she asks, picking up a silver brush. "You know I'm always nervous when they're here, and more so with this latest rumor." It's well known the Lords are suspicious of Olympias—perhaps even more than her own husband is. They've spread vicious rumors across the land that she's a witch, born of the beggars and scammers of the scattered Epirote nobility, an unfit queen. And the Lords take witches away for secret execution.

Philip lowers his eye, appraising her reflection in her mirror, her white-gold hair gleaming in the lamplight as she brushes it, the luscious figure just beyond the folds of her gossamer nightdress. Instinctively, she arches her back slightly. "They wouldn't dare poison my queen, but they're right about one thing," he mutters, approaching her from behind, a hungry look on his face. "All women are witches. Sometimes a man can't even be sure if his own children are his."

Olympias stiffens. There it is again. That insulting taunt. He doesn't seem to be serious, though, and runs his thick hand along her back, causing her gown to fall to one side, revealing her pale shoulder.

"Though High Lord Mordecai and I have known each other for twenty years, I won't let him meddle with my kingdom," he says, rubbing at his eye patch. "Lately he's been badgering me for the hellion. Can you imagine? The only one in the world in captivity. Five of my men died in the hunt for it. As always, Mordecai wants to recruit contestants who did well in the Blood Tournament—those two villagers, this year—and plans to stage a skills demonstration. I've told him he can do that much if he stops pestering me for everything else. Perhaps in a week they'll be gone."

Olympias squints her eyes in the mirror. A week. A long time to watch her back every moment. Even though there are only thirteen Aesarian Lords here, seeing them ride out of Pella will be like having a sack of stones cut from her neck. Or will it? There are hundreds—perhaps thousands—spread out all over the known world.

A drop of sweat trickles between her shoulder blades. Her handmaiden, pretty little Ariadne, sits in the corner pulling on a long rope attached to linen panels on the ceiling, which move back and forth with a low clacking sound, creating a slight breeze in the room. But it's not enough to make the temperature bearable. Will this hot, dry spell ever end? The entire palace is beginning to smell of sewage from chamber pots and latrines. Usually the fresh evening breeze rising off the Axios River right behind the palace is enough to clear the odor. But it's gotten so bad it will take a long, soaking rain to wash the filth and stench away.

Daphne is beginning to relax. A slight smile plays on her lips; she has survived another tasting. The queen chuckles to herself. Five years ago, Philip's constant ogling of the girl was so irritating to Olympias that she sent her to Epirus. Lately she has regretted giving in to her impassioned pleas to return. When she had to pick a taster from her several handmaidens, she knew immediately it would be Daphne.

"Would you care for some wine or sweets?" Olympias asks. Perhaps it's not too late to send the handmaidens away and do whatever is necessary to join the Council of State.

"No," Philip says, "I'd better get to sleep. Tomorrow will be an early day and a long march to the coast."

She smiles over her disappointment. The mood is broken, the moment missed. "May the gods grant you a safe sea voyage and victory in battle, my lord."

He grunts, and on his way out runs his left hand over Daphne's breasts. Daphne's horrified expression makes her look as if she has, indeed, just swallowed poison.

For once Olympias doesn't care. Even though she won't join the council, she feels happiness surge through her. Philip gone, maybe for as long as a year! Or possibly forever if he gets killed in battle or dies from camp fever, which kills more soldiers than swords and arrows. More likely, he'll catch an illness from that filthy whore of his in Byzantium.

Iris enters bearing a tray with a dozen golden cups of milk. The handmaidens set them on the floor throughout the room as Olympias removes her makeup with more of her jasmine-scented olive oil and splashes her face with lavender water. Iris opens the trap door next to the queen's bed, and all the ladies curtsey hastily, almost falling over one another to escape the room, then closing the door behind them.

As Olympias turns, a dozen beautiful snakes emerge from the trap door, their sinuous bodies whispering across the floor to drink the milk. Beings of wisdom, healing, and immortality, they serve the Mother Earth goddess and live deep in her womb, only emerging at night.

The largest one, emerald-green with gold diamonds, winds up the queen's dressing table and wraps itself around her mirror, its black tongue flickering. She runs her hand over it, feeling the cool, writhing body tingle against her skin.

"Here," she says, rolling up her sleeve.

The snake coils itself around her arm, and she feels its strength, its heavy muscularity. It could crush the breath out of her if it wanted to. During the day, she is the mistress; he is her pet. But at night, he is the master, she the slave.

The snake sways its head slightly, staring at her with alert, lidless dark eyes.

"Yes," she says. The snake opens its mouth impossibly wide, baring razor-sharp fangs. Hissing spray, it plunges them into the skin of her forearm. White-hot pain shoots down her arm as if it has been sliced open from shoulder to wrist, bone and muscle exposed. She gasps, closing her eyes, and slumps to the floor. The throbbing agony travels through her entire body; she arches her back and cries out.

The pain turns to spasms rolling through her, filling her with so much heat, she rips off her scarlet nightgown and lies writhing and naked on the cool marble.

After a moment, she goes still. She opens her eyes with effort and stares at the puncture marks on her arm, trying to focus. The snake has joined her on the floor and it curls around her now, as a word slowly begins to appear, throbbing in dark blue blood just beneath her pale skin.

Soon.

"Yes, soon," she says, laughing as the tears run down her face. So many years lost. But the waiting will be over soon.

The ritual will work only after the next full lunar eclipse when the heavens shift, and an invisible door opens, giving power to the spell. She has waited ten years for this moment. *Ten years.* It is more than just an eclipse—it signals the end of an era, the completion of another thousand-year cycle. According to the old priests and priestesses of the north, the Age of Gods is coming to an end, and in only a couple of days, they will enter a new, as yet undetermined Age. Many philosophers predict that during these great shifts, fates can be altered, curses lifted, and unthinkable feats achieved.

She may not possess blood magic herself, but she has the bones required by the ritual. She will spill the necessary blood. She just needs the new age to dawn for him to come back to her the way he was. It has been so long she has almost forgotten his face, the sound of his voice, the touch of his hand, the weight of his body when he embraced her. Soon he will be tall and broad-shouldered, forceful and strong. Soon she will be able to sit beside him in power and majesty, ruling the world together as they planned: he with his immortal blood, and she with the fire of her belief. Nothing will stand in her way. Nothing.

The snake thrusts its head under the small of her back, wrapping around her torso tightly. It slowly undulates all over her body, exploring the back of her knees, the palms of her hands, her earlobes. The scales feel sleek and cool against her overheated skin.

The oil lamps have long burned out when Riel finally coils around her legs like rope, and Olympias feels movement in her hair, against her arms and breasts. She cannot open her eyes, but she knows it is the other snakes, twining themselves around her to go to sleep.

CHAPTER TEN

CYN NOCKS HER ARROW IN THE BOWSTRING, looks up at the crow flying overhead—they've been gathering in great numbers lately—pulls the string back to her ear, and sends the arrow arcing into the clear blue sky. It strikes the crow in the breast, and the bird falls, flapping, to the ground.

She looks to Heph, but he's studying the springs of a catapult, totally ignoring her. The other men are sneaking glances whenever Diodotus bends over to examine a gear or check the strength of a rope. Heph's friend, Phrixos, in particular—the big one with the wide, friendly face—can't seem to take his eyes off her. And, after all, her outfit is chosen to get male attention—a leather breastplate, short leather skirt, and boots. But the other men aren't the reason she's here in the flat field that runs between the palace wall and the river, a field littered with catapults, siege engines, and battering rams.

"Fire!" Heph cries, stepping back, and two men release the catapult. With a loud groan, the eight-foot spoon-shaped arm arcs up and slams down on its face, flinging a large rock through the air. It soars soundlessly over the field and crashes down on the other side, raising plumes of dust.

Heph shades his eyes with his hand as two men at the end of the field plunge a long stick with a red flag on it next to the stone. This throw is definitely farther than the last, but Cyn thinks that with minor adjustments they can still get more distance out of the catapult.

"Not bad!" Heph says, nodding in approval to Telekles, as Diodotus grunts his approbation. "Pankratios! Menton!" Heph yells. "Winch the springs even tighter." One man turns the crank while the other heaves a rock into the cup.

Cyn makes a face. Not only could she do a better job than these men, she could command them as well as Heph or Alex. Of course, she's not allowed.

It wasn't always like this. Only a few years ago, Philip let her work with the soldiers on the catapults and siege engines, and the men liked having a cute little girl helping them. Now she isn't permitted because she is a woman. And women are supposed to weave and sew for recreation, not launch missiles. Last year Olympias set up a loom in Cyn's room and suggested she make her a wall hanging with it. Cyn smashed the loom with a hammer, sewed the broken wooden pieces onto a long strip of cloth, and delivered it to the queen with a note: *Olympias, I have indeed made a wall hanging for you with the loom.*

Now, the king and queen are waiting on Cyn's marriage. She has made it a point to scare away all her suitors, but she knows her antics have caused the king great embarrassment abroad, and that if she doesn't land a match soon, it would not be surprising if he threatened her with her own life.

Unless she can acquire the blood of true betrayal...and with it, Smoke magic.

Her mother died in vain, imprisoned in an unwanted marriage.

Cynane will not.

The smell of midsummer grass and hard baked earth wafts around her. She can feel the sun tanning her already golden skin, warming her hair, calming a bit of her frustration. Her leather clothing is sticky on her skin.

Nearby, more soldiers are loading a bolt-shooting catapult, which looks like an archer's bow laid flat on a wooden frame. One man fixes a seven-foot bolt in its cradle with the words *Greetings from Philip* stamped on its cruel iron tip, her father's idea of a joke.

She scans the sky for birds and, seeing none, turns back to the archery butt her slave hauled out here this morning, trailing the soldiers out of the city's west gate and north around the curve of the cliff-like walls. The square straw-stuffed canvas jacket is painted with concentric circles of different colors and placed on a wooden frame. She plucks an arrow from her quiver and shoots. It whistles through the air and embeds itself into the bull's-eye. Heph doesn't even turn his head.

He marches over to six soldiers dismantling a battering ram. For long distances, siege equipment is taken off its wheeled frame, the wooden parts, ropes, and springs transported in wagons. Well-trained soldiers need to know how to put them together and take them apart quickly before and after battle. But Cyn can see that the men are making a mess of dismantling the cowhide-covered wagon that protects the men swinging the giant tree trunk against an enemy gate. They are throwing the panels on the ground without paying attention to the numbers branded into the lower right corners. The lower panels are straight. The upper ones are curved. If the men don't stack them in the right order, it will take forever to put them back on again. Cyn wonders if the men even recognize numbers. They must be completely illiterate. If she were their commander…

Heph puts his left hand on the thick bristly hide of a panel and talks to the men.

Cyn lines up her shot and fires. The arrow whooshes through the air and sinks deeply into the hide between his thumb and forefinger.

That gets his attention.

Eyes blazing, Heph yanks the arrow out of the hide and strides over to her, the metal-tipped leather lappets of his skirt swinging. Even Cyn is a bit shocked by her own audacity—her look of embarrassment isn't totally feigned.

"I'm so sorry," she says. "That one went wild."

"You're the one who's going wild," he says as he shakes the arrow in her face. "Enemies surround Macedon from every side, and we're defenseless without Philip's army. This is deadly serious. There's no time for your games."

She finds she's excited by the heat of his anger, the storminess in his eyes, the heavy breathing and lips so close to hers. For an instant his eyes drop down from her face to her chest, and she knows he sees the sweat trickling between her breasts.

She looks at her boots. "Heph. I'm *eighteen* now," she says. "I know that in the past, we teased each other. But we were children. And I'm not a child anymore." She strategically adjusts her leather vest. "And for your information, that *was* a stray arrow—there's so much on my mind I lost my focus when I fired." She lifts her chin to look him in the eyes again.

As he studies her, she can feel that his anger is cooling. "What's on your mind?"

She shrugs. "Where do I even begin? I'm worried about Alex. Something's different. Something's *been* different since he became regent." Heph gives her an impatient look, and she pushes on. "And someone intentionally set the hellion loose, ruining your chances of winning the tournament. I don't know where I stand anymore. I don't know where any of us stands."

Heph looks away, squinting into the sun. "Things change," he says slowly, and Cyn feels a flash of triumph: she has found a point of soreness. But just as quickly, Heph shakes his head. "Alex is busy. He's regent. And that can't be the only reason you've been shadowing us all week."

She crosses her arms. "I know more about fighting than most of those men. And yet this is as close as I can get to actual battle. The Amazons—"

"Lived eight hundred years ago," he says. His face has now completely softened. "And were annihilated in the Trojan War after killing hundreds of Greeks." He smiles, and she's struck by how handsome he is. "But if they were still around, I'm sure you would have made an excellent Amazon. They were the best archers in the world."

She grins at him.

"I hesitate to give a word of advice about archery to an Amazon," he says, "but would you like a tip?"

She quirks her head, wondering what he could possibly teach her. He takes her bow and quiver from her, and slings the quiver over his left shoulder.

"I've seen you hit birds in motion," he explains, "but you're always standing still. The fact is that in battle your enemy isn't the only one in motion—you are, too, and you need to shoot from different postures quickly. Like this," he says, turning his back to the archery butt, twisting over his right shoulder, and shooting. The arrow strikes the bull's-eye. "And this." He plucks an arrow from his quiver and shoots over his left shoulder. "And this." He falls on the ground and shoots. "Now, you try."

Cyn feels a flash of heat through her entire body. She stares at Heph's three arrows in the bull's-eye along with several of her own. She takes her quiver and bow back, falls to the ground, and immediately shoots. Her arrow hits the edge of the butt, far wide of the mark. How embarrassing after she just compared herself to an Amazon. She utters a little noise of disgust.

"Here," Heph says, kneeling behind her. "When you are moving quickly your concentration must be the same as if you were standing still and had all day to take aim. Hold the bow a little closer, like this." He puts his arms around her from behind and she feels a shiver of excitement sweep over her. "Now, shut your eyes."

She shuts them. Heph smells of oiled leather and citrus cologne. It's a masculine smell, a good smell.

"Pretend this is a real battlefield," he says, his arms closing more tightly around her. They are bigger, stronger, than they appear from afar. "Wounded horses galloping wildly and whinnying in terror. Men throwing spears, slicing each other open with swords, and screaming in agony. The grass is on fire, black smoke obscuring your vision. You might be killed at any moment. But you are calm. Strong. Concentrating. Now, open your eyes and fire within a second."

She does. Her shot lands within a few inches of the bull's-eye. He stands up and dusts the dirt off his knees. "Just practice, Cyn," he says. "Run in circles and shoot. Shoot while leaping over a log. Throw yourself on your knees and onto the ground and shoot. But remember the power of concentration, of steadiness. If anybody can learn this, you can."

She stands up and nods. He's right, of course. But instead of making fun of her, he actually helped her. Not many people do that.

Come to think of it, no one does.

They stare at each other a long moment. Both start to speak

but are interrupted by Diodotus crying, "Fire!" as another rock goes hurtling across the field.

She pushes back her long black ringlets and looks around the field. She can't lose sight of the reason she's been seeking his attention in the first place. "Where's Alex?" she asks. "I haven't seen him with you all week. No time for old friends…?"

Heph wipes a trickle of sweat from his forehead. "He's in council meetings talking about trade, treaties, and taxes."

"And spending time with that girl he picked up at the tournament." She shakes her head. "Of course, I can't imagine he'd have the courage to face you after the trick he pulled with the hellion—" Her hand flies up to her mouth. "I shouldn't have—I didn't mean—"

Heph's good humor has vanished from his face as if she wiped it off with a sponge. "Alex had nothing to do with the hellion getting loose. He was sitting in the royal balcony the entire time."

"Yes, of course, you're right," Cyn hastily agrees. "That's what I said, too. You know how the servants like to gossip. Silly stories. You can't put any faith in them."

In the last eight days since the tournament, all the servants *have* been talking about why Bardas, the hunchbacked latrine cleaner, took the hellion the evening before the competition to a storeroom near the arena doors, somehow kept the ferocious beast quiet all night long, and then, at the critical point of the tournament, when everyone's attention was focused on the field, opened the gates to let it in. Unfortunately for Bardas, the hellion made a meal of him before leaping into the arena, so he couldn't be questioned.

It was easy to convince the slave he would gain his freedom and a sack of silver if he followed her instructions because King Philip secretly wanted to spice up the games. The night before the tournament, she administered the sleeping drug to the hellion, and then the two of them wheeled him to the storeroom where Cyn gave Bardas drugged wine. During the tournament, when the hellion woke, the creature killed the still-sleeping slave. Sword and shield in hand, Cyn opened the storeroom door and guided the hellion toward the arena gate.

"Servants tell nasty stories about their betters to cut them down to size," Heph says. But he sounds uncertain.

Tossing her hair, Cyn walks over to the butt to pull out her arrows. Heph walks with her. "Very true," Cyn says. "So many of them lie because they have nothing better to do. My handmaiden tried to feed me some story about a conspiracy between Alex and Katerina. She claims they had a plan to make Katerina's friend victorious in the tournament and then split the purse."

She yanks an arrow out of the butt and points with it to Jacob of Erissa, the tournament victor, running across the field toward the catapult, a smaller man behind him, both of them carrying huge rocks. "But as regent, Alex has access to all the money in the royal treasury. He wouldn't need to pull any tricks to get his hands on gold." She makes a face as she twists a particularly deeply embedded arrow out of the canvas.

Heph looks startled. "Alex has access to the royal treasury? I thought the council—"

Cyn looks at him and smirks. "Do you think Philip would let those old men on the council control the gold and not his own son?" She avoids Heph's eyes. She's well aware of Heph's dependence on Alex's generosity. Of course the prince doesn't have access to the treasury. But she doesn't have to convince Heph of her lie, only plant a small seed of doubt. She pulls out the last arrow and tosses the bunch of them into her quiver.

"So if Alex did release the hellion, it certainly wasn't for the gold," she goes on. "It would have to be for a different reason. Still, he could have gotten you killed…"

Heph scoffs. "Alex didn't release the hellion," he said. "Alex would never wish to harm me. That's the stupidest thing I've ever heard."

"I'm sure you must be right," she replies easily. "And my servants gossip about the silliest things, hardly any of it true." She bends down slowly near his knees, keeping her eyes on his, aware of her body the whole time. Then she picks up the sack with the birds she has shot, which is resting by his feet. When she stands up, they are face-to-face. She licks her lower lip. "As for the hellion, I think I'll give these to him. Walk with me?"

He hesitates only a moment, "All right. Give me a minute." Cyn watches Heph jog to Diodotus, observing his easy stride. Heph taps Diodotus on the shoulder and Cyn can just make out their conversation.

"I'm taking Princess Cynane back to the palace."

"Thank the Olympian gods!" the trainer growls. "Get her out of here so the men can concentrate. Their saliva is starting to dribble onto their uniforms." As she walks, arrows clattering in her quiver, she feels Heph's eyes on her back and can't help but smile.

They pass the barracks and the blacksmith's forge, making their way to the back gate and down a narrow staircase to the royal menagerie. Though not one for frescoes and statues, Philip appreciates the artistry of exotic creatures, mesmerized by the way sinew and bone take so many forms. Foreign kings have sent many animals as gifts: a black-and-white-striped horse from Ethiopia, a family of chattering monkeys from India, ostriches from Egypt, a kind of knobby-legged, brown-spotted African cow with an enormously long neck, and a majestic tiger from Persia.

They're both drawn to the hellion spread out in its cage,

panting slightly in the heat of the day. As they approach, one yellow eye opens and, after a moment, closes.

"What I don't understand is how someone could have smuggled the beast down into the arena," Heph says, shaking his head. It's all Cynane can do to not grin again. He might have said *someone*, but she can practically *see* him come to the realization that whoever pulled the stunt had to have been part of the royal family. That leaves a short list of suspects.

As if on cue, voices float into the menagerie enclosure on the warm air. It's the prince and Katerina, walking with their heads together. Heph stiffens when he sees them, then turns away, but Cyn studies them, detecting none of the physical spark you'd normally see between two young, attractive people. They aren't touching, or even walking that closely together, and both are more engaged with the animals than with each other. They seem…comfortable. It's a strange sight, and for a moment, Cyn can almost forget that Katerina is new to the palace. That she's an intruder. But whatever's happening between her and the prince doesn't really matter to Cyn. What matters is that she can use her, too.

She clucks in disgust. "Did you know that Alex invited the peasant girl to stay here at the palace indefinitely?"

Heph turns to her with a wrinkle in his brow. It's clear he *didn't* know. His eyes cloud over, looking as angry—and hungry—as the eyes of the beast in the cage beside them.

"I'm sorry," she says. "I thought Alex would have confided in you." Cyn turns and grabs hold of the bars, savoring the feel of cold iron between her fingers. She sees the yellow cat eye open again. "I remember when my closest friend found a man to spend all her time with… I was devastated. I thought our friendship was stronger than that." Lies. All lies. Cyn has never had a friend, not truly. "I'm beginning to see that that's not how the world works, is it?"

She pulls a stiffening crow out of her bag and drops it between the bars. In an instant, the hellion springs up and lunges at her hand, which she quickly withdraws. But it pushes its huge paws through the bars, and as Cyn turns away, its curved black claws sink into the back of her leather vest.

She gasps.

She had intended to fake a scream, but a real sound of pain and shock flies from her throat. Those claws dig into the flesh of her back, caught in her vest. The pain and danger have sent twin daggers of fear and excitement through her entire body, and she feels incredibly alive as Heph unsheathes his knife and, without thought or preparation, plunges it into the beast's shoulder.

There is blood, and a horrible, wild roar, as the hellion releases Cyn. Alex races to her side, setting her gently on the ground.

Ears flat against its head, the beast hisses so loudly the walls seem to shake as nearby monkeys screech in fear and warning. Saliva drips off the beast's fangs. Heph raises his knife again, a calm in his eyes that almost scares Cyn. It's the steadiness he told her about—unwavering. Unflinching. Powerful.

"Heph! Stop!" The prince's command seems to cut through the fog in Heph's eyes. Alex leaps up and pulls Heph's raised arm away from the cage. "What are you doing?"

Heph withdraws his arm from Alex's grip. "What do you mean, what am I doing? The beast attacked your sister."

The hellion lets out a cry between a shuddering roar and a whimper. It pads to a corner, trailing blood, then begins to lick its wound.

"You struck it far more than was necessary. It's behind bars, isn't it? I know you're still angry about last week." Alexander doesn't even have to name the tournament aloud for his words to inflame Heph's cheeks. "But it's wrong to take out your anger on a dumb animal."

The dark eyes that meet Alex's are full of that fog again—the fog of pride and anger. She knows that fog. It's stirring within her all the time.

After long seconds, Heph finally sheathes his knife. "Of course, Your Majesty." His words could slice a throat.

Katerina, meanwhile, has gone around the side of the cage and plunged her hand between the bars, laying it gently on the whimpering beast. Cyn fully expects to see the hellion twist its huge head and bite off the hand—the entire arm—but instead the hellion relaxes. Could there be some strange connection between the peasant girl and the monstrous beast? Kat's eyes are closed, and the hellion's breathing slows down; its whimper turns to a purr. For what seems like an eternity, the others stare in amazement, too, clearly afraid to move or say another word.

"Katerina," Alex says under his breath. "Remove…your…hand…slowly."

She looks at him with a strange expression of relief. "It appears the injury is superficial. I need some hot water, a needle and thread, and clean bandages. I think I can fix him up."

Alex gazes at her in wonder and looks back at Cyn, and then at the hellion again. "Only if we get my men to truss him up first. That's one of the most vicious creatures in the world. I'm surprised he didn't take your hand off."

Katerina shrugs. "I have a lot of experience with all kinds of animals," she replies, standing and shaking out her dress. Then she turns to Cyn and adds, "It's really the carelessness of those who *don't* that leads to injuries…and in this case, almost got the hellion killed."

For a moment, Cyn is too shocked to say anything. Who is this low-class girl with her peasant accent to tell Cyn, a royal princess, anything? Especially as she's sitting here, bleeding? Are her wounds less important even than an animal's?

The girl is not only making Cyn look like a fool, but doing so in front of Heph.

"So sorry," she says, disdainfully taking in the makeup and jewelry Katerina is wearing. In this moment, she couldn't care less that the girl belongs to the prince. She's never worried about insulting *him* before. What can he really do to her? "But I'm not accustomed to taking advice from a country mule, even if she happens to be dressed up in the finery of a parade horse. One with such a professed interest in beasts probably ought to be living among them and not in a palace."

Cyn is gratified to see Kat's expression change from anger to embarrassment, as if she, too, knows it's true.

Alex steps in between them. "That's enough, Cynane." He turns to Heph. "I don't understand your recent behavior," he says.

"And I don't understand *you*," Heph retorts.

Casting Heph a look of puzzled frustration, Alex shakes his head. "Please. Help my sister." Then he turns on his heel and walks away. His little peasant plaything quickly scrambles after him, as Heph stares at their retreating figures.

Swallowing her annoyance, Cyn takes a step forward and wobbles.

"Are you all right?" Heph asks, grabbing her arm.

"I'm just a little dizzy," she says. Her fingers feel the wet blood through her vest, a reminder of why she needs to find Smoke Blood: to become invincible to pain and death. "I think I need to lie down."

"I'll walk you to your room," Heph says, which is just what she wanted him to say.

In the hallway leading to her room she starts to slip toward the floor, hoping her swoon is realistic. He puts his arms around her and picks her up, carrying her the rest of the way.

Despite her height, she feels folded up and protected, surrounded by his warmth. She could fall asleep like this, feeling safe and cared for, for once, bouncing gently up and down as he walks, listening to the beat of his heart.

He kicks open the door and lays her carefully on the bed. "I'll call your maids," he says.

She sits up abruptly. "This is so silly," she says. "You know I'm no damsel in need of saving." She swings her legs over the bed but winces. "My shoulder," she says, quietly.

He sits down beside her. "Let me see." He gently unlaces the breastplate under her left arm, and unties the shoulder strap. The back half of the breastplate slips down, and the front half is dangling from her right shoulder, exposing part of her left breast. She could swear she hears his quick intake of breath.

He gently gathers her thick hair in his hands and drops it over her right shoulder. "Now, let's see. They're not too deep," he says, studying the puncture marks. She can feel his gaze tracing her skin.

"I'm disappointed," she retorts. "I was hoping for battle scars to match yours."

"Then you'll have to do better than this," he teases, but she feels the tenderness with which he lightly touches her shoulder blade and then neck. "But it should still be cleaned." He picks up a soft linen cloth and bowl of water from the washstand and brings them over to the bed. Carefully, he cleans the wounds. She feels his hot breath on her neck, heat emanating from his body, the cool water sending surprising shivers through her. His fingers on her skin seem to set it on fire.

He sets the cloth and water on the olive-wood table next to the bed. "I think you'll live now," he says, standing.

She rises and takes his hand. "I want you to know I really am a woman now, not a girl always trying to get attention."

He grins at her. "You could have fooled me today."

She smiles back. "Well, I always did have a bit of a crush on you, even if I did show it in funny ways as a kid."

"Like the time you put worms in my boots," he says, his eyes glittering in amusement.

"But then you put toads in my bed."

"But then you put a thorn underneath my horse's saddle. He threw me."

"But then you put unripe elderberry juice in my wine. I threw up."

"But then you nearly shot off my fingers with an arrow."

"Oh."

They stand there, staring at each other, his hand still in hers.

Heph is breathing quickly. His eyes stray down to her partially exposed breast. He's clearly conflicted about whether to stay or leave.

"I think… I should…go," he says, but doesn't make any move to do so.

"Haven't you ever wondered what it would be like?" she says.

"What?" he breathes.

"If we kissed. Don't you want to find out?" She leans toward him.

He closes the distance.

It's a warm, deep, lingering kiss: his lips on her hair, her neck, her eyes. She can smell the dirt of the practice fields on his skin, salty and earthy.

He pulls away. The warmth, the scent of him, everything is gone in an instant and she's left feeling chilled.

"Cyn," he says softly, "I have a duty to King Philip and to

Alex. You're the king's daughter, my best friend's sister. As beautiful as you are, it would be dishonorable..."

"You're right," she says, squaring her shoulders and lifting her chin stoically. Inside, her heart is singing. She knows he'll be back for more. "We have to fight this. Whatever *this* is."

He runs his fingers through his tangled curls and adjusts his tunic, then pauses for a second, like he plans to say something more.

Instead, he nods and slips away, closing the door softly behind him. It surprises Cyn to feel as if the room has just been plunged into darkness.

She flings herself on the bed and starts pummeling her pillow. Pretending it's Heph. Alex. Katerina. Olympias. Philip. All of them can go to Hades as far as she is concerned. Then she stops when she realizes she is angry most of all at herself.

She is, she knows, starting to feel a bit too fond of Heph.

Chapter Eleven

THE BARRACKS MESS HALL IS ODDLY EMPTY AS Jacob carries his breakfast tray over to the old, scarred wood table where Timaeus, the Tyrrhian who survived the tournament with him, is already seated, gnawing on a chicken leg. Philip has marched off with most of his soldiers; the usual laughter and backslapping, the scraping of chairs and clinking of crockery have vanished with them. Even some of the stench of sweat and spilled wine has been alleviated. In the far corner, a half-dozen remaining soldiers are playing dice next to plates heaped high with bread crusts and bones.

Jacob's shoulders and back ache from a week of training. The cut on his arm throbs and Jacob is reminded once again that he will need to find fresh bandages for the oozing wound. Wordlessly, he sets down his dishes and flops onto the bench beside Timaeus. The shorter man hardly stops the flow of his loud chewing and sucking and slurping to acknowledge him.

Perhaps he had been naive, but Jacob had been hoping to leave for Byzantium with the rest of the infantry. Yet despite all their hard work, neither Jacob nor Timaeus was chosen.

They're too new, too raw—that's what their trainer, Diodotus, told them. They had to stay here to continue their training and help the remaining men see to the defense of Pella. Jacob had thought that as the tournament victor, everything else would simply fall into place. Including the most elusive thing of all...

No. He refuses to think about her. He's wasted enough time poring over her many messages from the palace, trying to analyze what it means that the "prince has taken a liking to me."

He can't fathom (or bear to guess) how she has ended up at the heart of the palace and he has ended up...here. He feels helpless, reckless, like the time when his little brother Calas was learning to walk and fell into the superheated coals of the fire box below the kiln, burning his arm badly. Jacob saw it happening in slow motion—knew what was going to happen—but couldn't stop it in time.

Looking down at his plate, heaped high with fluffy bread, eggs prepared with eastern spices, and a slab of ham, Jacob knows he should feel grateful. Sometimes he still has a hard time convincing himself this isn't a dream: back home they might eat a rabbit raised in the backyard hutch, or fish and game he and Kat caught. But if the hunting was poor they ate only black barley bread, goat cheese, and olives. He'd never tasted beef before this week, or lamb chops in mint sauce. Just the other day he devoured an entire chicken stuffed with herbs and cheese. He can feel his body filling out, getting stronger, especially his arms and chest, though his stomach is still as hard and flat as the face of an anvil.

He takes a bite—even his jaw feels sore from yesterday's work—but the salty pork fat melting into his bread does nothing to calm the roiling in his chest.

Timaeus grunts in satisfaction, tossing the now-clean bone down on his plate. "You know why I risked a horrible death in the tournament?" he asks, stuffing a giant piece of rich honey cake into his mouth. He answers his own question, with his food half-chewed: "Because I was hungry. We never had much back home. I think that's why my growth got stunted." He takes another bite, crumbs spraying everywhere. "But I knew if I did well in the tournament I would get a position where they would feed me. You got the bag of gold, Jacob, but I get a bag of food every day, and that's almost as good."

Looking over at Tim, Jacob can't help but crack a half grin. Tim's filling out, too. His sunken chest seems the tiniest bit broader, his scrawny shoulders stronger. Despite the man's slurping, Jacob's grateful for Tim. He's not just the funny little acrobat Jacob encountered in the arena—he's clever, not much older than Jacob, and willing to work as hard as a man twice his size, even if he does always pepper his labor with lewd jokes. Ever since the tournament, the two of them have spent almost every moment together. That is, except the nights Tim has sought out the company of a certain milkmaid, Chloris, who—as far as Jacob can tell—is no more than a palace prostitute. Still, she seems to keep Tim happy, so Jacob has said nothing.

After all, he has needed Tim's friendship. Even with Kat's many encouraging notes, he's not sure he could have gotten through any of this on his own. Running, lifting boulders, riding, tossing javelins, waking at all hours—for the last eight days he's been forced to find the agonizing limits of his physical endurance and keep barreling ahead despite the pain, despite the exhaustion.

It's grueling, but there's a strange grace to it. When he's working his body that hard, a hot breeze whipping his hair into his face, sweat dripping from every pore, all his anger and unmet desires fly out of his mind. His favorite new thing is fighting with a training mace, an iron pipe with a round head at both ends that weighs exactly twice as much as a standard-issue military sword. If he and Timaeus can ever recuperate from their sore wrists, elbows, and shoulders, and get used to fighting with this weight, their real swords will effortlessly cleave through the air.

Jacob reaches for a fig and winces as the muscles around his cut flash hot with pain. Yesterday, during sword practice, Diodotus sliced open Jacob's arm—the repercussion for not trusting his instincts. But then last night it really gave him pain, throbbing so much he could hardly sleep. Today is a respite from hard physical labor: weapon cleaning and repair.

"I suppose we have to wait for the king to come back to be made part of the Hypaspists," Jacob says, scraping his plate. The Hypaspists, the elite fighting force that serves Philip directly, is the dream of many boys throughout the kingdom. To join these ranks is to rise in fortune and title. Jacob swallows his food. "And who knows how long that will be. I hear he could be gone as long as a year."

Timaeus gulps down some watered wine. "I'm afraid it will be a lot longer for the likes of you and me to join the Hypaspists," he says, slamming his mug down.

Jacob's knife drops from his hand and clatters onto the table. "What do you mean?" he asks.

Timaeus wipes his mouth with the back of his hand and says, "Do you think there's a man in the king's bodyguard from a village like Erissa? I don't even come from Tyrrhos itself. My family lives in a flea-bitten fishing hut on the beach, well outside of the village. All those elite guards you saw marching out the gates with Philip in red-crested helmets are from noble families. Sure, they can fight like Heracles, but they also can debate philosophy like Socrates, recite Homer's poetry, and play the lyre like Apollo." He holds up his hands to strum an imaginary lyre with a dreamy look on his face.

"I don't even know how to read. Do you?" Timaeus asks accusingly.

"Yes," Jacob says, almost embarrassed to admit what always made him so proud back among the farmers and laborers of Erissa. "My grandfather and his brother Epistor were well-to-do merchants who lost all their money when their ship foundered in a storm. Even though my father's a potter, he taught us all to read—even the girls."

Timaeus grunts and says, "Whatever the case, you and I are both insects to those bastards, horse turds on the heels of their fine leather boots."

Jacob looks at his eggs and ham, but they've lost their appeal. "I thought..."

"I know what you thought," Timaeus says, rolling his slice of ham into a ball and stuffing it into his mouth, "but I'm telling you as a friend that all we can expect from these asses is a place as regular palace guards or lowly infantrymen on the battlefield." He pounds himself on his chest and belches loudly.

"Look," he continues, "four years ago my brother was one of the top three finalists in the tournament. He was a small guy like me but he built himself into a Heracles with his training. Do you think the king made him one of the elite guards? No. He sent him to scout out a boar hunt, and the boar got him. Those lyre-playing little shits sent Aesop back to us as ashes in an urn."

The room seems to spin around Jacob. Is that what he will be doing? Rounding up animals in the woods for the king to hunt?

"I don't know about you, my friend, but I am not content with being a horse turd," Timaeus says, picking a piece of food from his teeth. "There's one thing we can do to get the status and wealth we want. We need to join the Aesarian Lords."

Jacob stares at him. He's seen the Lords stalking about the

palace the past week, proud, fierce, and vaguely menacing. He never imagined joining such a group. More importantly, he can't imagine they would want *him*.

"But if King Philip won't give us positions of honor, why would the Aesarian Lords?" he asks. "They seem even less likely to want two country boys in their ranks."

"Ah, but they *do*," Timaeus says, his eyes widening. "They sought us out last night after dinner but you were on prison watch."

Jacob grimaces. Nearly every evening, the soldiers are expected to take a watch on the town walls, where he sweats around flaming braziers half the night and tries not to fall asleep as the other guards play dice. But guarding the walls was better than watching the palace jail. Last night, a drunken palace gardener mooned a statue of Zeus and told the god to kiss his ass, and Jacob was forced to listen to his off-key singing for hours.

Tim bites into the ham and continues, "The Aesarian Lords liked the skills we displayed in the tournament, and they've been watching us train since then. They want young minds they can mold, strong bodies they can train. They don't care that we're not from inbred noble families. In fact, they like it better that we haven't had all the sense educated out of us. They want us both to join."

"And would the king even allow it?" Jacob asks. Technically they're his men now, even if they're not in his elite guard.

Tim shrugs. "It's one of the reasons the Lords came to visit in the first place. Some sort of bargaining chip, I suppose. In any case, I don't mind being a pawn in his game, so long as I land on the winning side."

Jacob leans back and crosses his arms. He looks at his friend's rubbery, comical little face, his bulging blue eyes, and over-large mouth, and bursts out laughing. "I can't imagine you in a black cape and a horned helmet," he says as he pictures the helmet falling over Timaeus's nose.

"I'll wear whatever fartass thing they want me to wear," Timaeus says. "I'll go naked and paint myself blue like the Celts if they give me a chance for a future."

He sighs deeply, looking straight into Jacob's eyes with an almost painful intensity. "Look, because I'm small and funny, no one is ever going to take me seriously. Except the Aesarian Lords. They can see past a man's background and look at what he has to offer. And they know my skills aren't just for entertainment. I can climb up a wall like a monkey. Squeeze between the bars of a jail cell window. Cartwheel my way across a battlefield severing heads as I go."

He skewers the two eggs on Jacob's plate with his knife and waves it in the air. "You, too, would rise quickly in their ranks. Just think. You would be *Lord Jacob.* You want to land that girl of yours? You'd better think about what I say."

That girl of yours. Jacob's hand goes up to the iron brooch Kat gave him for luck in the tournament. He touches the smooth, cool surface of the green river stone.

Abruptly, he stands up. "I'll consider it. But right now I need to make a…quick errand." He has to try to see Kat. It's been a week and he's been unable to sneak away from training, but now Jacob knows that any amount of mucking or feeding the pigs he'll receive as punishment for his tardiness will be worth it for just a moment of Kat. A moment to remind himself that she's real, and that she is still his Katerina who races with gazelles and makes up nonsense rhymes for his little brothers. "Tell Diodotus I'll be late—that I've got the stomach gripes."

Timaeus grins. "Sure. But I think you'll really have them once he's finished with you."

Jacob traces the path to Kat's room—the third door from

the outer staircase of the women's guest wing, as she had written him—feeling, as he has the last few mornings, like an imposter. He knocks, wondering if she won't be there. But he hears a light footstep—and his heart lifts.

The door is thrown open and she's miraculously there, fragrant and beautiful in a gold-trimmed peplos the color of sunset, her hair a cascade of carefully coiffed waves. Kat's whole face lights up, and she practically does a little dance. Then she grabs him with both arms and brings him through the doorway.

"The victor of the Blood Tournament!" she cries, sweeping him a low bow. "Perhaps I should fling myself on my knees to worship you." A huge grin spreads across her face.

He crosses his arms and grins back. "Perhaps you should."

She starts to kneel playfully, but he grabs her and pulls her close. She looks different, with her hair done and her face made up, and she smells of lavender and rose water. But he sees the outline of her mother's flower pendant below the sheer material of her gown and knows she's still his Kat. And now, finally, she's in his arms again. And all he wants is to recapture the moment in the pond, the kiss he's been replaying in his mind every day since.

"And you said I shouldn't have followed you," she says, disentangling herself and playfully swatting his chest. "At least now you have a witness to your victory. If you showed up in Erissa without one, no one would believe you. Like the time you said a fourteen-foot-tall bear chased you through the west meadow. Or was it a twenty-foot-tall bear? I think it kept growing each time you repeated the story."

"It did chase me, and it was a very, very tall bear. But forgive me if I didn't have time to pull out a measuring stick."

"At least you set better traps in the tournament than you

did on the road to Pella," she says, wagging her head from side to side teasingly.

"Rope is always better than vines," he retorts, wagging his head in the same way.

Smiling broadly, she stares at him, looking him up and down. "You look…different somehow."

"Must be my new hairdo," he says, running a hand through his straight brown hair as if he were a vain girl. "And the makeup." He flutters his eyelashes.

She laughs and takes his hand. "Yes, I know I look a little different, too. I'm not sure I like the makeup. It feels strange on my face. The first two days I washed it off and the hand-maidens yelled at me. And this hair feels like a marble sculpture glued on my head. I can't move my neck without the pins digging into me."

Jacob notices a sleeping pallet on the floor next to the huge four-poster bed.

"What's that?" he asks.

She looks embarrassed. "It's a maid's pallet they keep under the bed. I sank so deeply into that feather mattress I felt like I was drowning and kept waking up flailing my arms, trying to swim. So I sleep on the floor." She tugs his large, rough hand. "Come over here and sit down— you're not the only one who's had strange adventures recently!"

As Kat launches into her story about drunk, angry lords and pretty boys, Jacob glances around Kat's room, which smells of beeswax and lemon thyme. The gleaming floor of pink marble reflects the goddesses cavorting across the walls. Tortoiseshell studs dot the Nubian bed and a dressing table sits in the corner. Resting on it are tiny, exquisite jars of makeup that she never used back in Erissa, probably the things his mother always envied the olive merchant's wife for having: powdered malachite for green eyelids, black kohl for eyeliner, some sort of crushed eggshells—ostrich?—for face powder, and pulverized rose petals for lips and cheeks. He often heard Sotiria dreaming about these items she couldn't afford, reciting their ingredients as though they were the names of the gods themselves. And now Kat has them all, as gifts from the palace.

Not exactly a shared cloak by a small fire on the forest floor.

It seems as if in the space of a few days, she's traveled a million miles away from him, even though she says she doesn't like it. How could anyone not like it?

"And then Prince Alexander came up to investigate the commotion," Kat says. "He made the guards release me and invited me to stay as his guest in the palace."

The prince. A prickle of irritation breaks out on Jacob's neck and unthinkingly he picks at the wound on his arm.

"What happened?" she asks, noticing the nasty, oozing cut for the first time. She reaches a finger to the wound, but Jacob pulls away.

"It's nothing," he says, forcing himself into a grin. "Got it training."

Kat frowns, "It looks like it's starting to fester." Before he can react, she darts off her chair and grabs a jar from her dressing table. When she opens it, a powerful fragrance fills the room. Mint, citrus, rosemary, and other things, Jacob guesses. Ingredients from Arabia and beyond. She squats beside him, dips a finger in it, and rubs it on his wound, which starts to throb even worse. She looks around and snatches an underskirt from a chair, rips off a strip of linen, and wraps it around his arm. He thinks she's done and starts to pull his arm away, but she looks up at him with eyes that take his breath away and says, "Not yet."

She places both hands over and around the cut, resting her fingertips so lightly on his skin it is as if they are a whisper. She closes her eyes and Jacob feels warm where her hands wrap around him. No, not just warmth. Kindness. Forgiveness. Peace. He wonders what is happening. His exhaustion from seven days of nonstop training must be getting to him.

Despite the increasing heat in his arm, he shivers. He opens his eyes as she removes her hands. Quickly, he grasps them, not wanting to be away from her touch.

Her breath catches. "Don't take the bandage off until tomorrow," she whispers, looking into his eyes. Her lips part, just slightly, and he knows then—he's *certain*—she feels the heat coursing between them, too.

"Kat," he begins, clearing his throat and cursing himself for his nervousness, "all week, I've… I've wanted to see you, to tell you." He swallows hard. "Nothing has changed for me. I still want what I told you before. Back at the village. All of it. *You.*"

"Jacob," she says, his name trembling on her lips.

And then, he can simply wait no more. With a gentle tug of her hands, he draws her nearer, and leans in. Their mouths are inches apart, but still he hesitates for a moment, before closing the gap.

The warmth he felt before turns into scalding heat in his veins as he longs to press his entire body against hers, to hold her, to never let her go. He pushes her lips apart lightly with his tongue, and she responds with the faintest moan, almost falling into him. His hands are in her hair, ruining her beautiful coiffed curls. He doesn't care. He wants more of her. And she clearly feels the same way.

"Jacob," she murmurs again, her breath soft on his cheek.

He sinks to his knees beside her, about to lay her slowly down on the ground, when suddenly she is moving back, her eyes pained and unreadable.

"I can't. We have to stop. Jacob. You have to leave." The words come out in a rush.

He feels baffled. Dizzy. This can't be happening. She can't be pulling away from him...*again.*

"What? Why? Kat, why?"

"Because...you will be missed. And I—I— There are things I must do..." She gestures frantically, vaguely. And he knows—he knows she's lying. Or hiding something.

He clears his throat, suddenly cold. "Kat. What are you really doing here in the palace?"

She looks into his eyes and he senses she is almost pleading with him, but pleading for what? She abruptly looks away, still refusing to answer him, and he follows her gaze to the window with a view of the Poseidon Garden. The fountain is splashing, trickling, murmuring. Tickling something at the back of his mind.

"Is there something going on between you and the prince?" He feels ridiculous asking it...full of self-loathing and embarrassment...but maybe the reason he couldn't sleep last night wasn't just his arm. Maybe it was his suspicion...that there's something more she's not telling him. Something big. "Tell me truthfully, Kat." He's not going to break down. Certainly not in front of her. "At least you owe me that."

She turns her green gaze to him and he sees honesty in her eyes. "Nothing romantic, exactly. But there is—I do feel— some sort of connection with him. It's like we're old friends, that's all. As if we've always known each other. It makes me want to stay and...and find out more."

"You and I are the ones who have always known each other," he blurts out.

She has the grace to blush.

She's not going to get off easily, though, not when he finally has her alone, face-to-face. When he can see the pulse throbbing at her temple, smell the scent of her skin. Know in his heart if she's lying.

"He's never tried to kiss you, to touch you?" Jacob persists.

"No... I honestly don't think he's interested in kissing me."

Every instinct tells him she is speaking the truth, though he wonders how any man could spend days in Kat's company and not try to kiss her. Unless the man wasn't interested in girls at all.

He forges ahead. "Kat, I now have something to offer you—a large amount of gold. We could buy a house with it, here in Pella, and some nice furniture. Not like this, of course," he says, gesturing around to the exquisite objects in the room, "but comfortable enough. And we'd hire a servant to do the heavy work so you don't have to. Or you could, but only if you wanted to. Whatever you wanted. Whatever you want."

She's still smiling at him, but the smile seems fixed, some-how.

His mouth goes dry, but he stumbles on. "When the king comes back, he may promote me to his elite guard, which will mean honor and a good salary to keep up our lifestyle." He gulps and adds, "And there might even be better oppor-tunities for me."

She is still looking at him but the smile has faded and some-thing changes in her eyes. She starts chewing on the knuckle of her right thumb, a sign that she is nervous. The silence hangs thick between them, but Jacob is determined not to be the one to break it.

"There's no rush," she finally says. "Do we really have to address this now? Don't we both have things to do? You have to work hard to rise in your new profession. And I... I, too, have things to do." Her eyes take on a distraught look and she shifts her gaze back to her windowsill, where a sparrow pecks at bread crumbs she has put out.

"What do *you* have to do?" he says, his frustration rising. Why won't she let him in? He stands up and starts pacing.

"I suppose it was our fate that you and I both ended up here at the palace together but for different reasons," she says in a flat voice. "We are clearly in the hands of the gods."

"What does that mean?" he asks, exasperatedly running his fingers through his hair. "Kat, I'm trying to understand, but I have no idea what you're talking about."

She shrugs and doesn't look at him. That such a tiny gesture, the merest lift of her slender shoulders, should dismiss all his pleading, all his dreams, all his backbreaking hard work—he can't take it.

He grabs her by the shoulders and swings her around to face him. "Am I not good enough for you?"

"Don't be stupid!" she says, her cheeks reddening in anger. She's about to blurt something else, but stops herself. Her lips stay slightly parted. She sucks in a tiny breath. When she speaks again, it's so soft he has to lean in even closer to hear her. "You mean everything to me."

And it's true for him, too. She is everything to *him*. For the past few months—no, maybe even the last year or two—he's been biding his time, waiting for her to feel it, too, waiting until he's worthy of her, striving to become the man he needs to be, for her. She has been more than a girl to him—she has been a destiny, a driving force, a compass. It is because of her he has worked so hard, has pushed himself so far.

He doesn't know who he would be without her.

He lets his hands slide down her arms and stares at her, pulled toward her by an invisible force. He can feel the heat of her anger melting into something else. The skin on her exposed arms is soft, and for a moment he has the sense that he shouldn't be touching her, but he doesn't want to let go. He would give anything to be back with her in the fields outside their farm, covered with mud and grass stains, where everything between them was real and pure.

But he can see that it no longer is, and the thought leaves him feeling empty and lost. Directionless.

Finally, he drops his hands and backs away. "If you want to see me again, you come to me," he says. "I'm not coming back here. Not to this pretty birdcage the prince has you kept in."

"What?" she protests, taking a step toward him again, but he's already out the door.

I'm not good enough for her now that she's a guest of the prince, he says to himself as he jogs back to the training arena. *Well, we'll just see about that.*

The thoughts build a fury in him like a dust storm. He doesn't even want her bandage on his arm. Angrily, he rips it off.

He gasps, confused. Other than a slight pink mark, the wound is gone.

Timaeus and several other soldiers have spread out a large array of weapons on old hides. Even from a distance, Jacob can see them glinting in the sun. Tim's on his knees pouring honing oil on a whetstone as Jacob approaches. Then he picks up a sword and drags it diagonally across the stone from tip to hilt, first on one side, and then on the other.

Diodotus sits on a bale of hay with a long piece of grass between his lips and an old straw sun hat on his head, digging the dirt out of his fingernails with a knife. He looks up at Jacob. "Oh, Your Majesty," he says, standing up and bowing in mock servility, "how kind of you to grace us with your presence. Did you enjoy taking your time on the throne?" He straightens, spits out the grass, and scowls. "You'll have a lot worse than shit running down your leg in battle if you keep this up. And speaking of shit, while the other men are taking a break this afternoon you will be cleaning out the barracks latrines. Now get to work."

Timaeus, still honing the sword, snickers.

"So, you think that's funny, do you?" Diodotus says, storming over.

"No, sir," Timaeus says meekly, bending over the sword again.

"Anybody else who thinks that's funny will be helping Jacob muck out the latrines," Diodotus growls, wheeling around. A dozen heads bend closer to their work.

Knowing he's been pushing his luck and that an angry retort would only make things worse, Jacob kneels beside Timaeus and begins stripping the dried-out rawhide cords that bind spearheads to shafts. He dips new cords in water, soaking them thoroughly, and then ties them tightly over the junction of iron and wood. These new, supple thongs will more likely keep the spears intact in the crashing jostle of battle.

A pile of stiff horsehair lies next to Heirax, a stolid Thracian missing his front teeth, who has removed limp crests from a heap of bronze helmets and prepares to glue new crests in the slit on top. Other men are gathering up the weapons to be taken away for special repair; the armor will go to the blacksmith's and the leather to the tanner's.

Although it's still midmorning the day is already warm, and the air is redolent with the smells of glue and leather, oil and sweat, and sunbaked metal. From behind the barracks, Jacob hears clanking from the blacksmith's forge and a horse whinnying in the stables.

The heat in his head starts to cool as he works with the weapons. It is so easy to fix, to replace, to lubricate and strengthen. So much easier to understand where objects go wrong than where relationships do. He finishes the spears and starts on the bows, dipping his fingers into pots of beeswax to massage into the strings, keeping them supple and less likely to snap when his life might depend on them.

A shadow falls over Jacob, wide and tall on the golden-red sand, and there's a chill on his skin. The morning sun is blocked by the dark figures of three men wearing billowing capes despite the warmth, and tall horned helmets. Jacob rises, wiping his hands on his tunic, and looks into a thin, narrow face with pale gray eyes. The man's nose is long, aristocratic, and slightly curved to one side. He gestures for Tim and Jacob to follow him off a ways, with a slight nod of his head. Once they're a distance from the rest of the soldiers, the man turns to face them again.

"I am High Lord Mordecai," the man says. Jacob tries not to shudder. The voice has the tang of cold steel, but what really bothers him are the Lord's eyes—empty and glazed, not unlike the eyes of the deer corpse he and Kat once saw being pecked apart by vultures. Jacob forces himself not to look away.

"This is Lord Bastian," Mordecai says, nodding to a much younger man with a zigzag scar on his cheek. "And this," he says, gesturing to a barrel-chested man with a red face, "is Lord Aethon. We want to talk to you."

Jacob looks at the three men ranged before him and senses their chilling power. As tall and strong as he is—the victor of the Blood Tournament, he reminds himself—he feels small in their presence.

"Yes," he says, pulling back his shoulders. "I want to speak to you, too."

CHAPTER TWELVE

"WATCH IT, BOY.!" A FISHMONGER ROLLING AN
empty barrel knocks into Zo, and she stumbles forward a few
paces before she can catch herself. The bronze gong sounds
sourly in the air as a crush of people—merchants, shoppers,
worshippers, visitors—push to leave the walled city of Sardis
before its massive gates swing shut for the night. Zo nervously
checks the cap that covers her luxuriant hennaed hair. If she's
found out, all is lost.

It was Mandana's doing, of that she is certain. Mandana is
a hopeless romantic. Her favorite bedtime stories for Zo always involved true love triumphing against incredible odds.
In the days after Zo threw a tantrum about marrying Alexander of Macedon, she caught her old nurse staring at her
strangely and sighing. One day, an entire outfit of boy's clothing appeared on her bed. Another day, Zo found a fat pouch
of small-denomination coins—the kind that wouldn't attract
attention if she stayed at a hostel on the road—in her jewelry
box. Mandana, she guessed, was helping her run away, but in
such a fashion that she could honestly swear on the fiery altar

of Mithra—or on the rack of torture—that she had never even discussed it with Zo.

Now, caught in the throngs pushing toward the gate, Zo looks like a rather nondescript youth in wide brown trousers, a belted oatmeal-colored tunic, a thin brown cloak, and scuffed leather boots. Her grimy, sooty skin smells strangely sweet. To tone down her luminous complexion—which she bathes in milk every day—she smudged ashes from her perfume burner on her skin.

Zo looks ahead at the gate, made of purple-blue glazed bricks with golden lions. There, below the battlemented turrets, are rooms where she and the other royal women watch processions marching in and out of the city. She will never forget standing there when she was twelve watching the mother she had never known coming back from Bactria, an event she had both feared and longed for. She had pressed her face so hard against the lattices that she had red marks on her forehead and cheeks the rest of the day. Unfortunately, it was the first thing about her that Attoosheh noticed.

Then there was the time she and her best friend, Shirin, watched Artaxerxes, the Great King, enter with dazzling splendor to visit her uncle, King Shershah. Well into his seventies, Artaxerxes remained a warrior king still, his posture ramrod straight, his snow-white hair streaming out from under a golden helmet. In his train were two hundred of the prize horses—many of them rare breeds—that Artaxerxes collected from across the world. Zo—who routinely visited her uncle's stables to feed apples to her favorites—was amazed at the sleek, proud stallions wearing tall ostrich-feather hats, their gold-bedecked harnesses gleaming in the sun.

She and Shirin elbowed each other, laughing at tall black-skinned Nubian soldiers with ivory plugs in their ears, and the Indian regiment with their long hair and beards dyed green, perched on elephants that could hardly squeeze beneath the gate. Small and plump, with a round, comical face, Shirin had always been able to make Zo laugh, could always bring her out of the dark periods of sadness that threatened to engulf her, the times it became too hard knowing her mother had abandoned her to marry a faraway king. When Shirin died of the spotted sickness, Zo felt her heart break for a second time.

Now she is walking underneath the rather narrow, arched opening, wide enough to let in only one chariot at a time, or five men abreast, in case of attack. Someone behind her is pushing hard, forcing her to push the man in front of her who turns his head and curses at her. The crowd surges through—and she's on the Royal Road.

The Royal Road. One of the marvels of the modern world—one thousand, six hundred miles of hard-packed, well-maintained thoroughfare, wide enough for two carriages at once, with ferry crossings over rivers. It runs over mountains and desert, splitting off to Persepolis and to Babylon, the main road finally ending at the imperial Persian capital of Susa with an inn, market, and fresh horses every fifteen miles. The Persian kings built the road for their couriers to take messages from one end of the empire to the other. It's no wonder, Zo thinks, that even the Greeks are in awe of it. Almost a hundred years ago, the Greek historian Herodotus wrote, "Neither snow nor rain nor heat nor gloom of night stays these couriers from the swift completion of their appointed rounds."

Zo had traveled on its westernmost portion several times, when King Shershah took his court the fifty miles to his summer palace in Apasa, on the Mediterranean coast. It was an easy, two-day journey. Zo and her friends reclined on pillows gossiping in an enclosed *harmanaxa* that combined the grace and speed of a chariot with the capacity of a wagon. They spent the night at an opulent estate owned by a royal retainer. Once at Apasa, Zo and her friends swam in the ocean and played in the sand, heavily guarded by eunuchs and away from the prying eyes of men. That's where she taught Roxana how to build sand castles and dig for clams.

Roxana.

The very thought of leaving her sister behind is a stab in her heart. Zo needs to keep her thoughts firmly on the future—on her journey and her meeting with Cosmas. But her sister's face stays with her, and Zo barely takes in the carts, horses, and people flowing out before her onto the Royal Road like a spreading tide. That morning Roxana bounced into her room as usual, with her nurse, Jopata, a sweet woman with a face like a hatchet, right behind her. Zo was teaching Roxana to sew clothes for her small wooden dolls with painted faces, and her sister had proudly made several brightly colored outfits, with stitches that were way too big.

As Zo rearranged the pillows on the floor and brought out her sewing basket, Roxana looked at her wistfully and said, holding a doll in each hand, "Adeleh would miss Davar so much if she went away."

Zo was shocked. Did Roxana know of her plans? How could she? Mandana certainly wouldn't have told anyone. But perhaps there is an unspoken communication between people who love each other. "Davar wouldn't go away and leave Adeleh," she said slowly, feeling the bitterness of the lie. "Or if she did, it would be because she had something very important to do. She would think of Adeleh every day until she could come back. Come now," she said, forcing a smile that felt more like a grimace, "let me tell you a story."

Roxie plunked herself down cross-legged, looking up at Zo with her gap-toothed smile.

"Have you ever heard of the Pegasus?" Zo asked, remembering her favorite story Mandana told her when she was small.

Roxie nodded. "A white horse with wings who lived long ago. He could fly."

"Yes," Zo said, "but there are still some who live in the east, in emerald meadows, and at night they fly up to nests they make in flaming cliffs. If you ever get lost, or find yourself far from the one you love, you pray to the Pegasus to help you. And then, one night, you might hear horse's hooves on the door of your balcony. When you open it, you will see the Pegasus. If you climb on his back, he will fly you straight to the person you want to see most."

Her voice cracked and tears stung her eyes. She rubbed at them angrily. "I must tell Frava I don't like the new incense," she said. "It makes my eyes water. Here now," she said, picking up the sewing basket, "we must finish Adeleh's new dress."

When Jopata gently insisted they leave for the girl's music lesson, Zo hugged her sister again, and kissed her, and ruffled her dark hair, and kissed her one last time. Finally, Jopata, in a swirl of black robes and veils, firmly took Roxana's hand and led her away. The girl cast Zo a backward glance and opened her mouth as if she wanted to say something, but a second later, she had rounded the corner.

Up ahead a donkey pulling a cart brays loudly, refusing to go any further as several people behind it almost topple over and curse loudly. Wiping away a tear, Zo walks off the road, behind a man selling plums on a wooden table, to get around the obstacle. For a second, Zo thinks she hears Roxana calling her name. She looks around, seeing horses snorting and shifting their weight, people talking loudly to one another and shifting their packs, and finally the donkey cart creaking forward. Roxana isn't there. Of course she isn't. It's Zo's guilt at leaving her little sister behind.

"Forgive me, Roxie," she said an hour earlier as she stood on the threshold of a little-used palace servants' entrance. It was so unfair that she had to give up her sister to be with the man she loved. But at least it was *for* a man she loved. Zo reminds herself again and again that she would have had to leave for Macedon soon regardless. At least this way, she is following her heart. Her small, hesitant step onto the street was also the biggest stride she had ever made in her life. Her heart was beating so fast she thought it would explode. She thought alarm bells might sound, guards cry out, soldiers come running.

Nothing happened.

And so, throwing her shoulders back and keeping her chin down just like the servant boys she'd been studying closely all week, she walked past the law courts, the mint and treasury buildings, and then down into town, winding through stone streets of houses and shops selling wine and scent and live chickens in cages, expecting that any moment someone would recognize her.

No one gave her a second glance.

Now she feels bold, fearless, ready to take her fate in her hands and shape the rest of her life rather than let others do it for her.

Cosmas, she says silently, eagerly, *I'm coming*. Her heart beats faster as she imagines him taking her into his strong arms.

She shifts her coarse wool pack from one shoulder to the other. Inside are food and a pretty sky-blue dress and matching trousers she plans to wear for Cosmas.

Trundling beside her is a cart pulled by oxen with industrial-sized empty amphorae packed in straw. She recognizes the driver, Babak, a heavy man with a lazy eye; he delivers full jugs to the palace and takes the empty ones away. She pulls her cap further over her forehead and hunches forward, narrowly avoiding three mounted soldiers trying to force their way through the crowd toward the gate.

Years ago the bustling city expanded beyond the thick walls, and on the outside, too, are luxury villas and taverns, crowded living quarters and shops crammed side by side. Zo sees a merchant bringing in shiny brass cook pots hanging outside his shop, and a woman closing and barring the wooden shutters of a bakery.

On her right is a rather ramshackle building where three heavily made-up women in skimpy outfits lean against the walls in brazen poses. Two men ahead of her—farm laborers, by the looks of them—walk over to the women. Then all four of them go inside. Prostitutes.

Zo has heard about them, of course. She and her friends told each other gossip they heard from servants about people at court who were adulterous, or men who loved other men, or men who drank too much or gambled too much or frequented prostitutes. But she never actually saw a woman who sold her body. She walks closer to the one remaining against the wall for a better look. She's young, younger than Zo. Thinking Zo a boy, she saunters up to her, swinging her hips, but her eyes and her smile are as hard as those on marble statues.

Zo quickly ducks back into the knot of remaining travelers. How did a girl so young become a prostitute?

Had she been captured while out walking alone at night and forced into it?

Could Zo, too, end up in another town forced to lean against a wall and have sex with strangers for money?

She can't imagine there will be any criminals so close to Sardis, where first-time offenders lose noses or hands. Twice a year, King Shershah eats a lavish banquet with his counselors as they watch second-time thieves being hanged from eighty-foot tall gallows. Zo and the royal women are allowed to watch through louvered windows. But after she saw the first man kicking and swinging high in the air to the sounds of cheers, she had a sick feeling in the pit of her stomach and turned away.

She braces herself, and continues walking, trying to ignore the slow ache in the soles of her feet, radiating up her calves. After half a mile, the buildings spread out, and after that they are taken over by the city of the dead. Here the road is lined with mausoleums as big as houses, two or even three stories high, with sculptures and porches where families have picnics and pour wine to the departed. Some tombs have withered funeral wreaths on the doors, draped with the mourners' long hair, gray and black and brown.

Zo ducks behind a large multicolumned mausoleum with red marble lion statues guarding the door and picks her way through the smaller ones behind it. After a few moments, Zo recognizes the tomb she is searching for by the bronze statue on its roof of the thousand-eyed cattle watcher, Mithra, god of the cosmic forces and divine justice.

The mausoleum looks neglected. Dried leaves litter the porch and the heavy, ornate bronze door is discolored from lack of polish. Zo unsheathes her knife from her belt and pulls a lock of hair out from her cap. She cuts it near her scalp and ties it to the door handle.

"Shirin, I still mourn," she says. An evening breeze scuttles the dead leaves across the marble floor of the porch.

Zo remembers the time she and Shirin tried to henna delicate designs on their hands and feet themselves instead of having the slave do it. But they botched the job so badly it looked like they were scalded red and it took a week of scrubbing before it faded.

She remembers how she and Zo would laugh and laugh until their sides ached.

Two years ago when Shirin developed a fever, Zo's mother wanted her to leave her friend's bed because the sickness could

be catching. Zo refused to go; she sat there, day after day, bathing Shirin's face with cool cloths dipped in mint water, begging her to drink some wine or eat some egg and poppy broth.
When the girl died, Zo took a pair of shears and chopped all
her hair off at the scalp to adorn the funeral wreath. It was an
act of love and despair that infuriated Attoosheh, who said no
one would want to marry Zo until it grew back.

It has grown back now.

Zo takes her water flask and pours a libation in front of the
door. Since Shirin's death, she has been here four times with
her eunuchs and ladies to pour fine wine at the tomb, for the
dead are always thirsty.

"Shirin," Zo says, "come now and drink."

For a moment, she thinks she hears a voice in response, but
she isn't sure. A footstep, too. A rustle of clothing. Is it her
imagination or is there someone nearby? She heard talk in the
palace that beggars had taken to breaking into neglected mausoleums and living there, protected from wind and rain in a
snug stone house whose rightful tenants never bother them.

That she's alone with the dead doesn't frighten her. That
she's possibly alone with the living frightens her very much.

If it isn't a vagabond or criminal, it could be a guard from
the palace who has followed her and will take her back to
her uncle for a reward. She has tarried too long. It is twenty
miles to Cosmas's camp. She hopes to stand outside the nearest posting station at dawn when the portcullis is pulled up
so she can bathe and eat before walking the final five miles.

She ties her flask back on her belt, picks up a stout fallen
branch and walks briskly back to the road, looking over her
shoulder. There is only one other traveler on the road now:
Babak and his tired, plodding oxen. Everyone else who left
with her at the gate must be huddled around braziers of spit-

ted meat or unrolling a sleeping mat. No one wants to travel the road in the dark.

She falls in step a little behind Babak. He looks around warily and, seeing it is only a boy, looks back at the road.

All around her now are orchards of olives and fruit, and irrigated fields. On her left, a farmer urges his lowing cattle back to the barn, lightly hitting their flanks with a switch. To her right, smoke rises from a distant farmhouse, faint and blue in the purpling sky. The air smells fresh and clean, of pine trees on the hills and rich soil and green growing things. In the palace the air always smells of something man-made: heavy Arabian incense or smoke from charcoal braziers, cloying perfume or roasted meat.

She feels free. Adventurous. Excitement pumps through her like wine. So this is what the world is like without eunuchs and nurses and mothers and kings fussing over your every move. But then Babak and his rattling wine cart turn left and take the road up to the vineyard on the hill. Now there is no one left on the road except Zo.

The sun sets behind the slate-colored mountains, the last orange rays like fingers trying desperately to hold on. Then they, too, are gone, plunging the land in darkness.

There's a noise behind her, the snap of a twig or crunch of a leaf. She holds the branch like a weapon and whips around but doesn't see anything. She can't get out of her head the idea that someone has followed her from the palace, that every minute of her journey so far she has been tracked. She imagines King Shershah's face dark with rage as she is brought before him. She will be whipped, most likely, and starved into submission the way his daughter Darya was when she refused to marry the fat king of Pergamum. She will have to lose her pursuer if possible. If not, perhaps he would accept a bribe to go back without her. She sewed dozens of golden earrings and rings into the hem of her tunic.

Her moment of elation vanished, she squares her shoulders and walks more quickly, wondering if it was smart, leaving at sunset. Yet if she had left during the day someone would have noticed her absence and sent search parties out for her.

By the time they find out tomorrow, she will be far away.

She trudges on. Twenty miles, she tells herself. Only twenty miles to Cosmas's camp. If she becomes too tired to continue tonight, she can curl up in her cloak in the basketlike crown of an olive tree.

A brilliant moon is rising, just a sliver shy of a full moon, lighting the surrounding countryside like a divine torch. The dirt road gleams like pure silver. The Magi have predicted that tomorrow night there will be a total eclipse. Then the goddess Anahita and her shimmering sky chariot will be swallowed by the Evil Spirit, Angra Manyu, until Mithra squeezes him so hard he will spit her out again.

There are always festivities at solstices and equinoxes, meteor showers and eclipses: dancing, singing, and drinking, torchlight processions and prayers. Usually Zo and her friends dress in her best and watch the priests parade through town with the sacred fire.

Staring at the moon, Zo vows to make an offering of fine incense to Anahita as soon as she can, throwing it in the pure fire, untainted by the blood and meat that defiles the altars of Greeks and Hebrews alike.

She stops walking and, hands extended and palms raised, says a prayer: *Lady Anahita, Virgin Warrior Goddess of the skies and rivers, the life-increasing, herd-increasing, fold-increasing immortal, who makes prosperity for all countries, protect me tonight. Help me find my destiny.*

She pictures her arrival in his camp tomorrow, a travel-weary boy asking for Cosmas. Perhaps someone will point the way to his barracks or lead her to him on guard duty on a watchtower. Will he recognize her immediately from a distance? Or will she have to whip off her hat? What will his two best friends say?

She met them once though she led them to believe she was the palace butler's daughter. Now she pictures Feroz teasing Cosmas about his irresistibility to women, and Nasim staring at her with such intense interest that Cosmas playfully shoves him away and tells him to behave better with a lady. She will cook for Feroz and Nasim when she and Cosmas are living in one of the little cottages for married officers. That is, she will *learn* to cook.

There's a rustling in the wheat. She stops and strains to hear but there's only the sigh of the evening breeze rippling through the crops and a low trill of grasshoppers. Is she imagining things? Then she hears a sneeze.

"All right," she says, raising her stick, "I know you're in there. Come out so we can talk about this." She starts beating the wheat with her stick. Then she hears rapid footsteps behind her.

Before she can turn around something is whipped over her head and she is bundled to the ground. She tries to scream but her cries are muffled. She can't breathe. Will she suffocate before they take the bag off her head? The leather smells stale, pungent. She wants to throw up but there's no room for it; her vomit would choke her to death. She tries to calm her racing heart, slow her gasping breaths.

She flails her arms and legs but not for long. Rope is being wrapped quickly around her wrists so tightly it is cutting into them. Fear ratchets through her. She has an image of the hard-faced girl leaning up against the wall of the whorehouse. Then she has images of rape. Prostitution. Beatings. Living in filth. Never seeing Cosmas again. Or Roxana.

She's lifted none too gently and carried, bumping along. Panic drums loud in her ears but she tries to still her beating heart, tries to focus. She hears men's voices but can't tell what they are saying. Who are they? Robbers? How could she have been kidnapped by robbers only a few miles out of Sardis? If she gives them her gold jewelry, maybe they will leave her tied up in a field, and someone can free her tomorrow.

Finally, they put her down. They tear the bag off her head and she gratefully gulps in air until her breathing has returned to normal. The evening air feels cool against her cheek.

She looks up and sees a glitter of dark, calculating eyes. There are three of them. She feels like a wild animal trapped by hunters with spears. With her wrists bound together, she can't even try to fight. Wide-eyed, she looks around for a chance to flee.

But one of them puts a knife to her neck. "Listen, boy, if you make a move I'll slit your throat. Got that?" He jabs the point into her soft flesh for emphasis.

The moon slides from behind a cloud and Zo gasps. The man holding the knife is disfigured. Half his nose has been cut off, leaving a mass of grotesque red scars on a flat stump. This man has already been caught—and judicially punished— for committing a crime.

She nods. She can't escape. She can't fight. Her heart is hammering in her chest and perspiration is dampening her skin. She's fighting back tears.

"He doesn't look very strong," says a thin-faced man doubt-fully.

The noseless man says, "That's all right. We can still sell him for something."

Zo's heart sinks. Illegal slave traders.

Legal slave traders have a license from the empire to sell war captives. Before major battles, slave traders camp behind the opposing armies and erect auction blocks that will be used to bid on soldiers' captives. After the auction, the human merchandise is pushed into cages stacked on carts, and the captives are transported to the slave markets of major cities to become miners, or dock or field workers. A lucky few are sold into noble homes to administer the finances, educate the children, and run the households.

But illegal, unlicensed slave traders kidnap free people and sell them for whatever they can get to whoever wants them. No one believes a slave who claims to be free-born.

If she offered these illegal slave traders her gold jewelry in return for her freedom, they would probably take it and still sell her.

"Where's your money?" the third one says. He's fat and sweaty; she can see his bald head glistening in the moonlight.

She whispers hoarsely, "In my pouch."

He snatches the pouch off her belt and peers inside, sticking in a pudgy finger. "Look, Kansbar," he says approvingly, turning to the noseless one, "a nice amount of loose change."

"Let's look in the sack," Kansbar says. Zo has the feeling he's the leader.

They yank it off Zo's back and go rifling through it. The bald one snatches the loaf of bread and starts eating it. The thin-faced man grabs the figs.

"Whoa-ho!" cries Kansbar. "What's this?" He holds up Zo's sky-blue outfit, the one she was planning to wear for Cosmas.

"Maybe he was bringing it to his sweetheart," the bald one says, fingering the soft combed wool. "I think we can sell it for something. Good quality."

"Maybe he was going to wear it himself," the thin-faced one sneers.

The bald man is peering curiously at Zo's face. "There's something funny here," he says. He yanks the leather cap off her head and her glorious auburn hair tumbles out, betraying her.

"I knew there was something strange!" he cries triumphantly as the other two grunt in surprise and pleasure.

Zo's mind is racing. If fighting isn't an option, should she try to interact with them? Get them to like her? Tell them some hard-luck story of how her father killed her mother and threatened to kill her, too? How her stepfather raped her and gave her a horrible disease?

One thing she knows: she could never tell them she's the king's niece. They would be so afraid of retribution they would kill her and bury her the way kidnappers did to Princess Farah of Smyrna a few years ago. The princess and her three handmaidens were mistaken for wealthy farmers' daughters and abducted by slavers. When the men learned Farah was a princess, they killed them all except for one that was able to get away.

Better for Zo to live as a slave and wait for the chance to escape.

"All right, I'll take her over there, and when I'm done, I'll call you," the bald man says. His fat, filthy hands grab her shoulders as Zo recoils in disgust but Kansbar smacks them hard.

"Get your grubby hands off her," he says. "Let's see here." He spits on his cloak and rubs it on her cheek, holding her chin hard with his other hand. "Lookee!" he coos. "This is fine milk-white skin. Lady's skin. This isn't no peasant girl."

He sits back on his feet and considers. "When we get back to camp, we'll have Mother Aisha look at her. If she's a virgin, she'll fetch a high price. If she's not a virgin, we can all take a turn with her before we sell her." He turns slowly, making eye contact with each of the men. "But for now you'll keep your distance if you know what's good for you." The men grumble, but they agree.

Zo knows she's no virgin. She knows what they will do to her. She also knows she was incredibly stupid and naive to run away from the safety of the palace. She thinks of all the stories Mandana told her about war and pillaging, slavery and poverty and injustice. The world is frightening and cruel, especially to women. And Zo walked right into it like the greatest fool in the world.

"Come on," Kansbar says. "Let's get her to the wagon."

They pull Zo up and push her forward. She stifles a sob. It just can't get any worse than this.

And then it does.

A cry cleaves the darkness of the wheat field.

"Zo! Zo!"

It's Roxana, tumbling through the tall green stalks, her nurse Jopata behind her, arms outstretched as if trying to catch her. They must have followed her all this way, and only hidden in the tall meadow as the slavers approached.

Zo can't believe her eyes.

"Roxie! Go back!" she cries. "Go back! Now!"

But her sister runs up and throws her arms around her, even as a slaver is trying to drag Zo away. "Don't leave me behind, Zo!" she cries.

Zo looks at Jopata in astonishment.

"She had the feeling you were leaving, my lady," the nurse says, "and insisted on following you. I came to stop you, to bring you back—"

"But how—"

"We hid in the wine cart—"

The bald man who was holding Zo back now lets go of her and grabs Jopata, ripping off her black robe and veil. "This one's not young or pretty," he says, frowning. "This face would cause bronze to crack."

Zo sinks to her knees in the dirt beside the wagon, extending her bound wrists so Roxana can climb up on her shoulders. She holds her sister so tightly it is as if she's trying to absorb her into her own flesh to keep her safe.

Kansbar sighs. "And that one is too young to sell," he says, gesturing to Roxana. "It would be years before she was capable of work or anything else. I think we should kill both of them and keep the girl."

"No!" Zo screams. "I'll do anything, anything you want! Just let her go!"

Kansbar takes his knife and goes to Jopata. The old woman trembles in obvious terror. He raises it in the air, and it flashes with moonlight before falling. Zo presses Roxana's face into her shoulder so she can't see. It happens so quickly, Zo hardly has time to blink.

Jopata. So kind and helpful it was easy to forget her harsh features and love everything about her just as it was. She is dead now because of Zo.

Zo feels her throat tighten so much she can hardly breathe. Everything is a haze—flashes of metal and stained teeth, shadows, moonlight, a choking wind.

The three men gather around the body, rifling the clothing for any hidden valuables.

Zo wants to scream at the top of her lungs. But she can scream later. There's her sister to think about. And right now Zo sees a chance to escape. Not for both of them, but for Roxana.

Zo turns her back to the men and whispers to her sister, "Run, Roxie! Run very fast and quietly and hide. Go back to Sardis tomorrow. I will come soon."

She drops her silently to the ground and pushes her away.

Roxana looks as if she is going to refuse, but then she parts the wheat and disappears. Zo pretends that she is still holding her sister. She's behaving automatically, as though controlled by an external force—her own mind feels blank. "It will be all right, Roxana," she says to the night, "don't cry." She keeps talking, rocking, so the men will think the child is still in her arms.

After a few moments—is it enough?—Kansbar walks over to Zo, grabs her by the shoulder and roughly spins her around to face him. "Hey!" he cries, "the girl is gone." He gestures to the other men. "She might tell someone. Go and find her!" They stand up and bolt into the wheat.

His fist collides with Zo's jaw. Pain radiates through her head and she falls to the ground. "That's for letting the little runt get away," he says. He kneels down and holds a bloody knife to her cheek. "Say a word and I will cut out your tongue. Men will pay more for a woman who can't argue with them."

Zo hears the men trampling the wheat and cursing. She holds her breath. Will they find Roxana? She's so tiny, if she curls up in a quiet ball perhaps they will not.

Please, Lady Anahita, please keep her safe. I will make you such offerings...

A high-pitched scream echoes through the night. It seems to Zo that the wheat shudders in horror. Kansbar stands up, calling to his men. Shakily, Zo stands, too, ready to race through the field to her sister, but Kansbar grabs her.

Two men emerge from the thicket.

"All right," the bald one says. "We can go."

Zo feels her knees buckle as her vision fades. The moon silvering the wheat, the fiercely burning stars, everything dims. An ache hammers at her head, and with each painful throb there is a flash of blood red on the inside of her eyelids.

A terrible dream, she says to herself. *I am in my bed. When the*

cocks crow, I will wake as I always do. Roxie will come and we will
sew new dresses for her dolls…

Oblivion closes around her, and it is warm and dark. She
wants to stay in that place with no thoughts or feelings or
memories forever.

At some point, a cock crow slices into the warm, dark place.
Zo moves sleepily and feels a sudden soreness in her jaw. As
she stretches, she is aware of how hard her bed has become.
It's not at all like the luxurious goose-down mattress and pillows she sinks into every night. This feels more like a board.
It *is* a board. Zo lies still and breathes. There is no aroma of
the delicate perfume that Mandana sprinkles on her sheets
every night. Instead, there's the pungent smell of sweat and
old urine and, from farther off, a campfire. She hears the low
chirp of cicadas and frogs.

Her eyes fly open but she can't see anything. The world is
plunged in the inky darkness that comes right before dawn,
and the moon has set hours ago. She sits up slowly and puts
out her hands. They come in contact with something hard and
cold. Her fingers curl around the iron bars of a cage.

ACT THREE:
Desire and Deceit

All human actions have one or more of these
seven causes: chance, nature, compulsions,
habit, reason, passion and desire.

—Aristotle

Chapter Thirteen

TWO AESARIAN LORDS UNCLASP THEIR CAPES and stride onto the floor. Alex studies this new pair of combatants intently, his pulse pounding in his throat. Ever since becoming regent—and Heph's failure to win the tournament money—everything has changed, including all of his plans. How can they possibly go to the Fountain now, when they have no funds and no freedom? And when the country's fate could rest in Alex's hands?

Of course, his father wouldn't agree. Because his father sees no threat. But Alex sees one—no, *feels* one, senses one. It's like the time at Mieza when Aristotle lit a lamp wick soaked in rancid oil during an evening discussion. At first Alex was only vaguely aware that something might be wrong, brushing away the thought, wondering if he was imagining the sour smell. When he knew for sure, he still kept silent, realizing it was one of his tutor's lessons in perception and human reaction. Only when the room was filled with stench and smoke did anyone complain.

It's been like that the past several days, a slight odor associated with the Lords increasing slowly in intensity that either no one else is aware of, or if they are, they don't want to be the first one to mention it. Only this time, when foulness and smoke fill the air, it could mean betrayal. Lives lost. A nation threatened.

Alex refocuses on the Lords in front of him. Both wear the typical Aesarian uniform: black leather pants, boots, tooled breastplates, and their signature horned helmets of engraved steel. Black oryx horns, slender and curved as Arabian scimitars, adorn Lord Bastian's helmet, while notched beige ibex horns twist backward from Lord Gideon's.

Seated next to Alex, Kat waves an ostrich feather fan at Arrhidaeus who giggles, grabs it, and starts fanning her. Then he abruptly stops playing and, staring hard at the Aesarian Lords below, raises the fan to cover his face and sits back, whimpering. His maid Sarina—a dark, Egyptian beauty who rarely speaks, but is probably the kindest soul in the entire palace—holds Arri's arms gently at his sides to keep him still.

Alex turns his gaze to the warriors. While many scoff at the Lords' vow to rid the world of magic, and see them as relics of a former era, Alex knows that there's more to them than empty ritual. They are fierce fighters, skilled in acquiring allies from diverse countries and bringing influences from each into their battle tactics.

So far he has seen a dozen techniques he wants to try out with Heph. As the two contestants fix round iron practice buttons on their spear tips to blunt the blows, Alex casts a sidelong glance at his friend, who sits next to Cyn. Both have been watching the demonstration closely, pointing and whispering to each other behind their hands. Their shoulders seem to be welded together, and Cyn's hand rests on Heph's thigh.

Alex is surprised to see them on such friendly terms. When he first brought Heph home from the marketplace five years ago, Cyn took one look at the skinny, filthy boy and said he should sleep with the goats—though it was doubtful even they would have him. Until the day the boys left for school in Mieza, shortly after Alexander's thirteenth birthday, Cyn had either ignored or insulted Heph, playing the most appalling pranks on him. Together, Alex and Heph came up with ways to pay her back in kind. Seeing them now, acting like friends, like a *couple*, gives him an uneasy feeling in the pit of his stomach.

Ever since Heph lost the Blood Tournament, he has been behaving strangely—jumpy, irritable, and easily offended. Now, just when Alex has so much on his mind, Heph isn't there for him.

A warm breeze rattles the pegged-up canvas tent over the odeon, a small theater-in-the-round built on the far side of the sprawling palace complex. Given the relentless heat and burning sun, the one hundred or so spectators—nobility, high-level advisors, remaining military officers, priests, and priestesses—look grateful for the shade. Alex spots his mother on the queen's bench across from him, her fingers tracing the detailed embroidery on her sheer yellow gown. She looks worried. Beside her, her red-haired handmaiden Daphne stares at the warriors as if she were a starving woman and they were lamb chops. To his left, Phrixos and Telekles are bent forward, chins cupped in their hands, elbows on their knees. They have been studying every move with wide eyes and periodically elbow each other and comment.

In the center of the stage below, the two Lords bow to the audience, then to each other. They crouch, then begin to execute complicated twists and turns, swinging their shields and spears so quickly the weapons blur. Watching, Alex spots the same maneuvers he observed with the previous combatants: circles, semicircle left, semicircle right, figure eight, spiral. The men, Alex notices, are light and springy on their feet and flexible in the waist and back. The elegant, precise steps remind him of the intricate dances maidens perform at weddings, but they wield brutal force in their arms and shoulders. On a battlefield, those same graceful moves with a spear would skewer a man like meat on a spit, pierce an eye like a knife thrust into a hard-boiled egg, rupture arteries, and crack bones.

Alex feels a gentle pressure on his arm as Katerina nudges him. He realizes he was unconsciously rubbing his weaker leg. "They're so graceful," she whispers. "It makes me think of the harvest dances."

"I was thinking the same," Alex says. "Watch Lord Bastian. Any second, he's going to swing right, then circle left—ah, there he goes!" Lord Bastian swings the spear an inch away from Lord Gideon's throat, then draws back at the last second, a skill requiring both precision and lightning-fast reflexes.

Though Alex continues to watch the warriors' performance, he can't help but be momentarily distracted by the mystery of Kat. He steals a sideways glance at her profile—her long wavy hair twisted up in a complicated arrangement, accenting her cheekbones. She's thin but, he can tell, muscled and strong from years of being outdoors, of hunting for her own food. He can hardly fathom what her life must have been like before now.

But more than that, he can't read her the way he reads other people, despite how attuned to her he feels. The very first time he saw Katerina, bruised and dirty outside the arena, he knew that she was different. But different good, or different dangerous? That was the reason he invited her to the palace in the first place: to figure out why this village girl was unlike anyone else he had ever met. He still has no idea, but he feels connected to her in a way he's never felt with anyone, not even with Heph. Not even with his own mother.

The clanging of Aesarian weapons pulls his attention back to the performance, where he follows the Lords' moves, many designed to surprise an opponent. He could teach his men to do that.

Shifting in his seat, Alex watches the Lords show off their physical prowess. Allies, Philip calls them. But are they? After years of studying history, he knows that allies switch sides with alarming frequency. Many of Philip's own relatives were assassinated—not by declared enemies, but by close friends. Power, it seems, knows no loyalty, only self-interest. And only those who profess loyalty—who are considered allies—can get close enough to thrust a sword between the ribs.

Bastian and Gideon throw down their weapons, beat their chests with their right hands once, then extend them straight out in the Aesarian salute. The demonstration is over.

As the applause fades, Lord Bastian turns to the crowd. The ugly jagged scar across his otherwise proud, chiseled face only serves to make him seem more handsome, more fierce. When his gaze lights on Kat a moment too long, she looks away and shifts in her seat.

"Now that you have seen the might of the Aesarian Lords, does anyone wish to spar with me?" His lips twitch, as if he finds it laughable that a Macedonian warrior would think to challenge him. Alex hears ladies fanning themselves, the rustling of tent flaps in the breeze and someone coughing nervously.

"Come now," Bastian sneers. "Macedon is renowned as a country of brave men. Even those with unsightly injuries are known as warriors."

No one responds.

Unsightly injuries, Alex thinks, offended at Bastian's impudence. *Does he mean a king with one eye and a prince with a bad leg? Is he saying we're a country of cripples?* Alex is half-tempted to accept his challenge. Let them all know that even if Philip is gone, there is still a ruler here.

"As you wish," Bastian says, looking around the odeon and bowing slightly to the spectators, then to Alex.

Alex can feel all the hairs on his arm and neck standing on end. Yes, he's quite sure now: Bastian is definitely mocking Macedon's royal family and its soldiers.

"I accept your challenge," Alex says, standing. The crowd gasps—it's against protocol for royalty to perform for the public. Timid whispers behind hands rise to uneasy murmurings and head shaking. Someone begins to clap loudly. Others join in. A swell of applause rolls over the marble benches.

Kat places a hand on his arm and gives him a look of alarm, which he tries his best to ignore as he steps onto the floor. Lord Bastian tilts his head back and stares down his nose at him. He bows deeply. "An honor, my lord," he says, though his smirk suggests otherwise.

Alex unhooks his cape, and throws it toward the stands.

"Swords or spears?" Lord Bastian asks, gesturing to shining weapons laid out on the side.

"Swords," Alex says. Spears are fine for throwing from the top of a horse or piercing soldiers racing toward you at the beginning of a battle. But as Alex knows from the border skirmishes when he fought beside Philip, battle always comes down to the intense physical intimacy of fighting with swords, spraying and being sprayed by sweat and blood, feeling his weapon slide into a man's flesh and bone, looking into his eyes as the light fades and his last breath rattles in his throat.

Alex's heart pounds like a battle drum, loud and incessant. As he chooses a sword and fixes a button on top, he's afraid his palms are so sweaty he won't be able to hold on to it.

His first skirmish occurred when he was thirteen with a clan of feuding Thracians. He killed two men and wounded five. But they—and the others Alex has fought on summer military campaigns—were mostly untrained, undisciplined, and out of shape, a far cry from Lord Bastian. Still, he can't let anyone get away with such an overt insult.

He picks a shield and slides his left hand into the leather grip.

"The winner will be whoever hits his opponent three times or draws first blood?" Bastian asks.

Alex nods.

Though Alex has never practiced the Aesarian techniques, he has one great advantage over Bastian: Alex isn't winded. He's fresh, restless, and eager to fight.

Looking into his opponent's eyes, Alex anticipates Bastian's moves: the semicircle, the figure eight, the swivel to the left, then right. Alex knows a split second beforehand when Bastian's sword will peep out from his shield or swing behind his back or neck. As Alex parries Bastian's sword, he mirrors the Lord's steps, a bit clumsily at first, then with greater agility. Bastian sees that he has already learned and nods as though impressed, despite himself.

Alex licks his lips and tastes salty sweat creep into his mouth, but he cannot pause even for a moment to wipe his face. He needs every ounce of concentration just to keep up with Lord Bastian, let alone defeat him. He hears a cry from the crowd—someone urging him on—and he feels a surge of energy rush through him. As determination floods through his veins, his sword becomes a living creature, striking Bastian's sword and shield as if Alex had nothing to do with it.

The crowd roars in response, but it all seems to be happening in slow motion. A drop of sweat falls like a sparkling crystal through the air from Bastian's cheek onto his breastplate. Behind him a matron in a long green veil swigs from a painted clay wine cup, spilling some on her gown. In the top row, an old man sneezes, startling those near him. In the second row, Heph takes Cyn's hand and leads her to the exit.

Heph is going off with Cyn and not staying to watch Alex fight an Aesarian Lord? At such an important public moment for Alex, any friend of his should be there to cheer him on, but especially Heph, who trained with him all these years and rode beside him to battle.

Alex's blood brother, his best friend, isn't staying to watch.

His mouth parted in shock, Alex pauses to look at the backs of Cyn and Heph as they disappear into the exit tunnel. Lord Bastian raises his shield high as if to ward off a blow, and even though Alex knows his opponent's sword will thrust out from the shield's edge, he is slow to raise his shield, which suddenly feels like lead. The edge of Bastian's sword slices into Alex's right arm. Everyone in the audience gasps and stands up.

Bastian throws down his weapons. "I apologize, my Lord," he says, striding toward Alex. He doesn't sound at all sincere. "Should we call for a physician?"

Alex looks down at his arm. At first there is no blood, just a thin white line that turns to a thin red line. Now it's bleeding profusely, but the cut isn't so deep it will need to be sewn shut. "A scratch," he says, refusing to be mocked. In fact, it aches horribly, but he certainly isn't going to let Lord Bastian see that. What hurts Alex worse is that he allowed himself to be distracted by Heph and Cyn. If he ever lost his concentration like that on the battlefield, it could cost him his life.

"We can finish what we started another day, my lord," Bastian says, and his dark eyes shine with silent laughter.

Rage bubbles up in Alex. What other day? Why not finish it now? Why are Bastian's eyes so full of mockery? Why do they—

All sounds are silenced; all light fades. Alex is disembodied, traveling through the familiar tunnel of light, pulled forward by an unseen force.

At the other end, he emerges in a lamp-lit tavern or barracks, with carousing soldiers bathed in flickering shades of gold and brown. Bastian deftly substitutes dice from his pocket with dice from the table, and throws. Double snake eyes. The other men groan. With both arms he moves the pile of wagered coins toward himself, grinning.

This man cheats at dice.

Alex returns to the present with violent, wrenching speed. He finds himself back in his body, his ears ringing as though he has just dived deep beneath the sea's waves.

Lord Bastian has joined a knot of other Lords, and Kat is beside him, her cool fingers on his arm, examining the wound as Alex blinks, trying to clear his head.

But Olympias, like an enraged mother bear defending her cub, shoves Kat aside. "Remember your place," Olympias says. "Though I'm not sure what that is," she adds, her voice thin and sharp as a dagger.

A look of pure loathing comes over Kat's face and disappears so quickly that Alex isn't certain he actually saw the narrowed, burning eyes and hard mouth. She nods and walks away.

"Mother," he says, passing a hand over his forehead, "Katerina is my guest. You mustn't speak to her like that." Olympias is wrapping a handkerchief around the wound. The cream linen rapidly turns red.

"Never mind her. Why did you challenge him?" she hisses.

"For the honor of Macedon," he says, pulling away from her so that she's forced to take back the bloodied handkerchief. "And for my own honor." He is pleased with his performance except, of course, for his mistake at the end. A mistake he will never make again. His mind goes back to Heph. Why did he leave when he did?

Olympias stares at the blood-covered handkerchief in her hands, and, to Alex's surprise, folds it up and stuffs it quickly into the folds of her robes.

"Keep your distance from those carrion crows," she warns. "Their boundless greed only grows, and they no longer fear the law. They've recently demanded the archives and the hellion be released to them—that *I* be turned over to them."

"What did Father say?"

"He refused, of course," Olympias says. "But that's not the point. They have a confidence I cannot trust. I fear their plans. I fear their power."

For once Alex agrees with his mother, but he doesn't let his worries show.

"There's even a rumor they plan to poison me," she adds, her voice determinedly steady.

"There are always such rumors in a palace," Alex responds.

She kisses Alex's cheek, and Alex is surprised to feel wetness against his skin. His mother's tears mingle with his sweat. "Promise me you'll double your guards," she says. "Think about a taster."

Alex nods, about to reply when Radamanthos, the palace master of ceremonies, sweeps onto the floor. Olympias heads toward the exit as the former actor begins to thank the Aesarian Lords for the display. The Lords who participated come forward, acknowledging the applause with curt nods. Alex studies the men, all wearing the same uniform and cape but each with a unique pair of horns on his helmet. They come from across the known world and even parts of the unknown world.

Bastian, Alex knows, is a Samian, and Gideon, with his rich brown skin, must be an Ethiopian. But he's unsure of Mordecai's origin. He speaks with a Persian accent mixed with something else, and he doesn't have the same bearing as other

Persians Alex has met. One of today's competitors is a gigantic Gaul from the endless forests beyond the Western mountains, with long yellow braids and fierce blue eyes. There's even a Scythian from the legendary hill country north of the Euxine Sea, bowlegged like all his tribe from growing up on the back of a horse.

Fusing together the best men and military traditions of several nations must create a superior army. The most effective fighting force in the world.

Better even than Macedon's.

Riding a surge of heat and adrenaline—whether from the intensity of combat or the mortification of his public loss, Alex can't quite distinguish—he marches off the field and straight toward the royal library, angry suspicions swirling through his mind.

When he throws open the heavy door, a scribe looks up, startled, nearly dropping his quill. He scrambles to attention. "My Lord Alexander, how may I be of assistance?"

"Leonidas. Where is he?"

The slave bows his head and hurries through one of the many doors leading off the atrium.

It takes Alex's eyes a moment to adjust to the darkness: it's like another world in here. The atrium is cool and calm. Black and white pebbles swirl in a mosaic on the floor, and a rectangular blue pool ripples gently in the center under an open skylight.

A moment later, Leonidas emerges. An ascetic who doesn't believe in luxuries, Leonidas was Alex's tutor for seven years before he went to Aristotle's school at Mieza. Looking at his lined face and unkempt beard, Alex remembers long winter hikes through ice and snow wearing a summer tunic and sandals. The constant gnawing hunger that made it impossible to fall asleep. The memorization of long classic texts with a hard swat on the palm of his hand for every single error, no matter how small.

Though Alex never liked his tutor, he is grateful. Whether on a months-long campaign or in a daylong battle, Alex knows he can perform through heat and cold, hunger and thirst, exhaustion and pain, all because of Leonidas's training.

"My lord?" Leonidas says, his voice unrattled by the prince's sudden visit. His beetle-black eyes register clear distaste at Alex's luxurious purple tunic, embroidered with sixteen-pointed gold stars. Leonidas himself is dressed in a rough-woven unbleached robe.

"I need all records relating to the Aesarian Lords—history, correspondence, everything we have." Though Alex spent countless afternoons in the library with Leonidas growing up, he was mostly studying scrolls of epic and lyric poetry, history, philosophy, geography, mathematics, drama, and science. Leonidas gave him a few lessons on conducting royal correspondence, but only with documents related to Athens and Sparta, kingdoms with whom Macedon has the most trade and greatest rivalry.

"That has become very sensitive information," Leonidas says now, tapping a key ring hanging from his belt. His perfect enunciation and well-modulated tones remind Alex of all those times his tutor made him fill his mouth with river pebbles and then try to speak clearly. "Royal correspondence is kept under lock and key. You know that." He makes no move to unhook the key ring or lead Alex to the archives but remains standing there, stroking his gray beard thoughtfully.

Still treating me like a child, just like my parents, Alex thinks. He curls his fingers into a fist, resisting the urge to react. "I'm the regent while my father is away," he says, keeping his voice steady.

"Under advice of the council, of which I am a member," Leonidas counters coolly.

"I have heard of threats to the royal family," Alex says. "And the king...disagreed with the Lords on certain matters. When my father left, he took most of the army with him, but the Lords remain."

"Thirteen of them," Leonidas says, shrugging. "No great danger."

"Perhaps not," Alex says agreeably. "Though I imagine entire armies of them could be here in a few days' time. A certain teacher of mine once said power comes from knowing your enemies' strengths and your friends' weaknesses. It is a valuable lesson I have never forgotten."

Leonidas considers this. Finally, he unsnaps the key chain from his belt and beckons the prince to follow him through one of the doors radiating off the entrance hall. At the end of a long corridor he unlocks a door. The room, perhaps ten feet square, is dim. Leonidas stands on a stool and opens the shutters over the high barred window, allowing light to pour in. All four walls have diamond-shaped pigeonholes, a dozen or more scrolls thrust into each one.

"This is one of our royal correspondence archives," he says, jumping nimbly off the stool. "That wall is Persian, that one Carthaginian, over there Egyptian. That one," he said, gesturing to the wall to the left of the door, "has everything related to the Aesarian Lords."

Alex scoops out the scrolls and deposits them on the oak table as Leonidas pads from the room. The papyrus documents have been sewn together; one scroll might have twenty or thirty letters wrapped around a wooden rod. The earliest ones go back nearly two hundred years and were friendly. The Macedonian kings were pleased the Lords were restoring order after incursions by Persians and barbarian attacks and allowed them to take criminals and enemies away. They honored the Lords and rewarded them with gold.

Then, a hundred years ago, the Lords began questioning those accused of witchcraft and sorcery, especially women, whom they viewed with great suspicion. Only two letters later, the Lords moved from questioning to imprisonment. These people, they wrote, were the true danger to any king and any civilization. For what good is the best army in the world against unseen forces? Some kingdoms believed the Lords' reasoning and voluntarily agreed to do as they suggested: Athens, Sparta, Arcadia, even some Persian satrapies sought out magic wielders, and turned them over to the Lords. Other kingdoms—Boetia, Crete, Aetolia, Argolis—needed some persuasion. After the Lords terrorized these nations, their leaders called a truce and acquiesced to their demands. Now all kingdoms have Aesarian ministers, advisors, and generals in the highest echelons of power.

All kingdoms, except Macedon.

When he looked into Lord Bastian's eyes on the field today, Alex saw deceit.

A shiver runs up his spine.

He'll have a dagger in his belt, and a knife in each boot. From now on he'll sleep with a weapon in his bed.

He puts the scrolls back in their pigeonholes and walks out of the library into the main palace courtyard. After so much time in the softly lit archives, the late afternoon sun shines directly in his face, and he shades his eyes with his hand to look around. This is a space designed to impress visitors, with its multicolored marbles, colonnades, and bronze statues glinting on the orange-tiled roofs, but its current state of defense is hardly impressive.

Two soldiers play dice on the watchtower of the opened main palace gate. Farther below, the town gates, too, he knows, yawn wide, ready to welcome the enemy. Behind the palace, the barracks is two-thirds empty. At the main entrance to the palace, the guards on either side of the door look smart in their red-crested helmets holding red shields with white hawks in profile, beaks open and talons outstretched. One of them leans on his spear chatting to a blushing girl holding a basket of oranges. The other one's eyes are shut. He's taking a nap standing up.

Defenseless, he thinks with rising alarm. *We are defenseless. Utterly unprepared. Ready to be slaughtered.*

He walks briskly through the palace, analyzing how he would defend it in a siege. He couldn't. There are too many windows, too many doors. Philip tore down the dark, impregnable stone fortress of his fathers and built a pleasure palace of light and marble to show the world he was not only rich, but unafraid.

In his room, Alex opens his clothes chest and roots around his tunics and cloaks for his favorite dagger. This weapon, forged from Damascus steel in the blood of the last phoenix, is said to shatter not only bone, but also protective spells shielding the enemy.

But it is gone.

CHAPTER FOURTEEN

KAT MOVES HER LAST FLAT WHITE STONE TO THE next square on the *petteia* board, and immediately feels herself becoming trapped. Iris moves a black stone toward Kat's piece, and now two black stones have hemmed it in.

Then Iris picks up Kat's stone and sets it on the table next to all the others. "Game over," she says. Her smile is kind, but it stops at her eyes. And her words irk Kat. It has been too long already. Too long that she has dwelled in the palace unable to discover the truth. The desire for vengeance is growing, eating away at her from the inside, but she must be cautious. The maids only seem to be getting more wary around her as the days go by.

And she needs answers.

"Game over! Game over!" screeches a harsh voice from the window of the royal handmaidens' parlor. It's Odysseus, Iris's green-and-yellow parrot, poking his curved gray beak out of his ornate bronze cage. The handmaidens laugh. In Erissa, Kat heard of colorful talking birds from Africa, but never saw one until she met Odysseus.

As she and Iris clear the table of game pieces, Kat feels frustration rising inside her. It's embarrassing to lose so badly—again. The handmaidens must think she's a hopeless hayseed who can never learn anything.

She honestly can't tell if they've taken her under their wing today out of pity, or simply for their own amusement, but there have been plenty of times when they believe she's not listening, when she's sure she's heard them muttering about her. Probably speculating about the *true* nature of her relationship with the prince.

And it's natural. She, too, has wondered over and over again why the prince has taken an interest in her, and yet has left her alone at nights, has never once tried to force himself on her.

She is more out of place here, she knows, than Iris's parrot. She's no one—of no importance and no title. And yet she's a guest of the prince, adorned in fine jewelry, and treated like a lady—waited on by the same women whose trust and friendship she is trying to earn.

At least Daphne has been consistently kind to her, has spoken to her like an equal. So she's not quite as uncomfortable here as she would be with the noble court ladies, who look down their long noses at her and whisper behind their fans as she passes, some of them mimicking her country accent. Looking around the elegant room, though, she knows that she doesn't belong here, either. What did that nasty Princess Cynane tell her in the menagerie—that she was just a country mule dressed up as a parade horse?

She wants to scrub the makeup off her face, pull down her hair, throw on an old knee-length tunic, and bolt for home.

But she can't. She's here to learn the queen's secrets before killing her.

Why did Helen disappear the night of Alexander's birth? And why did Olympias track Helen down and kill her if not over the stolen scarf? And what was in the ivory-and-turquoise box? The questions are burning a ragged hole in her chest, and she's afraid of what may happen if they aren't sated soon.

And yet, she has tried everything and found only an impenetrable wall of guards, gossips, and secrets. If anyone knows the queen's past, it *should* be her handmaidens who are with her almost every moment of the day. These are the women who wash her in the bath, help her on the chamber pot, and provide clean bandages when she is menstruating. The women who know when Philip visits Olympias and inspect the sheets the next day to see if the couple enjoyed themselves.

But Kat has talked, subtly of course, so as not to draw suspicion, to *all* the older handmaidens who might have been there the night of Alexander's birth—Cassandra, Agatha, and Iris—and hasn't learned anything helpful. They seem too afraid—or simply too ignorant of the truth—to offer any insight.

And as for Olympias's private chambers, she hasn't even been able to breach the outer door of her suite. All entrances, inside and out, are too well guarded.

"Don't feel bad, Katerina," Daphne says, raising a painted cup of watered wine to her lips. Kat can't help feeling it's appropriate that Daphne's black glazed cup is adorned on the outside with white winged figures of Eros wielding a bow and arrow. The statuesque redhead is as interested in the opposite sex as they are in her. "If you can't capture men in *petteia*, at least you know how to do it in real life. The heir to the throne, no less."

The other women hoot and chuckle. Kat blushes.

"Speaking of capturing men," Ariadne says, reclining on one of the couches lining the dark red walls, "is anyone attending the Festival of the Lunar Eclipse tonight? I've heard some of the Aesarian Lords might come." She sighs and rolls a shining mahogany ringlet around her finger. "There's something about those uniforms."

"Where's it being held?" asks Agatha from a couch in the corner, plucking her lyre. An elegant forty-year-old widow, Agatha is an accomplished musician whose playing calms the queen's nerves. Kat tried strumming her instrument a few times, marveling at the gleaming cow horns rising from the top of a polished tortoiseshell, but she cringed at the jangling notes she coaxed out of the sheep gut strings.

"Where do you think?" Ariadne replies archly, her dewy dark eyes widening. "The andron."

"Oh, no," Daphne says. "That means it's going to be an orgy. Decent women never go to the andron."

Ariadne giggles.

"In that case, I suppose you are going?" Cassandra asks, her aging face puckering in scorn. She stabs a needle into her embroidery as if it were Daphne she were puncturing instead of a piece of linen.

Kat has an imaginary flash of what might go on in the andron, whatever that is, and just as quickly her mind goes back to Jacob's kiss in the pond. What would have happened if Calas hadn't interrupted them? Would she have had the strength to push away his strong arms, his hungry lips, the feel of his hot breath on her neck? She thought so many times about seeking him out in the barracks, but she knows she mustn't lead him on.

Still, the other day, when he appeared in her room, looking taller, stronger, and more confident than ever in his military uniform—when their bodies melted together and they kissed again—part of her wanted to tell him yes she would marry him, and pull him toward the bed...

With a jerky movement, Kat spills red wine all over her white peplos.

"Ha! Like a virgin bride's blood on the sheets," cries Iris.

"You are a virgin, aren't you?" Daphne asks, eyes sparkling. "I can tell, you know."

"Which young man do you have your eye on?" Agatha asks with kindness in her eyes.

"Alexander, of course," Daphne answers for her.

No. Not Alex. She has come to like what she knows of the prince, and how she feels in his presence, but he seems to her, strangely, like someone who could be a dear friend—and only that.

No, of course it is Jacob, and Jacob only, who has her heart. And she can't do what she wants to do with him because her mission is still hanging over her head. As soon as he stormed out the door the other day, saying he wouldn't seek her out again, the room seemed plunged in winter cold. The rich colors faded, and the birdsong from the garden was stilled. She never felt so alone in her life.

"—that everyone can see the prince never looks at you twice," Cassandra is saying crossly to Ariadne, "no matter how much you stare at him."

The two women glare at each other and Agatha gently lays her lyre on the couch between them, then says quietly, "Speaking of revelry, last night after the queen dismissed us, I heard those noises again."

The handmaidens' eyes grow wide. Iris munches on another candied plum and says cheerfully, "Well, with her husband always at war, maybe Her Majesty is…lonely. In a chaste way."

Cassandra's foot starts tapping again as she sniffs and says, "I don't think anyone could enjoy themselves that much alone."

"You should know," Daphne says, without missing a beat. "But with all those guards around her, I don't know how the queen could let in a lover. Unless it's one of her own guards who's supposed to be standing stiffly at attention *outside* her bedroom and instead is standing stiffly at attention *inside* her bedroom."

The women's whoops of laughter are silenced by a deep voice crying, "Ladies!"

Tall and elegant, Timandra, mistress of the maids, glides into the room. With her imposing square jaw and her robe of shimmering gray, along with a diaphanous veil sweeping from her carefully coiffured silver hair to the floor, she seems to Kat to be a goddess of the morning mist. "I am ashamed of you," she announces. "I should have you all whipped for such slander against Her Majesty."

Ariadne giggles again. "I wouldn't mind it if one of the visiting Aesarian Lords did the whipping."

Daphne smirks and raises an eyebrow. "After showing you his best *battle* tactics?"

Timandra scoffs. "Had you experienced the effects of real war, perhaps none of you would be making such comments."

"What? I was only joking," Ariadne protests.

Cassandra *tsk*s. "Have you forgotten? All seven of Timandra's nieces were brutally raped by Theban soldiers after the defeat at Neon, except the lucky one."

Kat remembers hearing of this battle when she was a child, though it happened before she was born. It changed the tides of the Third Sacred War in southern Greece.

"What happened to her?" Daphne asks.

"She was beheaded, of course."

Timandra clears her throat. "Had I a sword and armor, I'd rather fight any attacker than remain in the palace, vulnerable to the whims of the victors."

That quiets everyone.

"Victors! Victors!" shrieks the parrot. This time the women don't laugh but curtsey and, adjusting their silver-and-blue snake scarves, head for the door. Silently, Kat says goodbye to the bird, and as she does, she has a sudden sense of the bird's life, his—for lack of a better word—*feeling*. She feels him flying freely through lush jungles steaming with rain and chattering with life, almost as though it were her own body in flight. But the impression is momentary, then gone. Odysseus cocks his head to the side and stares out of the bars of his cage past the open window to an unattainable freedom.

But she's not free either, is she? She's a stranger who doesn't belong here, caged in the palace with her worst enemy until she finds the truth, a truth that will set her free to commit murder. And then what?

She turns to Timandra who, she heard, is nearly sixty and has lived at court for forty-five years. Looking into her strong, broad face, Kat has the distinct feeling she will tell her the truth, if she asks.

"Timandra," she says, nervously pushing the candied plum leaf plate around the table, "I was wondering if you could tell me about something that happened in the palace many years ago. It has to do with my…aunt, who was one of the queen's handmaidens at the time…" Sensing danger—after all, Olympias instructed the guards that day to search the premises, possibly to find Kat herself—Kat has told all the handmaidens but Iris it was her aunt who disappeared, not her mother.

Timandra shoots her a direct gray gaze. "Yes?"

"Her name was Helen, and she disappeared the night of Prince Alexander's birth. And I have been… I mean, my family, we've been trying to find out what happened that night. Where she might have gone."

"Helen." The name rolls lightly off Timandra's lips. "An excellent handmaiden. One of the best we ever had. Yes, she was assisting Her Majesty at the birth, and the next day no one could find her."

Kat already heard that much from Iris. "Was there anyone

else there that night, with Helen, who might have spoken to her, or seen anything that might have frightened her?"

Timandra frowns, and the vertical crease between her eyebrows deepens so that it looks like a spear. "Desmas," she says.

"Who?"

"The mistress of the royal laundry. Other than the midwife and Helen, Desmas was the first person in the queen's bedchamber after the birth. She had to roll the queen over, strip off the bloody, sweaty sheets, and put down new ones before the king came in. And she was furious with Helen about something or other that night, though it's been so long I can't remember what it was. Anyway, Desmas is the one you need to talk to. And from the looks of your peplos, you have a good reason to visit the laundry."

Entering the royal laundry is like walking straight into the underworld. Across the wide room, steaming cauldrons hiss and spit over roaring fires. Somber-faced bearded men push paddles around the bubbling vats, looking to Kat like Charon the ferryman paddling dead souls across the river Styx. Stupefied by the heat, servants wander about like shades of the dead carrying wet armfuls of laundry.

A large man in a loincloth stomps on piles of linens in a low tub as if he is making wine from grapes. In the corner, two men on either end of a sheet look as if they are engaged in a rope-pulling contest, twisting the material to wring out the last drop of water. At workbenches around the room, girls pound clothing with rocks, rub stains with sand, and massage olive oil onto tunics to soften the scratchiness of the wool.

A girl carrying a basket of neatly-folded laundry hurries by. "Excuse me," Kat says. When the girl doesn't stop, Kat calls out louder, "Excuse me!"

"I'm busy!" the girl snaps, then she looks over her shoulder.

Her eyes widen slightly as she takes in Kat's expensive clothing, and she walks back to her. "I apologize, my lady." Kat
sighs inwardly, but doesn't bother to correct the girl.

"I'm looking for Desmas. Do you know where I could
find her?"

"One moment," the girl says and walks away. While she's
waiting, Kat sees a man approach a wooden vat in the corner,
raise his tunic, and urinate into it.

A short, round woman shaped like a ball of wax walks up
to her. Sweaty strands of gray hair peep out from beneath a
wilted white cap and stick to her wide red face.

"Yes, my lady?" the woman inquires, looking her up and
down. "How can I be of service?"

Kat holds out the peplos with the purple-red blotch. Desmas
immediately takes it over to the tub of golden urine, scoops
some out with a ladle, and pours it on the stain, which starts
to fade at once. Then she orders a girl to take it outside to
bleach in the sun.

"Thank you," Kat says. Their cheap, unbleached tunics
back in Erissa never needed urine, perhaps the single advantage to being poor. "I'm a guest of the prince and don't want
to damage anything."

Desmas looks at her approvingly. "If so, you're the only
one in the palace who cares." She turns to a girl scrubbing a
tablecloth against a ribbed wooden board and yells, "Elpida!
More elbow grease or you'll never get those slobs' stains out!"

Kat feels her elaborate coiffure start to droop and a large
sweat stain form on the back of her peplos. She has to get out
of here quickly before she faints from the heat. "Desmas, I was
wondering if you knew my aunt, Helen, the queen's handmaiden," she says. "My family never knew what happened to

her." Beads of perspiration roll off Kat's forehead. She's melting like a honeycomb in a cook pot.

Desmas hmphs, eyeing Kat up and down, clearly wondering what the niece of a handmaiden is doing dressed as a lady. "I knew her—the thief."

Kat tries to keep her face blank of expression. "What did my m— my aunt steal?"

Desmas plants her red hands on her wide hips. "The last time I saw Helen was the night of the prince regent's birth. She was running down the halls with a bundle of Egyptian sheets—the beautiful, expensive ones used to line their majesties' beds. I never saw her again, but some time after that I heard the queen telling everyone that Helen left the palace because she was a thief. The gods only know what else she must have stolen."

But what else *could* Helen have stolen to justify her murder? Kat's thoughts are interrupted by a loud clatter. Elpida lies sprawled on the ground, the once-clean laundry scattered like a patchwork quilt. As Desmas scolds the girl, Kat quietly exits the washroom, her wet peplos clinging to her body.

Kat can't bring herself to believe that her mother—the woman who shared food with traveling strangers and gave away her best loom work to families with thread-worn blankets—was the same woman Desmas just described.

Kat stops in between rows of laundry hung out to dry and snapping in the breeze—sheets, tunics, and, oddly enough, gold-spangled costumes of some sort, probably for tonight's andron party. Studying the costumes, she realizes she's chewing her right thumb like a nervous nail-biting child and folds it inside her fist a few moments. Then she pulls her mother's silver Flower of Life pendant from beneath her peplos and holds it tightly, feeling her jaw tighten in determination. She's tired of feeling lost and helpless.

She needs to act. Tonight.

Daphne throws open the door of Kat's room and runs in with a linen bag. "I've got it!" she says excitedly, spilling the contents on the bed. There's a long blond wig made of horse-hair, a pair of soft deerskin boots, and a flimsy theatrical bow and quiver full of toy arrows. "These days, all the dancing girls pretend to be Amazons," Daphne says, pushing back a stray ringlet of long red hair and examining the gold-spangled outfit Kat snatched from the laundry line. "A couple of years ago, they all dressed as Persians."

Kat listens to Daphne's chatter as she dresses Kat in the costume, but it's hard for Kat to concentrate on the maid's excited descriptions of the andron when Kat has no intention of attending the festival. Kat's dancing girl outfit is a disguise—one that will allow her to slip unrecognized through the carousing palace inhabitants celebrating the first eclipse in more than ten years and the end of the Age of Gods. Tonight is a night when half the city will be huddled in temples, praying to the gods for protection, while the other half will be in the midst of adoring their own humanity—though it's unlikely that many of them actually believe the Age of Gods is coming to a close—if anything, most assume the Age *really* ended many hundreds of years ago. Still, tonight will be a night of drunken revelry, of empty halls and distracted guards. Kat is sure of it. This might be her only opportunity to kill the queen.

Daphne shoves the final pins into Kat's hair and adjusts the blond wig. Kat looks in the mirror and despite the gravity of her mission, smiles. The wig is not only unflattering; it also itches.

"Time for a dancing-girl face," Daphne says, opening several of Kat's cosmetic pots and pulling a makeup brush out of an agate jar. "Look down."

Kat looks down, and up, and everything else Daphne tells her to do as the older woman starts chattering about how handsome Lord Bastian is and how she nearly swooned watching him in the military skills demonstration.

"All right, you can look now," Daphne says. Kat turns to the mirror and sees that she has black eyebrows, bright blue eye shadow, and thick kohl around her eyelids. Olympias will never recognize her. Even Alex wouldn't. She barely recognizes herself.

"To complete your look." Daphne hands Kat the golden quiver of dull arrows. "And this," she adds, putting a glittery veil around Kat's lower face. "It isn't exactly Amazonian—in fact, it's from an old Persian costume—but you don't want anyone to recognize you."

"You're sure this outfit will get me in?" she asks, unhooking one side of the veil and feigning anxiousness.

Daphne laughs. "Every man loves a dancing girl! I can't imagine they would ever kick one out as pretty as you. Isn't this fun? It reminds me of the time we were celebrating Alexander's first birthday with a costume party for all the foreign ambassadors, and I watched Timandra dress Olympias as Helen of Troy."

Kat turns her head, surprised. "But Daphne, you've only been at the palace for two years."

"No," Daphne says, smoothing the wild blond horsehair curls on Kat's wig. "I was born here. My mother was handmaiden to the former queen, and as soon as Olympias married King Philip I was put in her service, young as I was. About five years ago Olympias sent me to Epirus as handmaiden to her brother's wife, the new queen. But I hated it there and was finally allowed to come back."

Maybe Daphne knows something about that night, even though she would have been very young at the time. Kat never asked her, thinking she was a relative newcomer to Pella.

"Daphne, do you remember a handmaiden named Helen who served Olympias about sixteen years ago?"

Daphne frowns and her voice takes on a sharp edge. "Yes, I do. Why do you ask?"

"She was…my aunt. I hear she disappeared the night of Prince Alexander's birth," Kat says. "Do you know anything about it? Why my aunt left and never came back?"

Daphne hesitates. "Well," she finally says, lowering her voice almost to a whisper, "I do know something about it. More, in fact, than I have ever told anyone." She looks over her shoulder as if afraid someone might be listening.

"What do you know?" Kat asks eagerly.

The redhead pauses and sighs. "It could be dangerous to tell the story. I might be risking my life. No one knows I saw."

Kat pauses for a moment as Daphne looks at her meaningfully. Finally it dawns on her—the girl wants payment. She goes to the trunk at the foot of her bed and rifles through her gowns until she finds the pouch of gold and silver she won betting on the Blood Tournament. She scoops some coins from it and hands them to Daphne.

"Here," she says. "I don't want to put you in danger without some reward."

Daphne beams with satisfaction and drops them in the embroidered pouch on her belt. "I was only nine," she recalls. "Old enough to understand what I saw, but young enough that people ignored me. I slept in a little room off the queen's bedroom to get her a chamber pot or glass of wine if she called me in the night. The queen's screaming woke me up. It lasted a long time. She wasn't just crying out in pain, she was saying a name: *Riel, Riel.* I thought it might be the name of a loved one, or a god, or a curse in some ancient language. I waited to be called, but no one did. Finally, I peered through the door and saw the midwife and Helen standing by the bed. The midwife had the baby prince wrapped in a blanket in her arms. But Helen had—"

Daphne stops suddenly and gasps. Her eyes widen in shock and her entire body tenses up, becoming as rigid as a board. White spittle appears on her lips and she falls to the floor, her body convulsing, arms and legs flailing, spine curving backward.

Kat grabs the girl's shoulders, trying to still her. "Daphne? Daphne!" she shouts, uncertain what to do other than turn the girl over so that she doesn't choke. Kat leaps up and grabs a wooden makeup stirrer from her vanity and tries to force it into Daphne's mouth to keep her from swallowing her tongue—perhaps she has the disease that causes people to fall to the ground in seizures.

The convulsions come to a shuddering stop, and Daphne, eyes wide open and glazed, is…dead.

Kat gasps and stifles a scream, which comes out instead more like a strangled whimper. She instinctively pushes herself away from the girl's body, whose eyes only moments before were lit up with secrets. She sits back on her heels, hands in her blond wig, willing herself not to throw up, feeling frozen to the spot.

All Kat can see is her own mother kneeling by the hearth, the surprise on her face as she is pierced by swords, then her body slumping backward to the floor, bloodied and still. The memory holds her prisoner; her arms feel like lead, her heart seems to stop beating.

She snaps back into the present and begins screaming for help, her voice sounding disembodied, like the voice of a scared child.

As a clamor echoes down the hall toward her room, a tiny movement in the dead girl's white robe catches Kat's eye. A slender green snake, flecked with gold, raises its head and stares at her. She gazes back at it, willing herself to *understand* it. But she cannot feel the animal's emotion, its need, the way she sometimes can. She feels instead a wall of silence, almost like an intentional resistance.

Unnerved, she backs up slowly and grabs a bronze lampstand, each of its eight curved arms holding a lit oil lamp in a basket shaped like a lotus blossom. As she angles the lampstand as a weapon, three of the clay lamps fall out and crack, spilling oil on the floor.

Most animals would have stolen away by now. But not the snake. Its black forked tongue flickers, and its dark eyes dilate.

What is this snake doing in the palace?

Her eyes dart to Daphne's shining silver scarf on the floor, with its pattern of blue snakes swallowing their tails. Woven in Epirus for the queen's handmaidens.

Of course: this living snake belongs to the queen.

And no disease killed Daphne, she realizes. It was the snake.

A snake bite that was perhaps not intended for Daphne, but for *her*. It was in her bedroom, after all.

Kat feels chilled to the core.

Just then, a series of slaves and servants burst into the room, and the creature slithers across the marble floor and disappears.

In the commotion over Daphne, no one questions Kat's garb, and within moments, the body has been lifted and removed from her chambers.

Kat stands alone now, completely at a loss. She keeps seeing Daphne's shocked face and wide-open eyes.

It could have been her.

Kat shivers, feeling sick all over again, but something starts to replace the tumult in her guts—rage. This was the queen's doing. She feels certain of it. No more procrastinating. She's got to see her plan through. Not just for herself, but for Daphne.

It's time to find Olympias.

The weight of a small knife sits comfortably on Kat's hip as she slips out the palace door and into the garden. Hearing heavy breathing and short whispers, she stops short. In the light of the full moon, she sees a couple embracing on a bench mostly hidden by hedges, both tall, tan, and dark-haired. She tries to slip past them, but hearing footsteps, they break apart.

It's Hephaestion. The would-be princeling who tried to have her thrown into a dungeon stands up, runs a hand through his rumpled hair, and straightens his tunic. He's staring at Kat, frowning. Has he recognized her despite her disguise?

"Excuse us" is all he says. The dim light makes his jaw seem even more angular and strong—she can tell that it is clenched.

Next to him is Princess Cynane, the nasty stuck-up shrew who angered the hellion the other day, then insulted Kat. These are the last two people in the world Kat wants to see right now.

Unlike Hephaestion, who seems unsettled by Kat's appearance, Cynane remains seated, her long legs stretched out below her rumpled tunic, exposing a great deal of thigh. She meets Kat's eyes and slowly smiles. She runs her tongue over her bottom lip, making no move to tame her hair or adjust her tunic, which has slipped off her shoulder.

"Would you like to join us?" Cynane purrs.

Kat shakes her head and hurries past, eyes firmly on the ground. Join them? No. As far as she's concerned, Hephaestion and Cynane deserve each other. Both of them are conceited, arrogant fools who have no idea how to treat people.

She continues down the garden path, past the towering statue of Poseidon reigning over a now silent fountain. There, at the other end, is the queen's bedroom. A few small slices of light escape from the slatted shutters of her windows and the double balcony doors, and trace their way across the stone balustrade. Kat looks for the usual guards, but tonight—as she hoped she would—all she sees are a spear, shield, and helmet resting against one of the columns. Kat takes a sharp breath. Could it really be this easy?

She approaches cautiously. Laughter ripples from behind the ornamental bushes.

"Have more," a man says, and a woman giggles.

Now. *Now.* The truth hits her, freezing her in her spot. This is her opportunity. She has to do it, no matter what happens to her afterward.

How might they torture and execute someone who killed the queen? She thrusts the question out of her mind. It doesn't matter. All that matters now is what she must do.

Her pulse picks up as she sees thick ropes of ivy climbing the walls on either side of the balcony. Without thinking twice— she knows the guard could return at any moment, along with his comrades—she throws her toy bow to the ground, removes her clattering quiver of toy arrows, and grasps the ivy with both hands. It stays firmly secured to the wall. She pulls herself up and within moments is on the balcony. Holding her breath, she slowly tries to push open the doors, but they are fastened together with a light latch. The slats are open, but pushed up against them are embroidered linen drapes.

Kat removes her small knife from its sheath, takes a moment to still the quaking in her hands, then pinches the drape and slowly pokes her knife into it. No sound comes from inside. Then she drags the knife a couple of inches, creating a slit to which she places her eye.

She holds her breath. At first she has a hard time understanding what she's seeing, her vision through the slit is so limited. Then she sees a stern-faced woman with long golden hair and sapphire eyes looking straight at her. She nearly throws herself off the balcony in fear before she realizes it's a wooden statue, one of the four painted goddesses serving as bedposts on the queen's luxurious bed.

Breathing deeply to calm her racing heart, Kat pinches the curtain and pulls it to the right.

At first, she sees nothing, but a quick movement at her periphery makes her look down. A dozen snakes drink milk from golden bowls on the floor. There is a hole in the floor, a trap door of some sort, and out of it emerges Olympias in a long, sheer white robe, carrying an ivory box inlaid with turquoise. Kat almost cries out. It is identical to the box Helen gave Olympias just before she was killed.

Kat tries to will herself to kick open the doors, to sink the knife into the queen's flesh and complete her mission, but she cannot move. She is frozen with a disturbed fascination as she watches the queen kneel on the floor and open the box, not three feet from Kat. Olympias smiles and pulls out the contents, examining them.

They are bones.

Kat stares in horror. They are small, and in the dim light, Kat can't make out what kind of creature they belong to. A cat? A puppy?

Then the queen removes a skull.

A human skull.

They are the bones of a baby.

Kat gasps loudly this time, and her knife slips from her fingers, falling onto the balcony with a clatter. The queen looks up at the drapes. She rises to stand, a look of pure fury on her white face.

Kat leaps over the balustrade for the ivy and starts to swing down but loses her grip and plunges the last ten feet, nearly leaving her long tangled wig in an ivy branch. Lying on her back, she can't get her breath. It's as if she's on the bottom of a pond, looking up, unable to inhale. She raises her hands and sees that she is still clenching leaves. Above her, the stars shimmer and twinkle. She forces herself to remain still, even when she hears the creak of the balcony doors. Kat stays in the shadow and watches the queen examine the slit in her curtain, then step out onto the balcony. Olympias looks down and picks up Kat's knife, its blade glinting in the moonlight. Then she looks into the garden.

Right. At. Her.

All of a sudden, gongs sound. Trumpets blare. Drums beat. And all around the palace, hundreds of voices cry out. Kat's heart nearly stops. Is it an alarm? Will soldiers rush into the courtyard and arrest her? This time there will be nothing Alexander can do to save her.

Then she realizes that Pella's temples are letting people know it's time to celebrate the eclipse. Olympias looks up at the moon, smiles, and returns to her room, closing and locking the balcony doors.

CHAPTER FIFTEEN

OLYMPIAS QUICKLY LAYS THE BONES BACK IN-side the box, wrapping them in the bloody handkerchief she retrieved from Alex during the demonstration.

That—the blood—had been the easy part.

The Aesarian Lords are getting bold, sneaking up to her balcony. Normally she would call the guards to search the garden—the entire palace, if need be. And for a second she reconsiders. It would set the Lords back a great deal if one of them was found skulking beneath a bush. She picks up the knife and holds it close to the candelabra's light. The blade is sharp enough but made of dark, dull iron that looks as if a village blacksmith had hammered it into shape. The handle is of undecorated bone. This is no Aesarian weapon, but a common peasant's tool.

And what peasant would have been standing on her balcony and dropped it? Olympias thinks about the two eyes she had just spotted, eyes that had a disconcerting familiarity...

As the queen's gaze falls on the box, she remembers that there *is* a peasant girl with palace access. That girl who had sat with Alex during the demonstration and who had looked at her son with the same bright eyes she'd seen in her garden tonight. She cannot remember her name, but it doesn't matter. There is no time for her now.

Olympias plucks up a tawny-colored snake from the floor and, sitting at her vanity, ties it into her thick hair. Then she picks up a small black one perched before a cup, licking the last drops of milk from its lips, and does the same. When she has the eleven smaller snakes in her hair, she takes the largest and wraps him around her neck like a shawl. She buckles on a gilt belt with a small leather pouch and a hand-tooled knife sheath. She grabs the ivory-and-turquoise box and a lantern, then sets out, using servants' passages to leave the palace. She can feel the snakes, alert, rising up in curiosity, and it is as if her handmaidens are lifting her thick tresses to curl or pin them.

The marketplace is so filled with revelers come to celebrate the full lunar eclipse that Olympias can hardly move. The shops, normally shuttered and dark after sunset, are ablaze with the hot light of cressets—iron baskets on tall poles filled with blazing wood—as their owners sell their wares. She smells Arabian incense and torch smoke, spilled wine and roasted meat.

She walks past the little wooden booths in the middle of the cresset-lit square selling papier-mâché masks of gods and animals, and picks up one of an ox. It's nicely painted but a flimsy thing that will be smashed to bits by dawn. She examines a small wooden drum covered with rawhide and thumps her fingers on it.

Olympias looks around at the torch-lit processions streaming toward all the major temples with black animals to sacrifice to the spirits of the Underworld as ransom for liberating the moon from its dark grip. She needs to join the long line of women heading for the eastern gate. Many of them wear animal costumes, the heads and pelts of wolves, deer, bulls, and mountain lions. In such a group, Olympias, with the living snakes writhing in her hair like Medusa, attracts little or no attention. In her unusual ceremonial garb, and under the cloak of darkness, no one even recognizes her as their queen.

The women sing or play harps, cymbals, or flutes. Some have bells on their ankles and wrists, which make a music all their own as they walk. Several carry the thyrsus, a long garlanded staff dripping with honey used to beat to death any man caught spying on their sacred rituals. They are the Bacchantes. Women devotees of the god of wine, madness, and orgies: Bacchus Dionysus, the Twice Born.

The train of lanterns and torches winds out of the city and up the ancient track. To honor Dionysus, most of the celebrants are already drunk, swaying, staggering, and laughing as they forget the words to the songs. In front of Olympias a woman falls down, sloshing wine all over her white robe like blood at a sacrifice. Her friend, laughing, helps her up.

In a flash of memory Olympias sees herself at the age of twelve falling down in a white robe stained with blood. Her name wasn't Olympias yet. It was Polyxena, daughter of Neoptolemus I, King of Epirus and a direct descendant of the hero Achilles who killed Hector, Prince of Troy. But her father was often away at war, and that night her stepmother beat her worse than ever before, for the unforgivable crime of not being her own flesh and blood. Fearing that this time the enraged woman would return and finish her off, she'd staggered through the dark, silent town, wheezing in pain from broken ribs. At the end of a street she saw a temple lit with torches and naked women whirling and dancing around a bonfire in front of it.

Unable to walk farther, she'd crawled toward it on bloody knees, her soft cries for help unheard amid the drums and flutes. She collapsed, barely conscious. After a time, gentle hands lifted her up and carried her, then laid her down and put a drink to her lips. It was wine, mixed with something else, something more potent. Soon, hands were stroking her, washing the blood off her. Kind voices murmured comforting words.

After a time she sat up, the stabbing pain in her ribs reduced to a low throb. Someone had put a snake mask on her head made from real snakeskin. Power surged through her from the animal spirit and even with the heavy mask, she suddenly felt lighter somehow. Wild. Free. She rose and joined the dance-like movement she didn't understand, but her body obeyed, casting grotesque shadows in the torchlight.

The pain in her ribs was gone now. Her young body no longer ached. She felt at once both weightless and grounded, both relaxed and yet aware of every part of her body. Ecstatic visions filled her mind of winged bird-headed gods hovering above the fire, of snakes turning into men, of marble statues on the temple roof climbing down the columns and joining the dance.

Intense rapture replaced the burning pain of the beating as she became one with the god. The High Priestess of Dionysus gave her a new name that night—Myrtale—her soul name, the name she bore until Philip changed it against her will after three years of marriage. The summer of Alexander's birth, the king's team of four black horses won the Olympic chariot races and he renamed her Olympias to always remind himself of his victory.

He could call her whatever he wanted. She would always be Myrtale, naked dancing queen of divine ecstasy. That first night the rituals changed her life, became her way out. This world became her everything.

Until Riel.

Now, in the forecourt of the old temple of Dionysus, among

ivy-clad fallen columns thrown down by Poseidon Earth-Shaker generations ago, the women drink deeply from goat-skins. A bonfire burns brightly, and one by one the revelers take off their clothes and fling them aside. In their state of ecstasy, the queen will not be recognized, and Olympias feels a sense of freedom and anonymity as she sets her lantern down and casts off her belt and robe, too, but holds the ivory box tightly to her chest as she joins the circle of naked women around the fire, spinning and twirling in wild abandon. Eyes glazed, they flick their heads backward, point at gods only they can see, and cry, *"Euoi! Euoi!"*

Behold the god.

The snakes in her hair curl and twist, hiss and spit, and one of them nuzzles the back of her neck. She shivers, feeling the night air touch every inch of her skin like a soft caress. But she hasn't been touched, not like that, in years. The thought takes her back nearly two decades, to when she and the high-born maidens of Epirus were engaged in the same ritual. She was not more than her son's age now—not even sixteen. Wheeling about the bonfire, she saw a man in the bushes staring at her, a man with glowing snake-green eyes. Myrtale had always known of her own beauty, but the look in his eyes both thrilled and terrified her. She stumbled out of the dance and pointed him out to the other maidens. But they couldn't see him and laughed at her for being drunk.

He seemed to have disappeared as quickly as he came. She made her way out of the cluster of dancers and found him not far off. She remembers the moonlight, how it gleamed off her bare skin and silver-blond hair. Though she'd now been part of the cult for three years, had experienced indescribable bodily pleasures and ecstasies of the mind, she still felt smaller away from the circle of revelry, from the noise and the wildness, the smoke and intoxication. Before this man, she felt all of her nakedness, as though every place his eyes touched, they singed. She felt vulnerable and exposed, but in a way that excited her. As though anything might happen next.

The way he looked at her took her breath away. He was tall, with strong cheekbones, a straight nose, and square jaw. His right eyebrow had a scar cutting it in half, earned in some battle perhaps. His hair color was something between antique gold and bronze. But it was his glittering green eyes that hypnotized her, just as a snake immobilizes its prey before striking. She knew in that moment he was more than a man. He was something not entirely of this world.

He extended his hand and, after only a moment's hesitation, she took it and went with him into the woods.

From that night on, Riel taught her everything: love, magic, and how to use them both to achieve immeasurable power. He was better than anything she'd ever drunk or inhaled or seen in a cloudy vision or experienced in an orgiastic haze. She couldn't get enough of him. It got to the point where every time they parted, she felt a deep, physical agony, an unquenchable need to be with him again. Without him she was incomplete, a shell.

So when, that same year, the warrior king, Philip of Macedon, visited Epirus and asked for her hand, she was revolted at the thought. He had already lost his eye and was as gruff and ugly as Riel was devastatingly handsome. Her father and stepmother pushed her to marry Philip, threatening her with the beating of her life if she refused. Though they knew little of the Dionysian cult she'd secretly joined, and her life there as Myrtale, they knew enough to realize this might be the last of her opportunities, despite how young she was.

"I will take their beating, and gladly," she told Riel. "I don't want his filthy hands on me."

They were in their usual trysting place, a cave in the hills outside the royal palace of Ambracia. They had to crawl in through a narrow passage. It was one of the wombs of the ancient earth goddess, Riel had told her: safe, silent, and secret. Like a womb, the walls were red, painted with ochre by a people so ancient they lived here before the birth of the Olympian gods. It looked to Myrtale like children had taken sticks of charcoal and drawn across the walls primitive black figures of humans throwing spears at horned animals.

She didn't like it here. The cave had a musty smell of time grown old. Sometimes it seemed the red walls were closing in on her. Every word they said was swallowed by the oppressive atmosphere. She fantasized about having him in her bed in the palace, fresh sea air blowing in the open windows, the sounds of crashing waves, and the clear cries of gulls. But that was impossible. If her father had any idea what she was doing with this man, he would kill her.

Riel's eyes gleamed with something like compassion as he said, "Philip is offering you power, Myrtale." His voice was as mesmerizing as his eyes, slow and deliberate, almost lulling her to sleep. She fought hard against the urge to give in to him, focusing on her rage until she almost spat her reply.

"Everyone knows queens have no more power than a brood mare."

"Except any colt you bear will be king. That is power, if you choose to use it." He slid his arms around her and she felt every muscle in her body tingle. She inhaled the scent of his neck, fresh pine and powdered amber and sandalwood oil. How could she leave this man for a smelly, one-eyed barbarian? Her rage turned to despair, roiling in her stomach, pounding in her head.

"But even for all the power in the world, I can't lose you!" She didn't want to cry, but tears rolled down her cheeks anyway.

He licked the tears off, then kissed her jaw, her ear, her neck.

"You won't lose me, my love," he said, running strong fingers through her hair, stroking her neck. "I will follow you. Advise you. It is quite simple, really. You follow power and I follow you."

And so she followed power. He followed her.

And then all their plans fell to pieces.

Now as she spins around the bonfire with the other women, a cold black tongue flicks against her ear, and Olympias-Myrtale-Polyxena feels a sob of pain and of hope rising in her chest.

The music ceases, the last notes jangling uneasily in the air. The dancers, too, slow, some of them bumping into one another. Holding her thyrsus high, the High Priestess of Dionysus points to the sky. The moon is starting to disappear, swallowed by the forces of Chaos and Night. A frightened silence descends on the group of revelers as Olympias, still clutching the box, picks up her clothing and lantern. She makes her way toward the back of the destroyed temple and down a flight of crooked stairs. This was the oracle's chamber, where the priestess would commune with the gods, inhaling fumes rising from a crack in the earth, and then prophesy to expectant crowds.

The oracle is gone; the fumes are gone. Even though the sacred spot is now the home of spiders and rats, the queen does not put on her clothes. Rituals are more effective when the supplicant is naked, a sign of humility before the gods and the forces of darkness. She kneels on the floor and opens the box. Inside is every tiny bone of a newborn baby.

She removes a knife and a pouch from her belt and lays them next to the box. From the pouch she removes a flower red as blood, black at the root. When she breaks the thick downy stalk, milk-white liquid spills out over the bones and onto Alex's dried blood on the handkerchief. She tears the petals and roots to shreds and throws them in the box.

Now she holds her breath. Everything has gone silent.

Then, after several minutes, a collective wail rises from the distant crowd as the moon disappears, swallowed whole, perhaps never to return.

The large green snake slides off her neck and coils itself on the floor, head raised. All the snakes in her hair, too, raise their heads, hissing and undulating in the darkness. She unsheathes the knife and cuts her arm, holding it over the box and dripping blood on the bones.

Nothing happens.

She feels herself beginning to shake but forces back tears. She cuts her arm again, deeper, and lets the red splatter onto the ivory. Still nothing.

"Please." The word scrapes from her throat like a moan. This has to work. It must. She may be a queen but in the eyes of the gods, she's nothing more than a beggar. Quivering. Naked. Covered in her own blood.

She puts her hands in her hair, struggling to stay focused, but her head feels light and fuzzy, and the disturbed snakes hiss and spit. The large snake weaves around the room, then stops in front of her, and its eyes dilate.

She chokes back a sob. "I'm so sorry," she whispers. "I don't understand." Her words are hardly more than a hiss themselves.

The snake lunges toward her, sinks its fangs deep into the flesh of her arm. As the excruciating pain courses through her, she collapses onto the buckled marble floor, convulsing. As the burning waves fade, she pushes herself up, straining in the dim light of the lantern to see the words written in dark blue blood beneath her ivory flesh.

She's still alive.

Olympias goes cold. It can't be true.

Outside there is a crash of cymbals, a wild lilt of flutes, and banging of drums. The women cheer and greet the return of the moon as Chaos disgorges it slowly.

Olympias slumps against the wall as the snakes in her hair rearrange themselves. The large one wraps its tail around her knees but its head is inches from her own, staring with lidless eyes.

"Still alive," she croaks, her speech slow and slurred. That means the bones she's been protecting for so long, waiting for so long to use—they are *the wrong ones*. A lie. It was all a lie.

Helen. A thief *and* a liar.

She should have known.

She touches the snake's head, pulls it close to her breast. She doesn't care that blood now stains her arms and collarbone. Rage boils within her, a familiar burn. The snake writhes against her as if it can feel the heat of her determination. Next time, she will not fail.

Chapter Sixteen

"I'VE ALWAYS WANTED YOU, HEPHAESTION," KAT *says coyly, looking up through thick lashes. A blush rises to her cheeks as she wrings her hands in embarrassment. "I...can't believe I just said that."*

They stand in the twilight, in the Poseidon Garden, the water splashing, the fragrance of the flowers wafting around them. Heph takes her gently in his arms. How can someone be so muscular and athletic and yet so soft? Her skin is as smooth as the rare shining cloth woven on the other side of the world. He strokes her cheek, gazes deeply into her eyes and buries his head in her neck, inhaling its sweet scent.

She wraps her arms around him. They're strong indeed for a girl. Too strong. She's crushing the breath out of him. He can't break free. "Katerina," he says, trying to pull away, "let me go."

From somewhere far away, Heph hears a scream, then feels hands shake his shoulders. Heph surges awake, only to realize the danger in his nightmare is real. Someone is straddling him, looming above in the darkness. Instinctively he grabs the wrists and flips the assailant off him, slamming his knees onto the man's chest and pinning his flailing arms to the bed.

"Heph, it's me!" says a woman's voice. Heph's throat feels raw as he rapidly blinks, trying to shake a sudden dizziness. He sees long black curls tumbled over the pillow and naked breasts that rise and fall as Cyn breaths heavily, trying to push him off her.

Cyn.

"Someone was in the room!" she says as she sits up. "He was next to the bed. Standing over you. He ran away when I screamed." She squints into the darkness, searching the shadows.

Heph grabs his sword before fumbling on the bedside table for his flint. He knocks over a wine goblet—empty, of course—and pushes aside a small clay lamp before he feels what he's looking for. He hits the flint against the steel, creating sparks which quickly turn to flame on the bits of tinder on a clay cup below. He surveys the room, striding toward the door. It's unlocked, though everything else is as it should be. Well, except for Cyn in his bed, the sheet now wrapped around her as she swings a gleaming leg off the mattress and hurries over to her tunic lying crumpled on the floor. Heph vaguely remembers being the one to pull it off her last night.

He drank too much unwatered wine at the feast. Cyn kept his goblet full, and when she began to kiss him, pink tongue darting into his mouth and licking the edges of his lips, hot breath on his neck, her body flush against his, he lost control of himself, and did the one thing he didn't want to do.

The dark room is spinning and the bitterness of nausea rises in his chest but he's not sure if it's because of the wine or Cyn. Probably the wine, he decides. His tongue feels as if it is growing thick fur. Cyn lets the sheet fall from her shoulders, and he catches a glimpse of her back before the midnight black of her tunic settles around her. He realizes that he is as naked as a statue of Olympian Apollo.

He grabs his own tunic puddled on the floor and quickly throws it over his head. "Are you sure you saw a man?" he asks.

"Yes," Cyn says. "I saw a figure standing over you, but I didn't see his face."

"You must have been dreaming," Heph says, thinking of his own disturbing nightmare, though it started with him kissing Kat, didn't it? The room smells of wine and perspiration and the scent of their skin mingled on the sheets. Seeing no immediate danger, he throws open the shutters and gulps in cool air to clear his head. Not a single light burns in the palace complex or in the city beyond the gates. It is as dead and dark as yesterday's hearth. Above him, stars shimmer savagely on the obsidian vault of the sky.

Cyn's dark eyes flash. "I don't think so," she says, and her hair swings forward as she bends down to retrieve her belt. She gasps and straightens up quickly, something glittering in her hand. "Heph, look!"

A dagger rests in her palm. Heph takes it and studies it in astonishment. He runs his fingers over the intricate design of a phoenix on the steel hilt, its eye a glowing ruby, its long pointed beak, and wings raised skyward. The bird rises from curling flames of solid gold near the steel blade. Heph's nausea returns full-force. "The phoenix dagger," he murmurs, a numb sense of foreboding creeping through his chest. "Alexander's favorite."

Cyn stares at him, her eyes unreadable. "I thought it looked familiar. But how did it get here?"

Heph is finding it difficult to swallow, even more difficult to think. His head throbs, and last night's wine rises, sour, in his throat. "I don't know," Heph answers honestly. His best friend's dagger, in his room. An intruder standing over him. All the facts seem cloaked in the haze of a dream, impossible to interpret. He hates the taste of this foreign feeling in his mouth—the bitter taste of suspicion.

But how could he suspect Alex?

He clears his throat, and takes another deep breath. "Obviously somebody stole his dagger." It's the only explanation. He spots his sandals on the floor and says, "Get dressed fast. We need to find who it was."

He can't look her in the eye.

Heph buckles on his sword belt and Cyn grabs one of the swords hanging on Heph's wall, then lights two lanterns. Out in the hall, Heph tries Alex's door to see if the intruder went in to harm the prince regent. It is securely locked, as Heph's door would have been if he hadn't lost control and forgotten to bolt it. He wonders if he should wake Alex to join the search but immediately rejects the idea—he would have to explain how Cyn came to see a man leaning over Heph's bed.

They walk quickly and quietly down the hallway, the transparent ox-horn lantern panels giving only a soft glow of light. Now and then they stop to listen, but the only sound is the usual scuttling of rats in the walls. Silently, they go down the main staircase to the ground floor. Still nothing. Frustrated, Heph turns to Cyn. "We should split up. You go right and I'll go left."

"Fine," she says, gently brushing past him, her wild hair grazing his arm. A few steps away, she pauses and turns around. "Yell if you find anything," she says, "and we'll rouse the guard." With that she walks off, the golden light of her lantern sliding away from him down the marble wall.

Heph stands rooted to the spot. The hallway lurches side to side like the time he was in an earthquake when he and his father were staying in a villa on the island of Rhodes. Then he had also felt like he was on a bucking horse as the walls and ceiling swayed around him. He ran outside and saw the

columns of the portico skitter off balance and come roaring
down in an explosion of dust.

He takes a deep breath. This is not an earthquake.

This is the Wrath of Dionysus. A common affliction that
occurs when the wine god punishes those who honor him
too enthusiastically.

He needs to clear his head and think. It's only after Cyn has
fled down the hall in the other direction that he realizes what
would have happened if she'd roused the guard too soon—if
King Philip found out about Cyn... He would surely have
Heph strung up and killed. Princesses must be virgins on their
wedding night. Her future husband could kill her or return
her to Philip, who would then be obligated to execute his
daughter. All of Macedon would be shamed. He's relieved, at
least, for Cyn's discretion.

A new wave of nausea washes over him. He has a flash of
memory of the last time he lost control—five years ago, shortly
after his parents' death. Only then it was to anger.

It was a cool, early spring day when he heard his sister
scream. When Heph rushed into her room, he saw Myron, his
father's cousin—their new *guardian*—pinning his sister Poly-
neices to the bed, ripping her dress, and kneeing her legs apart.
Rage swept through Heph's body as a red fog nearly obscured
his vision. Without thinking, Heph unsheathed his knife and
plunged it deep into the man's back, feeling the resistance of
flesh and muscle. Roaring in rage and pain, Myron stood up,
his hands pulling the knife from his own flesh. He turned toward Heph, murder in his eyes, as Poly pushed herself to the
far corner of the bed.

Unarmed, Heph reached for the only sharp object nearby—
Poly's pair of gilded embroidery scissors. It was a delicate
thing, in the shape of two facing herons, the blades their long
thin legs, but the pointed ends were as sharp as daggers. He

said a prayer, raised the scissors, and plunged them deep into Myron's neck. In that second when Heph murdered a family member, he became a moral outcast, hated by gods and men alike, and, perhaps, hunted by the law. He'd had to leave Poly, the estate, even his name behind, as he sought to outrun the vengeance of Myron's brothers. He doubts he will ever see his sister again. Only Alex can protect him from their vendetta and from public execution as a murderer.

This is what comes from losing control of your passions.

Heph hears quiet footsteps coming down the next corridor, and he quickly blows out his lantern. Shoulder blades touching the wall, he clutches his sword and waits. The light of a swaying lantern falls on the walls and he sees someone turn the corner. Heph relaxes. No assassin, just Katerina.

He steps out of the shadows. "What are you doing?"

Kat jumps, and her lantern swings wildly, causing dark shadows to spin around them. The image of Kat from his dream flashes across his mind. From now on, anytime she ever acts shy, sweet, or meek he will immediately know he is dreaming, as such a thing could never happen in real life.

"Hades' coins," Kat swears when she realizes it's only him. "What are *you* doing?"

"I asked first," Heph says, reaching a hand out to stop her lantern's dizzying arcs. In the now steady light, Heph sees smudges of eyeliner on her cheek, and the strands of hair escaping the leather band holding the rest in a knot above her head. His eyes slowly travel down her body, taking in raw scratches and fresh bruises.

Kat folds her arms. "I couldn't sleep."

"That's a likely story," he says, feeling a wave of wariness. "Did you toss and turn your way out of bed and onto the floor, scratching and bruising yourself on the way down?"

"What business is it of yours if I did?" she retorts. "You're not my father. I don't have to tell you anything."

"Someone came into my bedroom," he explains. "Just a few minutes ago. Was it you?"

It could hardly have been an assassin, as Cyn assumed it was. What possible motive would anyone have for removing Heph? And he knows that even if the prince misled him about the royal funds, it could only have been a misunderstanding. Alexander wouldn't lie to him with purpose, wouldn't betray him and their plans simply because he'd finally had his first taste of power. As tempting as it might be to see the logic in it, Heph refuses to believe his friend could be so changed.

Still, it's disturbing. Could someone be setting him up? Ever since the Aesarian Lords have come to visit, Heph has detected an air of caution in Alex. Perhaps their visitors are not to be trusted.

"You flatter yourself," Kat replies. "If I was going to crawl into some man's bed, it wouldn't be yours. I might sneak into your room one day, though, to borrow your jewelry."

Heph can't help noticing how beautiful Kat is when she's angry. Her eyes flash, and a bright spot of pink burns on each cheek. A small vein on her temple pulses with every beat of her heart. At the same time, her ridicule stings. Maybe he should only wear the jewelry at feasts when all the other men adorn themselves with torques and wrist cuffs.

"Katerina, this is serious," he says sternly and realizes he sounds very much like a father—a gruff, strict father—which isn't how he wants to sound at all.

"And I'm very serious about borrowing your jewelry. After all, you wear a lot more than I do." Her beautiful mouth smirks. "Perhaps the intruder was Princess Cynane. I saw you two in the alcove tonight. Are you keeping it secret? I won't be the one to tell Alex, but he's going to find out anyway."

"And I won't tell Alex you crept around the palace dressed as a dancing girl in a blond wig," he replies. "You still have some of that stupid makeup on your face, by the way. And you look terrible as a blonde."

They stare at each other, and Heph has the most perplexing, *overwhelming* desire to kiss her. She looks almost regal in the soft lantern light, even with her hair hastily knotted and on the verge of toppling over. A single hair rests on her lower lip, caught in the beeswax lip color dancing girls usually dab on for performances. It's ruining the gentle curve of her mouth, and without thinking, Heph's hand is near those perfect lips, brushing away the offending strand. Coming to his senses a moment too late, Heph freezes, his thumb still resting on the side of her mouth. To his surprise, Kat doesn't back away. She just stares, her lips slightly parted in surprise.

A scream pierces the night for a second time, and Heph stumbles away from Kat.

"Cyn!"

CHAPTER SEVENTEEN

CYN HASTILY DIPS THE HEM OF HER TUNIC IN the thick, sticky blood, trying to ignore the still-open eyes of the corpse lying before her. It's Heph's fault. She *had* to kill the beggar. She had no other choice.

The air down here in the storage cellar is cool and moist, and the metallic scent of blood is already mixing with the odor of wine and the scent of the spices, figs, and olives stacked on shelves along the walls.

She thought she had done enough. Setting the hellion loose in the Blood Tournament and blaming it on Alex. Lying to Heph about Alex's unlimited access to the Treasury's gold. And now, tonight—a night when he should be swayed by anything she said—"finding" the dagger she had stolen from Alex and crying out that she had seen an intruder.

But Heph had barely wavered. He was determined to think Alex innocent. Cyn quickly realized that if they didn't find the "intruder," Heph would begin to suspect Cyn herself. But hopefully the blood now sprinkled on her clothes will convince him that the man attacked Cyn, and not the other way around.

She finds she can't control the slight tremor in her arms and hopes Heph will take it for fear and not the urgency and anger that's boiling in her veins. All her plans are unraveling.

Hearing footsteps pounding down the stairs, Cyn leans over the body, cringing as she quickly adjusts its position and places a spare knife in its limp palm. Only a few minutes ago, the man had been sitting on the floor, nibbling cheese, and slurping wine from a cup, empty jugs scattered around. His patched clothes and gaunt frame told her he wasn't a soldier or a palace servant. Most likely, he was a common thief who'd snuck in to raid the royal cellars. She's glad she swung before she could change her mind. The head had come off with ease, her sword barely meeting resistance as the body crumpled to the floor.

Heph races into the room and Cyn is startled to see Katerina close behind him. What is *she* doing here, with Heph? Holding his lantern high, Heph surveys the scene. He walks over to the head, crouches down, picks it up by the hair, and studies it as Kat grimaces.

"I've never seen him before," he says, laying the head back down. "Have you?"

"No," Cyn says truthfully.

Heph stands up, his dark eyes probing her face. "Why did you kill him? We could have questioned him."

"He lunged at me! I didn't know what to do," she says, letting her voice tremble. "Heph, I was so scared." She covers her face to hide her lack of tears, praying to all the gods he will fall for her story, and that the nosy country girl won't ruin everything.

Peering through her fingers, she watches as Heph holds the lantern over the heap of bloody rags. He crinkles his nose.

"Smells awful. Dressed like a beggar. I don't think this is any assassin."

"It could be an assassin disguised as a harmless beggar," Cyn says. "But if it's not him, then you may still be in danger." She gives a delicate shudder.

Heph stares at her a long moment—long enough for Cyn to wonder if she has overplayed the weepy damsel— then straightens up. "I guess we'll never know since you beheaded him."

"I'm sorry," she says lamely.

Heph sighs and rubs his eyes. "The guards can't find you down here. They can't know you killed him. I'll say I did it. I saw an intruder, and when I found this man, he lunged at me with his knife." He turns to Kat, whose eyes flick between Heph and Cyn, clearly connecting what was left unsaid. "You, too, Kat, must return to your room. Both of you will be vulnerable to accusations—or at the very least, rumors that could be very damaging. *Neither* of you should be wandering about the palace at the dead of night. Go back, both of you, lock your doors, and tell no one about this."

For once, Cyn doesn't argue, but hurries back toward her room before glancing over her shoulder to make sure that neither Heph nor Kat nor anyone else has followed her. Then she makes a sharp turn down a nearly abandoned hallway to a small locked door. As Cyn twists the iron key, the rusty lock groans in protest, then releases. She opens the door and enters the small room, unused for ten years now. Something scurries into the shadows. She sets down her lantern and basket and sits cross-legged on the floor. This small room with its single window used to be a bathroom. In the center was a splendid red porphyry bathtub, mottled with black and gold crystals, where lesser royal women would bathe.

The bath is gone now, its ghostly outline still visible on

the floor, and a tile covers the drain through which the bath water flowed away toward the rain gutters. Except for Cyn, no one comes here. The room is considered unlucky, even cursed, because of what happened in there…

From her basket she takes a small bronze charcoal brazier and lights it with the lamp from her lantern. As it heats, she removes the other items left over from past attempts. A stone jug of pure white milk from an unblemished black cow. A container of brackish water from a stagnant pool that never sees sunlight. A small vial of foam from the mouths of mad dogs.

The charcoal is burning brightly now. She puts the bronze bowl on top of it, pours in all the milk, and tips in a few drops of the stagnant water and mad-dog foam. Then she throws in the skin of a snake to call the spirits of the Earth. The feather of an eagle to summon the spirits of the Air. A dried fish to conjure the spirits of Water. And a dried salamander, a magical creature known to live unharmed in flames, to command the spirits of Fire. These are the ingredients, according to scrolls in the archives, of a powerful incantation.

With her knife, she cuts off a fragment of her tunic, stained with the thick brown blood of the beggar, and throws that in. Will it work? Can she consider it the blood of true betrayal? She doesn't know. It's not what she's planned for, what she's been working on for these past weeks, weaseling her way into Heph's trust. He was supposed to turn against Alexander. It's the *prince's* blood that should have been shed, and—Cyn's certain—that would have been all the betrayal she needed.

But now, desperation drives her forward. She has a man's blood on her hands—the beggar's—and she may as well attempt the ritual. She has to maintain hope.

It's the only thing that has gotten her this far.

She removes from the basket a dried wreath of yew, the plant of death, and crowns herself with it.

The mixture roils to a boil. Its fumes burn her nostrils, but Cyn continues to inhale them, as the scrolls instructed, even though the room spins wildly around her. Finally, she dips a ladle into the brew, raises it, and intones the words her mother used to say to her as a kind of nursery rhyme:

"Ancient gods of smoke and might
In the darkness of the night
I drink the blood of betrayal true
Immortal power I will accrue."

Then she drinks. It's hard to swallow. Every part of her wants to gag, to spit it back up. But there's too much at stake. She forces it down, gulping hard and grimacing. The potion seems to kick her all the way down as her organs twist in revulsion. She clutches her stomach and groans. Sweat forms on her face and rolls onto her tunic.

Finally, the disgust passes. She takes her knife out of her belt and holds it against the inside of her left arm, near the bend in the elbow.

She slices her skin three inches. Pain floats inside and all around her, but she concentrates on the cut.

It isn't healing. It's bleeding more by the second. Throbbing.

The ritual didn't work. It couldn't have. She's not invincible. The pain roars through her.

She still needs the blood of true betrayal.

Cyn puts her head in her hands. With every day her life will get smaller. One day soon Philip will sell her like a prize sheep to the highest bidder. To be a *wife*. And *mother*. She grows nauseated at the thought. She will lead a life of frustration, resentment, and loneliness, never knowing power. Never having anything like the unbreakable bond Alex and Heph share.

She feels something hot on her cheeks and raises her hands

to them: tears. When was the last time she cried? Ten years. Ten years, too, since she had an unbreakable bond with someone. A bond that ended right here, in this little room.

Philip's first wife, Cyn's mother, Princess Audata of Illyria, was as tall and darkly beautiful as Olympias was petite and blonde, but her status was far lower than that of Olympias. The king decides which wife enjoys the title of Queen; all others have less honor, fewer servants, and less spending money. Still, Olympias was savagely jealous of Audata and did everything she could to show her up and put her down.

On days when Philip planned to spend the night with Audata—all kings with multiple wives kept a sleeping schedule supervised by their palace chief of protocol—Olympias would slip into her room and put a cat between her sheets. Invariably that evening a frustrated Philip would storm into Olympias's bedroom, complaining that Audata's eyes had swelled shut, and she had sneezed and sniffled him out of bed in the most unappealing way. The queen would openly boast about it the next morning over breakfast.

On the night when Philip feasted the Illyrian envoys, the ambassador toasted Audata, proud that one of their own was a wife of the powerful King Philip. Olympias immediately raised a toast to marital fidelity, implying that Audata was less than faithful. At that moment Audata, sickened by the unripe elderberry juice Olympias had arranged to put in her wine cup, vomited all over the table, utterly humiliated in front of her own people.

Most of the time, Audata never seemed to mind. "She's like a mosquito stinging Olympian Zeus," she would tell Cyn. "Annoying, but not truly harmful. She doesn't see how desperate it makes her look." Sometimes they made fun of Olympias's heavy makeup and elaborate hairstyles, her horrendous taste in furnishings, and relentless cattiness, and laughed until they cried.

Uninterested in palace intrigues, Audata preferred to spend her time with her daughter, teaching her the customs of Illyria, where women were trained as athletes, developing healthy, strong bodies to bring valiant warriors into the world. Cyn ran with her mother across the fields and up the rugged hills outside Pella, learning riding, archery, and spear throwing. And Audata told her stories. Of magic.

The night before her mother died, eight-year-old Cyn heard her arguing heatedly in her bedchamber.

"I must have it! You must show me how to get Smoke Blood! The Blood of True Betrayal is at my fingertips." But when Cyn peered around the door, her mother was alone, arguing, it seemed, with the air.

The next day Cyn found her mother pale as a lily in her bathtub, face below the bright red water with eyes open and black hair floating around her head like tangled seaweed. She put her arms under her mother's back to lift her up, afraid that her mother couldn't breathe with her face under the water.

Cyn cried desperately for help, and when Audata's handmaidens came in, they screeched for the guard and dragged her mother out of the tub, splashing red water over themselves and all across the floor. By the time they laid her down, it was obvious she was dead. She had been stabbed several times in the chest. Cyn felt tears, hot and salty, streaming down her face as she stood there silently, watching. Then they dried up completely.

Cyn never knew whom to blame. A suspicious King Philip? His envious blonde queen? Or the Aesarian Lords, those bloodhounds of magic who had heard of Audata's knowledge of ancient lore? Whoever it was, Cyn vowed never to be at the mercy of an enemy. Even in her bath—especially in her bath—she wears the dagger strapped to her calf.

She *will* acquire Smoke Blood, no matter how long it takes. No one will ever find *her* floating white as milk in a bath of blood.

Chapter Eighteen

IN THE DEEPEST, COLDEST RECESSES OF THE
Pellan palace, thirteen Aesarian Lords and two recruits stand
in front of an arched wooden door bound with iron. Lord Bastian unlocks it, and the Lords enter, most carrying torches but
two of them carrying black goats. Jacob and Timaeus look at
each other and follow.

When the men affix torches to the wall sconces, Jacob sees
the walls are made of human skulls. The vaulted ceiling is decorated with long bones—legs and arms. He shivers and hopes
the other men haven't noticed. It's ice-cold in here, and in
the flickering torchlight the skulls in the walls look like they
are laughing. Mildew hangs heavily in the air. Mildew and
something else, like the pungent scent of bittersweet decay.

"Recruits, come forward for your oath," Mordecai says.

Chests thrust out, Jacob and Timaeus walk boldly to the
center of the room and repeat the oath the High Lord renders.

"By the Titans who are overthrown but yet live, by the
Olympian gods who sleep but will wake, by the sacred Fountain of Youth in the Eastern Mountains, I swear utter loyalty

to the Aesarian Lords. If I keep this oath, I will become powerful, rich, and envied. If I break this oath, the Furies, goddesses of eternal vengeance, will pursue and scourge me in this life and beyond. I call to witness the three dread sisters: Alecto, the unnameable; Megaera, the grudging; and Tisiphone, vengeful destruction."

It is a fearful oath, and Jacob almost gags saying it. No one takes the Furies lightly. Most people never even utter their names, preferring to call them "the Kindly Ones" for fear that the goddesses will leave their Underworld home and haunt the soul who dares address them. The chill in the room increases, as well as the revolting odor. He wonders if the Furies are in the room, watching him, and he's smelling their foul stench.

High Lord Mordecai kneels and slits the throats of the goats who bleat weakly and fall to the floor, blood spurting from their necks. If the Furies are here, they will rush forward to drink the invisible essence of the blood.

"Recruits, come forward," he says, "and wash your hands in the sacrifice."

Jacob and Timaeus kneel and place their hands in the puddles of blood. It's hot and sticky and smells like copper. The goats' yellow eyes are open, glazed with death. Jacob looks up. The entire room is glazed with death. And what's coming next—the Ordeal by Fire—will be even worse.

But he can do it. So that he's good enough for Kat. So that she *sees* that he's good enough.

Ten minutes later, they are far from the dark Skull Room, and Jacob stands next to Timaeus in the crowded odeon, alight with torches. The canvas covering has been removed, and stars twinkle brightly overhead. Both recruits are stripped to the waist. This, the final test, is the greatest one. It must be held in a public place to show the bravery of the Aesarian Lords.

Jacob looks around for Kat among the faces flickering

golden in the torchlight, but he can only make out people in the first couple of rows. Then he sees Bastian staring at some- one and follows his gaze and spots her, sitting with a color- ful gossiping gaggle of the queen's handmaidens, though Kat is watching solemnly. Her eyes seem to be speaking to him, but he can't tell what they are saying. Jacob's gaze shifts to Prince Alexander, who looks intrigued by the ceremony, his eyes alive with interest. Next to him, his mother the queen nervously twists the flashing rings on her fingers.

Two brands on long iron handles are heating in the large brazier of burning coals. Jacob looks at these instruments of his torture calmly. Fear, he learned from his new brothers, intensifies pain. Fighting pain only magnifies it. He must ac- cept the agony, welcome it, even, as the price of victory. As the price of Kat.

Now, in front of the palace elite, they will be branded on the spot over their hearts. The brand consists of five flames representing fire, and a crescent moon for actions performed in the darkness of night.

High Lord Mordecai picks up a brand and walks toward Jacob.

"Only by fire and darkness is Aesarian forged," says Lord Mordecai as he pushes the brand into Jacob's flesh. The pain is unbearable. He wants to scream in agony and fall writhing to the ground. He hears a horrible sizzling sound and smells his own flesh cooking. His stomach convulses; vomit rises in his throat. Sweat pours down his face and neck. He grinds his teeth and clenches his hands until his nails tear into the soft skin of his palms.

A part of him slips away from the agony into that dark, secret place inside him, the place the Lords taught him over the past few days to go to when the body suffers. The pain is undeniably there, but farther away, as if someone is screaming in an adjoining room. He stands as still as rock, his face like iron as Mordecai removes the brand.

The High Lord takes the second brand from the brazier and pushes it into Tim's flesh. Jacob, still managing his own pain, is vaguely aware of his friend stiffening. But Tim, too, is silent other than a groan so slight that only Jacob, standing next to him, is aware of it.

"Behold how our warriors withstand pain!" High Lord Mordecai cries, raising the brands still bubbling with human flesh. The twelve other Lords unsheathe their swords and chant, "Aesarian! Aesarian!"

The air in front of Jacob turns red, then black, and he is afraid he will faint. He feels a hand on his shoulder, gently pushing him forward. It is over. He and Tim walk over to chairs of honor at the rear of the circular floor, heads held high.

Lord Mordecai cries, "Bring out the Hemlock Torch!"

Jacob, sweat rolling down his face from the throbbing pain of the brand, casts a sideways look at Timaeus, who raises an eyebrow in response. Neither one of them has ever heard of a Hemlock Torch.

From the arched entrance under the seats, Lord Acamas comes out, his black horns twisting high above his head. He's a wiry man—his limbs like large ropes braided together—with bulging, unblinking brown eyes that seem to stare through a person's skin, right into his organs. Jacob has always felt wretchedly uncomfortable in his presence.

Lord Acamas holds with both hands a long torch. Except it's not made of wood. It's made of iron. And the flame isn't orange-gold. It's a dazzling white that gives off no smoke, no hiss or sizzle of burning oil.

A murmur of excitement ripples through the spectators.

High Lord Mordecai clears his throat. "This device is the

most powerful tool in the world for detecting the presence of foul magic. By this torch, which we have been perfecting for years, we will discover and root out every source of evil magic left, in every kingdom, until all the land is cleansed."

Jacob finds he is holding his breath. Though he knows the Aesarian Lords are a brotherhood dedicated to the removal of all magic from the world, he hasn't actually seen them speak about magic directly yet. Back in Erissa, it never occurred to him that there *could* still be magic left in the world—he believed, along with most people he knew, that it had died out many thousands of years ago. And he certainly hadn't understood magic to be evil, though he'd never spent much thought on it. Why would he?

But now, everything he knows about the world around him has begun to change. And he's eager to see proof of what the Aesarian Lords can really do.

The flame leaps up, tripling its size, and becomes bright red. The audience gasps. Jacob studies High Lord Mordecai, who is nodding gravely as if the change in color was expected. Then the flame becomes purplish, and the High Lord frowns. All at once it turns black, though it isn't doused; it has become a living thing, twisting and turning, roiling and popping, exploding its blackness in a wide arc throughout the odeon.

Lord Acamas screams and drops the torch as the sound of an explosion deafens the spectators and all the torches are snuffed out. The very air is sucked away. Jacob finds himself gasping for breath. He looks up at the sky and sees that the stars no longer twinkle. Even their light is gone.

He hears screams, the sound of running feet. Panicked people dash for the exits, for air and light. But he can't move. Perhaps this is part of the ritual, a test to see how they react.

The stars shine again, dully at first, and he can finally breathe. A palace slave relights the torches. Those spectators that haven't run off look around nervously, hoping for more spectacle, thinking this is part of a wonderful show. They don't have long to wait.

He hears a rustle and looks up to see what seems like entire flocks circling the odeon. People point and cry out, many making a mad dash as the birds swoop counterclockwise, flapping and chattering. The noise is deafening, and Jacob feels like he is drowning in a sea of sound and feathers. It seems to go on forever.

Finally, it stops. Jacob takes his hands away from his head and looks up. The last crow circles the odeon and flies after its companions, calling raucously. All sign of them is gone except for black feathers on the white marble floor.

The Lords and the few remaining spectators pick themselves up and look around. Jacob needs to find Kat—has she been harmed in the melee?—and takes a few steps forward. He trips over something. An Aesarian helmet with twisted black horns. Lord Acamas's helmet.

All that remains of the torch-bearer, and the torch itself, is a pile of ash and bone and a twist of iron.

Jacob shudders, rooted to the spot.

High Lord Mordecai's thin voice breaks the stunned silence. "Elder Lords to council!"

The rest is a blur as Jacob and Timaeus are hurried from the odeon to their room by Lord Ambiorix, the enormous Gaul.

Jacob has hardly any time to process what he has just witnessed. The Hemlock Torch, burning black. The crows.

Whatever that was, he knows it isn't what the Lords had planned for. The device itself seems to have been destroyed by its own dark flame.

"Here," the Gaul says breathlessly as he shoves a pile of clothes into Jacob's arms. "Uniforms. You will find your helmets inside, along with a special drink to heal your wounds. I must go to the others."

Before Jacob can ask the blond Lord what happened, what that shadow *was*, the door clicks shut. Jacob turns to Tim. "What happened out there?" he asks.

"As long as they never ask me to hold another Hemlock Torch, I guess it doesn't matter," Timaeus says with a quick little shrug, but he hastily takes a large swig from the jar left for them, and an amber-colored liquid drips down his chin.

"How can you joke about this?" Jacob joins him at the table and picks up an iron-bound black leather helmet. "Aren't you as chilled by what you saw as I am?" He runs his hand up and down the small cow horns, about six inches long and white except for black tips. In time, a Lord will be presented with his own unique pair through an act of great loyalty or cleverness.

Tim sighs. "All I know is I'm grateful I don't need to be in the meeting they're having now. They will inform us when we need to know more. For now, it's not our problem, is it?"

"How can it *not* be our problem?" Jacob examines the supple black leather cape Lord Ambiorix had shoved at him. Waterproof, it is lightweight in summer and lined with fur in winter. Right now it is plain, but in the future, after battles and victories, badges will be added: lightning bolts, a red hand, flames, a skull, a horned demon, a snake biting its own tail, a man hanging upside down, and nine swords.

"Well, I don't care how many crows invade their ceremonies," Tim says, finally putting the jug down, "or how many skulls they decorate their meeting rooms with as long as one of them isn't mine. I'll be happy if they feed me, pay me, and give me a helmet with horns. Think how much taller I'll look."

More jokes. Jacob sighs. The little man slips his new helmet on his head and looks at his reflection in the bronze tray. "Hard as rock," he says, knocking on one of his horns as if it were a door, "just as a certain milkmaid likes it," he says. "And *you* should test out *your* horns. It's a night for celebration!"

Jacob shakes his head, scowling. The need to know more about the torch, and about magic, burns in him almost as strong as the fiery brand that mutilated his flesh.

"Tim, there must be some way we can learn more about what just happened. What the Aesarian brothers have in store for us."

Tim shrugs. "I suppose you could always do a little snooping. Chloris says the walls are full of secret passageways, specially designed by the king."

"What?" Jacob quickly stands up. "Can she be trusted? How does she—" But he doesn't finish his question. Of course Chloris, if anyone, would know of the king's private corridors—and any way to access royal men when discretion is called for.

"Has she told you how to access these passageways?"

Tim scratches behind his ear. Then he laughs. "She did mention one, now that I think of it. Something to do with a herm—one of those fertility statues—and a hidden lever. Good luck, brother. While you're off spying, I'll be accessing *other* private areas."

Jacob snorts. "Give Chloris my regards, then."

He hurries out the door toward the herm. Jacob knows where it is—the leering, lascivious bearded face on top of a tapered plinth stands out in the palace, different from so many of the queen's graceful commissions that line the halls. Arriving at the herm, Jacob studies it, then runs his hand along the back of the plinth until he feels a knob. He applies a bit of pressure and hears a click. A panel in the wall swings open— one of the hidden entrances to Philip's secret labyrinth of tunnels and halls, peppered with peepholes and vents. The path twists and turns, and soon he hears muffled voices echoing down the tunnel. He puts his ear against the wall.

"—destroyed! And Lord Acamas so completely consumed he was turned to ash. Nothing like this has ever happened!"

Holding his lantern high, Jacob sees a tiny sliding panel, a spyhole, which must be concealed in a wall fresco on the other side. He slides it open and sees that the Lords are in a room that he remembers from his tour of the palace when he joined the guard. Adjoining the bedroom King Philip reserves for guests of honor, this smaller chamber is used by ambassadors and visiting dignitaries for private discussions about how to deal with the king on issues of trade, war, and taxation. High Lord Mordecai paces furiously back and forth. Lord Bastian sits next to the round table, spinning his jeweled dagger in circles. Lord Gideon, a frown on his broad dark face, leans against the wall, his powerful arms crossed.

"And the crows," Bastian says, sending his dagger spinning again. "Birds of darkness drawn by a great intensity of magic. I've read about the swarms, of course, but thought such a thing no longer possible."

"Our suspicions are correct, then," Gideon says in a rich, authoritative voice. "There is a dangerous amount of blood magic in this palace. I was not at all surprised when the Hemlock Torch burned red, were you?" The others shake their heads.

"I would have been astonished if it had stayed white," Bastian says, stopping his dagger's wild spin by slapping his hand down on it. He looks up. "We have suspected for some time that Philip might be hiding something dark here."

Mordecai stops pacing. "There is so much magic here it destroyed Plato's torch. Capturing the source is the only thing that can save us from what we all fear. What we saw tonight is only a sliver of the horrors that could await... The beating heart of this evil must be the queen with her snakes, her spells, and rituals. We need to capture—"

"What was that?" Gideon's deep voice cuts through.

"What?"

"I think that painting of Zeus just winked at me." Jacob hears the scrape of a chair, and barely manages to slide the peephole shut. His heart pounding, Jacob grabs his lantern and races through the dark corridors. He doesn't understand most of what he's heard, but he knows that what he saw today— that destruction, that darkness—was evil, and that the Aesarian Lords believe the source comes from the palace.

Pella is in danger.

Kat is in danger.

CHAPTER NINETEEN

AS THE WOODEN WHEELS OF THE CART GRIND forward into the twilight, Zofia lies numbly in the corner of her cage, as far away as she can from the puddle in the other corner. The slavers let the prisoners out only at sunrise and sundown, and even though they are allowed only a cupful of water each day, everyone needs to urinate more than twice. The first day Zo held it so long she was trembling with pain until one of the two girls in the neighboring cage whispered it is better to just let it out, that she would get used to the smell.

Since her capture—she has lost count of the days—she has shaken uncontrollably with fear, cried for Roxana, and prayed to every god she ever heard of. Now she feels panic rising, bubbling up from the pit of her empty, aching stomach. She wants to scream, to pull her hair out, and bang her head against the bars of her cage until she knocks herself unconscious. But she's too afraid of what might happen to her then.

She takes several deep breaths, trying to force her thoughts away from the slavers and her bleak future. In the palace, her favorite escape was to think of Cosmas. Of his face. His kisses.

His smell of leather and horses and a tunic beaten clean with river rocks.

But it's different now. Now her thoughts slide to the food she used to eat in the palace. Rich, fluffy bread made with grape syrup. Lamb-and-spinach stew with pomegranate seeds floating in it like tiny red boats. Chicken with oranges, cinnamon, and walnuts. She's had only mouthfuls of something bordering on food the past four days, enough to keep her alive but not enough to give her the strength to escape.

And she's almost delirious from thirst; her throat is parched and her lips cracked and bleeding. She thinks of the fountains splashing and spraying in every courtyard and garden in the Sardis palace. Some of the king's main rooms even have waterfalls cascading over walls and splashing down the center of steps, as well as channels of water rushing through the middle of the floor.

She thinks of the palace smells. The perfume and incense and flowers everywhere instead of piss and sweat and worse. She thinks of the luxury she never appreciated before, of slipping a clean garment over her head instead of wearing the filthy, ripped boy's tunic and trousers.

"Zo, are you all right?" says a voice. Zo is too tired to sit up and look. "You were moaning, and we're worried about you."

It's Arzu, the girl with hair like a raven's wing and intelligent brown eyes. Her voice is lower, more like that of an adult; Arzu could pass for twenty, while Minoo, another captive, looks and sounds like she's twelve, with a high-pitched breathy voice, frizzy brown curls, and huge blue eyes. In fact, both of them are fifteen and best friends.

"Yes," she lies, "I'm all right."

When Zo awoke that awful first morning, the girls tried to calm her. They said they had been captured two days earlier when they went looking for Minoo's dog after dark. They also told her they overheard the men talking about where they were taking the prisoners—a camp in the forest, a secret village of murderers and thieves, where buyers would come and bid on new slaves.

The three boys and the old woman arrived in cages later that day when Zo's captors met up with four more slavers. Zo found the men just as disgusting as the three who'd captured her. One was missing an eye, another a hand. Their long hair was oily and, by the way the men scratched at it, presumably lice-ridden. They poked and pinched Zo and the two other girls through the bars of the cages, laughing at them.

The three boys—each locked in a different cage to prevent them from rushing their captors—are kept on the second cart. Zo can't talk to them because she would have to yell. Whenever the slavers hear the prisoners talking to each other, they bang on the bars with swords threatening brutal punishment. But the old woman was transferred to Zo's cart, her cage set on the other side of Zo's. At first Zo was glad of someone to talk to on both sides. But the crone hasn't answered Zo's questions, hasn't spoken a word to her. She either mutters to herself or sings a haunting wordless melody, rocking back and forth.

The old woman's singing slides into a raspy voice that seems to crawl on the night breeze into Zo's ears.

"You lie, Princess," she says in a staccato voice. "You are not all right."

Zo turns toward the old woman, but in the pale shaft of moonlight can barely make out what she is seeing. A hunched form with wild, gleaming silver hair. How does she know she is a princess? The hairs on her neck stand on end.

"No," Zo whispers. "No, I'm not."

"I am Kohinoor, and they caught me gathering herbs by the full moon."

"What?" Zo's head is spinning from lack of food and water.

"You asked me my name and how they caught me. My name is Kohinoor and I was gathering herbs by the full moon."

Zo laughs harshly. "I asked you those questions days ago. And you answer me now?"

The old woman cackles. "Questions are answered not when you want an answer but when the time for answers is right."

Zo forces herself to crawl to the other side of her cage and look through the bars at Kohinoor, who pushes aside her stringy hair and peers back at Zo with cloudy purple eyes. Zo gasps. An oracle, perhaps? Old Mandana told Zo about oracles—those cursed humans blessed by the gods to prophesy with their immortal voice. Artaxerxes, the King of Kings, keeps an oracle, and even the Aesarian Lords bow to her divine revelations.

But perhaps this woman is merely a soothsayer, someone who can see wisps of the future. King Shershah kept a soothsayer at his court before Zo was born. He handed her over to the Aesarian Lords as compensation for rooting out horse thieves and cattle raiders. As far as Zo knows, the Aesarian Lords swept the land clean of all fortune-tellers, witches, and sorcerers, and of all those rumored to be magic, even if they had no power at all.

But wealthy people still want to know their future and would pay a high price for Kohinoor on the chance that she is a true soothsayer. That must be why the slavers haven't killed a woman too old to be a laborer or bedmate, as they had Jopata, who was middle-aged and ugly, and Roxana, who was so young.

Roxana. Zo's throat almost closes up with pain. It's her fault that the little girl is dead.

"Kohinoor, can you tell me if my sister Roxana has reached Paradise yet?" she asks, wondering if it's foolish to hope that the woman truly can see the future. "Does she forgive me?"

But the old woman turns away and laughs.

Not an oracle, then. Not even a soothsayer. Just an addled, powerless woman who probably calls every girl "princess." Zo curls into a tight ball, feeling the scrap of moldy bread in her belly churn. As the night darkens around her, a cool wind makes her shiver in her sweat-soaked tunic, and the sounds of Roxie's screams in the wheat field echo in her ears.

In the depths of the night, camped near a small village, she wakes to screaming again. But this time it doesn't stop when she sits up and clears her head.

"Arzu! Minoo!" she whispers hoarsely. "What is happening? Can you see?"

"Some commotion outside the village," Minoo says. "Kansbar and two others are running down to see what's going on." Twisting her head, Zo sees three men running away from the campfire toward torches in the distance while the other four remain to guard the prisoners. Her pulse leaps into her throat. Could it possibly mean that someone is coming to rescue them? The countryside, she knows, is patrolled by imperial soldiers devoted to catching criminals.

But when the three slavers return, there is no rescue. Just an argument.

"We need to leave this place now," Kansbar says, kicking dirt into the fire to put out the last glowing embers.

"I don't see why," the thin one says. "Just because the townsfolk arrested a woman—"

"—to give to the Aesarian Lords for having Earth Blood," Kansbar replies.

Earth Blood? Zo has heard of it, she dimly remembers. It's one of the two rumored types of magic blood, though of course she never believed such stories.

Kansbar continues, "That means the Lords will be coming this way. They'll arrest us as soon as they look at us. They cart off thieves and bandits just the same as if we were witches rooting for bones in a graveyard. The Great King has given them permission to arrest any lawbreakers they find."

"Perhaps we could sell them the soothsayer," the thin one suggests. "Maybe they would pay more than our wealthy client."

"You fool, they would take her by force and us, too. The gods only know what they do with the people they take. Besides, if she's not a soothsayer, then they might punish us for lying."

"Either way, they won't be here tonight," the thin one retorts. "The village will have to send a message to them, wherever they are. Let's get a good night's sleep and leave at first light."

"I agree," says the man with one hand, his companions grunting in agreement. "The Lords won't come for days. I'm exhausted from traveling on that horrible bumpy track. There are more potholes than dirt on it."

Kansbar whips his knife from his belt and pushes it against the man's throat. "Listen, you bag of dung," he says, his voice hoarse with anger, "we're moving camp. Now! I'll cut off your other hand if you don't start packing up this minute." He turns to the thin one. "You, too," he says. "And the rest of you. Start packing!"

Within minutes, they are off, the tired horses plodding down the bumpy path into the woods. "Kohinoor," Zo whispers.

The old woman grunts.

"We must hope the Aesarian Lords don't get their hands on *you*," Zo says urgently. It's clear they wouldn't take kindly to a woman who gathers herbs by the full moon, a time when all plants have greater magical powers, no matter how dim and faded with age she may be.

Kohinoor chuckles in the darkness, a sound that reminds Zo of wooden shutters bumping in a stiff wind. "They won't," she says. Her thin voice is almost singing as she continues, "I can see my future and there are no dark Lords in it. Just a merciful lord who will not turn me over to my enemies but will send me home to my bats."

Zo shudders. "You mustn't say you see the future," she implores the woman. "It will only make it worse for you."

The woman laughs again, a dry whisper in the dark night. "But I do see the future, Princess. It is impossible to deny your true self. You should know this, Zofia of Sardis."

Zo blinks her eyes in astonishment. Kohinoor must be a soothsayer if she knows who Zo is.

And if Kohinoor's prediction for herself is true, then it is possible that Zo, too, will find her way out of this calamity. Perhaps the same merciful lord will set her free. For a second, Zo allows herself to imagine the kind of home she would like to have with Cosmas. A little thatched-roof cottage surrounded by a flower-and-herb garden and a stable with a beloved horse munching hay. A well with fresh water—she licks her lips just thinking about it—and a thick stew bubbling in a black cauldron on the hearth.

"Can you see my future?" Zo asks, hating the hope in her voice.

"Give me your hand."

Zo stretches her hand through the bars of her cage and Kohinoor's.

Kohinoor's hands are as cold and dry as the skin of a lizard, and Zo resists the urge to snatch her hand back. Nails like brittle claws trace her palm and then stop. Zo waits so long in the silence she wonders if Kohinoor has fallen asleep.

"What do you see?" she asks, her heart pounding.

"You are carrying a child," the old woman says. She starts singing an eerie lullaby that sends shivers up Zo's spine.

Zo instinctively puts her hands to her belly. Child? But she had been with Cosmas only once. One glorious night. Could she be fruitful just from that? And yet, even as the thought sinks in, she can *sense* the truth of it, the slight ache in her lower belly which she attributed only to hunger and the pain of being entrapped.

The truth sinks in with an awful thud. Enslaved. Expecting.

What would the slavers do to her when they found out? Force her to drink something to abort the child, most likely. A poison that, if it doesn't kill her immediately, might burn her womb and prevent her from ever bearing a child again. Old Mandana told her such tales, long ago, in that other life.

The woman makes an odd little cooing sound. "There's more, Zofia of Sardis," she croaks. "Your blood will mix with that of Prince Alexander of Macedon. It is fated."

Zo exhales sharply. "No, you're wrong."

"It is fated."

Zo leans her head against the bars. One part of her heart wants to believe that the woman is truly a soothsayer. That means she will get out of the filth and hunger and thirst and cramped legs she can't stretch out or stand on, and from the stinking puddle on the floor. The other half of Zo refuses to believe—*can't* believe. For what would Alexander—or his barbarous father—do to the baby if they discovered she was with child before wedding him? They would expose it. Set the newborn on the hillside outside the city walls where all unwanted infants are placed at sunset. Sometimes childless couples come by and choose one to raise as their own. Those that are left behind are eaten by wolves. Then King Philip would kill her or return her in shame to her uncle.

And if Kohinoor is right, then she will never be with Cosmas. He may never even know of their child.

And that is unacceptable.

Better to believe that Kohinoor's "predictions" come from observation. Zo has been unwell on several mornings and, if Zo is completely honest with herself, she had wondered why her monthly bleeding had not yet come. As for knowing her name, Zo is sure that the disappearance of the king's niece is probably known by all locals now.

Kohinoor is nothing more than a fraud with an eye for detail.

"If you choose to disbelieve, Princess, it matters not." The woman's voice breaks Zo's thoughts. "Your blood will mix with Macedon. And that slaver?" Here she points to one of the men walking beside the wagon in front of them, his thin silhouette a spear in the darkness. "His death will come in a single grain of wheat. And I will go home."

Kohinoor is silent for the rest of the night, but Zo cannot escape the screaming in her own head.

The next morning, Zo wakes to men's shouts. When she looks out from her cage, she sees the thin slaver Kohinoor mentioned last night lying on the ground. Dead. The rest of the slavers stand around his body.

"What happened?" Zo asks Minoo, who watches the commotion with interest.

"He gave Kansbar an unsatisfactory breakfast," the girl says. "Kansbar said his food was rotten, and he flicked a grain of wheat from his porridge into Haresh's eye. Haresh attacked Kansbar, but obviously, no one stands a chance against Kansbar..." Zo isn't listening anymore. A single grain of wheat. Kohinoor had known.

Zo leans against the bars and, taking advantage of the slavers' distraction, calls out cautiously to the old soothsayer.

"Wise woman, I believe," Zo says, her voice flat. "Is there any way I can escape my fate? A chance I can reunite with my true love?"

The old crone cackles. "You will see the child's father again, but only once before his death. You will be the cause of his death."

"There has to be a way!" Zo says. "There must be something I can do. A sacrifice to the gods, a trade."

"The gods are asleep, Princess, but..." Kohinoor seems to be thinking about what to tell her. "The only way to undo the threads of fate that have been woven for you is to find the Spirit Eaters, who can negotiate with those goddesses who spin out, weave, and cut the threads of our fate."

"Where do I find these Spirit Eaters?" Zo asks.

A wheezing sigh comes from the other cage. "If they still exist, you will find them in the Eastern Mountains. That is where the Spirit Eaters sprang up from a fissure in the rocks, and there they still live. That is where you must go."

It's crazy. Crazy to believe the old woman—and if she's right in her predictions, to believe there's a way to change them.

But then, does Zo dare risk *not* believing her?

To calm herself, Zo squeezes the gold ornaments carefully sewn into the hem of her tunic—earrings and pendants and rings—hard things in the soft folds of cloth. It is her secret from the greedy slavers, her power.

Her hope.

The following day, the slavers make camp at a small clearing in the woods next to a spring. Zo hears the water first, a sound so spontaneously happy it is like a child's laughter. Licking her dry lips, she peers out of her cage and sees a tiny waterfall splashing cheerfully over mossy gray stones into a round turquoise pond about fifteen feet across, which splashes down another waterfall into a chattering stream.

It's cruel for her captors to let the prisoners hear and see the fresh, pure water—feel it, even, as a slight breeze-borne mist coats her dusty face—without giving them some.

"Water!" Zo cries, pushing her outstretched arms and nose through the bars. "For mercy's sake! Give us water!"

"Shut up!" the man with one eye says, raising a stick to whack her arms. Zo huddles against the far side of her cage, and wraps her arms around her knees. She turns her head away from all the beautiful water and looks down the forest path, willing herself to shut out the sound of her captors splashing their faces and letting their thirsty horses drink. Coming toward them on the trail, she sees a dark smudge. To Zo's tired eyes, it almost looks like the dust clouds that heralded the return of soldiers to Sardis.

Zo's head aches with dizziness as she pretends that the cloud coming closer is a group of imperial guards coming to her rescue. She wishes it so much, that she almost hears the rhythmic pounding of hooves. It's a dream, she knows, caused by hunger and thirst. Zo watches as in her dream Kansbar suddenly runs from the bank and barks orders to his men, who scramble to arm themselves.

Two of the men ignore him, hop on horses, and start to race off into the woods; but arrows strike both riders, who fall off their mounts and hit the ground dead.

Kansbar nears her cage as an arrow enters his back, the pointed barb coming out of his chest. He stumbles forward, his body hitting Zo's cage as he drops to the ground.

Zo tentatively puts her finger in the droplet of blood smeared across the iron bar, and draws her finger back. It's wet. This isn't a dream—it's real.

At that moment, riders—eight of them—gallop into the clearing. Who are they? Rival slavers? Aesarian Lords?

No. Zo sees that they are imperial Persian soldiers. Tears of relief stream down her face. They are saved.

On their tall horses, the soldiers have the advantage of speed and height over the remaining four panic-stricken slavers who are running wildly around waving swords in the air. One soldiers thrusts a spear into the gut of the fat, bald one; another shoots an arrow into the eye of the thin-faced one.

Zo is now grasping the bars so tightly her knuckles are turning white. The men who killed Roxana are dead.

Within minutes of the soldiers' arrival, in a swirl of screams, curses, horses' hooves, and flying dirt, all the slavers lie dead on the ground, blood mingling with dust. Zo feels no joy, only a sense of cold justice looking at the lifeless bodies. Nothing can bring her sister back.

The man who seems to be the commander rides over to the cages and cries to his men, "Let them out! I want to talk to them." Soldiers leap off their horses and smash the locks with the hilts of their swords. The chains, as they are pulled from the bars, make a crusty scraping sound that is more beautiful to Zo than harp music.

When Zo sees the door of her cage open, a sob rises in her chest. On her knees, she scrambles forward, and the soldier grabs her by the arms and helps her slide off the cart to the ground. She almost falls—her legs are so cramped from not being able to stand up—but he holds her up.

The other prisoners are dropping to the ground, crying with happiness, uttering thanks to the soldiers and prayers of gratitude to the gods. Zo gets her first good look at the three boys—tall and handsome, with shoulder-length dark hair. All three have bruised faces and split lips.

The commander unhooks his chin strap, flings off his

pointed helmet, and looks at the prisoners. He's young, Zo sees. Maybe twenty. His face is angular and handsome, streaked with sweat and dust, his hair a damp brown tangle.

"How many do we have here?" he asks.

"Seven, my lord," says a soldier.

The commander looks from prisoner to prisoner. "I am Ochus, Commander of the Fifteenth Cavalry, great-grandson of Artaxerxes III, the King of Kings. We have been tracking these slave traders for five days now. Tell me, who among you is a slave and who is free?"

"We're not slaves!" cries one of the boys. "We're brothers who were late coming home from harvesting our father's wheat field. These men put leather bags over our faces and abducted us. I can take you to the farm of our father, Johar! It is between the villages of Doma and Marzut."

"We're not slaves, either," says Minoo. "We live in the village of Pazan with our families."

The commander nods and walks over to Kohinoor whom he eyes with interest. "And you?" he asks. "Usually slavers don't take old people."

She raises her cloudy purple eyes to his and smiles slowly, and he understands. "Ah," he says. "I see you have special gifts they wanted to sell."

He turns to Zo. "What about you?"

She can hardly tell him the truth—that she is the niece of King Shershah of Sardis who stupidly ran away at night to marry a common soldier and was captured by slave traders. Back home she would have to tell her uncle and her mother that because of her, Roxana and Jopata have been killed. *And* that she's with child. Word would get back to the Great King Artaxerxes that the man he allows to rule Sardis can't even manage his own family.

Her return would be a disgrace in so many ways she can't

even imagine how they will punish her. Even if they let her go back to her old life, she would always be listening for the sound of Roxana skipping on the floor and the little nonsense songs she sang to her dolls. She would always be looking at everything that moved—a shadow, a bird—hoping it was the small figure she loved so much but knowing it couldn't be.

No. There is no going home.

Two vultures hover over the body of Kansbar, frightening one of the horses who snorts loudly and shakes its bridle. The soldier standing next to it rubs its muzzle like a mother calming a fretful baby. Zo recognizes the horse as a honey-colored Thessalian with a wild mane and flashing eyes, a horse rarely seen in Persia as cultured people look down on all things from the Greek mainland. Still, Thessalian horses are known for their stamina, and King Shershah has some.

Zo sweeps her gaze around the horses encircling them. They are wearing gilded cheek rosettes, red saddles with high horns and cantles embossed with silver, and scarlet saddlecloths fringed with bullion. There are two Thessalians; two white Arabians with high cheekbones and finely chiseled profiles; a ram-headed Nisaian with flaring nostrils and a switching tail; a gentle, muscular Kirruri; and two elegant Medeans on impossibly long, shapely legs. It's a rare and valuable herd for an army regiment. Then she remembers Shershah saying Artaxerxes had the largest stables in the world with the finest horses and recalls watching his magnificent procession coming through the gates of Sardis. Even his lowliest soldiers had mounts worth a king's ransom.

"Are you all right?" Ochus asks with concern. "We will get you food and water in a few minutes." Apparently she hesitated so long in answering him he thought she was incapable of doing so.

"Thank you," she says, licking her lips at the thought of

water. Her voice sounds as if she has just swallowed sawdust. "The slavers hardly gave us anything to eat or drink the past several days. To answer your question, I am the daughter of a horse breeder." She spins the lie quickly, with ease, as though it's simply another bedtime tale she's read over and over to Roxana. "I was going with my father and his men to look at some unusual horses in the foothills. The slavers killed all the men in my party, even my father..." Her voices catches, and her lower lip trembles, and though she's making up the story, the distress she feels is all too real. "And they captured me."

Ochus sighs and sweeps his arms in a gesture to include all the prisoners. "They all claim to be free," he says to his men, shrugging. "I've never been to a slave market yet where anyone admits they are legally slaves."

He scratches the back of his neck and looks into the trees, frowning. "We'll take our grandmother here," he says, gesturing to Kohinoor, "to her home, so no further harm will befall her."

Zo is struck by the fact that the soothsayer was right. A merciful lord is rescuing her. The captain won't hand her over to the Aesarian Lords.

"As for the rest of you," he adds, turning to them with a maddening grin, "we will take you all to Miletus and confine you while we send investigators to look into your stories. If you are free, we will return you to your homes. If we cannot substantiate your stories, we will sell you as runaway slaves to raise revenue for the empire."

This stops Zo in her tracks. Now, despite her dramatic rescue, she's in the same position she was before. She will be sold as a slave once they find out there is no family horse-breeding farm and no one to swear to her identity.

She needs to be in a position where she can go to the Eastern Mountains to change her fate. Then, she will make her way back to Cosmas's camp, have their child, and sink into happy obscurity as his wife.

"The prisoners will sit under that tree while we clean up," Ochus says, pointing to a large, wide-armed oak. "Give them water first, then food. They look as if they need it immediately." Leaning on the soldiers, the exhausted band staggers over and sits down in the dirt. Soldiers fill large goatskins with fresh water from the pond and give one to every prisoner except Zo. "There are no more goatskins, miss," a soldier tells her. "When one of the other prisoners has finished in a few minutes, we will refill it and give it to you."

Zo licks her lips again, fighting back tears. A few minutes of *agony*. None of the others greedily slurping water seems in a hurry to let her share their goatskin. She wants to scream in rage as she sees water coursing down Minoo's chin and throat as she tilts the water bag back. Minoo is *wasting* the water. Zo thinks about grabbing it from Minoo, or crawling to the spring and sticking her head in, though she doubts she has enough strength to do anything except sit and wait.

A shadow blocks out the sun. She looks up. Kneeling before her is the commander, Ochus, his bronze helmet filled with cool clear water from the spring.

"Drink," he says, tipping it toward her as a few bright drops fall like glittering diamonds on her knees.

Right now the water is worth much more to her than diamonds. She puts her hands on top of his and drinks in long luxurious gulps. It tastes better than the finest spiced Carian wine. When she is finally sated, she takes the helmet from him and dumps the rest of the water over her head, feeling deliciously cool and a little bit cleaner.

Ochus laughs. "A good idea," he says, taking the helmet.

A soldier hands Zo a wooden bowl with olives, dates, and goat cheese. Her fingers are filthy—why hadn't she washed *them* with the helmet water?—but she digs in heartily, laughing out loud at the image of a eunuch pouring rose water over her already scrubbed and scented fingers before and after her meals. As she gulps down the black olives, she realizes that she never appreciated them before. Olives are the most boring staple of any Persian table, even the poorest. Now she realizes that they are as rich and flavorful as meat. She sighs with delight as she bites into the salty tanginess of goat cheese and the potent sweetness of dates.

Her shrunken stomach is quickly full, and she leans back against the tree trunk, knowing she must come up with a plan to escape. Some soldiers wave away vultures and pick over the dead bodies for valuables while others examine the slavers' horses and carts. But they cast frequent glances at the prisoners and will probably lock them up at night.

Her gaze keeps going back to the soldiers' horses. And then she has an idea. She rises unsteadily to her feet and walks over to Ochus, who is standing next to the pond in just his baggy red-and-white-checked trousers and tall brown boots, his mail shirt and green tunic on the ground behind him. He is dipping his helmet into the water and sluicing himself with it, then rubbing his skin with a towel. He has a broad chest, muscular arms, and an incredibly well-defined stomach, though the smooth tan skin is marred by several jagged scars.

He pours a helmetful of water over his head, sets the helmet down, and runs his hands through his hair, working out the dust and sweat. Water is running down his face and neck in rivulets.

"Commander Ochus," she says. He opens his eyes. They are golden brown, the color of dark honey, but bright and shrewd. Completely different from the luminous depth of Cosmas's eyes, she notes. His nose leans toward his left cheek—it must have been broken in a battle or a brawl. She senses that this man is a bundle of raw, impatient ambition and hesitates, wondering if her lies will work with him.

He picks up the towel, squeezes the water out of his hair, and wipes his eyes. "Yes?" he says, blinking.

"Your horses are…magnificent."

He smiles and tosses the towel on the ground. "The king, my great-grandfather, is probably the greatest horse collector and breeder in the civilized world."

She looks back at the horses. The soldiers have taken grain bags from the slavers' carts and emptied them into feed bags, which they are now strapping onto the horses' necks.

"I suppose it's not surprising," she says. "Two hundred years ago, the favorite white stallion of the Great King's ancestor, Cyrus the Great, drowned while crossing a river. Cyrus was devastated by the loss. He ordered his army to spend an entire summer draining the river into so many runoff channels that he, in effect, killed it as punishment. Only a Persian king would kill a river for a horse."

He grins, revealing straight white teeth. "It's a story my great-grandfather often tells, and one that the daughter of a horse breeder would know. Don't worry, girl. We will get you back to your farm soon. Is your mother still alive? Do you have family to look after you?"

"Yes," she says, looking at the ground. "It's just… I don't want to go back without finishing what my father set out to do. Knowing the Great King's love of horses, my father wanted to give him the rarest horse he could find. He sent word out far and wide about finding a suitable stallion as a gift. And he heard from some peasants about a herd of Pegasi. We were going there to find and capture one. But then we were ambushed."

Ochus's left eyebrow flies up. "Pegasi? All the Pegasi died two hundred years ago or more."

"No," she says, keeping her voice steady and remembering old Mandana's tales. "According to a group of shepherds my father spoke to, there is a Pegasus herd in a valley near the Flaming Cliffs of the Eastern Mountains. They graze in the meadowlands, but whenever anyone tries to catch one, they fly up to their nests."

His bright gaze bores into her, as if he is searching for a lie. "And you know where these Flaming Cliffs are?"

"My father had a map," she lies smoothly, amazed at his gullibility. Maybe he is the Great King's great-grandson, and maybe he can track and kill a motley group of slavers, but he's really very stupid. How could cliffs be flaming? The whole story is ridiculous. "I studied it with him, but the map was lost when we were ambushed. The cliffs are well east of here, up a track that leads north off the Royal Road. I think I can find them." She shifts her weight from one foot to the other. "Could we not capture one to give to the Great King? It would fulfill my father's last wish. And it would surely help you rise in your great-grandfather's favor."

Ochus tilts his head to the left, stares at her, and says, "You speak beautiful Persian for a farm girl. You have the accent of a wealthy city lady."

Zo's heart beats fast. She looks down at her stained, ripped boy's tunic and trousers and then grins up at him sheepishly. "I suppose it must come as a surprise, given these rags the slavers gave me, but my family grew wealthy from horse breeding. You must know that most Persians would prefer to have a splendid horse and a decrepit house to owning a luxurious palace and a broken-down nag. My father hired me a tutor who had worked with noble families."

Those burning eyes study her a long moment, then he cries, "Men! We will rest here tonight and fill our water bags. Parviz!"

A stocky man runs forward. "Yes, my lord?"

"Tomorrow you will be in charge of the regiment to take grandmother home and the other prisoners back to Miletus. Tomorrow at first light I want Payem and Javed saddled up with a mount for this girl. I am going on a special expedition and will meet you there when it is complete."

Zo is flushed with relief. Surely on their scramble eastward she will be able to escape, to save herself and her baby. To change her fate from marrying Alexander. To be with Cosmas.

Ochus picks up his mail shirt and tunic and starts walking back to the camp. He stops suddenly, turns and walks back to her. "What is your name?" he says.

"Zo...tasha," she replies. "My name is Zotasha, but call me Zo."

"Well, Zotasha-but-call-me-Zo," he says, his mouth twisting in mirth...or disgust, as he takes in her state, "you're filthy. If you are going to be my traveling companion, you will need to bathe in the pond—once we have filled our water bags, that is." He walks away to check his mare.

Zo flushes scarlet red. What a rude thing to say. All the prisoners stink. After tracking the slavers all day, Ochus himself doesn't smell that great. Great King Artaxerxes probably doesn't even know the name of this great-grandson, fathered by some lesser son's lesser son to a palace scullery girl or peasant woman who caught his fancy.

She'll be free of him soon, though. She'll lead him on the wildest goose chase ever, after an extinct flying horse in a place that doesn't exist, and when he isn't paying attention, she'll escape as if it were she who had wings.

ACT FOUR:
FATED

We become brave
by performing brave actions.
—Aristotle

CHAPTER TWENTY

"BUT IT WAS A POSSIBLE ASSASSINATION ATTEMPT," Alex says again, keeping his voice calm. He slides the phoenix dagger Heph returned to him into the center of the table. "We must investigate further. It's already been several days since it occurred, but you refused to meet with me." He resists rubbing his temples. He hasn't been sleeping much at all, and the exhaustion weighs down on his shoulders, but he won't let that show.

Theopompus runs a plump, well-manicured hand through his oiled and curled hair. A sensualist who delights in all physical pleasures, he is the king's minister of provisions, obtaining wine and foodstuffs for the army and civilians. Lately, though, he's been provisioning himself a bit too much. "We were at my hunting lodge," he says with a slow drawl, affecting boredom. "Except for Leonidas who, if rumor be correct, was here at the palace." He pauses and smiles. "Whipping himself."

Laughter rumbles around the polished ebony table of the small council chamber. Leonidas's hard black eyes narrow and his mouth twists to the right, but he doesn't stand up for himself. Alex clasps his hands tightly in his lap in a pretense of calm.

"The poor beggar probably stole the prince's dagger earlier in the day," Theopompus continues, "got drunk in the wine cellar, started wandering around the palace, and dropped it in Hephaestion's room before he went back downstairs to his wine. It's not exactly a matter of state." The brilliant jewels in his many rings flash as he reaches across the table for a dish of olives stuffed with lamb meat.

"It is odd, though," General Kadmus says, "that a thief would only steal the prince's dagger." His shrewd gray gaze sweeps the table, boring into the eyes of every other man there. "As Prince Alexander says, the thief left gold rings and arm bands, a silver writing box encrusted with lapis lazuli, and a silk tunic that traveled from the other side of the world. Why take only the dagger? And once he stole it, why not leave the palace immediately? Why go down to the wine cellar and eat cheese?"

General Kadmus, tan and wiry, hoped to go to Byzantium with Philip, but the king chose his other general, Parmenion, instead. Since Philip's departure, Alex senses that Kadmus—as ambitious as he is energetic—is not only disappointed but bored. An ally, perhaps.

"Maybe a servant stole the dagger from you, my lord," says Hagnon, the finance minister. His alert face, with a small beak of a nose and nervously darting brown eyes, reminds Alex of a sparrow. Even his voice is an annoying chirp. "Then he lost his nerve and replaced it in Hephaestion's room, knowing your friend would return it to you. You're lucky to get it back, my lord. It's valued at two hundred drachmas."

Hagnon fixes a value to everything. It occurs to Alexander that the man would probably sell his mother for an *obol* and consider it a deal. "And the figure Hephaestion saw looming

over him when he woke?" Alex asks, working his jaw, trying
to contain his impatience.

Leonidas drums his fingers on the table slowly. "The Council of State is well aware of the lamentable practice that young
men, in particular, have of keeping their doors unbolted so
their 'friends' can drop in to drink wine and...explore. The
night in question was the Festival of the Lunar Eclipse. Plenty
of young people were roaming at indecent hours, going who-
knows-where to do we-know-what."

More chuckles from around the table. Leonidas takes a sip
of water from his unglazed clay cup. "Hephaestion admits to
having drunk too much unwatered wine that night," he said,
glancing sideways at Theopompus, pouring himself a healthy
serving of unwatered wine from an *oenochoe* on the table. "Perhaps he imagined the figure."

Alex clenches his jaw as he looks around the table. He wonders if one of them—or perhaps two or three—are accepting
bribes from the enemy. Why else would they be treating an
assassination attempt so lightly?

Theopompus takes a swig of wine and immediately spits it
out, spraying the table. "Hagnon, this isn't wine! It's vinegar.
No—it's sheep's piss!"

"I got it at a very good price," Hagnon says waspishly.

Theopompus snaps his fingers. In an instant, a servant who
has been waiting motionless in the corner is at his side. "In
my office, there is an amphora of Chian," the minister says.
"Pour it into the...the Achilles *oenochoe*. And bring it before
we die of thirst. Or poison." He glares at Hagnon and leans
back in his chair as the slender legs squeal in protest.

Alex studies him. While most wealthy men's robes have a
richly embroidered border of another material, Theopompus's
robe is *all* border, glistening with gold and silver thread against
a turquoise-colored background. He has braided small tur-

quoise gemstones into his blond beard in the Persian fashion and even sports huge turquoise-and-gold earrings.

A man who appreciates the trappings of wealth might be an easy target for treachery.

"Everyone needs to bolt their doors at night and behave themselves. It's quite simple," Leonidas says.

Alex clasps his hands so hard it hurts. "A good suggestion," he replies calmly, nodding, "and one that everyone should abide by. However, I am wondering if it could have been an Aesarian Lord who tried to harm Hephaestion, my right-hand man, as a warning. The tension between the Lords and Macedon has risen lately. We are the only nation that has steadfastly refused to hand over suspected sorcerers and ancient documents about magic, refused to play their games and succumb to their fearmongering. And now the king and most of the army is gone. I worry about the Lords' intentions. They were extremely angry the other night when their sacred torch exploded. They won't tell us what it means, but I know it bodes ill for us."

Silver-bearded Gordias, the minister of religion, rouses himself from his nap, raises a trembling hand, and croaks, "I believe Father Zeus sent a bolt of lightning. It happens from time to time when he is displeased."

Theopompus cocks his head to one side and says, "My Lord Prince, it is true that enemies can become friends and friends enemies with very little warning. But the Aesarian Lords are extremely powerful outside of Macedon. If we do suspect them, we must proceed with great caution."

"The prince is brave and wants to prove himself in his father's absence," Hagnon says. "But imagining that our allies are out to attack us is not the proper path to pursue. My lord, with all due respect, you are as yet young and unwise in statecraft. Unwarranted suspicion can turn your friends into your enemies."

"A wise king must suspect everyone, *particularly* those who claim to be his friends," Alex rejoins heatedly, his patience finally eroded. He gets up and starts pacing the room, hating the slight limp that becomes more apparent the more agitated he gets. But he can no longer sit still. "How many Macedonian kings have been assassinated? Who killed Alcetas II, Craterus, Archeleus, and Alexander II? Was it a Spartan, a Persian, a Thracian? No, the assassins were all Macedonians. More than that, they were brothers, nephews, *friends*."

"True, but there are only fifteen Lords here," Leonidas says, folding his hands on the table, "counting the two new ones."

"Fourteen," Gordias says, nudging him. "Remember, the other night the one exploded—"

"There are only *fourteen* Lords here," Leonidas continues, frowning, "while we still have two hundred men at arms training every day under our General Kadmus."

"As history has proved repeatedly, only one man is needed for an assassination," Alex points out, feeling as if he is trying to persuade a flock of uncomprehending sheep that wolves might be coming. No, *are* coming, are prowling, fangs exposed, just beyond their walls. And maybe some within. "I am armed every moment of the day and night. I will double my mother's guard and place a guard on Arrhidaeus—he'd be the perfect puppet king. Any assassination or abduction of the royal family would be immediately followed by an attacking army, which would be hidden nearby. If the men were disguised as peasants or merchants, they could walk right in through the open gates of Pella and into the palace."

General Kadmus nods in agreement. "We will increase the watch at all towers and gates of the palace and the town."

Alex's eyes meet his. Understanding flashes between the two. Allies.

Theopompus, who misses nothing, has seen the glance. He watches Alexander carefully. A man whose vaunted position is based on pleasing others doesn't wish to displease the heir to the throne. "My Lord Prince," he says, smiling graciously, "as you know, I recently returned from a most delightful embassy to Sardis. Soon your thoughts will be turned to more pleasant princely duties than battle, and our friend Gordias here will sacrifice not to Ares, but to Eros on your behalf."

My bride, Alexander thinks. At least now he knows she's a Persian from Sardis. Probably a fat, silly girl with an entourage of fatter, sillier eunuchs, all of them wearing trousers, the true sign of a barbarian.

A servant enters the chamber with a magnificent red-and-white figure *oenochoe*, the heroes and goddesses delicately painted against a glazed black background.

"Oh! Thanks be to all the gods," Theopompus cries, clapping his hands. "I thought I was going to faint from thirst. Here, fill my cup."

An eerie giggle rises from beneath the council table. Shocked, everyone around it bends down to peer beneath it. In the center is Arrhidaeus, sitting cross-legged and rocking back and forth.

"Good gods!" Hagnon cries. "Someone call the guard to drag this idiot out from there."

"No," Alex says, standing. "He is a royal prince. How dare you disrespect him? Let him be." Hagnon looks as if he has just been slapped.

"Well, then, I think this meeting is adjourned," says Theopompus, standing. He starts to head for the door in a rustle of blue silk and a cloud of perfume, then turns, grabs his wine cup, and leaves with the others.

Alex crawls under the table and sits cross-legged next to his half brother. "Arri," he snaps, trying and failing to mask his irritation. "What are you doing here?"

Arrhidaeus holds out two fists. It's a game they often play where Alex has to guess which fist has the pebble inside. Alex stifles a sigh. He has no time for childish games now. Not with Macedon threatened by Persia in the east, Byzantium in the north, and an uneasy alliance with Athens in the south. And he can clearly see a glint in the boy's left hand where the object peeks out. He taps his brother's right hand. Grinning, Arrhidaeus opens it, and pushes his left hand toward Alex, willing him to tap that one, too.

Alex complies, thinking it must be a shiny pebble or loose nail, but when the boy opens it, Alex sees a finely chiseled agate cameo of Artaxerxes, the Great King of the Persians, in a frame of shining gold studded with enormous rubies, pearls, and emeralds. As Alex takes it, Arri claps.

Alex stares at it. Whose is it? It looks like something belonging to Theopompus. Was it a gift for arranging the Persian girl's marriage to Alex? Could it be a foreign envoy's donation to Gordias for performing religious rites? Part of the miser Hagnon's hidden treasure everyone whispers about?

Or is it evidence of something else?

"Arri, where did you find this?" Alex asks, his voice tight and urgent.

"I d-don't remember," he says, shaking his head back and forth. "Somewhere." Alex knows there is no use in trying to coax or threaten more information out of Arri. Sometimes the boy will remember something days—even weeks—after you ask him, and come running to you with the answer when you can't even remember the question.

Could the jewel be a bribe to a traitor? But a bribe from whom? If Alex is marrying a Persian princess, there is no threat from that side for the time being. A chill settles in his stomach when he remembers the Aesarian Lords' ancient fortress, Nekrana, is lodged deep in the Eastern Mountains, Persian territory. Perhaps this is an Aesarian bribe.

He puts a hand to his forehead and tries to rub away the beginning of a headache, fighting away voices that tell him he is unable to think clearly in his father's absence. Too young to rule. Suspicious of his own shadow.

He wonders if someone innocently lost this cameo—if it became unpinned from a robe—and how he can find out. Alex looks up at planks of unstained wood held together by square pegs, thinking. If there is no guilt involved and someone lost a jewel of this value, they will be frantic to find it. They will publicize a large reward and search relentlessly for it. If no one mentions it in the next day or so, it was a secret gift, a bribe, and Alex will know there is a traitor in the palace.

Clutching the jeweled hilt of his phoenix dagger, Alexander storms out of the palace and strides toward the stables. He knows he won't feel calm, won't be able to think straight, until he's riding Bucephalus. On the back of his favorite horse, head and shoulders above the crowd and moving with the strength of beast and man combined, only then does he feel the true authority of being a prince. Only then does he believe he can accomplish his greatest dream.

The light is dim inside the stables; the shutters are closed against the coming storm and a lantern hangs on a hook from the central beam between the rows of stalls.

Kithos, sandy-haired and freckle-faced, stops raking hay and horse droppings when he sees Alex and grins. "My lord, he's already got a visitor," Kithos says.

"Really?" Alex says. "I hope the poor man still has both hands." It's difficult for anyone else to get near the horse as

Bucephalus kicks and bites anybody except Alex—even Kithos, whom all the other horses adore.

He starts to walk toward the stalls, down a long corridor. Some horses have pushed their heads over the chest-high doors of their stalls, eyes half-closed and nostrils twitching at the ripe smells of approaching rain.

At the far end, in the corner stall, he sees the opened door and pauses. Normally Bucephalus would bolt if his door were open, trampling anyone who tried to stop him. Quietly, Alex approaches and peers in. Katerina stands there, stroking the black stallion's soft muzzle, telling him how beautiful he is. The horse swings his huge head against her shoulder and nuzzles it.

"Katerina?" Alex says.

She turns, and the horse whickers as Alex steps toward them. Alex holds up his hand, and the stallion gently bumps him, pushing his forelock against Alex's palm, begging for a rub.

"Yes, boy, yes," Alex says, fluffing the stiff black mane. He turns to Kat. She's smiling at him, but he can see she's been crying. Her eyes are swollen and red. She's hiding something; that much he knows, even though he can't read her.

He had pictured himself galloping into fresh clean wind, alone with his thoughts, but he can't very well saddle his horse and leave an obviously upset Kat.

"I'm going for a ride," he says. "Would you like to join me?"

"I think it's finally going to rain," she says. In the distance there is a low rumble of thunder.

"I need to get out of here," he replies. "And I love the rain."

She smiles. "I do, too," she says. "In Erissa, I used to dance in it until my foster parents dragged me inside, fearing I would be struck by lightning."

"Let's go, then," he says, excited by the thought of riding with Kat.

Moments later, they race across the fields behind the tall palace walls, Kat's arms tightly around Alex's waist. The river Axios slides by, the color of iron, just like the sky.

Alex pulls up, slides off, and helps Kat down. A brisk wind whistles along the river, making the trees bend and sway with the lithe grace of acrobats.

"It's so beautiful here," she says, watching two jewel-colored bee-eaters—a blur of green, red, and gold—flap hastily toward the safety of their nest. "Why are there no houses along the river?"

"It floods often," he says, turning back to the walls. "See how high the wall is back here with no gates or windows? Five years ago it rained for a month and the river went almost halfway to the top. The palace and city are built on hills not just for defense, but also to stay dry."

Kat studies the walls as if trying to imagine such a flood. "What's that?" she asks, pointing to a tall conical tower in the distance.

"That," he says, "is where our astrologers study the stars."

"We have a stargazer in Erissa named Laertes who does that for us," Kat replies, nodding. "The most important constellation for us is the Pleiades, the seven beautiful sisters Father Zeus turned into stars. When they set in the west just before dawn, it means it's time to harvest the crops. If we wait much longer, there will be a frost and our crops will die."

Alex laughs. "What a quaint story!" he says, shaking his head.

"It's not quaint when your life depends on it," Kat snaps.

Alex feels a blush crawling up his neck. What a snobby, condescending thing he just said, bringing up the staggering gulf of birth that separates them. A peasant girl. A future king. How stupid of him. "I'm sorry. I didn't mean…" He gestures helplessly.

"I know you didn't," Kat says, waving her hand as if at a fly.

"It's just that our astrologers up there in that tower are more concerned with lineage and destiny than the land. In the library's archives, there are records of the birth of every member of the royal family so the astrologers can cast their horoscopes throughout their lives. Based on these horoscopes, temple priests propitiate angry gods who rule over different sections of the night sky of one's birth."

Kat smiles. "I suppose if any of the gods ruling over the sky of my birth is angry, I'll find out the hard way."

In response, thunder rumbles like the low growl of a vicious dog. Over the fields on the other side of the river, massive black clouds, heavy and swollen with rain, tear across the sky.

Bucephalus's eyes roll as he snorts and backs up. Alex rubs his head and whispers gently, "It's all right, boy." Turning to Kat, he says, "Despite his bravery in battle, Bucephalus spooks easily. I first saw him three years ago, shortly before Heph and I left for Mieza with Aristotle. The Persian horse trader boasted that he was bringing the most beautiful stallion in the world to Pella in the hopes of selling him to my father for thirteen talents of gold. Black as night with sky-blue eyes and a white star on the forehead that looked like the head of an ox." Alex rubs the white spot and the horse nickers in pleasure.

"As *Bucephalus* means *Oxhead*, it seems appropriate!" Kat says. "Did you name him? Or did he come with the name?"

Alex smiles. "I did. I don't think he had a name when I got him. When the breeder brought him into the main palace courtyard, he asked who wanted to ride this splendid horse fit for a king. Of course, that was a joke because no one could ride him. Dozens of the strongest warriors tried, and the horse threw them off as if they were weightless dolls. My father said the horse was worthless and should be put down, but the desperate horse merchant said he would give the horse for free to anyone who could tame him."

"And then you said, 'Father, I can tame him.'"

He turns and stares at her. "Did I already tell you this story?"

"No, I heard it in Erissa a couple of years ago."

"People know of it there?"

She grins. "I think people have heard of it everywhere. And when you said you could tame him, everyone laughed—your father most of all. You were less than half the size of the warriors who had been thrown. But it's not just size or strength that wins a battle," she says.

"It's intelligence." They say it at the same time, and smile at the coincidence.

"I didn't have to be Socrates to see what was scaring the horse," Alex says. "It was a cloudless day, and he was terrified of his huge black shadow moving on the sand and of the flapping capes of the men who tried to mount him. I took off my cape and turned him to face the sun, so he couldn't see his shadow anymore."

Kat says, "And then, to everyone's surprise, you hopped up on his back and started riding him around and around the courtyard, and then through the main gate and out of Pella into the countryside."

Alex chuckles at the memory, one of his favorites. "That's right. I came back six hours later, long after they had sent out a search party to find my dead body by the side of the road, thrown and trampled by the untamable horse. My mother was prostrate on her bed in hysterics."

Something dark passes over Kat's face at the mention of his mother, but he can't read her eyes. "Bucephalus is the most magnificent horse in the world," she says simply, placing her hand on the animal's muzzle.

"People have said he is the closest thing to a Pegasus."

"How I would love to see a Pegasus!" Kat says. "But that's not likely, is it?"

"The last ones were seen centuries ago far to the east of here, in Persia." Near the Fountain of Youth on the map. The place he has yearned to find for so long. But how could he seek it now, when his responsibilities lie here? He wonders if Kat understands how trapped he is in his own life. All at once he has an overpowering desire to tell her about his frustration at being a puppet regent, at no one taking him seriously, and of the journey he longs to make. He hasn't been able to talk to Heph lately. Something tells him he can confide in Kat.

"Kat, there is a place far from here, in the Eastern Mountains of Persia, with a fountain that could make me the most powerful leader the world has ever seen." He watches her carefully, searching for any sign of mockery, but there's none. He pushes on. "A leader powerful enough to unite the warring kingdoms. That's why I was hoping Heph would win the Blood Tournament. We needed the gold to go on our journey."

She looks at him a long moment. "Yes," she says, nodding. "I understand about life-changing journeys."

He picks a piece of straw out of the horse's mane as the first fat raindrops plop down. "I think if I came back from that journey—a dangerous one requiring both courage and cleverness—my father and his counselors wouldn't treat me like a child. I just came from a council meeting, and they acted as if I were ten years old. It was infuriating. I thought it was my duty to stay here and support Pella, but how can I when I'm not taken seriously?"

She nods slowly, and he knows she understands his burning need for respect. Suddenly he wants to tell her something else—the very thing he's tried so hard to hide from everyone else.

"There's more. I was born with a scar," he says quickly before he can change his mind. When he raises his tunic to reveal the long purple scar twisting about his thigh, she doesn't react with revulsion as most people do. Her mouth parts in surprise—not pity, he is sure of that—and she extends her hand, as if she wants to touch the scar, before letting it drop by her side.

"I hear this fountain can heal all kinds of wounds and weaknesses," he says. "I want it to heal my leg, Kat. To make me perfect, the way a king should be."

She stares at him, and her face shows signs of an interior struggle, before she finally says, "Let's go back. I want to show you something that might help."

They swing onto Bucephalus and gallop through the increasing downpour. Alex feels as if he is being washed clean by heaven itself. He inhales the air, moist with the fresh, earthy smell of rain, and listens to its loud rushing whisper. His body rocks easily with Bucephalus's gait and Alex forgets his own crippled leg. He feels Kat's soft cheek leaning against his neck, feels the pressure of her arms around his waist. He feels completely comfortable in his own skin.

When they arrive at the stables, they quickly rub down Bucephalus and dry off the leather saddle before leaving the stallion happily munching on an apple. The two of them run through puddles and mud until they arrive at the main palace building, their clothing molded to their bodies, their hair like wet snakes clinging to their skulls, mud splattered up to their knees.

Kat unlocks her door and the two of them enter. A maid has closed and bolted the louvered shutters, and the indoor light is the color of tarnished silver. While Kat rifles through her clothing trunk, Alex lights some tinder on a side table and all the lamps. It smells nice in here, not like the heavy incense of his mother's room. Here it smells of clean linen and beeswax furniture polish mixed with lemon. He closes his eyes and inhales. He could fall asleep here and not wake for a long time.

When he turns to face her she is holding out a large leather pouch that he has seen somewhere before. "At least one of us should be able to repair the damage of the past," she says. "These are my winnings from betting on Jacob in the Blood Tournament. Take them and find what you are looking for."

He stands as still as a statue. "That's not why I told you about my journey," he says.

"I know that."

"I can't take it," he says. "It's your money. You need it."

"I want you to have it. Please."

"Think what this could buy in Erissa, Kat," he says, ignoring the outstretched purse as he puts his hands on her shoulders. "An entire farm, I'd wager. Think what this could do for your family."

She shakes her head. "Jacob will take care of them with his earnings as an, an—Aesarian Lord." She almost chokes on the last word. *So that's it*, Alex thinks. *That's what she must have been crying about in the stables just before I arrived. Jacob.*

"I don't really need the money, at least not at the moment, and you do," Kat continues. "You've given so much to me. Live your dream. Get the respect you deserve. And if anything happens, please remember me...kindly."

There's something so sincere in her face, so authentic in her voice, that in spite of himself he takes the pouch. It's heavy.

"I don't know if I can go right away," he says, thinking of the Lords. "I may have something else to do first."

"It doesn't matter," she says. "It's there for you whenever you need it."

"I'll pay you back. I'll double these winnings when I return."

She nods. "Go now, Alexander, please. I need some time to myself."

There's more he should say, but he isn't sure what. He opens the door to the hall and two maids, Iris and Ariadne, arms full of fresh linens, tumble into the room. Dark curls bouncing, Ariadne recovers her balance but Iris falls flat on the floor, her hiked-up peplos revealing plump little legs.

"Your Highness!" Iris cries, hastily picking herself and the linens up. "Forgive us. We were just going to change Lady Katerina's bedclothes."

Kat has a bright pink spot burning on each cheek. Alex hopes his own face betrays nothing, as he nods to the ladies and exits.

His wet sandals smack loudly against the marble floors as he leaves the women's wing and heads toward his room. He stops at a hall window, unbolts the shutters, and opens them. Wind slaps his face like an angry hand. Lightning illuminates the courtyard for a moment, bright as noon on a clear day, and just as quickly it fades to nearly black. A moment later, a booming thunderclap rattles the entire palace.

Love, he thinks with astonishment. He loves Katerina, the wild, fierce, mysterious village girl. But he doesn't know what kind of love it is. What he *does* know is that she loves him, too. If she didn't, she wouldn't have just given him everything she had.

CHAPTER TWENTY-ONE

THE MORNING IS SO DARK IT IS HARDLY A MORN-
ing at all. Rain hammers the roofs and wind sighs through
the courtyards. Ever since the storm began, the palace seems
to be under a spell, its inhabitants like bears who crawl into a
cave and sleep away the winter months. But one figure hurries through the puddles.

The hellion purrs loudly as Kat approaches its cage. It paces
toward her, the long chain that runs from its hind leg to a bolt
in the cage floor clinking slightly like coins in the pouch she
gave Alex yesterday. The master of the menagerie, horrified
that the beast escaped during the Blood Tournament, decided
to chain it down despite Kat's protests.

Though the shoulder wound is completely healed, Kat visits the creature every day, sitting with it despite the strenu-
ous objections of the menagerie master and the prince. Being
around this wild, dangerous creature gives her courage. And
she needs courage. After seeing Olympias resurrect the box
of bones—the same box that had belonged to Helen—she has

hardly been able to sleep. What horrors has that woman committed? What more does she intend to do?

In the week since that night, Kat has observed Olympias taking private meetings with advisors and, in one case, an Aesarian Lord.

Though the Lord came to the queen out of uniform, Kat recognized him as Bastian, the one with the jagged scar. He has a shifty energy Kat doesn't trust. He strikes her as the kind of person who simply can't adhere to any one allegiance but is always looking out for his own interests. Someone who could easily betray his friends without a second thought.

At first Kat assumed that the queen was carrying on some sort of…*relationship*…with him, but according to the handmaidens' gossip, the queen has always feared and detested the Lords. Certainly something strange is going on between the two, and it's just further evidence of the complex secrets the queen must be hiding.

Kat can only hope that the queen doesn't suspect she was the one spying on her that night on the balcony.

She leans in toward the bars of the cage, rain pummeling her hair and streaming into her eyes. If she were to actually wrap her fingers around these bars, the hellion would surely take her hands off in a single pounce. What she has with the creature is a tentative trust, a sort of truce.

She can feel the beast's fury, its desire to fly free and wild— the urge tears through her own veins, making her pulse throb. She knows it yearns to stretch its wings even as muscles strain against gusts of wind. It wants to drift on air currents as it stalks prey from above. It wants to tear into soft flesh, swallow still-beating hearts and feel blood warming its gullet.

We are all caged and wounded in our own way, Kat thinks, staring into the animal's glassy yellow-green eyes.

It licks its fangs, staring back.

She thinks about the most wounded of all. *Jacob*. Has she lost him forever? Her foster brother. Her best friend. The boy, she now admits to herself, that she has loved since that cold winter day when she was five. Helen was showing Sotiria a new bolt of cloth when Kat started chasing Jacob around the fire pit. She tripped, fell, and burned her arm badly. Jacob held her as Helen put a cool wet cloth on the burn. Jacob was safety. *As long as I have you*, she used to think, feeling the warm pressure of his hand squeezing her shoulder, *I'll be all right*.

If only she had folded herself against his chest, her heartbeat next to his like that day in the pond. If only she had trusted him and told him the truth about her mission.

If only she had said yes.

But she couldn't. Of course she couldn't. She has a mission she must see through—perhaps not as wild and far-reaching as Alexander's, but one she must fulfill just as urgently as he must his. That was partly why she gave him the winnings. It could in no way make up for what she was planning to do, but it was all she could think of. And she feels for him—not just guilt, but something else. An affinity between them. An empathy.

With Jacob, she wants everything—his arms, his kisses, his loyalty forever. With Alexander, she craves nothing other than his presence. And yet that craving is surprisingly strong for someone she has only known a short time. She wonders if her feelings for Jacob could change someday. If she could find herself falling in love with the prince.

But of course, even if she could, it wouldn't matter. Not after what she intends to do.

She thinks of what Alexander told her yesterday about the alignment of the stars. All the tangled secrets spring from the same point in time: the prince's birth. It's a long shot, but Kat knows she must find the records from that night. The astrological charts of his birth would certainly be kept in the library, and might contain notations regarding the nature of what happened that night—not just cosmically, but within the palace. An astrologer might even have been in the room when the prince was born.

Through the rain, she sees a tiny form scurrying along the ground, dangerously close to the hellion's cage. She recognizes it as Heracles, the rat that Arrhidaeus named and always carries with him. Quickly, she scoops up the rat before it enters through the cage bars. She hears the hellion hiss loudly as it lunges toward them, stopping short at the bars. Heracles trembles in her hands as she turns away, leaving the hellion stalking restlessly in her wake.

The courtyards are empty in the steady drizzle as she detours around deep puddles. Everyone is shuttered away in lamplit rooms as if it were the dead of winter. The plants, so wilted and tired ever since she arrived in Pella, are already rejuvenated, standing taller, their green arms reaching toward the life-giving sky. Three pink-gray mourning doves eye her from the branch of a laurel tree as she bends down and lets Heracles scurry his way back to his owner, feeling the small animal's relief trail in the air behind it.

Tugging her deerskin cloak close, Kat hurries through the monumental courtyard. Like the rest of the palace, it's empty except for two guards in front of the main entrance. Rain courses down their bronze cuirasses, and the red horsehair crests of their helmets sag, limp as wet feathers. Two girls bolt out of a doorway and race across the square, a shared cloak over their heads, laughing and shrieking as their sandals slap into cold puddles, spraying their gowns.

At the far end, the gold marble facade of the royal library gleams in the rain. Picking up her skirts, Kat walks up the steps, through the entranceway columns, and pushes open a small bronze-studded door set within a much larger one. She enters a dim, cool world, as the atrium windows facing the square are tightly shuttered. Rain falls through the oculus in the roof into the blue rectangular pool below, making little bubbles and rings in the water. Bearded statues peer at her from niches set in ochre-colored walls.

There is a small desk near the entrance, its chair pushed away at an angle. On the desk is a stack of documents, a white quill across a half-written piece of papyrus and an open inkpot.

"Hello?" she calls out. "Anyone here?" No reply. Looking around, Kat notices double doors on the other side of the pool. Figuring that must be the main section, she pushes them open to a dim, cavernous room with long tables and tall ladders on wheels. Each table has a flint-and-tinder set, which she uses to light a small handheld clay lamp.

As she makes her way around the room, Kat trips. Looking down at the black marble-and-amber floor, she sees a leather bucket filled to the brim with sand. Kat understands. They have one at the farm in Erissa, too, near the hearth. If anything caught fire, they would throw sand on it, which smothers the flames far better than water. Here in the library, if a reader knocked over a burning lamp, spilling oil on dry old scrolls, the entire building would go up like the tinder she just lit.

Holding her lamp high, she wanders around reading the labels.

Under Comedy, she tugs a scroll from a pigeonhole and unrolls it. *The Clouds* by Aristophanes of Athens. She scans it and sees a line in which the philosopher Socrates says to a student, "Well, if a little tummy like yours could let off a fart like that, what do you think an infinity of air can do? That's how thunder comes about." She laughs, and wishes she could read more, but time for fun is over. She puts the script away. Today she will find the truth.

She continues her investigation. Tragedy. Maps. Medicine. Animal Husbandry. Farming. Politics. History. Poetry. Mathematics. Music. Philosophy. Science. Religion.

Nothing about astrology or the royal family. Then she sees a small door at the far end of the room. Before she is even halfway there she notices the heavy lock and chain on the doorknob. Could the clues she seeks sit just a few feet beyond that door? It would make sense for the prince's astrological records to be locked up. Enemies could use information about his stars to put spells or curses on him. Curious, Kat gives an experimental tug on the chain.

"Hey now!" cries a sharp voice from across the room. "How did you get in here?"

She turns to see two guards striding toward her, one tall and slender with one black eyebrow that runs straight across his face like a thick line of paint. The other one, shorter and stockier, has such terrible acne it reminds her of the red rose bush in the Poseidon Garden.

Kat quickly releases the chains. "I'm so sorry. There was no one out front. Where is the librarian?"

The taller man raises his spear to the level of her heart, and Kat involuntarily takes a step back, hitting the door hard and rattling the lock. "Scrolls have disappeared," he says, the spear still steady, "and Leonidas asked for an increase of guards." Kat feels a slight pressure on her collarbone. Without looking down, she knows it's the spearhead's razor sharp tip pressing against her skin.

The shorter guard grins. "I will be happy to tell Master Leonidas that the thief has been found, and now we can go back to our *proper* work."

"I'm not a thief," she protests. "I'm a guest of the prince—"

"Quiet," he snaps. "You can tell your story to the jail's warden."

Jail? Kat feels her heart thudding in her chest as the guards grab either arm. How could they possibly arrest her for something she didn't do?

The answer comes to her quickly: this was a setup.

Not by the Aesarian Lords, but by the queen. Kat had been foolish to think that Olympias hadn't seen her in the garden that night.

Can she get word to Alex to stop this? He could—

Her thoughts are interrupted by a scurrying sound, followed by squeaking. Pairs of dark eyes look up at her from the floor. Rats! Kat sees half a dozen brown rats have emerged from the walls, twitching their pink noses and wringing their small pink paws.

The guards either don't see them or are so used to rats in the palace they don't care. As they begin to pull Kat from the room, one of the rats leaps onto the cape of the taller guard, crawls up to the shoulders, and bites the man on the back of the neck just below his helmet. He screams and drops Kat's arm. Dozens of rats swarm, attacking the guards.

The guards scream and holler, each trying to help the other shake the gnawing, clawing rodents from their limbs and cloaks. When more rats stream into the room like a raging river of swirling brown fur and beady black eyes, the guards are forced to retreat.

Kat stands breathless in the middle of the sea of rats as in one movement half of them turn to her. She waits for them to rush her next, but they recede into the walls like brown water draining away. "Thank you," she whispers as the last tail flicks out of sight.

Kat pulls up her hood, covering her face, and swiftly heads toward the atrium. Thank the gods, it's empty. Hiding behind a column on the library portico, she realizes more guards could come charging out of any of the dozen doors onto the courtyard at any moment. She ducks around the side of the library, through a narrow door in a marble wall, and finds herself in a small, unkempt walled garden piled with old rusted wheelbarrows and hoes. Numerous windows open onto it from the library, the shutters closed against the rain. But one small window is barred.

It's the window to the locked room. Thinking about the library's layout, she's sure of it. She stands on her tiptoes, reaches up, and grabs the bars. They're wobbly as loose teeth, with cement crumbling around their bases. She spies a wheelbarrow full of shovels, drags it over, turns it upside down, and stands on it. Using a shovel, she pries off three of the bars, hauls herself up, and kicks open the shutters. Then she drops silently to the floor. It's a small room, perhaps ten feet square. On one side are a battered old table and two decrepit chairs. Everything is terribly dusty, as if no one has been here in years.

She pushes the deerskin cape back from her shoulders and looks around. Green canvas covers what she presumes are the scrolls, protecting them from dust, moisture, and light. She raises one. Behind it are diamond-shaped pigeonholes stuffed with crumbling documents.

The light is dim, but she has no flint and tinder. So she gently pulls out a few scrolls and opens them next to the high window.

"To curse a rival in love," the first one advises, "write the name on a lead tablet, fold it, and leave it in a cave, a ruined city, or an old battlefield with a jug of good wine. The ghosts that live there will drink the wine and work on your curse."

She frowns. How ridiculous. That's not magic. That's superstition. She unrolls the scroll, scanning the other pages. It is like a recipe book filled with curses against business and love rivals, disorderly neighbors, corrupt politicians, and nasty stepparents.

She opens another scroll.

"To speak with the souls of the dead: dig a trench two feet deep in an abandoned cemetery. Pour into it honey, milk, wine, and water. Slaughter two black sheep so their blood runs into the ditch. This attracts the shades of the dead in flocks and by drinking the blood they regain for a short time the ability to communicate with the living."

Kat shivers and rolls it back up. She continues to search through scrolls, finding information on how to interpret dreams. Calm seas when sailing. Heal fevers. Bring rain to end a drought. Call fish into your nets. Make your hens lay twice as many eggs.

What nonsense. Finally, she comes to a pigeonhole of astrological charts for the royal family. Amyntas, Perdiccas—dead kings, perhaps? Her heart races when she finds one labeled Prince Alexander III. But when she unrolls it she sees only charts and drawings: constellations, phases of the moon, planetary exaltations, and conjunctions. She doesn't understand a word of it.

She picks up another scroll and sees that the leather cover is stamped with a design: a six-petaled flower inside a circle.

She pulls her mother's Flower of Life necklace out of her peplos and compares it to the stamped leather.

Identical.

She opens it carefully. The papyrus is yellowed with age, and the faded brown letters are written in an archaic style and language.

The Blood Magics is the title. On the first page she reads:

"Man is comprised of two parts, the Mind and the Body. Some individuals are born with an inherent understanding of these parts in their blood."

She unrolls it to the next page. "Earth Blood pertains to the physical, and all those living things with an unconscious mind such as rocks, trees, air, and water. A powerful Earth Blood may control the weather or cause the earth to tremble or even heal mortal wounds. Their powers might surprise them and first show themselves later in life.

"Snake Blood is of the mind, and each of its manifestations connects to human memory, character, and communication. On rare occasions, Snake Bloods may understand animals and even communicate with them. Rarer still are reports from Caria of a sorceress called Ada, knowledgeable about Snake Bloods, who believes in their ability to transform into different creatures."

Kat lays down the scroll, thinking. A special ability to understand animals. Communicate with them. She wants to shake off the heavy weight of suspicion that alights on her heart. She thinks of the horses that saved her life. The gazelle that seemed to talk to her. The rats' strange behavior today. And how her Carian-born mother admonished Kat sharply whenever Kat spoke of animals' thoughts. She wishes she could talk to Helen right now.

Kat unrolls the scroll a bit farther.

"Some say there must be a third blood magic that pertains to the third element of Man: the Spirit. Rumors from the East speak of a people with the ability to fly and alter fate, but little is known of this most mysterious of magics."

The scroll ends there, and Kat sighs. Though interesting, it hasn't been much help. She rolls her hopes up along with the parchment and puts it away before reaching for the next one: *The Blood and Bones Ritual.*

"This most potent ritual may be used to reverse any curse or enchantment, though it comes at great cost. These rites can only occur in times of great change, when one Age dies and another is born. And they must involve the blood and bones of one's own offspring..."

Kat thinks of the turquoise and ivory box Olympias took from Helen that day. The same box Olympias held mere hours before the lunar eclipse that marked the end of the Age of Gods, at least according to philosophers. The box that contained the bones of an infant.

A shudder passes up her spine so intense it is as if someone is dragging a knife up her backbone, nicking every single vertebra from her tailbone up to her skull.

What enchantment did the queen need to reverse? And did those bones belong to *the queen's own child*?

Suddenly she hears a key turning in the lock, and a moment later the door is flung open. The Aesarian Lord with the scar on his cheek—Lord Bastian—stands there, grinning, almost as though he has followed her here on purpose.

She rises unsteadily from her chair.

"Well, well, what are you doing in here?" he asks, even though he seems to have known he would find her within.

"I...was curious," she says. "To see what people aren't supposed to see."

"There's a reason for that, you know." He looks her up and down. "I've seen you around the palace with Prince Alexander. I've noticed you," he says as if it is the greatest compliment in the world. He's now standing so close to Kat that she feels his warm, damp breath against her forehead. Lord Bastian leans down. "I wonder," he says, "do royal prostitutes taste better than the rest?" He lunges for Kat, and before she can stop him, his tongue is down her throat.

She twists her head right and left to get away from his hungry mouth—and can't. Finally, he releases her an instant and Kat's right fist punches him hard in the nose, feeling gristle shatter beneath her knuckles. Surprised, Bastian lurches back, blood dripping down his face. Kat runs to the other side of the table, smashes the old chair against the shelves and in her left hand holds up a pointed, splintered leg as a club. She's just itching to crack it over his head which, for once, is without its horned helmet. Swearing, he pushes the table over and charges toward her as dozens of scrolls fall to the floor in a cloud of dust.

Voices float through the little door to the library.

"In here!" someone cries. "In the archives!"

Bastian grins slowly. "No," he says, running his tongue over his teeth. "Royal sluts are the same as your average whore." Before Kat can stop him, he grabs her again and shoves her to the ground. Quickly, he hoists himself to the window's ledge, and disappears.

Two guards—different guards, not the ones bitten by rats—rush in followed by a tanned gray-bearded man in a homespun robe carrying a torch. The bearded man walks up to Kat crumpled on the floor and, looking down at her, considers her calmly. Finally, he says, "You're that...friend...of Prince Alexander's, aren't you? Why are you in the archives?"

"I..." What reason can she give?

"Search her," the man orders.

"Yes, Master Leonidas."

One of the guards rifles through Kat's gray robe, rough hands searching private places, which brings tears to her eyes. The other one unties the leather pouch from her belt and opens it. Inside are the linen handkerchief and ivory comb she put there this morning, as well as the key to this very room—the one she saw Bastian holding only moments ago, when he entered—and a small stone vial Kat has never seen before.

The guard hands it to Leonidas, who uncorks it and sniffs. His eyes widen and he grimaces.

"Wolfsbane," he says, carefully recorking it and tucking it into the folds of his robe. He studies her, frowning. "Prince Alexander warned the council that there were rumors of an assassination attempt. The queen found a knife on her balcony a few days ago, and this morning the queen's new handmaiden fell unconscious after tasting Her Majesty's breakfast. It's not known if she will survive. But this," he says, fingering the vial, "this is meant to kill."

"It's not mine!" Kat cries, as the guards pinion her arms. "I've never seen it before in my life!" Even as she says it, she knows it sounds ridiculous. She can see the disbelieving contempt on the men's faces. How did it get there? The answer comes immediately. *Bastian.* He planted both the poison and the key on her.

The guards haul her to the door.

"Lord Bastian was here!" she says, struggling, dragging her feet, twisting her shoulders. "He pushed me against the shelves and must have put the poison in my pouch. I fought him... Look at the overturned table! Look at the chair! We struggled!"

Leonidas turns to stare at her again. "Perhaps you made this mess to convince us you weren't alone. Last week on the night of the lunar eclipse, there was an attempt on the life of Lord Hephaestion. A dagger was also discovered outside the queen's chambers. You were seen, that same night, wandering the palace. I have a report from Hephaestion himself. Is that a coincidence?"

"Yes," she cries, knowing how weak she sounds. "I swear—"

"Save your breath," Leonidas cuts her off. "I think you were sent here by someone—King Artaxerxes perhaps—to kill the royal family. And if knives and poison didn't work, you were told to find magical means—curses and incantations— in these scrolls." Leonidas bends down to examine the heap of torn scrolls and sighs. He looks ancient in the dark room, the torchlight throwing into relief the deep contours around his eyes. Turning away from Kat, he commands, "Take her away. Tell the queen her poisoner has been caught."

Quickly, the guards drag Kat out of the library and into the drizzling main square. They take her out a small door on the other side of the abandoned garden, down a narrow street, and into a low building. A guard stands near a wooden door carrying an empty food tray. He looks up in surprise.

"Prisoner for you, Heirax," says the guard holding Kat's left arm.

The soldier carrying the tray sets it down on a table and eyes Kat doubtfully. He's solidly built, with stringy brown hair and missing several important teeth. "Yes, sir," he says, pulling a key off a hook next to an open cell with a clean straw pallet and a little square barred window.

"No," the guard says. "Not that cell. Downstairs."

Heirax looks up sharply, lines creasing his low forehead. "Are you sure, sir? A girl like that, she wouldn't last—"

"For trying to assassinate the royal family."

The man's eyes narrow as he looks at Kat. "All right, then." He lights a torch and leads the way down a dark and winding staircase.

Heart hammering, Kat feels the temperature plummet with each step. She is innocent of the poison, but the knife the queen found on her balcony—the knife she had dropped before she could use it to kill—*was* hers. Could Olympias know that? Could she have asked Bastian to plant the vial on Kat as revenge for a possible assassination attempt? Or does she just want Kat—whom she clearly despises—out of the way, out of Alex's life, without looking as if she had a hand in it?

Cobwebs tickle Kat's face as she's dragged roughly through the darkness, and she sneezes at the smell of mildew and rot. It reminds her of the time she and Jacob were out hunting and she fell down an old well. Badly scratched and bruised and with a sprained ankle, she felt swallowed by icy darkness and damp stone, looking up at a small circle of pale light far above her. Panicking, she screamed and beat her hands bloody on the walls until Jacob found her and rescued her with rope made of strong vines.

Jacob, she says silently, tears stinging her eyes. But Jacob doesn't know where she is. So how can he possibly rescue her?

At the bottom of the stairs, Heirax takes a key off an iron hook next to a door and opens it. The other man pushes Kat in. She gets a glimpse of slimy walls, filthy straw, and hundreds of black pellet-like rat droppings before they lock it. Footsteps fade away on the stairs, and the door slams shut.

CHAPTER TWENTY-TWO

HEPH DRAGS THE BLADE OF HIS DAGGER OVER the whetstone and holds it up in the dim twilight drifting in from the open window of his bedroom. That ought to do it. He pushes the tip ever so slightly into the finger of his left hand and is rewarded by a tiny drop of blood. Sharp enough.

A gust of wind blows rain onto the small wooden table. Everyone else in the palace has closed their shutters, but Heph wants the rain and fresh air to clear his mind.

Something has been bothering Heph ever since he found the beheaded beggar in the wine cellar, though he can't put his finger on it. Leaning back in his chair, he goes over the events again. Hearing Cyn's cry. Rushing downstairs and seeing the bloody body sprawled on the floor, the staring head a few feet away. Cyn looking terrified for the first time ever.

What was wrong about it?

Another gust blows fresh air into his room, and he inhales deeply. The storm has washed away the palace smells of dust and sweat and filthy chamber pots and replaced them with the clean smell of rain.

The smell! That's it. The beheaded beggar reeked like a chamber pot. Heph could smell him several yards away. Yet there was no odor in Heph's bedroom when the intruder dropped Alex's dagger. If the intruder in his room had indeed been the beggar, the room would have stunk.

Cyn had beheaded an innocent man. Had she done it out of fear? The man was armed only with a small knife. If any woman in the palace could have disarmed him or bravely held him at bay while reinforcements arrived, it would have been Cyn. But why would she want to kill a stranger? If they were still young, he might have thought this part of one of her elaborate pranks, but the urgency and intensity in her voice were all too real. Heph knows he should talk to her about it, but she refuses to see him.

And if the intruder wasn't the beggar, who could it have been? Not Alex. Of course not Alex.

Booted footsteps coming down the hall bring him back to the present. Someone knocks hard on his door.

"Enter!" he calls.

It's Telekles. "My lord," he says, removing his helmet and pushing hair off his forehead. His normally golden locks are so saturated they are brown, and the usually stiff horsehair helmet crest is a sodden mess. In fact, every part of him is dripping. "Leonidas has had Prince Alexander's friend, Katerina, arrested and placed in the dungeon."

Heph pushes his chair back and stands up. "What!" he cries. "On what charge?"

"Breaking into the archives," Telekles replies. "Stealing library scrolls and..." His keen blue eyes study his sopping boots, which have left wet footprints across Heph's floor tiles.

"And?"

"Attempting to assassinate the royal family, sir." He looks up. "The queen wants to personally question Katerina. Apparently they found a vial of poison on her. That, combined with your report of having seen her wandering the halls..."

"What does the prince say?" Heph asks, trying to remember exactly what he told the council about seeing Katerina on the night of his assassination attempt. He hadn't wanted anyone to know about that night, to find out about him and Princess Cynane, and then leap to their own conclusions about Alexander's friend.

He had wanted to protect both girls' reputations by keeping their whereabouts a secret, but one of the palace guards had said he heard Heph talking in the halls—and a woman's scream—and Heph had been asked to file a report. He'd been tempted to lie, but he'd figured as long as he claimed to have seen only Kat, and far from his own chambers, she'd be safe from suspicion.

He'd been wrong.

"The prince doesn't know yet," Telekes replies. "He's on the other side of Pella. The Aesarian Lords are leaving, and he is seeing them off at the southern gate."

Leaving? At sunset *and* in pouring rain? That doesn't make any sense, either. Journeys are planned days in advance: horses are examined for good health, their hooves examined for cracks, their saddles and reins oiled by grooms. The traveling baskets tied to either side of the horses are carefully packed with supplies: food, water, wine, blankets, and oats. Journeys are embarked upon at dawn on a day that promises good weather.

The whole thing reeks.

Just like the beggar who was never in Heph's room.

"When will the queen question her?"

"Within the hour, my lord. And with the queen's methods of questioning—well, the prince's guest is unlikely to survive the night."

The prince's guest.

Heph knows what it is like to owe one's entire life to royalty's whim. It could easily be him one day, waiting as an innocent in the dungeon for the queen's arrival, with Alex unable—or unwilling—to do anything.

Now Heph pictures Kat shivering and scared in the dark, in the filth. *No,* Heph tells himself firmly. *Alex would never want his guest to be harmed while under his protection.*

Deep down, Heph feels a stir of determination he can't quite name—a fire in his gut that he knows isn't just linked to Alexander's wishes, but to the sparkling, tempermental peasant girl herself. She has a strange power over him, a power he finds both fascinating and loathful, the way she has strangely haunted his dreams and unnerved him...

As usual, when that fire sparks in his veins, he can do nothing but obey. He has to help her, even if he can't—and doesn't want to—understand exactly why. And if he's going to help her, he'd better do it now, because by the time the queen gets to her, it'll be too late.

Heph needs to get her out *now.*

And he knows a way.

Lighting an oil lamp from the one already lit on the table, Heph opens the door to the dungeon and makes his way down the winding stairs. It was ridiculously easy to get rid of the guard on duty. He told Heirax that Telekles wanted to see him about a disciplinary matter in the barracks. Telekles would keep him there for an hour at least, discussing infractions while on watch ranging from falling asleep to drinking to gambling to punching a fellow guard—all of them true.

At the bottom of the stairs, Heph grabs a resin-soaked torch from a wall sconce and lights it. There are several cells down here, each with its key on a hook next to the door. The stench hits him like a punch to the gut. It's a foul stew of accumulated death, decay, vomit, and feces. Trying not to retch, Heph holds the torch high and looks around. The stone walls ooze with something that looks and smells like pus—slimy and yellow. Anyone could easily die in such a place in a few days.

He knocks softly on the closest door. "Katerina!" he calls softly.

"Yes!" comes the instant reply. "I'm here!"

He thrusts the key in, hears the lock turn, and pushes the door open, cringing at the bloodcurdling scraping of the hinges. There, huddled on the floor against the wall, is Katerina.

"Hephaestion," she says, a smile lighting up her face.

He offers her a hand and she stands unsteadily. "Come with me," he says, pulling her out the door. "I can get you out of here."

"But how—"

"Hush."

He locks the door behind them and hangs the huge iron key on the hook beside it. Then, grabbing her by the hand, he says, "This way. I know a secret path out of the palace."

He leads her down a corridor to the right, past several other cells. It seems they have come to a dead end, but there's a waist-high wooden panel in the wall. Heph kneels and removes it. Beyond is a passage that angles sharply downward.

"Drainage if the dungeon cells are flooded," he says. "We'll have to crawl for a bit."

She nods.

Holding the torch, Heph crawls forward awkwardly, like a wounded animal dragging itself. Katerina scoots in and pulls the wooden panel into place behind her. The tunnel is barely tall enough for them to crawl on all fours. Heph feels closed in. Trapped. Unable to breathe. But it doesn't matter as long as he is getting Katerina to safety. Momentary doubts come to him as they make their way through the darkness. Will there be a manhunt triggered upon her release? Is he putting her in even greater danger? What about himself?

He may not have Alexander's intuition—or his authority—but he knows when he feels something is right or wrong. And though Kat has been everything from distracting to infuriating to mysterious to the enticing, maddening figure in his dreams, he believes her to be good. And Lord Bastian, he senses, is not. It's as simple as that.

The determination sending heat coursing through his veins right now is enough to keep him going, to stop the questions that surface before they unnerve him.

It's what Alexander has always called pride, or passion, or even hotheadedness. His greatest strength and his greatest weakness.

He crawls for an eternity, knees scraping dirt and grit. Finally he feels cool air ahead. At last, the end. He slips out of the tunnel and reaches back to help Katerina. Heph's torch casts eerie shadows on the damp stone walls of a spacious hallway.

"Where are we?" she whispers. Water trickles nearby.

"Storerooms beneath the old fortress of Alexander's forefathers," Heph says, gesturing to an open door. They peek in and he holds his torch high. Hundreds of empty amphorae lie at crazy angles. They are wider, more bulbous than other amphorae. Cobwebs festoon them like decorative draperies at a feast. The light from Heph's torch disturbs several huge black spiders, who creep sideways from their webs into the black open mouths of the amphorae.

"Quickly, we must hurry," he urges.

She nods. He takes her hand and they break into a run.

"Where are we going?" she asks, looking up.

"This corridor becomes another drainage channel, though

it's tall enough to walk upright in. Look, down here." The floor slopes sharply downward. "That was how they kept the storerooms dry in the old fortress," he explains, "by channeling the water down to the Axios River. Alex and I found this place years ago exploring down here. It's not used anymore. This tunnel has been completely forgotten."

They reach the end of the tunnel, and Heph sets his torch in a wall sconce. He pushes on an ancient wooden door that opens into tall bushes. Then he and Katerina fight their way through scratchy brush into a field that goes down to the river. It's stopped raining, and heavy clouds roll away from a glowing half-moon.

Katerina looks around in wonder and says, "I was here yesterday. Riding. I didn't know there was a door in the wall." She stares up at him questioningly. Moonlight shimmers silver in her hair. He wonders if she would taste of starlight if he kissed her. It would be so easy to reach out and trace her cheekbone, trail a finger down to her lips.

He leans forward but stops himself. Barely. *Never again*, he tells himself angrily. *Remember what happened with Cyn.* The restraint is physical, a battle within him. "Here," he says instead, his voice rough as he unbuckles his dagger and hands it to her. "You might need a weapon."

She slips the sheath onto her own belt and says, "Lord Bastian attacked me. I think he slipped the wolfsbane into my pouch to get rid of it, but I fear he was going to poison Alexander. You have to warn him."

Heph swears softly. "I will," he promises.

"And tell the prince...thank you. And goodbye."

"I will," Heph promises again. "But where will you go? Not Erissa. They will be looking for you there."

Kat's eyes flick around the dark night. "No, not Erissa," she says sadly, "but I have an idea."

Heph waits for her to continue, but she reveals nothing. At last he says, "At least you have your winnings."

She bites her lip and looks down. Only then does he notice she doesn't have the pouch on her belt. Of course she doesn't. No one would carry that much gold around with them. It's probably hidden somewhere in her room.

Heph sighs. "Where is it?" he asks. "I can find it and keep it for you. Get it to you later."

She shakes her head. "I gave it to Alexander. He needs it for...a special project."

Something slimy crawls from Heph's thoughts and into his chest. And for the second time that night, he thinks of Cyn. "I see. So you were working with Alex this whole time." He is shocked to find himself trembling. "You and Jacob and Alex rigged the tournament to get that money. *You're* the one who's so friendly with the hellion. Was it also you who let him into the arena to try to kill me?"

"What in Hades' name are you talking about?" Katerina says, sudden fire in her voice. "I don't know *how* the hellion got inside the arena, but even if it hadn't, Jacob *still* would have won. You're good with a sword, but you're not very inventive, are you? Strategy is not your strong point."

"My strategy just got you out of a dungeon," he retorts. She stares at him angrily, obviously ready to launch another insult. "Go," he says before she can say anything else and give away their cover. "Just go, Katerina."

And she does, slipping away silently into the silver shadows. A moonbeam hits the spot where she stood. It looks achingly empty.

CHAPTER TWENTY-THREE

"WHERE IS SHE NOW?" ALEX DEMANDS.

A cool breeze blows through the small bedroom window, and a shaft of moonlight breaks through ragged silver-edged clouds.

Heph, his hair tousled and tunic askew, sets his oil lamp down on the table and shakes his head. "I don't know. That's why I couldn't sleep."

"Maybe she went back to Erissa," Alex suggests.

"No, I told her not to go there. They'll be looking for her there."

Heph is right about that. As soon as Heirax informed the council that the prisoner escaped, Leonidas ordered soldiers to ride to Erissa the following day.

Alex crosses his arms over his chest. "Let me get this straight. Without saying a word to me, you helped my guest escape—after she'd been accused of carrying poison with her."

Heph bristles. "There was no time for plotting and discussing. I had to act."

"Alone?"

Heph rounds on him, eyes blazing. "Yes, alone! *You're* the one who's been telling everyone you're tired of me, that I'm like a weight around your neck. *You're* the one people are saying arranged for the hellion to be turned loose in the Blood Tournament to kill me. You told me you had no access to the royal treasury and that was why we must delay our travels. And maybe *you're* the one who actually did try to kill me in my bed and dropped *your* dagger on the floor. Is it really so surprising I prefer to do things alone now?" He slams his fist into the wall, winces and examines his bruised knuckles.

Alex feels as if Heph punched him instead of the wall. "I have no idea what you're talking about," he says angrily. "I never said I was tired of you. I had nothing to do with the hellion ruining the Blood Tournament. I *don't* have access to the treasury—you well know that! And someone stole my dagger from my clothing trunk. What kind of an idiot are you to accuse me of these things?" He feels his fists tighten. "Besides, *you're* the one who left the odeon when I was fighting Lord Bastian. Do you know how insulting that was? Could you imagine me leaving the Blood Tournament for a little game of *petteia* while you're out there fighting for your honor and your life?"

"That was Cyn," Heph says, massaging his sore hand. "She felt sick and asked me to walk her to her room. Otherwise I never would have left when you were fighting Lord Bastian. Never. Even with everything between us…changing."

Alex raises an eyebrow. "Cyn…" he says slowly. "I've never heard of Cyn being sick in her life, not even when everyone else in the palace had the sweating sickness. Have you?"

Heph thinks a moment, then shakes his head.

"And who told you that I was bored with you?" Alex persists. "That I set the hellion loose to kill you? That I had direct access to the treasury?"

Heph looks like a pig bladder with the air taken out of it. "Cyn," he whispers so low Alex hardly hears it.

"Cyn. Who was missing from her seat in the royal box during the tournament."

Heph's mouth opens and closes. "Yes." He says the word so quietly it's almost like an exhale.

Alex runs a hand through his hair. Cyn knew where he kept that dagger. She could have stolen it and put it on Heph's floor. "Did you really see the figure looming over you with the knife? Or did Cyn say she saw it?" Alex asks.

Grimacing, Heph just shakes his head again. Alex stares at the dark eyes trying to avoid his and sees—

What he sees makes him look away quickly.

So that's it. Heph and Cyn. Like *that*.

He clears his throat. "And you went into the wine cellar looking for an assassin, and killed the beggar," he says.

Heph hesitates, then says, "Yes." But Alex knows better. Cyn. Everything was Cyn's doing. Because of her interference, two innocent people are dead: the hunchback slave killed by the hellion, and the drunken beggar in the wine cellar. But at least now he knows what has been going on.

As for Cynane, he'll have to find the right punishment for her later...once he discovers her motives. For this was clearly more than a childish prank.

He feels the knots in his taut muscles relaxing as if Nikiforus, the royal masseur, was kneading oil into them with his massive hands. "Aristotle taught us to always look for the common denominator in any problem," he says. "Mathematical. Scientific. Political. Social. And it would seem that here the common denominator is..."

"Cyn," Heph replies softly.

Alex folds his arms and nods. "Cyn," he says.

But still Heph can't meet his eyes.

"Heph," Alex presses. "Why didn't you just tell me?"

His friend's face burns red. "I couldn't. I was ashamed of my...our relations. I—"

"It's your duty only to tell me the truth, at all times. If you're too proud to let me in, I cannot trust you. Do I have your word that it won't happen again?"

It's Heph's turn to nod, relief flooding his face. He finally looks at Alex, with fierceness in his eyes. "I swear it."

"Good," Alex says. "Because we simply can't risk anything—especially not the folly of pride—getting in our way." He can hear the words of Aristotle and Leonidas in his head as he says these words, and is surprised to realize how true they are.

"In any case," he goes on, "in addition to Kat's disappearance and Cyn's treachery, we have another problem. One that affects not only us but all of Pella. All of Macedon."

He looks out the small window at rooftops gleaming from the rain, then back to Heph. "Here's what I think. I think that Lord Bastian was out to kill me and the queen. He—or another Lord—had already slipped poison into my mother's breakfast. Luckily, Mother had a taster, though the poor girl is still unconscious. When the Lords realized their plans weren't working, Bastian slipped the poison into Kat's pouch and all the Lords left Pella."

"Yes," Heph replies, nodding. "That makes sense."

"It's so clear, isn't it, Heph?" Alex says. "The Aesarian Lords are our enemies. Where are they going? Why leave now? I saw them leave through the southern gate, but that doesn't mean anything. They could have doubled back and joined a camp nearby. There could be an entire army waiting to attack the city once they've poisoned me. Since their assassination plot didn't work, they are likely desperate."

"Maybe it's time to talk to the council again about the Lords," Heph suggests.

Alex shakes his head. "Someone in the palace—I think in the council itself—is in the pay of the Aesarian Lords. Yesterday after a council meeting, I found Arrhidaeus sitting under the table holding an extremely valuable Persian jewel. If anyone had obtained it honestly, worn it openly, and lost it, there would have been a frantic search. A large reward. But no one has even mentioned it."

Heph knots his brow. "It's more dangerous to have one enemy inside the palace than an army of thousands outside the walls."

"Correct. So we will have to get proof of an invasion without alerting the council of our plans, plans that the traitor could sabotage."

Heph considers. "How will you get it?"

"If there is an army near Pella," Alex says slowly, "it shouldn't be too hard to find, especially since High Lord Mordecai's group left in a rainstorm. All those horses and heavy wagons will have made deep ruts in the mud."

Heph nods. "It'll be easy to track them, I agree," he says. "But once we find them, they will kill us. And launch an immediate attack on Pella."

"We have to be stealthy," Alex says. He grins. "I think I will go hunting."

Heph stares for a moment, then grins back. "I haven't been hunting in several weeks," he says. "Perhaps we could track some sinister creatures with tall horns."

"The Lords will have scouts in the trees looking for any intruders," Alex says. "We need to create a diversion to distract the Lords while you and I—and General Kadmus, I think—do the reconnaissance."

Heph considers a moment. "Telekles," he says. "And Phrixos.

With that chubby, good-natured face, Phrixos can play a harm-less country bumpkin better than anyone."

"Good," Alex agrees. "A hunting party of five. Nothing threatening. We'll need to look like ordinary Pellans out for a ride. Borrow horses—they mustn't be from the royal sta-bles—and wear servants' clothing. If their scouts see us, they won't know who we are."

"I'll tell the men," Heph says, and Alex feels a surge of con-fidence. When he and Hephaestion are working in tandem again, nothing can stop them.

"We should be ready to leave at dawn."

Cantering out of the city's southern gate the next morning, Alex's spirits are high—almost as if he were going on the hunt-ing expedition they were outfitted for. A large straw basket on either side of Phrixos's saddle sways with the horse's gait. A flask of wine juts out of one, and Alex manages to maneu-ver his mare close enough to poke it back in without breaking stride. Bows and arrows clatter in Telekles's old leather pan-niers. All five men wear dusty patched cloaks and slouched felt hats and ride rather elderly swaybacked creatures who prefer nibbling at grass to racing across the fields.

As Alex suspected, it's easy to follow the tracks of the Aesarian Lords in the mud. Continuing on the main road, the hunters ride past the few houses and taverns outside the walls and negotiate their way around heavy crop-laden ox-carts plodding toward the city. The grass and trees stand tall from the past days' drenching rain, and the oppressive heat has lifted. The whole world smells clean.

After another couple of miles, the Aesarian Lords' tracks veer off the road and across a field. Now the hunters are fol-lowing grass crushed beneath hooves and wheels. The tracks curve slowly to the right until they head back the way they came: toward Pella.

Alex pulls his mount to a stop and the others pull up beside him. "They've turned back. Toward the city," he says, noticing something sticking out of the mud at his feet. He hops off his horse and picks it up. It's a badge from an Aesarian cape: a bronze lightning bolt about four inches long. He holds it up to Kadmus, who eyes it and grunts.

Alex scans the horizon—an army can't be camped too far from the road, heavy equipment would get stuck in the hidden quagmires these meadows are known for—and sees a thick band of trees in the distance. He knows the place from real hunting expeditions, and it's a good place to hide; there's a shallow depression beyond the trees where campfires and torches would be hidden from view.

Alex says, "They're in the field on the other side of those trees."

Kadmus turns to Phrixos and Telekles. "The three of us will go left, quietly, and once we disappear from sight, you two go right, making as much noise as you can to attract the attention of their scouts. You must appear harmless—unless you want arrows through your hearts. Don't go near the woods. If you see the camp, they will *have* to kill you or at least take you prisoner."

"Which they would do, reluctantly," Alex adds. "If you disappeared, your families would come out looking for you, and that's not what the Lords want. Their attack on Pella is based on complete secrecy."

Phrixos pulls a hunting horn from his saddle bag and laughs. "We will look to all the world like two fools chasing our dinner through the meadow."

Alex, Heph, and Kadmus dig their heels into their horses' sides and gallop to the left. After a time, they hear Phrixos's hunting horn and the excited cries of the two decoys chasing game. The other three men enter the band of trees and tie up their horses. Then, silently, they walk between birches and elms toward the bowl-shaped depression in the field beyond.

The smell of campfires and roasting meat wafts through the trees, along with gruff male voices and steady hammering. The three men pad silently to the other side of the trees and peer out.

Below is an enormous military camp, with at least two hundred men and dozens of campfires. As Alex watches, he sees a small regiment of travel-stained Lords on sweat-covered horses joining the ranks from the other side and knows that the Lords' numbers will only continue to swell. A makeshift forge has been set up where a blacksmith is hammering weapons. Alex sees wagons, their canvas coverings rolled back as men check the dismantled parts of siege engines, catapults, and battering rams. Others in small groups hone swords and polish armor.

It's enough, Alex knows, to besiege Pella for months.

An hour later, Alex is looking at the stunned faces around the table in the small council chamber, where he has just marched into an ongoing meeting, mud still covering his hunting attire. "The Lords will shortly attack Pella," he announces, nearly out of breath.

He has already decided on the way here: even if there is a traitor in this room, the only way to sniff out the mole will be to share what he knows—and see if there's a leak.

"And from the looks of their equipment, it seems they are prepared for a long siege," General Kadmus adds, entering behind him.

"We must propitiate the gods so this doesn't happen," says Gordias, his entire body shaking like a leaf. Alex knows he's old enough to remember Sparta's yearlong siege of Athens sixty years ago. When the food was gone, the Athenians ate all their horses and donkeys. Then their dogs and cats, and every insect, bird, or rat they could find. By the time the victors entered the gates, they found a silent city of walking skeletons gnawing on human bones.

Leonidas sits up sharply. "If this is true, we must send a messenger immediately to King Philip with word of this treachery. If he is not becalmed, his ships should be back here in less than a month, during which time we can ration food. We must bring in people and crops from beyond the walls before the Lords entrench themselves around the city. When Philip returns, he can attack their army from the rear."

"I saw their siege equipment with my own eyes," General Kadmus says, slamming his fist on the table in irritation. "Why permit catapults to fling death onto houses and temples and citizens? We should launch a surprise attack before they have time to set up their siege."

"Pella doesn't have enough men," Theopompus cuts in. "The king took most of them with him."

"We will have the element of surprise—" Kadmus begins.

"Let us not debate further. We must vote," Gordias says. It is a statement, not a suggestion.

"I vote for an attack as soon as we can call up the volunteers and prepare the men," Kadmus says, his voice filling the room.

This is followed by silence. Alex knows he needs two more votes.

"I vote against it," Leonidas says. "We have yet to confirm your suspicions and if you lose that battle, Kadmus, we will have no one to guard the walls or defend the city at all. Pella will quickly fall into Aesarian hands."

Alex's entire body practically shakes with fury. "The suspicions *are* confirmed. We're just back from the fields, and—"

"I agree with Prince Alexander," Gordias cuts in again,

with greater urgency now. "The Lords have broken the law of *xenia*, imposed by Father Zeus himself, who often visits people disguised as a beggar. If the guest and host treat each other well, they are both blessed. If one breaks this law, the gods punish him. Let us serve as the gods' instruments in punishing the sacrilegious Aesarian Lords."

Now Alex needs one more vote.

Theopompus turns to the minister of finance. "Hagnon?" he asks.

Hagnon flaps and twitters and plucks nervously at his robe. "I... I... We should do the safest thing—preserve Pella and all inside it," he says. "Rash decisions will always come back to haunt us. I agree with Leonidas. Let us send messengers to Philip immediately, then shut ourselves in and wait for the king and his army to rescue us. If catapults are raining stones down on us, we can live in our cellars and storerooms."

Two against two.

Theopompus has the tie-breaking vote. Alex tries to steel himself for failure. The minister of provisions will vote no.

Theopompus leans forward in his chair, his turquoise eyes bright. "You all know I stand for negotiation, conciliation, and friendship among nations," he says, his white teeth flashing in a way that makes him look wolflike. "But when so-called friends and allies plan an unprovoked attack, I say we crush them so thoroughly no ally of ours will ever consider such betrayal again. I think that even though we are outmanned, with the element of surprise we can still defeat them. Macedonians are too proud to hide in cellars."

Kadmus stands and claps Theopompus on the back. Gordias raises a translucent hand in blessing, while Leonidas and Hagnon sink deeper into their chairs.

"With all due respect to General Kadmus," Alex says, standing and pushing his chair back, "I will lead the troops."

"You are too young," Leonidas snaps before the word *troops* has fully left Alex's mouth. "You have never been to war before, my lord, other than some border clashes with cattle thieves. I hardly think they're on the same level as the Aesarian Lords, the best fighting force in the world. Let General Kadmus lead. At least he's been in *real* battles."

Looking at the pinched faces around the table, Alex feels his anger solidifying into something else.

Power.

"*I* am the heir to the throne of Macedon," he says. His penetrating gaze rests on one after the other, causing them each in turn to flinch. "*I* will be your next king. While you sat here and quibbled like crones, it was *I* who suspected the Lords' treachery and reconnoitered their camp. Without *me*, Pella would be under the Aesarian boot in a matter of days." He tosses the mud-caked Aesarian emblem onto the table. The bronze lightning bolt spins as it slides to a stop in front of Leonidas.

Kadmus stands up. "I will follow you, my Lord Prince, along with my men. And gladly."

There is a loud silence from the others, which Alex understands is a grudging assent.

"We will convene a council of war immediately," Kadmus continues. "Prince Alexander, Lord Hephaestion, let us go to the barracks and strategize. We must move quickly."

"But not *too* quickly," Alex counters. "The Aesarian Lords are known as fierce fighters, but their many allies across the land are both a benefit and a detriment. It will take them time to gather reinforcements. We can use that time to our advantage." He looks around the room. All the men are now nodding in agreement. "And there's one more thing. Let us acknowledge that Katerina of Erissa is innocent of trying to poison the royal family. It should now be clear that one of our treacherous guests—most likely Lord Bastian—had the vial of wolfsbane and slipped it into her pouch. Knowing her innocence, some god—" he studiously avoids looking at Heph "—must have helped her escape. I want her name cleared so she can return to Pella unmolested."

The five heads around the table nod.

As Alex and Heph walk past the training arena to the barracks, Phrixos and Telekles catch up with them. Phrixos waves a game bag. "Two rabbits!" he says.

"Yes, Phrixos's arrow actually hit its mark. For the first time ever," says Telekles. "Perhaps his eyes were shut this time."

Phrixos playfully shoves his friend away as Alex smiles in relief. "Did you see the Lords?" he asks.

"Oh, yes," Telekles says, "we saw movement in the trees. They watched us boast about the stew our wives would cook, but didn't make a move to stop us as we turned our horses around and headed back."

Alex nods. "That's what I thought. Thanks to you both, but before you enjoy that rabbit stew, go upstairs to Kadmus's office and join us for a council of war." The men nod and enter the barracks.

He turns to Heph. "The rabbits have given me an idea. One that traitor in the council—if there is one—needn't hear."

Heph raises an eyebrow.

"I've figured out the linchpin to our plan. High Lord Mordecai."

"What about him?"

"We will capture him. *Alive.* We need their highest-ranking man as a hostage. One who knows the workings of their precious torch. Why *its* destruction means they need to destroy *us.* It's our *petteia* stone."

Heph begins to protest. "But do we even need—"

Alex raises a hand. "Heph, this is but the first battle, of what may be many. This is simply our first strategic play."

Heph nods. "Very well."

Alex grins. "Though this isn't exactly traveling through Persia to find the Fountain of Youth, it's still going to be a good adventure. And I'm glad you're by my side, Hephaestion."

Heph grins back and clasps Alex's right shoulder. Alex knows that all the distance and awkwardness of the past couple of weeks is over. Their friendship is as strong as ever. A stab of pain runs through Alex's happiness as he realizes that even though Heph is back, Kat is gone. He will look for her as soon as he can. He will send scouts and messengers to every village in Macedon if need be, and if that fails, to every place in the Greek world.

But right now, he needs to plan a battle.

CHAPTER TWENTY-FOUR

KAT WAKES SUDDENLY, STIFF AND CRAMPED, BUT her senses at full alert. She cautiously stretches her leg—and almost tumbles out of the olive tree that had been her bed for the night. She rights herself quickly, and slowly kneads the pins out of her calves as she surveys the area. The river glimmers beneath her like a band of beaten silver in the dawn's pink-gray light. Herons swoop on insects and pluck out fish. Through the olive tree's branches, Kat can just make out a kestrel lazily circling the sky. It shrieks, and the sound pierces the morning air.

Kat feels her heartbeat return to normal as she realizes the kestrel's haunting cry must have been what roused her. Gingerly, she scrambles down the tree and moves to the riverbank. Her reflection no longer looks like that of a palace girl, but more like the Kat that first arrived in Pella—mud-splattered, with tangled hair. She scoops up clean water and splashes her face. Can it have been only two days ago that she escaped through the tunnels with Hephaestion?

She had told him she had an idea...and she wasn't completely lying. She wanted to go to Caria—her mother's birth-place—but she was too embarrassed by *why* she wanted to go there to admit her plan: that she wanted to learn more about magic. She thinks back to her increasing abilities with animals; the Flower of Life necklace and the *Blood Magics* scroll; and Helen's warnings to keep her special inclinations hidden. Events have surged to a crescendo, and now an urgency to know more throbs in her veins. For once there is something bigger than her vision of vengeance. Something greater to discover, to live for, to conquer. And besides, if Olympias is now suspicious of her, there's no way Kat will be able to fulfill her original plans at the moment. The best she can do is equip herself with knowledge.

She will go to Caria, a territory she knows lies on the southwestern shores of Persia, across the sea. And she will look for rumors of the sorceress, Ada, whom she read about in the library.

Except...how *can* she? She hardly knows her way around the outskirts of Pella, let alone how to find the port.

She feels her cheeks redden with frustration, and she quickly dunks her entire head into the coolness of the river. Surfacing, she flips her hair, sending droplets skyward.

She had been furious when Hephaestion accused her of cheating and diminished Jacob's victory. In a storm of pride and stubbornness, she refused to ask for directions toward Pella's port. *Reckless*, she can almost hear Sotiria scolding her. *As stubborn as Midas.*

And yet, it can't be that hard to find the port, can it? When the queen's new bolts of Egyptian linen trundled into the palace last week, Alexander told Kat that they had come on a ship that docked in the lake between Pella and the sea. Everyone knows the sea is toward the east. If she keeps following the river, she should be able to find it eventually.

Kat sits back on her heels. She knows she should be grateful—she could be dead, like Daphne, or stuck in that horrible prison cell forever, rotting away in darkness. Instead, she's free... But she's starving. Yesterday she ate only a handful of wild berries. Her stomach growls loudly in protest at its emptiness. And even if she finds the lake, she has no idea how to get to Caria from there. She can't return to Sotiria's house, not with the knowledge of how far Jacob has gone to try to prove himself to her—so far as to swear fealty to the Aesarian Lords. She can't return to the palace—she's a suspected assassin. She's all alone.

The kestrel silently glides down and perches on a nearby log. *Well*, Kat thinks ruefully, *not* all *alone*.

The kestrel stares at her with surprising intensity. With a flap of its powerful black-and-tan-speckled wings, it swoops downstream, toward the Aegean Sea, turns around, and flies right back, closer to her, perhaps a yard from her face, and stares at her again.

Its eyes are as dark, round, and hard as ripe elderberries, and a band of yellow brightens the bridge of its neat, curved gray beak.

Follow me.

It's talking. In language. Not *out loud*, exactly, but in her mind she seems to know what it wants.

Just like the gazelle. Twice now in the same month, and with so much clarity. Kat's always had a connection with animals, but they've never sounded so...*human* before. Her green eyes lock on to its black ones. Then she drops her gaze. Who is she to question a sign? After two weeks in the palace, she has failed at every effort to discover the secrets of Helen's disappearance. Perhaps the gods are frustrated with Kat and are sending a bird to lead her to answers she's too stupid to find for herself.

"All right," she says aloud. "I will."

The kestrel leads Kat on a continuing path east, into the rose-gold warmth of the rising sun. The walk is pleasant. Jewel-colored dragonflies buzz about the river reeds, and minnows dart through the shallow water. Eventually they reach a hill, and Kat's stomach rumbles again as her muscles strain upward. The kestrel circles back, seemingly insisting that she move quickly. "Palace life must be making you soft," she mutters to herself as her legs begin to burn.

At the hill's crest, Kat looks down on a round sapphire-blue lake. Across the water, a frowning cliffside fortress hovers above it like a low dark cloud. At the foot of the hill, Kat sees eight bobbing vessels bump against wooden piers, their sails snapping in the breeze. Men clatter up and down wobbling gangplanks bringing cargo on board while others climb the rigging as nimbly as if they were spiders moving about their webs.

The port.

The kestrel flies above the ships in a wide circle, diving gracefully toward the mast of one before veering sharply and drifting upward as it catches a current. It seems Kat has found a ride.

The sun pricks at Kat's skin even through the protective awning, and she takes a sip of wine, trying to calm her frantic pulse. Seated next to old Demetrias, she breathes in the fresh air as *The Siren* sails down the river toward the sea, hoping it will calm her and give her the courage she needs. The mermaid figurehead bobs ahead, naked breasts thrust boldly forward, blond hair streaming behind, and a long blue fish tail that ends just about the ship's eyes. All the ships have large blue eyes painted on either side of the prow so the spirit of the ship can see its way through the waters and safely reach land.

The ship is about a hundred feet in length with a comfortable well-rounded line. Two sailors scrambling up the rigging unfurl the red-and-white-striped sail at the top of the main mast, while two others position a matching square sail at the very back of the ship.

"Hey now, Kat! Demetrias." She turns to Captain Fotis striding across the merchant's coop toward her. Again, she is struck by his eyes. A pale gray, they look like chunks of ice and contrast strangely with his weathered face. His brown hair is streaked with sun, his body muscular and lithe. Kat can't tell if he's twenty-five with old skin or forty-five with a young body.

Captain Fotis walks past her to inspect the ropes lashing the lumber together—and the entire heap of it to the mast. If the knots come loose in rough seas, the precious logs destined for Persia could seriously injure both crew and passengers. Macedonian timber, Kat knows, is prized in the Persian Empire. It's not as expensive as the magnificent cedars of Lebanon, but a great improvement over the scrubby, scraggly trees of most satrapies. When Erissan landowners want to clear their woods to grow crops, their trees usually end up in Persia. Satisfied with the ropes, the captain returns to the steering paddle, his eyes sweeping across the horizon.

Kat is grateful to Captain Fotis. Not many would allow an unaccompanied young girl onto their ship, even if she had paid far more than the actual price of passage. The cost had been Heph's dagger—a beautiful weapon stylized in the shape of a gold horse's head, its mane a curl of silver, its eye a glowing brown topaz. It was far more than a weapon—it was a finely crafted, incredibly expensive work of art. Seeing it pass into the captain's weathered hands, Kat had felt a pang of guilt. She'd treated Heph badly. He was right. Without him, she would be rotting in a jail cell at this very moment instead of sailing toward Caria for answers.

Kat takes a swig of water and another of wine before pouring more for Demetrias, the old man with a curling beard and a kind face, who very much resembles Jacob's great-uncle Epistor back in Erissa. He, too, liked to tell stories. She tears off a hunk of smooth, pale yellow cheese, slaps it on a piece of thick wheat bread and bites into it. The captain has even given her leftover cold meat from last night's dinner at the port tavern—lamb on the bone.

"Have some lamb," she says to Demetrias. The old man smiles and shoves his dish of figs her way.

"Eat quick, before Leukas swipes them," he says, eyeing the barefoot sailor swinging down from the ropes like a monkey. "He's known to have a criminally sweet tooth."

He grins, his warm dark eyes looking like two raisins on a scarred leather bag.

"How do you know so much about everyone on the ship?" Kat asks. So far Demetrias has told her that Captain Fotis has three wives in three different ports who don't know about one another, and that one of *The Siren*'s sailors was told by an oracle that he was fated to die on land so he never left the water, even when in harbor during a terrible storm.

"I was a sailor myself for thirty years," he says, looking wistfully at the sea. "But once you're in your forties, your bones ache and your vision blurs. You can't spot land on the horizon. You can't lift as much cargo anymore or climb the rigging as fast. So I saved my money and bought a bee farm in the hill country of Macedon. I have fifty jugs of honey belowdecks."

Demetrias opens a small flagon and drizzles some honey on her bread. It is a shining clear amber color and the morning sun sparkles through it as it falls onto the bread.

"My honey is highly valued by the nobles of Caria. I should

make a good profit," Demetrias says, lazily stretching out his wrinkled brown legs and waggling his toes. "I could afford the cabin, but I like sleeping on deck, waking to see the glint of starshine on water, just like I used to."

"How long does the journey last?" Kat pictures heaving seas tossing the ship, lightning striking the mast, and loose tree trunks rolling about and crushing everyone on deck.

Demetrias shrugs. "Depends on the weather. If it stays fair, we should reach land tomorrow."

Kat cranes her head and is relieved to see the kestrel gliding alongside the ship.

With her stomach full and the coop's gentle rocking, Kat slips into a deep sleep, though her dreams are full as ever of bones and ash, of Daphne convulsing and foaming at the mouth before her eyes. Of Jacob reciting his oath to the Aesarian Lords. Of Olympias's sinister green eyes when she realized she was being spied on, that night Kat stood precariously on her balcony, watching her.

When she wakes the sun is high overhead and the decks are wet with spray. She quickly sits upright and sees more water than she has ever seen in her life at one time. She squints, trying to get her bearings, feeling as though the world has changed while she slept, and she may no longer belong in it. "Is this the Aegean Sea?" she asks Demetrias.

"No," he says, chuckling. "It's the Thermaic Gulf. Do you see that thin green strip of land on the horizon? That's Sithonia. There are three peninsulas reaching like fingers toward the Aegean. They are all still part of Macedon."

Macedon. She thinks of Alexander, for whom she has come to care greatly in such a short amount of time. And Hephaestion, who has mostly baffled and annoyed her, but who came to her rescue when no one else did. She thinks of his curls and his seriousness and strong jaw and his pride, the last of which she sensed when she first met him and has teased him about at every opportunity. It hasn't occurred to her until now, as the water pushes her farther and farther away from Pella and her brief life in the palace, how much she herself has changed.

A couple hours later the water becomes choppy, the color of slate. And the land disappears entirely from view.

"The Aegean," Demetrias says, sighing with satisfaction.

Kat settles easily into the lazy rhythm of ship life, enjoying the clear night sky and the morning's sunrise. She listens eagerly to the many stories Demetrias shares about the islands they pass. Some are full of whitewashed houses on sloping hills while others are just blue lagoons and vineyards. When Demetrias points out Chios, Kat hurries over to the side of the boat so as to better see Homer's birthplace and the home of the finest wine in the world. Shortly after, they pass Samos, a rich island covered with emerald-green trees and two large mountains in its center. King Philip's palace has some precious Samian marble, red streaked with gold. The huge harbor bristles with masts close together like the quills of an enraged porcupine.

By midafternoon they approach Halicarnassus, Caria's port city. At first Kat can't see the harbor, only white marble breakwaters curving far into the water from the right and left like a mother's protective arms. On the hill beyond, she sees an enormously tall white building, which looks as if some god has perched a many-pillared temple on top of a one-hundred-foot-tall rectangular plinth of gleaming white marble. Bronze statues of human figures stand between the columns and around the edges of the steeply pitched red roof. On the top a bronze chariot pulled by four horses shines like fire in the sunlight.

"What's that?" she asks, pointing at it.

"A wonder of the known world—the Mausoleum," Demetrias says. "Built by Queen Artemisia as a tomb for her husband, King Mausolus. Can you see the two figures in the chariot on top? That's the king and queen. Artemisia's grief was so intense at the death of her husband that she drank a potion of his bones and ashes to have something of him inside her. When she died, her ashes were laid next to his. That structure is a poem in stone to love and loss."

Kat thinks of her own love and loss. Her mother. Her family in Erissa. Jacob. Alexander. Surprisingly, there's even a twinge for Hephaestion. She doesn't know how she will ever see any of them again. But she can't think about that now.

As the ship edges between the two breakwaters, Kat can hardly believe her eyes. She has never seen any town so huge. So colorful. So rich. So alive. It makes Pella look insignificant, and Erissa nonexistent.

"Do you see?" Demetrias asks. "The harbor is nearly circular. It's like the floor of a theater. And the hills rising around it are the seats." He casts a worried look at the dozens of ships in the harbor—mostly merchant vessels, but also some fishing boats and two gaudily painted Persian military triremes—and says, "Now we have to hope we can find a berth, or we might have to wait until tomorrow to dock."

Fortune smiles upon *The Siren*, and an hour later, Kat finds herself on firm land, surrounded by fruit peddlers and money changers with strange foreign currency. "Come," Demetrias says. "It will be a while before the Persian officials arrive to inspect my honey. We can wait in my favorite tavern."

Kat is tempted—the chance to explore the wonders of Caria, to examine the wide gold collars of coral and turquoise sold by the Egyptian merchants and copper ingots from Rhodes—but above the noise of the docks, she hears the shriek of a kestrel. She looks up, and Demetrias follows her gaze.

"She has followed us from Macedon," Demetrias says, squinting up at the circling bird of prey. "I have never seen a falcon follow a ship before. Their prey is on land or on shore, but never in the middle of the sea." He lowers his gaze. "She's here for you, isn't she? Guiding you?"

After a pause, she says, "I think so."

He chuckles. "Maybe it's the great enchantress Ada herself," he says, "who lives in a secret fortress in the mountains up there." He gestures past the Mausoleum. "At least, that's the legend." He kisses Kat gently on the forehead and slips her a few silver drachmas. "May the gods go with you," he says, before disappearing into the crowd.

In the marketplace, Kat buys a goatskin water bag, a waterproof pack, and a dozen hard-boiled eggs. She has no idea how long she will be walking; that depends on the falcon. To be on the safe side, she adds dates, figs, and pickled herring wrapped in thick leaves, a loaf of hearty brown bread, and a bag of walnuts.

Then, thinking about the sailors' wrinkled skin, she purchases a *petasos*, a wide-brimmed felt hat popular with travelers. Kat never minded the sun before; a golden tan looked healthy and attractive, but speckled, wrinkled skin is a different matter altogether. If Kat tightens the adjustable chin strap of the *petasos*, she can secure the hat against sun, wind, or rain. In pleasant weather, if she loosens the strap all the way, the hat hangs down her back and won't get lost.

The falcon glides up the wide central road of the city, and she follows it past shops selling dazzling displays of jewelry, gilt sandals, fine armaments, and embroidered cloth. Every time she stops to stare, the bird flies back and utters a piercing cry, urging her forward. She fills her goatskin in a cool fountain where veiled women draw water in polished jugs, and makes her way past marble statues commemorating the city's great men and women. Halfway up the hill, she is confronted by the Mausoleum. She cranes her neck to look up at it.

A poem in stone to love and loss.

Her stomach twists, and she quickly skirts the Mausoleum and walks past a large bath complex. In the front courtyard, men carrying towels and flasks of oil turn to stare at her and one of them whistles appreciatively. She hurries past a Greek temple to Ares next to an Egyptian temple to a god called Osiris. As she passes walled homes—palaces, really—she hears the mournful cries of peacocks in the trees.

At the very top of the road, next to the gate, a Greek theater is carved into the hill. Kat looks up to see steeply rising marble benches. She turns and looks back down at the city, the circular harbor shining in the sun, the silver-blue stretches of water beyond the curving white stone breakwaters and dark gray humpbacked islands in the distance.

And then she sees the kestrel circling overhead. It tilts its broad speckled wings and flies directly over the square double towers of the city gate that leads toward the mountains beyond.

She follows it through the gate and up the winding, over-grown path, enjoying the sweet scent of wild thyme and sage crushed beneath her feet. She climbs upward as the ground falls away to her left, revealing a deep valley with rows of fig and olive trees.

The kestrel cries harshly, urging her forward onto a path so steep she can't climb it without grabbing on to rocks and sap-lings along the way. Her calves scream in pain, and her breath comes in ragged gasps. A sturdy branch lies across her path; she picks it up and uses it as a staff, plunging it into the ground to keep her balance. She hears water and finds that the path runs parallel to a twisting stream and countless small waterfalls. She pauses on a ledge to fill her goatskin again and drinks deeply from it. The late afternoon sky is cloudless and the hard, bold blue of lapis lazuli. The air up here is pure and cool; there is a kind of ecstasy to it.

Panting, she comes to a wide waterfall about twenty feet high, splashing into an oval basin. The bird flies behind the shimmering curtain of light and water and disappears.

Kat reaches the side of the waterfall and sees there is a space about two feet wide where she can step behind the sheets of water. Cold droplets spray her face as she skirts the tumbling wet wall and finds herself in a cave. Rippling reflections of light through water glimmer and shift on the walls. The sound of the rushing deluge echoes so loudly it is almost deafening. The kestrel is nowhere to be seen. She can only assume it has flown through an opening at the back of the cave.

Cautiously, she enters, expecting to find herself sinking into darkness, but torches light the way along the winding corridor. Whoever is here, they are expecting her. She continues upward for what seems like a mile. Sometimes other tunnels branch off to the right and left, but only one path is lit by torches, their dancing flames beckoning her onward. Whispers echo off the walls around her, words, snatches of conversation that she can't quite make out. *They were all devoured— The evil has awakened— When the true warrior comes...* The words bounce around her and seem to lodge inside her head. Dizzy from the noise, she puts her hands to her ears, wanting only to curl up in a ball and make it stop.

But she presses on. She can't stop now. Maybe all her questions will be answered at the end of this tunnel. Every mystery solved. A path of action made clear.

Finally she emerges from the dark heaviness of the rock into a huge torch-lit room. She thinks she hears a whisper, *She's here...here...here...*but wonders if it's only in her imagination.

When her eyes adjust, she sees thousands of small glowing jewels—*eyes*—staring at her from the shadows. It takes her a moment to understand they are all birds of prey perched on silver bars protruding from the walls. Some of them impatiently nibble feathers while others lazily stretch their wings, but all are intently aware of her.

A spot of blackness on the floor before her ripples and grows. Heart hammering, Kat steps back. It rises like a black marble column and becomes a woman in a gown of black-and-white feathers and a matching headdress, the feathers fanning out behind her head.

"Finally," the woman says in a rich, warm voice, "you have arrived."

ACT FIVE:

BATTLE

You will never do anything in this world
without courage. It is the greatest quality
of the mind next to honor.

—Aristotle

Chapter Twenty-Five

THE WIND PICKS UP, BLOWING JACOB'S HAIR back from his face as his horse gallops down the road toward Pella. The moon hasn't risen yet, and the stars' shine, while dazzling in the sky, does little to light the path. It wasn't easy to take a horse and leave the battle camp without the Aesarian night watch noticing. Timaeus used his slingshot to make the guards run in one direction, looking for intruders or spies, while Jacob bolted in the other direction and untied the horse.

He's risking everything, but he has no choice. Three days ago, the Lords suddenly departed Pella in a driving rainstorm without telling Jacob or Timaeus where they were headed. About five miles from the city they left the road and turned around completely, heading back toward town. Behind a wooded hill, they all arrived at a camp where some hundred men had already set up tents and dug latrines. At first, Jacob wondered why there were far more tents and latrines than men, but his questions were answered the next morning.

At daybreak, the first reinforcements arrived sporting the intricate tattoos of the north. By noon, more Aesarian Lords had joined the camp. Some had accents from the east, while others spoke with a southern lilt, but all came with wagons loaded with siege equipment. Each hour, the pile of weapons—spears, arrows, swords, shields, and missiles—grew as if the blacksmith god, Hephaestus, and his metal giants were producing them in his Olympian forge.

There are enough weapons to easily slaughter hundreds of Macedonian soldiers.

Thousands of Macedonian civilians.

Ever since the conversation he overheard at the palace, Jacob has known that the Lords will stop at nothing to root out the evil magic there. But when Jacob asked Lord Bastian about their new mission, the reply was much as Jacob had expected and feared: "New recruits follow orders. They don't ask questions. But be assured that what you do is honorable, right, and will save the world from a fate worse than Lycaon's. We seek out those with blood magic in order to cleanse the world of their evil."

Jacob shuddered as he remembered the story of the prideful, violent king who dared to serve Zeus human flesh, and was punished by being turned into a wolf while Zeus slayed his fifty sons with lightning bolts.

The rise and fall of kingdoms has never really interested Jacob. He's a soldier now, sworn to follow the orders of his superior Aesarian Lords. He won't betray his brothers by alerting the Macedonians of their plans. After all, the dark magic he witnessed himself during the induction ceremony was enough to prove to him that an evil does lurk within the palace, and should be extinguished. He can't shake the disturbing image of Lord Acamas, the Hemlock Torch bearer, and the pile of ashes he so quickly became.

No, he won't betray their plans.

But he *will* get her out.

Kat.

Urgency throbs through his entire body, and he longs to explode through woods and fields, crash through the gates, swing Kat up onto the horse, and ride far, far away to a place with no princes, fatal torches, or crows. Frustration wells up inside him, and when his horse stumbles, nearly knocking Jacob to the ground, he feels like a catapult spring ready to release.

Maybe this isn't even necessary, he tells himself, trying hard to calm down. The word in camp today was that the Macedonians had increased their watch day and night. The town gates no longer yawn open while the guards play dice. They are only partially open during the day, the soldiers checking all men for Aesarian brands and all carts for hidden weapons. Today the Aesarian Elder Council, their invasion plans thwarted, met for hours in High Lord Mordecai's tent, and sometimes loud voices rang out in anger.

Diligently splitting wood nearby, Timaeus overheard that the camp will move to a defensible position near a mountain pass a few miles away, and any attack on Pella will wait while reinforcements arrive from the west. And that Lord Bastian is in trouble for failing in his attempt to poison Queen Olympias—because a girl stopped him, forcing him to frame her and flee. Now Bastian's attempt has alerted the Macedonians to danger. He's had serious warnings from the Elder Council that his position within the brotherhood will remain tenuous until he can come up with a brilliant plan for invasion.

The way Bastian stormed around camp all evening, ready to punch anyone who happened to walk in front of him, Jacob is fairly certain he can't come up with one. Maybe the town is invulnerable, and Kat isn't in any danger.

But he can't take that chance.

A half mile outside of town, he ties his horse to a tree and runs the rest of the way past a few dark houses and shops. Tiptoeing between rows of strung-up cucumber vines in a vegetable garden, Jacob hears the furious barking of a dog, which is, mercifully, chained to a post. Jacob ducks as its owner throws open the shutters and curses.

As usual, the portcullis of the main city gate is down for the night, but something is off, different from Jacob's nights on the walls: they are populated. The turrets on either side bristle with armed men, their bronze helmets glowing amber in the light of cressets. He creeps closer and squints. That one, with the quiver and bow slung over his shoulder, must be Telekles. No other soldier would have long gold hair streaming behind his helmet like a horse's mane. A burly man with a battered face leans his spear against the wall, removes his helmet, and runs a hand over his grizzled head. Diodotus.

Jacob inhales sharply. These are men who know him. Who would recognize him as an Aesarian Lord. The fact that he's left his horned helmet and black cape in his tent won't fool them at all if they catch him.

With a growing sense of alarm, Jacob looks at the large bell hanging from the inner wall of the gate. Its curving brass reflects the torchlight—it's been polished recently. The Lords were right. The town is on high alert.

And somewhere within its walls walks the one thing he cares about more than anything else, completely unaware of the harm that might come to her.

He circles the city wall looking for trees close by that he could climb, but there aren't any, just thick bushes and spindly saplings. And then, at the rear of the palace wall along the riverbank, he sees a young tree that he could climb up perhaps as far as fifteen feet, if he balanced his weight carefully. Above that point, he thinks he makes out uneven bricks in the wall—shadows in the starlight, really—but maybe they are bricks he could cling to and use as a foothold to haul himself up. It is a chance. The only chance he has to save Kat.

He pulls himself up the tree as far as it will hold him. Then he sweeps his right hand across the pitted surface of the bricks and grabs hold of one jutting out of the wall. As he lifts himself up, his left foot slides up and down until it, too, finds a narrow ledge. He feels like a blind insect crawling perilously high, an insect without wings. If he falls now, he will break his legs or his back. He can't think about it. He doesn't look down.

The outstretched fingers of his right hand find a new brick to grab, and his foot another one over there—too far to the left to be comfortable—so that he is almost spread-eagled. He looks up. Maybe only another ten or twelve feet to reach the top. He can make it. He's almost there. He raises his right hand…

Below him a branch cracks sharply and footsteps echo through the night. He freezes, clinging to the wall like moss.

Voices drift toward him on the cool air.

"Mosquitoes," says a man directly beneath him, as Jacob hears the resounding slap of a hand against skin. "I've never had so many blithering mosquitoes on night watch before."

"That's because we never had to watch these fields before," says his companion in a low, gruff voice. "And those recent rains turned them into a swamp. A mosquito breeding ground. They don't bother me, though."

Jacob twists his head to the right and looks down. Panic slices through him as he realizes how far up he is. Below him are two soldiers. They have no torches, but he can make out their crested helmets and what looks like an alarm bell rolled out on wheels. What the second soldier said was true. This riverbank wasn't part of the night watch when Jacob was on it. Why is it now? There's nothing to guard back here.

His fingertips, grasping the corners of the jutting bricks, are starting to ache.

The first one sighs. "I guess you smell too bad for them to like you, Haemon. I'm going to be itching and scratching for days."

"You see? There are advantages to not bathing," Haemon chuckles.

"Except the girls run from you as if you were a pile of sheep's dung. Which you smell like."

"Not always. Last week I had that pretty waitress…"

Jacob focuses on leaning in. The slightest relaxation outward would send him hurtling to the ground. He puts his forehead against the wall, his shoulders screaming.

"…that one was pretty, but not as pretty as that peasant girl the prince was so taken by."

Jacob lifts his head and wonders… No. There must be numerous girls Alexander has flirted with.

"You mean the girl who's the reason behind this stupid new night shift? You're the tenth person to mention her tonight! If she isn't more tempting than Helen of Troy, change the subject because I'm sick of hearing about her."

"Tempting? She's more beautiful than any of the palace ladies! *Bountiful*, if you know what I mean. If I'd known she was going to escape prison, I might have first had a taste of her."

The guard must have swatted at Haemon, because Jacob hears a soft *thud*, followed by a yelp.

"What? I have a taste for country girls!"

"Well *I* would have at least searched her. I heard she escaped wearing some sort of flower necklace. Heirax said it looked valuable."

Stunned, Jacob nearly falls. A flower necklace? It must be Kat they're talking about!

Kat who escaped.

Kat who caused the prince to order extra guardsmen at this part of the wall.

It all makes a certain kind of sense. And yet he hardly knows what to think. Kat—*his Kat*—was imprisoned, and has fled!

"Did you hear something?" Haemon asks.

"When do I not hear something on watch? Owls, rodents, bats, you farting…"

Jacob is surprised they can't hear his heart, which is pounding like a war drum. He takes a deep, silent breath to clear his mind.

What was Kat doing in the dungeon? Could she have been the girl Bastian framed with poison? But no matter what, at least she is safe from the invasion. Wherever she is, she will not be a battle prize. She will not be sold, tortured, raped, or killed. She will not starve to death in a siege.

Jacob's fingers are starting to grow numb from clutching the edges of the bricks so tightly. In a few minutes he won't be able to feel them at all. Slowly, carefully, he flexes his right hand and then his left. That's a bit better, but now his legs are starting to cramp. His back and shoulders are straining to keep close to the wall.

Something flaps clumsily toward him and lands near his right hand. It's small and black with beady eyes.

A bat. Jacob has always had a wild fear of bats, even though he knows they're harmless. It inches closer to his hand, making a little squeaking noise. A part of Jacob wants to let go and fall backward just to avoid the creature. He can't seem to get his breath; if he gulps in air the way he wants to the soldiers below will hear him. Sweat pours off his face, trickles down his back. Part of him wants to laugh. Here he is, the winner of the Blood Tournament, terrified of a four-inch blind mouse with wings.

Directly below him, one of the guards pushes away shrubs

in front of the wall. Jacob hears creaky hinges and, looking down, sees a golden glow of light. There must be a torch in the tunnel.

"I don't know about you," says Haemon, "but I'm not crawling back through that little tunnel when our relief comes."

With a groan, the door slams shut. "I hate small spaces. I'm going to walk around town and go in the main gate like a human being, rather than slithering on my belly like a snake."

The guards' voices grow fainter as they continue their patrol. The bat is now inches from Jacob's hand. When they are out of earshot, he flicks it away, and it spirals into the air, squawking loudly at the rejection.

Jacob begins the laborious process of climbing down. He knows where the uneven bricks are—that part is easy—but his limbs are stiff and sore and almost numb from holding that uncomfortable position for so long. And they're slick with nervous sweat. When his right hand reaches for the brick he knows is there, it slips, and he's hanging from his left hand, swinging high in the air, until his left foot finds its perch.

Finally, he reaches the tree and swings to the ground. He creeps back through the bushes, around the city wall, and down the main road toward the grove where he left his horse. Relief courses through his body as he rides back to camp. The sound of the mare's hooves on the road seem to say, *Kat is safe, Kat is safe, Kat is safe.*

He's so distracted it takes him a moment to recognize a second set of hooves thundering toward him in the darkness. No, several sets of hooves. Have the Macedonian guards seen him? Why are they coming toward him, not chasing him from behind? He turns his horse to the right, kicking her hard, and gallops across a field as his heart hammers in his chest. He *can't* be arrested by the Macedonians. But the hooves are coming closer, and a man cries, "Halt if you value your life!"

If he doesn't pull up, he will feel an arrow or spear piercing his back.

His head spinning with the horror of what awaits him, he reins in his horse as four shadowy men on horseback surround him.

Bastian pulls up first and grabs the reins of Jacob's horse so violently the animal whinnies and tries to rear up, nearly sending Jacob hurtling to the ground. The others approach: Ambiorix, his long blond braids gleaming silver in the starlight; Turshu, his bow legs wrapped so tightly around the horse's belly they seem to be part of it; and Timaeus. Jacob looks from face to face. It's not as bad as being captured by Macedonians. But almost.

"Betraying us to the enemy?" Bastian asks. "The Aesarian sentence for treachery in our ranks is the slowest, most painful death."

Jacob knows what that is. The Lords told him and Timaeus about it in their training: being skinned alive in such a skillful way that the victim lives—for a time—without any skin at all, as a mass of exposed fat and muscle and bone.

"A moment!" Timaeus says, pulling his horse up next to Jacob's. "I thought it was the Aesarian way to hear a man out before condemning him."

"Very well," Bastian says. "Tell us, *Lord* Jacob, why you secretly left our camp tonight and we find you coming *back* from Pella? You were under strict orders to remain in camp after dark."

"I am new, my Lord, and have much to prove," Jacob says, trying to keep his voice calm and slow when it wants to slide into a terrified squeak. "My family is poor, my father a potter. I feel the weight of my upbringing on my shoulders."

Bastian's face remains a cool stone mask. Jacob knows he should slow down, but cold sweat drips down his face as he pictures himself pinned between two posts, a man-shaped blob of pulsating, bloody muscle. He hears himself ramble, "I seek only honor. I want to prove myself to the Brotherhood—earn your respect and earn my place."

"Your place is in a grave," Bastian says, handing the reins of Jacob's horse to Turshu and sliding his sword out of its hilt with a scraping whisper.

"Give the boy a chance, Bastian," Ambiorix says, his horse shuffling a bit too close to the others and then stepping backward. "I remember an ambitious recruit who risked his life against orders and has a scar on his face as proof. Go on, Jacob."

"I heard in camp today that the Macedonians increased the watch and searched everyone entering town," Jacob explains. "I knew the Elder Council was meeting to find a solution. I wanted to help, to reconnoiter the city defenses at night." He wonders if he is babbling, if he sounds stupid. Even worse, if he sounds guilty.

"We have already done that," Bastian says, rolling his eyes. "We have studied every gate, every tower, the weapons, the men, the equipment, horses, and training. We did this while we were still guests of the king, and since we left our spies have continued to do so. Do you think we're fools?"

Jacob shakes his head. There is one thing he can say to save his life: the information he has that Bastian sorely needs to keep his honor and his place on the Elder Council. "Not at all, my lord. But I learned of a way into the palace complex itself, by the northern wall."

"There is no northern gate of Pella," Turshu interrupts. "There are no roads there, just the fields that flood often. There's only a sheer wall."

"There are tunnels that lead from the outside directly into the palace," Jacob says. "There is a door hidden behind the shrubs that leads through ancient drainage tunnels up to the jail."

Jacob watches Bastian's face. The Lord doesn't speak, but he seems to be listening. Jacob rushes on, "Right now that door is guarded by two men. From my time in the guard, I know there are probably two more men up in the jail where it ends."

Lord Bastian considers a moment as his horse snorts and shifts its weight impatiently from side to side. "Tell me, can we take horses in the tunnel?" he asks. "An entire invading force?"

Jacob shakes his head. "No, my lord. The two guards I overheard said that men have to crawl on their bellies through it."

Lord Ambiorix moves the reins from one hand to the other and says, "The Elder Council must know of this."

"Yes," Bastian agrees. He tilts his head back and studies Jacob with shrewd dark eyes. "You will join us, Lord Jacob. You have done well." Turshu releases Jacob's mare's reins, and Jacob kicks the horse into an easy canter.

Kat is safe. He's impressed his brothers. He should feel alive with joy, but as he rides away from the palace and toward camp, he can't help but wonder if he's just sentenced an entire city to death.

CHAPTER TWENTY-SIX

CYN SITS IN ALEX'S FAVORITE CHAIR BY THE flickering light of a dozen lamps until, at last, she hears her half brother's footsteps echo in the hall outside his room. She knows they are his footsteps because there is a tiny hesitation just before he puts his left foot down, all that's left of the limp he works so hard to hide. No one notices it.

Except for her.

The door opens and Alex enters holding a lantern, its ox-horn panel raised. The flames inside reflect off the gold rosettes of his leather scabbard, making them twinkle in the dim light. Cyn stiffens. He never used to wear a sword around the palace. He also never used to patrol with the guards until the early hours of the morning.

He looks like he has barely slept in days, and the effect is, she hates to admit, powerful. He seems older. Stronger. More serious.

"I thought you were a divine visitation of the goddess Athena," he says calmly. Cyn is dressed for war with leather combat boots laced up to her knees, a military skirt of leather lappets, a bronze breastplate carefully molded with lifelike breasts, and a black crested helmet. Her sword is buckled around her waist, and her dagger hides in her boot. Her battle shield leans against the tortoiseshell table next to her chair. "If you went to Athens like that, sculptors would pay you a fortune to pose for them."

He sets his lamp on the table beside her and tilts his head. "It's unusual for you to visit me. When was the last time? Was it five years ago when I caught you putting a dead rat in my bed? Though you were here more recently, I think. Stealing my phoenix dagger."

For a painful moment, anger and embarrassment wash over her like a poisonous tide, leaving her feeling burned and gasping. Alex knows. Which means Heph knows.

"I don't know what you're talking about," she says, standing, glad that she's as tall as Alex and can look straight into his strange-colored eyes. "I am here to inform you that I will ride with you to the Aesarian Lords' camp."

"Ah." He crosses his arms and considers her for a long moment before speaking. "There are two reasons I will turn you down."

"And what are they, my Prince Regent?" Cyn asks through clenched teeth, hating her little brother's power over her. His condescension.

"First, though you are well trained, you have never been in battle."

"You haven't, either," she snaps, the frustration and helplessness making her feel like a thwarted child. It's all she can do not to stamp her foot.

For a second, Cyn thinks she sees a hesitation, a flicker of his eyes, but in the next second it passes. "I've ridden out with Father," Alex says. "I've fought cattle raiders by his side. It may not have been the full fury of battle, but it was practice. I am prepared." He rubs the back of his neck and shakes his head. "The Lords are a different matter altogether. If your first real fight to the death is with them, it will probably be your last."

"The second reason?" she asks, so furious she is only vaguely aware of the sounds in the hall.

"Trust," Alex says, and though his voice is calm his eyes shine with anger. "With you riding behind me, I would have to worry about defending both my front and my back, difficult even for the greatest warrior."

"I didn't know you—"

The door opens and two royal guards race in, swords drawn. "What is—?" Alex begins, turning toward them, as the words die on his lips.

In an instant Cyn realizes they are not there to protect him. They are there to kill him.

Time stands still. For a moment, Cyn wonders if she should stand back and let the men kill Alex, but only for a moment. She's filled with unexpected rage at the audacity of the enemy sneaking into the palace to kill the prince, her brother, rather than in an honorable battle. Macedon would never live down the disgrace of such weakness. She picks up a chair and throws it at the oncoming guards, buying time for both her and Alex to draw their swords. She yanks her brother's shield off the wall and throws it to him just as the men rush him.

Alex deftly parries one blow with his shield, the other with his sword. The two assassins are intent on Alex. Their mistake. Cyn slashes at one of the men, meeting his sword with a resounding clang. Cyn and her opponent break apart from Alex as their swords press together. He is taller than she is by a few inches and weighs some eighty pounds more, but she is lithe and swift, springing back easily, circling and wheeling in a blur of motion, her eyes always on both his sword and shield, knowing every moment where they are and where they are headed.

She spins to the left and hits him hard in the face with the edge of her shield. Blood streams from his nose and mouth.

"Bitch," he grunts, spitting out a tooth. He attacks her with an inhuman rage, unleashing the most furious onslaught that she has ever known. For the first time, Cyn is fighting for her life. The thought thrills her. Her senses heighten, and she feels blood pumping in the veins of her neck and smells the man's sour sweat as he heaves the shield and swings the sword. Once more he takes advantage of his weight and pushes toward her with his huge shield, and she is forced to fall back. A few more steps and she will be trapped in the corner.

Cyn takes in her situation at a glance. There is a chair behind her. Above it is a loop of iron chain used to raise and lower Alex's circular iron chandelier in the middle of his ceiling. His slave hasn't lit the wicks. She jumps onto the chair and lunges for the chain. Clutching the iron, she swings out and kicks the man hard in the face with both feet. Stunned, he staggers back. Cyn quickly releases the chain, but it is already too late. The hook in the ceiling holding the chandelier gives way to her weight and it rips out.

The heavy iron fixture hits her attacker's shoulder as lamps tumble out, spilling their oil on him, and he is momentarily knocked off balance. Cyn quickly wraps the now-loose chain around his neck and pulls tight.

Bellowing, he shoves the fingers of one hand between the chain and his neck while his other hand reaches behind his back to grab her. He bends forward, trying to throw her over his shoulder, managing to drag them both toward the other battle in the room. Cyn is vaguely aware of Alex and the other soldier in a furious swordfight, but she can only hope her strong grip on the chain around the guard's neck will cause him to faint before he manages to break free or flings her against the wall. As they pass a table, she grabs a lit lamp and puts the flame to the oil-stained sleeve of his tunic. It goes up like a torch.

Letting go of the chain, Cyn falls to the floor and rolls away from him. Screaming, the man beats at his sleeve, but flames jump to his beard, which is also saturated with lamp oil. With a roar, he tosses off his helmet and beats at his face, even as a flame licks at his hair. On the other side of the room, the man's companion freezes in horror. Alex takes advantage of this distraction to stab him through the heart. He slumps to the ground, blood darkening his leather breastplate.

Cyn's opponent howls in agony. Blinded by flames and smoke, the burning man lurches toward her. She lifts her sword and he runs right into it. He falls to the floor, writhing as the flames turn his face into a blistering, bubbling mess.

Leaning on her shield, she looks at him and smiles. "Call me 'bitch' again," she says.

But the man doesn't hear her. Alex has put his sword through the man's neck, ending his misery. He picks up a bucket of sand near the wall and pours it on the flames still eating into the head and arms, and the fire flickers and goes out. Alex then returns to the man he killed, carefully avoiding slick puddles of lamp oil and blood. "Help me take off his breastplate," Alex says, rolling the body over. He undoes the laces in the back.

Cyn swiftly joins her half brother and rips the bloodstained tunic down the front. Though the death wound has obscured part of it, Cyn can clearly make out an Aesarian brand. Five fingers of flame and a crescent moon.

"Aesarian Lords," Alexander says, wiping his bloody hands on the bottom of the man's tunic. He and Cyn come to the realization simultaneously: the Lords must have doubled back,

found a way to infiltrate the city, and disguised themselves
as guards. "I must find the queen." Alex rushes out the room
without giving Cyn a second glance.

She walks back to the man she killed, staring at the melted
mess of flesh in front of her. It's funny how the Aesarian's death
has made her feel so alive. She wants to kill another one. If
these men made it in, there might be others.

From far off, Cyn hears the bell signaling an attack. She
quickly slips from the room, staying in the shadows as she
hurries after Alex. Down the hall, she hears the pounding of
feet and the clanging of armor as the king's guards respond
to the alarm. She joins a throng of people streaming into the
courtyard with lanterns, torches, and weapons as soldiers shout
orders and civilians cry out in fear.

She's about to join the guards when a movement in her peripheral vision stops her.

Across the courtyard, the library door is open, just slightly.
Who would be in the library in the dead of night?

Cyn unsheathes her sword, picks up her shield, and runs
in long strides across the courtyard, up the steps and into the
dark library atrium. She stops and listens. She hears only the
gentle lapping of the pool's water against the edges.

And then, that high-pitched, anxious whine she'd recognize anywhere.

Arrhidaeus.

She may have little love for her addle-minded brother, but
he's of the royal house of Macedon. *Her* royal house. How
dare the Lords infiltrate the palace to lay hands on any of her
family?

Cyn creeps forward, crouching low, and slips through the
half-open doors to the main reading room. After a few moments of breathless silence, she makes out voices and the rustle
of papers. Lamplight dances in the archives to her left.

In the flickering shadows, she spots the lock and chain thrown haphazardly on the floor. The intruders must have waited until the alarm sounded and the guards left their stations. As Cyn approaches, her back against the shelves, she sees men rapidly unrolling scrolls. Arrhidaeus is tied to a chair, gagged, his eyes wide. The men throw some of the scrolls into a large canvas sack and discard others onto a heap on the floor. They all wear swords. But they are sheathed. They have no idea an attack is coming.

With the ululating battle cry of the ancient Amazons, she leaps into the room, plunging her sword into the chest of the closest intruder. Her blade is blocked by something hard beneath his tunic—a bronze breastplate, most likely. Cyn tries to aim at his face, but the man whirls around, hitting her with the sack as he unsheathes his sword. His two companions unsheathe their weapons as well, but they are hampered by the smallness of the room.

One of them lunges toward her, and their swords meet. The man beside him slashes at her, but she raises her shield to parry the blows. The third man is stuck behind the other two, unable to fight. Arri's chair tumbles over in the shuffle and his whimpering takes on new heights.

She is uncertain how long it goes on—two minutes? ten?—as she fights her two opponents. She sees the third man, the one in the back, leap onto the table and wonders if he will try to jump on her. If so, her sword is prepared to skewer him like a piece of meat on a spit as he comes down. Instead, he hurls something at her, something hard and big that sails over his comrades' heads, hits her on the side of her face, and crashes to the floor. It's a huge scroll with heavy wooden rollers in the center, big as the rolling pins bakers use.

It doesn't injure her—her helmet has absorbed most of the blow—but it throws her off balance. As she tries to steady herself, a man jumps on her and topples her to the ground. In one fluid movement, she stretches her legs up and back, and plucks the dagger from her boot. She sinks it deep into his neck.

Yelling, the other two Lords pull his lifeless body off her, and she is on her feet again, gripping her sword and shield. There is little room for maneuvering in the small chamber half taken up by the old table and the body, but Cyn manages a hard thrust into—and through, she thinks—the breastplate of one man, who falls backward onto the table, knocking off an oil lamp, but it is only a graze because he leaps up almost immediately and redoubles his attack.

"Faustus!" he cries in between thrusting and parrying. "Take the scrolls!"

Cyn inhales deeply, trying to keep her breath steady even as her lungs scream in exhaustion. She smells perfume mingled with sweat and blood. And smoke.

Flames rise high behind the two remaining men as Cyn dashes over to Arri and unbinds him. Tears streak his face, and he immediately begins coughing and sputtering.

"Run, boy. When you can, run," she whispers.

She swivels back around, seeing that the oil lamp has caught the pile of discarded scrolls on fire. It's rapidly turning into a bonfire to rival those of summer solstice. She tries to force them closer to the flames, but the men push forward, hammering her sword and shield so that she can't defend herself. Dimly, in her peripheral vision, she sees Arri dart between one of the men's legs, crawling to the door, to safety.

With a circular motion, the man on her right twists her sword out of her hand and onto the floor. The other pushes her onto the pile of burning scrolls, and hastily overturns the heavy library table, pinning her to the heat and ash.

"Grab the sack and let's take it to Bastian," he says, as Cyn feels the unbearable agony of her flesh burning. She shoves the heavy table off her and lets out such a bloodcurdling scream that for a moment the men stop and look at her. She sees them through a cloud of smoke and dancing flames.

Oddly, a numbness has descended on her; she feels nothing. And despite the thick smoke now filling the air, causing the other guards to cough and choke, she is able to breathe freely. In fact, she finds she is able to stand and walk through the flames, as though they aren't touching her.

"Maybe she is a goddess," Faustus says, his voice shaking.

"A witch, more likely. Now *that* would interest the Elder Council."

She is consumed with wonder. Is it possible? Could it be the spell with the beggar's blood worked after all? Has she become invincible to pain…and even death? After all these years, did she succeed in finding the blood of true betrayal?

Still utterly confused, she barely reacts when Faustus grabs her hard and quickly binds her hands behind her back. She can't possibly have acquired Smoke magic.

Has she?

The other man ties a kerchief around her mouth. She has no idea where they are taking her. As they push her into the main room, absurd laughter bubbles up her throat but chokes on the gag.

"This place is going up like a torch," the one soldier says, looking behind at the inferno in the archives. "Let's get out of here."

As the men drag Cyn out of the library, she sees dozens of people in the main palace courtyard gesturing and crying out that the library is on fire. One of the men yells out, "The enemy set fire to the library! Bring sand and water!" He shoves Cyn down the stairs and through a gate into the small unused courtyard behind the library, then through another gate and into the narrow street beyond. Her captors push and jostle her rudely until they eventually push her onto the little porch in front of the jail. The men knock five times on the door. She hears a bolt slide, and a second later the door opens and she is shoved inside. On the floor in front of her, two Macedonian guards, stripped of their uniforms, lie in pools of blood.

She looks around the torch-lit room and sees six Aesarian Lords. One of them steps forward, and it takes her a moment to recognize him: the usually self-assured Lord Bastian. Cyn is surprised to see a tick in his forehead and watches as beads of sweat form on his upper lip. He was much more handsome at the banquet, she recalls. To think he once flirted with her...

"What's this?" Bastian asks her captors.

"She attacked us, my lord," says one, setting down the sack of stolen scrolls, "and killed Lord Ajax. And she—she..."

"She what?" Bastian approaches Cyn, looking her up and down.

"She seemed to resist the fire. She walked through flames."

"This *girl* killed Ajax and walked through flames?"

"Yes, sir. The library is on fire, but we managed to take many scrolls that might be of interest to the council."

Five sharp raps pound at the door, and a man opens it. Cyn twists her neck to look up and sees two ungainly women holding baskets step into the jail office. They pluck off their long sheer veils and long dark curls, revealing short hair and scarred faces.

"My lord," says the one with a grizzled crew cut, "our men cannot open the palace gates. And even if we could, we couldn't open the city gates to let in the army. Prince Alexander has issued orders that any civilian approaching the gates from inside the palace or the town is to be killed."

Bastian knits his dark brows together and nods. "Prince Alexander? What of Lords Melampos and Kebes? Were they not successful in killing the prince?"

"They are dead, my lord," the other man in an ill-fitting peplos replies. "Slain by the prince and his sister."

"His *sister*?" He turns to Cyn. "Menos, remove her gag."

It's all Cyn can do to not bite down on the rough fingers that pull her gag from her mouth. When at last it's gone, she takes in a clear, deep breath before she flashes Bastian a brilliant smile. "I'm disappointed," she says. "I thought your warriors were supposedly the best in the—" Cyn's cheek stings and she tastes the salt of her blood as Bastian's palm connects with the side of her face.

"A disappointing night," Bastian says, scowling at her, then at his men. "A few scrolls and a girl."

"Not just any girl, my lord," says the man still holding Cyn. "King Philip's daughter. A royal princess for ransom. A woman whose flesh is not burned by flames. Look how her skin bears only the faintest marks, as though the fire barely touched her."

Bastian looks at Cyn again, and for the first time all night, he smiles.

CHAPTER TWENTY-SEVEN

ZO KICKS HER HORSE AND STRUGGLES TO KEEP up with the three men ahead of her, who have pulled up and are looking back at her with impatience. Her thighs burn and she can feel bruises blooming where they connect with the saddle. At the end of each day, she has a hard time standing and wonders if her legs are permanently bowed. Each one feels like half a perfect circle.

It's not that she hasn't ridden before, but not ten hours a day pounding down a hard-packed road. Every night she looks forward to the posting station where wrinkled old women throw buckets of hot scented water on her and massage her skin with sponges and bristle brushes until it glows. The hot baths are the only thing that makes life bearable on this unending journey to nowhere to find a creature that long ago became extinct.

"The Eastern Mountains," Ochus says, gesturing to the purple-gray peaks in the distance as Zo pulls up beside him.

Zo stares ahead at the long, seemingly endless chain. Kohinoor said the only way Zo could avoid marrying Alexander of Macedon and reunite with Cosmas—without risking his death—was to find the Spirit Eaters in the Eastern Mountains and ask them to change her fate. *But* where *in the Eastern Mountains?* she wonders. And is her belief in Kohinoor's words going to damn her in the end? Or is it the only thing keeping her alive even now?

The range stretches some eight hundred miles from central Asia Minor deep into the heart of the Persian Empire, sweeping north into the land of nomads between the two great inland seas. She imagines herself alone, stumbling blindly up and down mountains, hungry and exhausted, and once again a prime target for rogue slave traders.

At least she has money—gold, actually—that she could trade for food or a place to sleep. She fingers the jewelry in her sky-blue hem. When Ochus found the tunic and trousers outfit she had planned to wear for Cosmas in the slavers' bags, he threw it to her and suggested she change out of her filthy rags. When the prince wasn't looking, she ripped the gold from her ragged tunic and sewed it into the hem and waistband of her clean outfit, pretending she was making some alterations.

"You said your father's map showed a track off to the north of the Royal Road that winds east up into the mountains," Ochus says. "He was told the Pegasus herd lives in a valley that way, is that right?" His eyes narrow as he looks at her.

Zo nods. That was what Mandana told her in her fairy stories. Or something close to it. Come to think of it, Mandana also told her of evil jinns that lived under mushroom caps. And water sprites that reached up from ponds and pulled you into the depths with long green wet arms, and—

"Come on," Ochus says. His two men—Javed and Payem— kick their horses into a trot, and Zo reluctantly follows.

A caravan of wagons plods toward them from the east. In one of them, merchants in strange, colorfully embroidered at-

tire sit cross-legged on cushions under awnings and sip wine
from tiny cups. Zo has seen many such caravans the past few
days, carrying treasures like lapis lazuli, spices, perfumes, and
that rare shimmering cloth spun by worms in trees at the end
of the world.

A cry comes from behind them.

"King's post!"

Everyone obediently shuffles to the side of the road as a
man in a blue postal uniform thunders past on a straining stallion. "King's men!" comes another cry. Ochus gestures to his
group to stay where they are as a cavalry regiment rides by,
kicking up clods of dust in their wake.

Later in the day, a *harmanaxa* rumbles past them. Peals of
female laughter echo through the tasseled scarlet curtains. Zo
knows that inside are the female members of a noble family, reclining on carpets and pillows. A twinge of pain passes
through her. How she enjoyed riding in her uncle's *harmanaxa*
with Shirin and Roxana.

Riding beside the vehicle are several eunuchs wearing
wide-brimmed hats to protect their delicate complexions.
Zo even misses her busybody eunuchs, who always followed
her around and fretted over her. Frava, so greedy for sweet-
meats he carried candied dates in his pouch. Chosroes, so easily insulted, always borrowing jewelry and scarves from the
women and sobbing when they refused his requests. Darkly
handsome Erfan who missed what he lost as a child to slavers'
knives and tried his best to look and act like a normal man.

But that life was an age ago, and a world away. She will
never live in a palace with eunuchs again or travel in a *harmanaxa*. She looks back over her shoulder with longing, but
wagon and riders have all disappeared.

After a few more agonizing miles, they arrive at the next
posting station, a fortified mud brick building with no exterior

windows except arrow slits in the corner towers and a nasty-looking portcullis that rattles down at sunset. Zo knows she's been lucky. They have stayed in a station each night. Though each one feels very much like the other, Zo has found them clean and comfortable with large stables that provide fresh horses for the royal mail, guards who watch brimming merchants' wagons, and a tavern with food, drink, and gossip.

Zo pulls her horse to a stop and waits for Ochus to dismount, but he shades his eyes and looks at the sun. "We could stop early today," he says, "or we could continue and camp outside. We won't make the next posting station before dark."

"I've had enough of soft living," Javed says, his large toothy mouth sliding into a grin as he rubs some of the road's dust out of his eyes. Zo groans inwardly. Riding fifteen or twenty miles a day isn't what she calls soft living, no matter how comfortable the posting stations.

"Payem?"

"Agreed," Payem says, nodding his dark curly head.

"What about you, Zotasha?" Ochus asks. Zo's pretty certain she sees his mouth twitch, and her irritation rises. Almost every word he speaks to her mocks her in some way. *Cosmas*, she thinks, *I miss you.* She longs for her lover's shyness, his kindness. There is something quiet and comfortable about him, whereas the man she now rides with radiates energy so fiercely it's almost like the prickly heat from a fire.

"It's up to you, horse master's daughter," Ochus says, taking obvious delight in her hesitation. Before Zo can think it through, the answer has slipped out of her mouth. "We should ride on."

"Well, then," Ochus says. "We ride on!" He squeezes his horse and it breaks out into a long, loping canter.

Great Mithras, what have I done? Zo reluctantly kicks her horse forward, blisters screaming on her backside, feet, and fingers. As she rides, a thought creeps into her mind. Though her back muscles ache, this might be the perfect chance to escape. And she must escape. She must find the fabled Spirit Eaters, or die trying. She has nothing to go home to, and there's no way Ochus will allow her to live when he discovers she's been leading him astray.

And she has an unborn child to save.

The soldiers never leave her alone. Sometimes she catches Ochus talking quietly with Javed and Payem, the three of them staring at her and nodding slightly. The men share a room while Zo is permitted her own, but before she blows out the lamps, Ochus locks the door and pockets the key. Even when Zo uses the latrine or bath at a posting station, one of the men accompanies her and waits outside.

When the sun casts long shadows in front of the horses, they turn off the road and across a field before they settle in a patch of forest where they collect wood for a fire and eat their traveler's food: dried beef, smoked fish, cucumbers, and almonds. As the stars begin to shine, they wrap themselves in their cloaks.

"Payem, keep the first watch," Ochus says. "When the moon is high, wake me."

Zo knows they are watching *her*, to make sure she doesn't escape. But after a hard day's ride, it must be nearly impossible to stay awake in the rich blackness of the night, with the wind whispering lullabies in the gently swaying trees all around them, and the crickets singing softly. She rolls over and pretends to sleep. She will stay awake longer than Payem and run.

When she wakes, she curses herself for nodding off. She sits up silently and looks around. All three men are on their sides, breathing deeply. So much for the watch.

Now.

She unravels herself from her cloak and gingerly stands up.

She bites her lip to keep down a muffled moan as her legs stretch, but she slowly walks away from the tent and into the sable embrace of night.

She walks for a short while, feeling cold and achy, lost and alone, but determined to get as far as possible from camp, when suddenly, somewhere very close to her, a growl slices through the blackness of the night.

Goddess Anahita, what now? Zo looks around nervously. She stands perfectly still in the brush, holding her breath. As her eyes strain through the darkness, she finally makes out a dark shape and two golden eyes. A mountain lion. One bite will snap her neck in two. Before she can move, it utters an unearthly howl. Huge paws stretch and fangs gleam in the moonlight as it springs into the air.

Zo throws herself to the ground as a scream lodges in her throat. Something whizzes past her from the side and the animal cries out in pain, twists while still in the air, and lands several feet from her. Ochus is beside her, holding a burning torch in one hand, a spear in the other. Several feet away, Javed notches another arrow and on the other side, Payem holds his long curved sword.

The mountain lion, an arrow sticking out of its thigh, bellows in furious pain. It pounces on Javed before the man can fire his arrow. The soldier screams in agony. Payem runs toward them, sword raised, but the animal turns to defend against this new threat. Then Ochus is in the midst of the fracas, holding his torch high to make sure his spear pierces the mountain lion and not his friends. Crouched behind a bush with her hands over her head, Zo can hardly see what's going on in the wavering light of a single torch in a desert of darkness. The air is full of screams, but Zo is unsure which is man and which is beast.

Finally, she sees three still bodies on the ground: Javed, Payem...

...and the mountain lion.

Still holding the torch, Ochus turns to her. "Take off your trousers."

"What?" she asks in disbelief.

"We need bandages. These men are seriously injured."

She slips out of her trousers and throws them to Ochus. The gold. She's just thrown him her gold sewn into the waistband.

"Here, hold this," he says, handing her the torch.

He takes his knife out of its sheath and cuts a strip from the leg of the blue trousers which he wraps tightly around Payem's bleeding thigh, murmuring words of comfort and hope to the groaning man. Then he cuts off the waistband, frowns, and rips it open. Gold rings and earrings tumble out, shimmering in the torchlight.

His accusing eyes rise to meet hers with a flicker of disgust. He says nothing, however, and bends down to bind the yawning wound in Javed's stomach. The man isn't moving or making a sound. Ochus touches his neck for long moments before he proclaims his verdict. "He's dead."

Zo wants to sink into the ground. Kind Javed, with those big white horses' teeth—

Ochus yanks her up hard by the elbow. "I knew you weren't a horse master's daughter. I've known it since our first day on the road. If you were, you wouldn't have toppled off your horse like a cripple every night. And now this gold." He holds an earring to the torchlight. "Royal gold by the looks of it." An intricate gold amphora covered with exquisitely tiny granulation dangles from a large gold disk, its center a huge glowing ruby.

"I think you're a thief running away with jewelry stolen from a palace." He pulls her roughly toward him by the tunic and grabs the hem, feeling the bumps and lumps inside. "More gold," he says as his fingers explore the seams of her tunic, running his hands along the edges of her body, the tops of her thighs. "There's a king's ransom in here."

"I was running away from my family," she says, backing away, fighting the tears that sting her eyes. She can't let him see her cry. A sob rising from the pit of her stomach threatens to choke her, a howl of pain for Roxana and Jopata, for Cosmas and the baby inside her. She's suddenly shaking like a leaf and doesn't want to talk. She wants to scream. But she has to convince him to let her go.

"A very wealthy family," she continues, trying to control her shaky voice, "and the slavers kidnapped me. Take the gold, but just let me go."

He studies her. "And the Pegasus? Was that a lie?"

"My nurse is from the Eastern Mountains," she says, and it's a relief for once to say something true. "She told me stories of the Pegasus who lived in a valley near the Flaming Cliffs. That is no lie."

"How can I believe a liar who says she is not lying?" he asks, pacing around her. Zo tenses, trying to stay calm. She knows full well that he could sell her at the slave market and keep a handsome profit. Or he could return her, a thieving handmaiden, to a palace and get a reward. Or he could simply strangle her now and keep all the gold.

A sob escapes Zo's throat, but Ochus continues as though he hasn't heard her. "Then again, there's always the slim chance that you do know something about a Pegasus. If we find it, you can keep your gold and earn your freedom."

He stops his pacing and looks at her. "If this journey is a wild-goose chase, I will keep your gold, and you will remain as my slave for the rest of your life. If you so much as look at me wrongly, I will whip you for disobedience. The way I see it," he says with eyes gleaming golden in the moonlight just like the mountain lion's, "either way, I win."

Zo was tempted to slam the torch onto his head. No one in the palace—not her mother, not even the king—ever talked to her like that.

"Now sit next to Payem and see if he can drink some water," Ochus orders, taking the torch from her. She complies, unhooking her goatskin water bag from her belt. Just because she hates his commander doesn't mean she will ignore Payem. The man's breath is ragged, and his eyes remain closed. He doesn't open his lips when Zo tries to get him to drink, and the water streams onto his chin.

Ochus holds the light over the tawny, sinuous body of the mountain lion. "This will make a beautiful battle cloak." He kneels, sets the torch into the ground, and starts skinning the animal.

Unable to watch, Zo sits next to the wounded man and feels something hot and wet on her face. *So many dead because of me.*

She looks at the dying man's face, so like a baby's in sleep. Does Payem have a woman back home who loves him as much as Zo loves Cosmas? A child, perhaps, who will grow up fatherless? Elderly parents? He whimpers, and she instinctively cradles his head in her lap, awkwardly stroking his cold brow.

Ochus slices skin from muscle and bone, taking extra care with the mountain lion's head. The air reeks from coppery blood and foul guts, and she wonders if she is going to vomit. She finds herself singing a melody Mandana used to soothe her with, during nights when she missed her mother and couldn't sleep. Whether it's for Payem's sake or her own, she can't say.

"Breathe me in my love
And hold me tight
I am here with you in the darkness of the night
I will give you golden rings
And you will grow as tall as kings"

Suddenly she realizes Payem's heavy breathing has stopped. Payem is dead. The chubby-cheeked man with the smiling eyes and dark curling hair. Another one dead. Because of her.

She stops singing.

Her only escape now is death. She must follow the path she has sent all those others on. She has just killed Ochus's two best men, and there's no Pegasus left in the world. She will be a slave again.

No, she thinks with a fury that surprises her. *Never again.*

She sees Ochus's spear on the ground, its iron tip gleaming in the torchlight. Death might be her only escape, but it need not be her own death. She reaches for the spear and balances it in her hand. She can do it. She *must* do it. She raises the spear, preparing to plunge it through Ochus's back.

But she hesitates, and before she can lower the spear point, Ochus turns and hurls himself into the wooden shaft, knocking it out of her hands. He launches himself onto her, hurling her to the ground. He's on top of her, pinning her hands next to her head. His hands are slick with blood and now so are hers.

She twists, kneeing him in the groin. He cries out and redoubles his effort. They're both sweating, grappling, a tumble of arms and legs and hot panting breath.

At the same instant, they both stop. Time stands suspended as Zo examines Ochus's face up close. The fine hair curling softly at his jaw. The faint freckles that are almost lost in the tanned skin. The dust clinging to his eyelashes. Then his golden eyes, alert and narrow, crinkle. Her behavior amuses him.

Zo spits a thick wad of saliva into his face.

Ochus finally laughs out loud. "Good thing I have chains and fetters in my saddlebag," he says.

"Order us some food," Ochus says. "I am going to arrange the burials and sell the extra horses." As he swaggers away, he turns his head over his shoulder and calls out one more order, "And Zo, my darling, don't go anywhere. Remember, I'm trusting you."

Zo scowls and clenches her hands into fists; the chain connecting her wrist to the fretted wooden side of the low couch clinks gently. They are back on the Royal Road at a posting station. After a night of fitful sleep outdoors—he had chained her wrist to his—he made her help him swing the stiff bodies of Javed and Payem over their horses and tie them there under blankets. Now he is using some of her gold to make sure they receive lavish burials.

At least this morning he got rid of that blood-smeared lion skin with pieces of fat and muscle hanging off the sides; he left it at a foul-smelling tannery. Shackled to Ochus, Zo was forced to enter the shop, endure the stench, and listen to how the pelt would be soaked in urine and animal brains and pounded with dung. Her rising nausea reminded her that she carries a child.

Now, however, she's ravenous, and delectable smells rise from the low tables around her. She looks around and sees many Persian imperial guards in their red-and-white-checked trousers and green tunics—*goddess Anahita*, how she misses Cosmas—and imperial couriers in their bright blue uniforms. Across the crowded room, a bright-eyed courier leaning on a pile of cushions raises a glass to her and winks. She looks away quickly.

"My name is Bahar," says a woman's voice. "We have lamb today and goat stew along with fruit and salads. Would you like some wine first?" Zo looks up and sees a plump woman carrying a tray of clay wine goblets. Strands of wiry gray hair escape from her bun and stick to her sweaty face.

"Wine, yes, for two," Zo says, hoping the drink will soothe the subtle cramps she has begun to feel in her belly—early signs of the secret life stirring inside her. She reaches up to take one of the goblets and then realizes she can't.

Bahar purses her lips at the sight of Zo's manacled hand, but she squats and sets two goblets down on the low table. Zo decides she's probably seen stranger things on the Royal Road, a river of filth and splendor where all mankind swims past— kings, beggars, merchants, murderers, whores, and thieves. And add to that enslaved kings' nieces who are with child, and conceited cavalry captains. Zo could probably tell this woman any story, and she wouldn't bat an eye.

"A moment, Bahar," Zo says as the woman turns to go. "My nurse told me long ago about a race of sorcerers called Spirit Eaters. Have you heard of them?"

Bahar places her tray on the table and makes a fist with the pinky and pointer fingers straight out like the horns of a bull, the ancient sign to protect against evil. "From what I hear, it is true," she says, leaning close. "About a hundred and fifty miles east of here, there is a track north off the Royal Road through Korama, the land of magical stones. The Spirit Eaters live there, an ancient people with the secretive ways of the mountain folk, those still in touch with the old gods."

"Why do they have such a frightening name?" Zo asks.

Bahar shrugs. "Some say they aren't even human, but powerful *jinn*. Others say they are a peaceful tribe called the Hunor who want to be left alone and tell scary stories to keep people away." Bahar looks at her curiously. "If so, it works. Few travelers ever go there, and most never return."

"Ah, there's my girl," Ochus says, grinning as he pushes past several fat merchants getting up from a table. "Such an obedient woman. She always stays exactly where I tell her to." Bahar inclines her head to Ochus and bustles off to wait on a table of drunk merchants. "Well, my dearest love," he says to Zo, "are you hungry?"

Dinner is a humiliating affair, beginning with Zo holding her manacled hands over a bowl as Bahar pours warm scented water over them and laughs out loud. Zo glares at Ochus, who gives her an infuriating grin. Then, as she tries to reach for the platters of sliced meat, fruit, and vegetables, her chains clank against the wooden table as diners nearby turn, point at her, and laugh. Finally, she settles the chains gracefully on the cushions at her side, but that means she's dependent on Ochus for everything, needing him to refill her wine cup, dip her bread in yogurt, and push the platters closer to her so she can reach them. As bad as it is, though, Zo dreads the end of dinner.

With a scrape of metal against wood, Ochus stands up and unlocks Zo from the couch. "Ready, my darling?" he asks.

"You're insufferable."

He grins. "But I have so much fun! If you promise to behave, I'll let you carry your own chains to the room." He hands her the end of the link, and Zo tries to hide how grateful she is that she won't be led to their room like a pet gibbon on a leash. She keeps her posture princess-straight as she follows him up the stairs and enters their tiny rented room as he locks the door and pockets the key.

There's only one bed.

He removes his shirt and starts washing himself with the

basin and towel on the table. She stands awkwardly—she's certainly not going to get on the bed—and has nowhere to look but at his broad, muscled back, gleaming smooth and golden in the lamplight except for some battle scars. He turns toward her, and she sees his broad shoulders, large arm muscles, and strong chest. *Goddess Anahita*, his stomach is as chiseled as the statue of Apollo she and Shirin saw when they snuck into the Greek merchants' temple. She thought such a stomach was reserved for gods, not mortals. She saw it before, when he was bathing at the pond shortly after rescuing her, but she had been so exhausted she hadn't really noticed just how incredible… To her horror, he sees her staring and smiles knowingly. A hot blush rises to her cheeks and she looks at the floor, furious at herself.

"Here," he says, "is a fresh towel for you. Let me remove your chains so you can wash."

He lies on the bed and stares at her as she turns her back to him and quickly washes her hands and face, and then reaches awkwardly beneath her tunic to wash her chest and underarms.

"Is that all?" he asks, approaching her. "I was hoping for more."

Her heart pounds as he grabs her wrists and she expects him to throw her on the bed. But all he does is snap her fetters back on her wrists, pushing the key deep down in his trousers pocket.

"If you get up and move around, I will hear you," he says in a taunting voice, as if he is talking to a naughty child. As he blows out the lamp, he adds, "And if you try anything—" he leans down close to her, tracing his finger along her jaw "—I will wrap those chains around this lovely neck."

She only lets out a breath once he has moved away, taking his side of the bed. Within moments he's sleeping; she can tell by the slow rhythmic breathing. She, however, is kept awake by the thumping of her heart, by the heat of his body, and his closeness. It reminds her of the night she spent curled against Cosmas, feeling his warmth and inhaling his scent. Loneliness settles on Zo's chest, smothering her. Shirin, Roxana, Cosmas...she's lost them all.

As she rolls over to the far side of the bed, the chains clank against themselves. She tries to suppress a shuddering sob and closes her eyes tight. She thinks of Cosmas and can almost feel his soft breath on her neck as he wipes away the sadness and pulls the blanket tight, his warm hand on her back, soothing her.

Right before she slips into a tear-induced sleep, she prays as fervently as she has ever prayed for anything in her life.

Holy goddess, help me get to the man I love.

When Zo wakes the next morning, the comfort is still there. She nestles deeper under the covers and tilts her head slightly before she realizes where she is: tucked under Ochus's chin, his palm resting on the curve of her back.

Just as quickly as she begins to savor his warmth, he rolls over, facing the other way, and she feels more cold, exposed, and alone than ever.

Outside the tiny open window, the sky is just starting to turn from black to pale silver as dawn breaks.

And then, something strange happens.

White feathers brush against the window frame, and are gone. It must have been the biggest bird in the world. A stork, perhaps? A pelican?

Careful to silence the clinking of her chains, Zo lifts them and quietly edges her way out of the bed, toward the window, shivering. She could swear she feels another faint stirring inside her, deep in her belly, as she pokes her head outside the window. She can just make out, at a distance, the body of what looks like a white mare...a white mare with *wings*...leaping into the tree line, just as the sun breaks over the horizon and she's blinded by its sudden light.

When she blinks, the beast—the image, the fantasy, whatever it was—has flown.

Chapter Twenty-Eight

KAT OPENS HER EYES AND SEES BARS OF LIGHT on the dirt floor. She's stiff. Her neck and back ache, and for a few moments she isn't sure where she is. Then she sits up, looks around, and groans. In a cell. A tiny stone cell high up a cliff, a chill wind whistling in through the narrow window.

She stands, slowly and painfully, and looks out through the iron bars. Yesterday she had no idea how high she climbed, but now she can see she's on top of the world. The sun is rising behind the mountains, streaking the summits and clouds with rose and amethyst, orange and gold, and painting the valleys below her with deep purple shadows.

She yanks on the bars in anger, but they don't budge. Even if they did, there's a three-thousand-foot drop straight down to the valley below. She's Ada's prisoner. Trapped like an animal in a pen. No sooner had Ada welcomed her the evening before than servants appeared on either side of her wearing long robes covered in feathers. She couldn't be sure if they were men or women with their shoulder-length black hair, beak-like noses, and yellow eyes, but they grabbed her by her arms and dragged her into this cell, their cold fingers digging into her flesh like talons.

Why did Ada put her here? How long will she remain? She stupidly thought the kestrel was guiding her to decipher the secrets of her mother's past. Instead, she's in prison. Again. She slides down the wall and sits in the dirt, her elbows on her knees, her head in her hands.

At first she isn't sure that she has heard anything at all, other than the wind dancing through clefts in the cliff face. But when she looks up, she sees it.

A scorpion. Black. With six beady eyes, eight legs, two enormous claws, and a curled-up tail shaking in what seems to be anger.

Go away, she says aloud. *I wish you no harm.*

Another one, this one so much bigger it has difficulty squeezing itself below the door, follows it. And then several more. Alarmed, she pushes herself against the wall, curling her legs beneath her gown. She has only seen the creatures once before, when she'd traveled three days south of Erissa with Sotiria. She was warned then that their stings are poisonous—and often deadly.

She swallows nervously.

I am no danger to you, she says again, this time with her mind. *Leave me alone, I beg you.*

It doesn't work.

She gasps as dozens—no, hundreds of scorpions—stream into the cell, surrounding her, some of them climbing up the walls, several of them climbing up her robe, all of them avoiding the bright bars of light on the floor. Though she wants to be brave, her entire body begins to shake as she curls even tighter into the corner.

This can be no accident. Someone has sent these creatures to do her harm.

Ada.

Kat sits perfectly still, knowing any sudden movement could be perceived as a threat to their safety that must be stung to death.

She tries to still her pounding heart.

She remembers running beside the gazelle. Remembers the rats who came to her rescue in the library, and the kestrel that seemed to speak to her with its mind, calling to her. Then she closes her eyes, trying to breathe through her rising panic as she does her best to feel the feelings of the scorpions.

A deep, gnawing hunger courses through her, a craving for living prey.

It's working.

She feels herself flexing enormous pincers, searching for information in the air and along the ground. At the same time, she is in her own body, watching as the scorpions approach her, a few clinging to the edges of her robe. She concentrates on the largest scorpion's mind again, curls and uncurls her segmented tail with the long barbed stinger on the end. She scuttles backward a bit. It's too light in here. Where is her dark nest beneath the rock? She must return and wait for night, then come out and find something better to eat.

Yes, go, she tells her scorpion self, all her scorpion selves in the room. *The light stings our eyes. This one here is no food for us, no threat to us.*

It's working.

The scorpions on her robe drop gracefully to the floor as the others turn and creep beneath the door. She has a glimpse of them draining away, and a moment later she, too, is one with the scorpions, and squeezes beneath the door into a dark tunnel where the light doesn't hurt her eyes. There is a hole at the bottom of the wall, and here all the other scorpions enter, one by one. Back home to safety and gentle darkness.

She hesitates. Ada. She must find Ada, who has the key to her cell. She will carry it back there and set it on the floor so that when she awakes in her human body, she can escape. If Ada tries to prevent her from taking the key, Kat will sting her.

A strong instinct leads her through palace corridors: right, left, right again. She has never noticed before how many cracks are on a polished floor, how many little chips in the stone, how much dust and dirt. Her eight legs step neatly over an eyelash, and a bit later on, an insect wing. For a disconcerting moment, she is in her cell, shaking like a leaf, eyes closed, but then she is standing before what she knows must be Ada's room, her tail bristling in rage, the stinger aimed at the door. She can tell by the smell. She flattens herself and crawls underneath.

The golden marble floor stretches before her like an endless desert. Determined, she scuttles forward, noticing a tiny black feather that must have fallen off Ada's gown, a sprinkle of crushed eggshell face powder near her vanity table. Finally, she crawls up a carved ebony leg of the enormous bed. But there is no woman on the endless fields of green wool embroidered with colorful flowers.

A giant hand scoops her up. Kat, as the scorpion, swivels around, tail raised and shaking. A large smiling face appears and blows her a kiss. Kat feels as if she is falling from the sky, waving all her legs, her tail, her pincers, until she hits the ground hard, and finds herself back in her human body, in the cell.

She looks around in a panic. No scorpions. No Ada. Just bars of light on the floor and the ceaseless whining of a cool wind. She flexes her hands and feet, two of each, thank the gods. It all must have been a strangely real dream that left her heart pounding and her head spinning. But no, the scorpions had been real. How did they flee?

She feels sick and dizzy, like she might throw up.

A moment later, the door unlocks.

Ada stands in the doorway. Today her gown and headdress are peacock feathers, a shining teal green with dozens of royal blue eyes that seem to be staring at Kat in surprise. Kat scrambles to a standing position and takes a good hard look at this woman who last evening seemed to rise like a sword out of a dark spot on the floor.

Ada is perhaps forty, her thick black hair threaded with silver. Her ivory skin is flawless, like pale marble, except for lines about her mouth when she smiles, which she is doing now. Her eyes are black as coal with a glowing white ring in the center. Kat looks away sharply. There is something in those strange eyes that makes her feel as if she is tumbling into a whirlpool.

"Now you and I can talk," Ada says.

"Talk?" Kat says, her anger rising. "You want to talk after you just tried to kill me by sending hundreds of scorpions into my cell?"

Ada shakes her head, and the tall peacock feathers undulate gracefully.

"I had no intention of killing you, silly girl. I was testing you. And you passed my test. It has been proven."

"What's been proven?" Kat asks, terrified. She wants to look Ada in the eyes but...can't. She stares at her cheekbones instead.

Ada looks cautiously around. "Come with me," she says, "for even walls have ears. Well, maybe not literally. But the creatures within them do."

Ada leads Kat down a dark tunnel and through a door to a courtyard. There's a rectangular blue pool in the center, with a fountain splashing. All around are flowering trees with brightly colored birds beginning to rustle and call with the dawn. Kat starts to walk to a group of stone benches, feeling weak from hunger and long travel, and hardly having slept a wink in that cold cell, but Ada's voice yanks her away. "Not here," she says.

They pass through a small door in a wall and find themselves on a desolate, barren spot jutting out over cliffs on three sides. To their right, a frothy waterfall tumbles down over jagged rocks, reminding Kat of a sheer linen veil tossed about by the wind. The water is loud, making it unlikely any human or creature here could eavesdrop on their conversation. Kat looks down at the valley far below, emerald-green, a shining silver river meandering across it.

They are standing too close to the edge. Kat starts to take a step backward, but Ada grabs her wrist.

"There was, long ago, in the time before time, a great battle between gods and monsters," Ada begins, looking straight ahead. "The gods won but lost much of their power and became almost mortal, mating with humans."

Kat sneaks a sidelong glance at Ada. What nonsense is she talking about?

"From that mating there developed the two kinds of blood magic, passed down through families, though often skipping many generations. Snake Blood is the magic of the mind, Earth Blood the magic of the physical body. These magics come literally in one's blood—they are inherited."

Kat read something almost identical in the archives when she was searching for information on Alexander's astrology. And there was something about Caria, wasn't there? She wracks her mind. Yes, it was, *Rarer still are reports from Caria of Snake Bloods' ability to transform into different creatures.*

Still, just because it was written in that old scroll doesn't mean it's true. "Everyone knows there was a great deal of magic in the past," she says, waving her hand dismissively. "But it died out long ago."

Ada shakes her head, and the stiff breeze ruffles the feathers in her headdress and on her robe. "Not all of it died out. There are still some with great power who walk among us, even though they might not be aware of it themselves."

Kat feels prickles rising up the back of her neck. She doesn't want to hear what is coming next. She wants to get far away from this dangerous wind-whipped perch, from this strange woman.

Ada continues. "Earth Bloods often have the power of healing, but their strongest abilities lie in controlling rocks and trees, wind and water and earth, those things of nature that are alive in their own way, yet not consciously, not of the mind. Snake Bloods have great affinity with animals, any living thing with thoughts and feelings. Humans, too. They can communicate with other living creatures, even, in rare cases, become one." She turns to Kat and says icily, "Like a scorpion, for instance."

Kat's blood freezes in her veins. She tries to inhale but can't.

Then Ada says the words Kat doesn't want to hear. "You, Katerina, are Snake Blood, as I am, too. But you, I think, will become more powerful even than I. Perhaps the most powerful in many generations. That is why you must be trained. If you remain untrained, your abilities can lead you into danger. What if I had stepped on you in your scorpion form? Your human body in the cell would have fallen over dead."

Kat inhales deeply as a burst of wind whips her hair into her face.

"I don't believe it," Kat says through gritted teeth. "It must have been a dream. Magic that powerful doesn't exist anymore."

Ada raises an arched black eyebrow and smiles. "Really?" she says, as she puts both arms straight out, her long fingers spread wide. She shuts her eyes and bows her head. Kat senses the energy coursing through her, hot and pulsating. She takes a couple of steps away from her.

At first she thinks Ada has whistled up a stiffer wind. There's a rushing sound coming from the other side of the waterfall. If that's all she can do, Kat isn't impressed. Every village has stories of hags who can fiddle with the weather.

But then the entire sky is blotted out by tens of thousands of tiny black buzzing creatures swooping in circles in front of them.

Locusts.

The locusts stop their large loops and form themselves into the shape of a giant woman with arms outstretched, her hip-length black hair rippling around her shoulders and behind her back.

Beads of perspiration slide down Ada's temples. This spectacle is costing her a great deal of energy. Kat stares at the fifty-foot-tall woman made of locusts, and it seems to stare back, waving its arms at her. It looks to its left, starts as if alarmed, then races across the sky, its shapely legs pumping hard.

It's running from birds. Thousands of blackbirds swoop into the mass of locusts to devour them, wheeling and diving. The chattering insects disperse across the sky, the screeching birds hot on their trail, until they become too small to see, disappearing into the blue-gray distance.

Kat stares in wonder, not wanting to believe what she is seeing, that this is the work of one person—a sorceress. After years of being told to keep her affinity for animals hidden, it seems bold, foolish, *crazy* to make such a demonstration of it here. And yet, it awes her, too. Ada's power moves with such freedom.

And she knows, deep down, that something within *her* is stirring in response. That Ada is right. That she, too, is Snake Blood.

Just as the realization sinks in, a crushing despair knocks the breath out of her...

She hears the screams of her mother, sees the scene of her murder, her blood on the dirt floor mixing with wine. Kat feels the dread, the despair, overtaking her, freezing her. She feels as if she is plunging straight down into black waters, boulders attached to her feet. Bent over, weak, and aching, she sees her mother die all over again. She is alone in the darkness. She cries for her mother. For Jacob, who has gone his separate way, unable to forgive her for her secrets. She cries for Prince Alexander, with whom in such a short time she found so much in common, such an unexpected sense of *belonging*. She cries even for herself, alone at the very ends of the world.

Then, just as she can feel the very bottom of the darkness swallowing her forever, turning her blind, seizing her heart, she is, suddenly, lifted.

Into golden air. She rises. Dazzling light moves through her in giant waves, cleansing her, and she laughs with pure joy. Even though it is too bright for her to see anything, she feels as if she is feasting with Helen and Jacob, her family back in Erissa, and Alex. As if everyone is alive and happy and together forever.

The joy, too, fades, but not entirely. Kat strains to see through the light as it dims, and makes out Ada, staring at her intently.

"Now are you impressed?" she asks, twisting her mouth.

Kat sways, once again dizzy, and aware how close she is to the edge of the cliffs, to the wild waterfall, to certain death. "You did that?" she asks, breathless. "But...how could you?"

"Snake Bloods can, with great training, interfere with and control the emotions of others," Ada says. "Controlling the ebb and tide of people's minds is a great power, perhaps the greatest. But this is why you must train. Magic in and of itself is neither good nor evil; it is neutral. Yet because of our own folly or wisdom, it can be incredibly dangerous or incredibly powerful."

Kat puts her hands to her ears. "I don't want to hear any more. I don't want to be a Snake Blood. I don't want to train in magic. I just want to go home."

"And where is home?" Ada says, her cool voice winding its way into Kat's ears.

Where *is* home? "I don't know anymore," she says, hating the pain and uncertainty in her voice.

"Listen, Katerina," Ada says, bending so close her lips are practically on Kat's ear, "I knew your mother, Helen. She and I were friends."

Kat looks up, a mixture of hope and wariness warring within her. Can this witch possibly be telling the truth? "You were?"

"She knew—months before your birth—that you would be Snake Blood. She knew of all the dangers that came with that. She didn't want you to know about it until you were ready. And now you are."

Kat blinks away unexpected tears. The endless sky is like the inside of an oyster shell, white and gray, purple and gold. Kat smells rain in the blustering wind. The day has hardly begun and already a storm is brewing.

"How did she know I would be Snake Blood?" Kat asks, one of hundreds of questions she has. "Was she Snake Blood?"

"No," Ada says, "she wasn't Snake Blood, but she was a powerful oracle who could see much of the future. She was born here, in Caria, and we grew up together. Even when she was very young, she would go into a trance and prophesy. Her visions were so clear and correct that her fame grew far and wide. Many sacred sites vied for her services. She ended up at the Temple of Dodona in Epirus. Have you heard of it?"

Kat gasps. Everyone in the world has heard of the Temple of Dodona, whose prophetess is second in greatness only to the Oracle of Delphi.

Her *mother* was the Oracle of Dodona. And never told her. At first she feels angry, betrayed. But then she remembers how young she was when Helen died. Too young to learn these things.

"Why did she leave?" Kat asks. "I thought oracles usually stayed at their temples for life."

"They generally do. But a certain Epirote princess took the oracle with her to Pella when she went to marry King Philip, ostensibly as her handmaiden, though in truth to keep a prophetess at hand."

"Olympias." Kat hisses the name. "The queen's handmaidens told me how much time she spent with my mother alone, closeted together. They thought it was because they were best friends."

"No," Ada says firmly. "Helen told me the queen was always seeking information about the future. Your mother wasn't happy there. Still, she stayed until she had to leave."

Kat turns to Ada, willing herself to look into those strange white-ringed black eyes that stir up so many shifting emotions.

"What happened?" she asks, terrified of the answer.

"Oracles aren't allowed to have lovers, Katerina. They must keep themselves pure vessels for the gods to enter and speak through them."

Kat turns away and her whole body sags. "She was with child…"

"Yes. It was early, and she wasn't showing. But she knew. She knew you were coming. That much she confessed to me. A child born of darkness, a forbidden girl child. She obtained permission from the queen to visit relatives in Caria, but she really came to ask my advice about where to hide a baby that would be born with Snake Blood. She knew the child must be hidden, kept out of the way of the Aesarian Lords and their spies. When she got to Halicarnassus, she found that I was being tried by the Lords as a Snake Blood. She saved my life. She pretended to go into a trance and speak with the voice of the god, threatening the Lords with doom and destruction if they didn't let me go."

In the far distance, lightning tears through the sky.

"And they let you go."

"They did, reluctantly. I knew they would be back, though, and created this refuge up here. No one can enter unless I allow it. As for your mother, I told her to go to the village of Erissa, a dull little place far off the beaten path. Evidently she did so on the night of the prince's birth, when the entire palace was rejoicing and she wouldn't be missed for some time. I sent a kestrel to watch over her and report back to me. He saw her that night, riding for Erissa as if the Furies were chasing her."

Now, finally, Kat is getting answers. Helen needed to leave the palace before her pregnancy showed, and took advantage of the confusion surrounding Alexander's birth. That night she rode to Erissa to protect her unborn child. Olympias was furious with her and finally tracked her down and killed her for leaving.

"And who was my father?" Kat asks. Clearly it wasn't the wandering wool merchant Helen told her about, who, she'd claimed, died shortly after Kat's birth. "Did she say?"

"She would never tell me, but she asked me for help, for a spell. I'm afraid…" Ada shakes her head. "I'm afraid she wanted harm done to your father. Wanted his silence."

Kat gulps, wondering what all this could mean.

In all of her swirling thoughts and emotions, one detail keeps snagging.

"What was in the ivory-and-turquoise box?" she asks. "Why did Olympias want it?"

"What box?" Ada asks.

"When Olympias found us, Mother dug up a box and gave it to the queen. The queen had Mother killed anyway. When I was at the palace I was spying on the queen and saw her open that box. Inside were a baby's bones, Ada. Did Mother put them there? Or the queen, later?"

Ada frowns. "I don't know anything about the box," she says. Thunder booms in the distance. "It seems Helen had many secrets, Katerina, and perhaps together you and I can yet discover them."

The next week—or is it more?—flies by in a blur. It is the most exhilarating and exhausting time Kat has ever known. So much activity is packed into each day that she wonders if Ada has somehow slowed time down, stretched it to cram two days of work into one. She has never seen the sun crawl so imperceptibly across the sky before. But still she pushes herself, hard. For her mother's sake. For Daphne's. For all the unreasonable suffering that could have been stopped if Kat had achieved her mission and killed the queen.

Since the magic of the mind can leave the body weak and vulnerable, Ada emphasizes physical strength and flexibility. Kat climbs up jagged mountain peaks, shimmies down ropes dangling off cliffs, races for hours through mountain meadows, and swims in icy streams that numb her limbs.

"We are all creatures of the body and the mind," Ada says one day as Kat staggers back to the palace, wet, freezing, bruised, and more than a little angry. "Most humans think the body is predominant. It is heavy, hungry, tired, or in pain. It is like a cranky child always needing something. Its goal—

almost always a successful one—is to keep the mind focused on the body, and not on its own powers."

Kat can only agree. Her body is complaining so loudly about a dozen different discomforts she can't think of anything else at all.

Ada continues, "Those with blood magic know how to shift the balance. Snake Bloods move the power back to the mind, which should control the body, not be at its mercy."

In her sessions of mind training, with Ada by her side, Kat slips into the body of a bird, wheeling and circling above the plain below, floating on air currents with hundreds of other birds, feeling the breeze stream through her feathers in an exultation of freedom she could never have imagined possible. She becomes a fish, waving her fins in the shimmering watery world of the mountain river. She transforms into a worm, painstakingly carving a path through rich black earth.

In each experience, she has flashes of herself in her human form, sitting in a trance in her bedroom, wearing her mother's Flower of Life necklace rubbed with lotus oil, a sedative that stills the ceaseless chattering of the mind and helps Kat remain in control.

One day Ada takes Kat into a long bright chamber with arched windows on two sides. She flings off her feathered robes, revealing long muscular limbs, and throws Kat a sword.

"What? Me? A sword?" Kat says. She might be scrappy in a fistfight, but she never learned sword fighting—what village girl would?—and only sparred with Jacob now and then using rusty dull weapons. It wasn't much fun as he was always afraid of hurting her.

"Yes. You. A sword," Ada mimics sarcastically.

After teaching Kat basic moves, Ada says, "The greatest success in sword fighting doesn't come from watching where your opponent will swing the sword, but reading his mind, knowing where he will move it before he even starts to. The ability to do this, Katerina, is more important than years of sword practice. Now I will open my mind wide, concentrating on my next move, and I want you to enter my thoughts and defend yourself accordingly."

I will stab her in the stomach.

Kat raises her shield in front of her torso just as Ada starts to swing her sword.

"Good. Again."

I will slash her in the neck.

Kat raises her sword and blocks Ada's well before it nears her neck.

"Good. Again." And so the practice goes, speeding up until they are a blur of swords and shields. Sweat flies off Kat, her heart pounds and her arms and legs ache, but she has never felt so powerful before. Soon Ada's thoughts are no longer words or directives, just flashes of instinct that Kat perceives as though they were her own.

A large dappled bird flaps lazily into the room from an open window and settles on a chair, where it begins to preen itself. Kat wonders what kind of bird—

Ada's blunted sword point pushes hard into Kat's throat.

Kat cries out, stumbling back, choking. She blinks hot tears away at the pain. She can hardly swallow.

"That will get you killed in a real fight," Ada says, eyes flashing in rage. "You cannot rely on the physical to defend yourself. You don't have the bodily strength or years of weapons training your opponents will have. We can assume they will be men with muscles of iron who outweigh you two to one. Men who could snap your bones with one hand, who could pick you up and toss you across the room like a rag doll. Your only advantage is staying in your enemy's mind. The moment you come out of his mind, you are dead."

At the end of each day, as the sun finally slides behind the mountain peaks, Kat is so physically and emotionally exhausted she can barely move. When she falls into bed, she's asleep before her head hits the pillow.

Today Ada has instructed her to experiment with her own memories. She is sitting in her bedroom, slivers of daylight creeping in through closed shutters, the room aglow with dozens of flickering oil lamps. The blue smoke of incense rises lazily from a burner, its scent calming her fractious thoughts, relaxing her aching body.

"Once you can access your own memories, you may be able to enter those of others," Ada says, and her voice is low and hypnotic. "Though you will never be able to enter the mind of another Snake Blood unless invited to. Now, go into the silence within you and ask to see your past. Remember, *everything* exists in the silence."

Kat hears a swoosh of feathers and a door quietly closing. She retreats into the silent caverns of her mind. It is dark there, and warm. She floats peacefully for a long time.

I'm going to be in the tournament, Jacob says, grinning sheepishly, and her heart leaps to see him the way he used to be when the world was still good, standing in the lane near their house, his tousled brown hair and unbleached tunic still damp from the pond where they kissed so passionately. He runs his hand over her cheek. *I'll come back once I have something to offer. Something to offer...you.*

Is she really with him now? He seems so real. His fingertips on her cheek are warm and gentle. Can she change things, keep them the way they were that last, wonderful day?

No, because when she puts a hand out to touch his face, it changes into his father's face, and the hand stretching out in front of her is very small, a plump beige starfish of a hand. *You will live with us now,* Cleon says, tears in his dark eyes. He enfolds her hand in his large calloused one. *We will be your family and take care of you.*

She puts her arms around him, feels the violent wracking sorrow of his embrace, and when she pulls back, she sees her mother's smiling face. *Are you ready for dinner?* Helen asks brightly, her blue eyes smiling. *I have something special for you!*

She reaches to touch her mother's face but the hand is truly tiny now, and she can't even see it, just flex her fingers in the warm, liquid darkness. She somersaults slowly and hears the comforting beating of hearts. But then there is movement, disruption. She is being tightly squeezed and cannot move or stretch. She opens her mouth to scream but no sound comes out. Then she tumbles into blinding light and rough hands. She feels something cold and wet on her skin, and voices rise around her like loud rushing water. Somehow she knows, without knowing, that this is her birth. And she's experiencing it both as she did then *and* as she is now. Because it's more than a memory. This is her blood magic, growing stronger. Like when she was in the scorpion's body and, somehow, her own, at the same time.

Amid the noise there is a thin choking wail. Her own wail. She is wrapped in something warm and placed in someone's arms.

Sobbing, she opens her eyes and blinks. She sees large green eyes looking into her own. Green eyes. But Helen had blue eyes.

Helen had blue eyes.

Helen had blue eyes…

Kat's screams are one with the baby's wails. And mixed in with that are the cries of someone else…the cries of another baby beside her.

"Kill the girl," says a harsh voice, a voice she recognizes.

"Not here!" says a softer voice she also knows. "The

Furies would haunt this place if an innocent were killed here. Let me take her into the country, offer the proper sacrifices."

There is a pause as Kat waves her tiny red fists, sobbing helplessly.

"Very well. Wrap her in these sheets. Don't let anyone see you taking her away. And take that ivory jewelry box on my table to bring me proof. The prophecy must not be fulfilled."

The words come to her from afar, dimly, swirling together in her infant mind, uninterpretable.

Kat looks around wildly, but her eyes can't really focus. There is too much light. She is trapped here, on the day of her birth. She can't get out. Can't come back to the present. She screams at the top of her lungs because she is trapped, with those horrible green eyes that want to kill her...

A strong, sweet smell right below her nose jolts her out of her terror. She yanks her head back and opens her eyes. Her body is convulsing—arms and legs moving jerkily of their own accord—and she shakes with cold even as sweat runs in rivulets down her face. Ada holds the lotus flower to her nose again. She has a hand behind Kat's head, steadying her.

"Breathe, deeply, yes," she says.

Kat inhales and feels her body begin, slowly, to calm, though she is still trembling.

Ada crushes the flower petals and rubs them into Kat's lotus necklace. "What did you see that upset you so?" Ada whispers.

Kat opens her mouth to speak but realizes she can't describe it. Not yet. The memories are too fresh, too painful. Every baby must be frightened by birth, she knows, leaving the cozy quiet of the womb for a world of bruising light and crashing sound. But what really horrifies Kat is the vision of the green eyes.

Because she knows who those eyes belong to...

Sweat pours down her forehead again, and she feels faint.

"This is a lesson for you," Ada says. "When you slip out of yourself, either into your past or into another living thing, you can get stuck there forever unless someone calls you out, as I just did, or unless you are so well trained you can free yourself. This is why even though you have made much progress, there is still much for you to learn. I will let you rest now, Katerina. We'll talk later."

After Ada withdraws, Kat opens the shutters, letting in shining daylight and fresh mountain air. She blows out the lamps and incense burner and bathes her face in cool mint water. Exhausted, she lies down...

But she cannot rest. Whether her eyes are closed or open, whether she is lying on her left side or her right, she always sees the same thing.

Green eyes.

But it can't be. Because that would mean that everything is a lie.

It is a lie.

And even Ada doesn't know. For even Ada believes that Helen was Kat's mother.

Kat swallows hard, recalling word for word the Blood and Bones Ritual she read in the archives, a spell to reverse a curse.

These rites can only occur in times of great change, when one Age dies and another is born. And they must involve the blood and bones of one's own offspring...

She doesn't know what curse, but she knows enough to make her feel physically sick. Trembling in horror, she sits up and looks at the palms of her hands, tracing the delicate blue veins of her wrists. She clenches them into fists, knowing what she must do.

She must return to Pella.

CHAPTER TWENTY-NINE

IN THE TREE-SHROUDED GLADE OF THE SOUTHern hill, Alexander peers down at the Macedonian camp, watching the three torches move slowly from tent to tent, firelight glinting off the bronze helmets of men sitting and sleeping around each fire. In the darkness of the new moon, the men seem ready for dawn's battle, but the camp is one of ghosts.

His army set up old helmets and capes on wooden crosses jammed into the ground or put them on empty pallets. They brought gentle, quiet oxen and fixed baskets with damp, burning straw on one of their horns and let them wander the campsite, mimicking the slow walk of generals the night before battle. After helping themselves to the water in the amphorae and pretending to get drunk and argue, one by one all the men slipped away, some to one hill, some to the other, leading horses with burlap shoes on their hooves and muzzles on their mouths to deaden any noise. There's not a single man in the camp. Alex prays they are not found out.

War. Real war. This is it—what they've been training for

and dreaming about. Not skirmishes with Thracian cattle raiders or Illyrian rebels, but full-out war with a powerful enemy. And more than that for him—it's his first battle as general. Everything—life and death, victory or defeat, freedom or slavery—is riding on his decisions, his commands.

He has always fantasized about this moment. But now that it's here, he isn't sure how he feels. It's one thing to imagine deeds of valor on the battlefield over a mug of wine with friends, another to stare war in its ugly, gaping face. If he loses, the Aesarian Lords will rule Macedon, crushing the joy out of everything. Every town square will hold a tribunal for witch trials.

He thinks of the thousands of people behind the city walls—the long line of citizens who entered the palace gates with oxen and goats, lambs and donkeys, carts of wine, and barrels of olives. He had sent heralds to warn those outside Pella's walls of an imminent attack. While city people hide behind high walls, farmers are murdered and enslaved, their womenfolk killed, their animals and crops stolen, their olive trees cut down, the wells poisoned, the buildings burned. Ten families are camped out in the throne room alone.

"Did you sleep?"

Heph's voice startles Alex from his thoughts.

"Not much," Alex admits. What he can't explain, either to himself or to Heph, is that interspersed with obsessive strategizing about today's upcoming battle, images of Kat kept haunting him in the night. Fear for her safety. This peasant girl he knew for a mere couple of weeks. It makes no sense to him, but he knows there's something special about her, about their connection, and he can't help worry that her absence is a bad omen for the events of today.

And then, of course, there's Cynane's disappearance. Much as he may dislike his half sister, her presumed kidnapping by the Lords was a strange choice, and he suspects they have larger plans in store. For once, he pities Cyn, knowing it may take more than this one battle before he's able to rescue her from their foes.

He tries his best to push these thoughts away. He certainly can't express any doubts to Hephaestion—or any of his men. He mustn't let the mind's many weaknesses get in his way. He's silent for a minute before he says, simply, "So much depends on us."

"I am praying for mist," Heph whispers back. "Remember when we were here the summer before Mieza? There was always a thick dawn mist covering that field, like three feet of snow."

Alex nods. It burned off within half an hour after sunrise, but that might be all the time they need.

Around them, the men begin to wake and prepare for battle. Somewhere nearby, lark song, pure and sweet, warbles through the darkness. Other birds reply, tweeting and chirping. The entire world is stirring as the air turns from black to deepest silver. Then the sun crests the horizon, revealing a milky-white soup on the plain below, just as they hoped. Above the mist, bronze helmets gleam like carnelians in the orange rays of the rising sun, and red Macedonian capes swing slightly in the early morning breeze. Tall Macedonian guards stand watch on either side of the catapult and on the edges of the camp, but they, too, are just capes and helmets on sticks.

While high on the hill, the true Macedonian soldiers hurry to their positions.

It's time. Time to gain the reputation of a victorious general that he has always dreamed of. He feels a rush of exhilaration. Every part of him is alive with energy.

"Archers at the ready!" Alex whispers, and each man whispers the command to his neighbors. Heph, the best archer in the army, is front and center, behind a chest-high bush. Alex watches as he confidently sets an arrow in his bow.

"Hold your fire until I give the order!" Alex says quietly, and he once again hears the command whispered down the line of men like the hiss of a snake retreating. They've all been informed of the plan. If they recognize High Lord Mordecai by his helmet—the only Aesarian with bronze horns—they must hold fire at all costs, band together and surround him. Each soldier has been outfitted with a ram's horn, with a shrill whistling note that will soar over battle screams and alert the others to Mordecai's whereabouts. This is their one priority in addition to driving back the troops. Alex knows that Mordecai has answers about the Hemlock Torch. And he might be used as a trade-in for Cynane in the future. No, they can't risk losing this opportunity, if at all possible.

They wait. Each second seems like an eternity. Alex clenches and unclenches his fists, trying to stay in the moment, to stay focused. The greatest danger is to let the mind take over, with all its worries, when it's the body's turn to act.

His heart is beating in his chest like a battle drum. The enemy must attack before the mist disappears.

"Brotherhood! Righteousness! Aesarians!" come the enemy cries from the plain below.

From their vantage point, the Macedonian army watches—breath held in unison—as dozens of Aesarian horsemen and hundreds of cavalrymen race through the pass between the hills toward the fake Macedonian camp, their legs and waists invisible in the swirling mist so that they almost resemble the mythic centaurs—heads and torsos of men, with bodies of horses— their black battle flags with five red flames and a white crescent moon flapping as they ride. The front row of horsemen lets loose a deadly rain of arrows on the camp, seemingly unaware that the "soldiers" remain upright. They are too intent on attack to notice the "men" are in fact just capes hung on wooden crosses—too intent on demolishing this pitiful force led by an inexperienced boy.

Laughter rises in Alex's throat. He's tricked the world's greatest warriors. But he reminds himself this is just the beginning. Within minutes he will have to prove himself on the field of battle.

The Lords are careening all over the camp now, hacking and slashing at the fake soldiers, throwing spears into empty capes. Then everything stops. They realize they have been deceived. Alex keeps his bow steady as he watches. Soon, it will be time to strike. The Aesarian horsemen wheel their whinnying horses around in tight circles. The foot soldiers turn right and left, looking for a living soldier to kill.

"A trick!" one cries.

"Deceit!" shouts another.

"Fire!" Alex shouts, and his voice itself is like an arrow, finally released. He feels all the tension of the wait flying out of him as anticipation becomes action, and he's on fire now, all heat, more alive than he has ever felt before.

Macedonian arrows whine through the air. Alex has aimed his at a tall Aesarian Lord on a brown horse and he watches as it digs deep into the man's neck. The Lord falls to the ground, lost in the mist, as his horse bellows in fear and gallops off.

A deadly hail of black arrows descends from both hills as the archers fire again and again. Some miss their mark entirely; others hit horses who throw their riders and race away, trampling foot soldiers. Some arrows bounce harmlessly off shields and helmets and breastplates, or bite deep into arms and legs, wounding the Lords, slowing them down for hand-to-hand combat. A few plunge into necks or eyes, killing their targets instantly.

"Tortoise!" cries the Aesarian commander, who blows five

short notes on a bronze trumpet. Immediately the remains of the cavalry skitter beyond arrow range while those on foot form up in a square, the front rows holding up their shields in front of them, the inside rows holding them over their heads. They do, in fact, look much like a giant tortoise shell from afar. No arrow can puncture this phalanx.

Alex takes a quick count of the arrows in his quiver and looks around at his men. The Macedonians are almost out of arrows anyway. In a flash, he realizes: it's time for real battle. They're all waiting on him. "Advance!" he commands.

Kadmus blows the war trumpet three times, and it's echoed by a horn on the other hill. Macedonians come streaming down both hills on horse and on foot crying, *"Alala! Alala!"* at the top of their lungs. Alala, the daughter of Polemus, the demon of war, is the goddess of the war cry. Hundreds of men scream her name.

Below him, Bucephalus pounds the mud into obedience, the animal's energy flying up through Alexander's body as though it were part of his own. He feels wind in his face and his horse's sweat spraying from its mane, and the sensation is exulting.

This is what he was born for.

The Aesarian infantry unlocks itself from its tortoise formation and spreads across the field. Behind it, the cavalry races toward the Macedonian charge. Alex sees the entire field as though it's one large, moving organism—all angles and arcs, all speed and rhythm—a giant mathematical puzzle of arms and legs and beasts, of swords and shields and breastplates and helmets, of spraying blood and cries of agony.

Within the chaos, he quickly picks a target: a Lord on a piebald horse about thirty feet away, speeding toward him with his spear raised. Alexander and his enemy throw their spears at the same moment. Alex's spear sinks into the man's groin, while the enemy's spear tears through Alex's royal shield with such force he is nearly knocked off Bucephalus, but the enemy's terrified horse rears, throwing his fatally wounded rider to the ground.

Alex has a moment—only a moment—to wrench the spear from his shield. It entered right above the arm holster. An inch lower and Alex would have lost his lower left arm. As it is, his shield now has a small hole in it, but at least he has another seven-foot spear to throw, a great advantage when enemies have already thrown theirs and are attacking with swords only three feet long.

He looks around at his forces. His left is losing ground slightly, but his center is attacking the advancing Lords on the side as they swoop in. He nods in approval. His men are doing exactly what they trained to do. His right is actually advancing. He is surrounded by war cries, screams of pain, pounding hooves, and whinnying horses, but those noises fade and he mostly hears his own breathing, his own heartbeat.

Heph. Where is Heph?

He scans the nearby men and doesn't see Heph. But he does spot a foot soldier fighting hand-to-hand with Diodotus. It's a desperate battle between two evenly matched enemies. Alex races over and throws as hard as he can at the Aesarian's back. The spear pieces the armor and the man, its iron tip emerging from his chest. He drops. Diodotus grins at Alex as he canters to his side. "Looks like my spear training has paid off!" he says as he bends down, puts his boot on the dead man's back, and wrenches out the spear. He throws it to Alex who catches it handily.

He has no time to gloat, however, as another Lord runs toward him, his spear raised high, aiming not for Alex but his horse. Alexander feels a spike of panic, but before he can react, suddenly, Heph is there, galloping at full speed. He aims his spear at the white flesh of the man's underarm, that soft unguarded spot between bronze breastplate and leather arm guard. It sinks in. The man's raised spear falls to the ground, the man following after it.

The army... What is his army doing? He wishes he could be a bird, looking down, seeing clearly what is happening all around him. Right now all he sees is chaos, small pockets of men fighting. A runaway horse with an arrow in its shoulder careens into Bucephalus, who rears and throws Alex.

When he picks himself up, a man stands in front of him, his face twisted into a leering snarl. Lord Bastian. The same man who two weeks ago indicated Macedonians were a race of cripples, too cowardly to field a challenger in their skills demonstration. Alex lost that bout, but he's not going to lose this one. Because this one is to the death.

Alex raises his sword and the two men slowly circle each other. "When we sparred that day in the odeon, you said we could finish what we started another day," Alex says, his voice hoarse with anger. "Today is the day."

"It is no great victory to kill a cripple, a coddled princely weakling," Bastian scoffs.

"Nor is it a feat of valor to kill a crook who cheats at dice," Alex says, gratified to see the flash of uncertainty in his opponent's eyes. He swings his sword and it rings down on Bastian's.

All pretense of chivalrous politeness is gone. This is a fight to the death. Again and again their swords meet or crack onto each other's shields. Alex is alert for Aesarian tricks. The sword thrusting out from the edge of the shield or swinging behind the waist as the warrior turns. Bastian makes all the moves Alex saw in the skills demonstration, and he is ready for them. He senses Bastian's increasing anger as he easily parries blows meant to kill. But Alex's grin masks the pain in his shield arm as it grows weak and fatigued under the endless attack.

Suddenly a spear embeds itself in the back of Alex's shield with such force it cracks and he drops it. In that split second Bastian knocks the sword out of his other hand. Bastian raises his own sword for the kill, and Alex, defenseless now, knows he is going to die. As the sword comes crashing down, another Aesarian Lord, three arrows sticking out of his back like porcupine quills, stumbles in front of Alex and takes the blow on his shoulder. Alex rolls out of the way, picks up his sword, and looks for Bastian, but he is gone.

In fact, they're all gone, or going. Alex hears an Aesarian trumpet bleating commands and sees the backs of countless black capes and horned helmets racing away from him, back into the pass between the two hills where they came from an eternity ago. As the Aesarians retreat, jubilant Macedonians race after them, cutting down those they reach from behind.

It's a trick. Alex is sure of it.

Heph pulls up beside Alex, drawing Bucephalus by the reins. There is a nasty cut on his arm, but other than that he appears unscathed. Alex feels a warm surge of relief.

"That was too easy," Alex says, his mouth a tight line, as he swings onto his horse. "Retreat!" he cries, pulling out his trumpet and blowing it five times. Across the battlefield, other trumpets pick up the signal and repeat it. The men, perplexed, stop chasing the retreating enemy and fall back.

Kadmus, on a brown horse now, pulls up beside Alex. "They're regrouping," he says, and Alex notices deep dents in his breastplate and a slash on his leg. "There will be reinforcements back there, fresh men, many of them on fresh horses. Our men are mostly unhorsed at this point, wounded, and exhausted."

"Of course," Alex says grimly. "We knew it wouldn't be an

easy victory, even with our initial deception. But at least we have time to reform. Battle formation for pincer movement!" he cries, and blows the trumpet four short times. The trumpet is echoed across the field. "Archers at the ready! Catapult at the ready!" Men repeat his orders across the battlefield so everyone can hear.

"We will soften them up as they come toward us," Alex says. "Heph, lead my left. Kadmus will lead the right. Arrows first. Heph, you can hit a bird's eye at five hundred paces."

"Where's your shield?" Heph asks.

"Broken."

Heph hands him his. "Go," he says. "I'll find another one. The men need you now."

Alex grins, slides his arm in the leather straps, and kicks Bucephalus into a gallop. He surveys the entire battlefield, the Macedonian and Aesarian dead and wounded, the number of horses remaining, the condition of the men's weapons, and most of all, their fighting spirit. He orders that all those unable to continue fighting be carried off to the side on shields where physicians can attend them. He asks questions, issues orders, and stops often to praise his men by name. For years he worked to remember every soldier's name in his father's army. For this day. For this moment.

"Clytias, you have fought well today!" he cries to a sweaty bearded man leaning on his spear. "Your father's shade is proud of you! Make sure to hold this side firm when they attack."

The soldier beams up at him and says, "I will, my lord!"

Alex wheels his horse around and sees a man with a bloody bandage on his arm, blood streaming out beneath it. "Alcon! That's a nasty wound. Do you wish to leave the field?"

"It's but a scratch, my lord," the man says gamely. "I fight for honor."

"I am proud to have you on my side," Alex says. "Make sure

your men fight together as a unit, not as individuals. You are all parts of a whole." The man nods, glorying in the praise. "And you know the protocol."

He nods again. "When we spot the High Lord, we blow the horn, surround, and isolate."

"That's right."

Back and forth Alex flies, purple cape flapping behind him, reconnoitering the entire field, encouraging, instructing, analyzing. Some of the men he sees have lost weapons in the fray.

"Find your spears!" he cries. "Get your arrows! If your shield is damaged, find a better one! Helmet and shield straps must hold tight!"

Many Macedonians race across the battlefield picking up replacements for weapons that have been lost or damaged. Some of the soldiers—Macedonian and Aesarian alike—are still alive when Alexander's men yank spears and arrows out of their bodies, and groan in anguish as the iron rips from flesh.

Then the army is facing the pass. Their center is intentionally weak—only two rows of men, a tempting target for the enemy, but there are eight long rows on the left and right flanks. If the Lords crash through the center, the two sides will wheel in like pincers, attempting to crush them.

Wafted on a light breeze is the smell of blood and sweat.

Just as the Macedonians are ready, the Aesarian army lines up in the pass. At first Alex isn't too concerned about their size, but then they stream onto the plain like black flood waters, spreading out in a deadly deluge. They are outnumbered two to one. No… They keep coming. And coming. Three to one. The Macedonians inhale sharply as if with one breath.

This is the end. They cannot win this. The Lords will surround the entire Macedonian force and beat them into a smaller and smaller circle. Alex feels his whole body stiffening, turning to stone as if he has looked Medusa in the eye. Because looking at Medusa is death. And at this moment he is looking at his own death, and the death of everyone, everything he holds dear.

He is paralyzed, his heart beating so fast he can hardly catch his breath. Hundreds of faces turn from the advancing army toward him. They are looking to him for guidance. For encouragement. He must say something. Must do something. Everyone is depending on him. If he shows fear, they are not only dead, but their memory will be disgraced.

Anger wells up in him. Anger at himself. This is his first great battle. Does he *want* it to be easy? Doesn't he want his fame to spread far and wide as having won against insurmountable odds?

He relaxes, smiles broadly, and cries as he raises his sword to the sky. "Thank the gods for such a chance to win eternal glory!"

The men grin back and wave their swords. "Thank the gods for glory!" they cry. "Thank the gods!"

They turn to the enemy, eager now to fight. Alex holds his sword high, ready to kick Bucephalus and race toward the enemy. In those few seconds the world is absolutely silent except for the sounds of horses nickering and pawing the ground.

And the rattling of cart wheels.

Out of the burning mist, a low, hideous growl sounds. Alex turns around and sees a sight so strange he wonders if he is having another vision.

There, at the far right side of the battlefield, sending up plumes of dust on the track behind her, is Timandra, mistress of the maids, in full battle armor, silver hair streaming over a bronze breastplate, driving a cart loaded with old wine amphorae. Two other women sit beside her. He recognizes one as Sarina, Arri's maid, usually known for her silence and patience, suddenly looking powerful and fierce, her dark skin gleaming in the sun. The other woman must be another of the queen's ladies-in-waiting, and looks like she's about to faint right off the wagon.

A second cart appears. In the driver's position, also geared up in full battle armor...is Katerina.

She has returned.

And in a cage on that cart paces the hellion, its wings tucked, hissing, and lashing at the bars.

What in Hades' name are the *women* doing?

He can't wait to find out. He lowers his sword and cries, "Advance!"

CHAPTER THIRTY

THE ARMIES RACE TOWARD EACH OTHER LIKE two seas roaring across the plain and clashing violently in the middle. A foot soldier slashes up at Hephaestion, who raises his shield, and the sword tears a hole right through the cowhide. Heph hacks at the man, who falls.

Ahead of him, Phrixos has lost his mount and is fighting two Lords by himself. Heph races toward them, but an Aesarian horseman thunders up to him, cutting him off. Heph raises his damaged shield and his sword and gallops toward his adversary. An arrow hits Heph's horse in the thick leather padding around his belly and he rears up in fear, sending Heph crashing to the ground before cantering off.

Before he can rise, he sees a Lord above him, swinging a cruelly spiked mace on a chain. Heph has only time to raise his shield and pray the mace doesn't crash down on the damaged section. It doesn't, but it splinters the entire shield, cracking it like an eggshell above Heph, the spikes only a fraction of an inch from his face. He doesn't move, wanting the Lord to think he's dead, knowing the man won't be able to pull his mace out of the shield easily. It's clearly stuck in the tangle of splintered wood and shredded cowhide. Grunting in frustration, the Lord finally pulls the entire shield off Heph, who follows right behind it, springing up with his sword, slicing his throat.

Where's Alex? Heph looks for a purple cape waving over a black horse, but just then a wounded horse careens wildly into him, knocking him to the ground. He rises, looking for his sword, but a Lord almost twice Heph's size wraps thick strong hands around his neck, crushing his throat. Heph remembers a move Diodotus taught him and head butts the man as hard as he can, smashing his nose and loosening his teeth. The Lord reels backward, blood pouring onto his chin, as Heph plucks his sword from the ground and runs him through.

Heph's head rings with pain and he sinks to the blood-soaked ground. This isn't how his first battle is supposed to be. He is supposed to help Alex achieve victory. Win the prince's eternal gratitude. Be envied and admired and...safe.

But here he is in the dirt with a splitting headache.

Still feeling disoriented, he forces himself to rise again. He's suddenly assaulted by smells: horses covered with dust and lather, sweet crushed grass and thick salty blood, oiled bronze, the sour sweat of fear, and, oddly, the comforting aromas of warm leather and the smoke from last night's campfires. He's surrounded by battle cries and the shrieks of dying men. Riderless horses rear and wheel and gallop past him. Swords flash orange in the sun. The dawn mist is shriveling up like curls of white smoke when water is thrown on a hearth.

Heph stumbles forward and sees a severed hand, fingers spread, on the ground above a sword. It looks to him like a hairy brown spider that will crawl away.

Strange laughter rises in his throat and he wonders if he is losing his mind. He rubs his throbbing forehead. His throat aches, and his mouth is filled with dust. He scans the field. The bulk of both armies have surged away from him, the Aesarians encircling the Macedonians. He needs to rally men to attack the Aesarians from behind, drawing them away from the Macedonian center. He needs to help Alex.

He quickly grabs a shield from a fallen Macedonian soldier just as a Lord with bronze horns jumps in front of him, sword raised.

High Lord Mordecai.

Instinctively, Heph parries the blow, circles, and lunges, feeling that he is coming back to himself. He has to come back to himself if he is going to survive this encounter. He knows he must signal to the Macedonians so that they can fall into proper formation and isolate Mordecai—Alexander's plan hinges on Heph's ability to capture the leader alive.

Despite his age—the High Lord must be in his forties—he is strong *and* flexible, an unusual combination, and his swordsmanship is lightning-fast. As Heph defends himself, he has no chance to reach for the ram's horn on his belt. But failing Alexander isn't an option.

With a ferocious bust of energy, Heph attacks Mordecai, letting his muscles, hard from endless hours of training, respond before his mind grasps his next move. The High Lord stumbles, and Heph lunges—

—to meet with air.

An Aesarian tactic. Lord Mordecai intentionally fell, only to roll over, spring up, and thrust his sword toward Heph's throat. The tip of the Aesarian sword scratches Heph's cheek and splits the chin strap of his helmet. A moment later, his helmet falls off and rolls around on the ground like a dropped bronze coin.

"Could it be?" the High Lord says, his cold gray eyes glinting. "Alexander's mindless minion."

Heph backs away. Now any blow to his head will kill him. He needs his men to come to help him. He needs to give the signal. He lowers his sword, his thumb brushing against the curving shell-like twist of ram's horn hanging from a leather thong on his belt. And hesitates.

"Blow your little horn, boy," Mordecai mocks in his thin, reedy voice. "Call for reinforcements. Shame yourself that you could not best a graying man."

Still Heph hesitates. His sword is warm in his hand. The horn dangles from its thong.

"Go on," Mordecai sneers, raising his battle blade for the deathblow. "Let them all see how worthless you are—the second-rate, pretty leech that will take any scrap thrown at him. Alexander's chamber pot."

Heph forgets the ram's horn. He forgets duty. His sword, alive in his hands, lashes into Mordecai, sinking into flesh, severing sinew, hitting bone. He has become something other than himself. He has become pure rage. A red mist swims in front of his eyes, like the day he fended off the hellion in the menagerie. Like the day he killed his sister's attacker.

Again and again, Heph's sword bites into the High Lord's neck, long after life's light has left the broken man.

Suddenly Heph feels sick looking at the mangled body in front of him. The body Alex needed alive. Heph promised the prince that his pride would never cloud his actions, but he's failed his prince and his friend—again.

Alexander cannot know.

Something hurtles through the air at Heph, and he instinctively raises his shield and steps back, thinking it is a missile, but it's a helmet. Either some god or one of Heph's men saw his danger and tossed him a dead Macedonian's helmet. He grabs the helmet and straps it securely to his head.

Another enemy soldier rushes Heph from the left...then spots the bronze horns lying bloody on the ground.

"The High Lord is dead!" The cry is heard by others, and soon the news echoes across the battlefield. The Aesarian thrust wavers, then the formation nearest Heph scatters as the loss of their leader hits them.

"Regroup!" comes the cry of several voices, followed by trumpets blaring orders.

In the broken wave of Aesarian Lords, Heph looks around, trying to regain his bearings, to figure out how to explain himself to the prince, when suddenly, standing near the catapult, he sees...

Katerina.

He blinks, wiping the sweat and mud from his eyes. It can't be.

She's wearing a helmet. And breastplate. A sword in her belt. Standing near the catapult and grinning at him.

He rubs his eyes again. She's still there.

"Kat," Heph says, finally gaining control of himself. "What are you— No matter. You've got to get away from here with the other women. Now!" He points to the Aesarian army hacking at the Macedonians. "You'll all be killed."

Kat turns to two women at the catapult and cries, "Release!" To Heph's amazement, it's not a rock that goes sailing through the air, but an old amphora, the fat-bellied wide-mouthed kind from the old storage room beneath the prison. Men point at the giant wine jug flying through the air, some of them laughing. It crashes among Aesarian horses encircling the Macedonian phalanx. The Aesarians turn back, see three women loading another amphora into the sling, and their laughter ripples across the battlefield.

"Are you crazy?" Heph shouts.

"Just wait," she says sternly as another amphora flies into

the Aesarian line. "I didn't race back across an entire sea in under two days to argue."

It crashes down between horses to more laughter. But suddenly several horses rear up shrieking in fear and pain, as riders try to control them. Again and again the women launch the amphorae. Instead of advancing toward the surrounded Macedonians, the Lords' cavalry is bubbling with confusion as horses shrieking in pain throw their riders and race across the field toward the Macedonians. Some of the men scream, grasping at their faces, where writhing black forms have landed. Even horses that aren't hurt sense the panic in the column, hear the whinnies of their comrades, and smell fear and danger. The Aesarian cavalry is suddenly useless.

Heph storms over to the heap of amphora yet to be thrown from the catapult, picks one up, removes a cheesecloth cover, and looks in. At a roiling, hissing, slithering mass of scorpions and snakes.

"Infantry advance!" cries an Aesarian commander. And two hundred men with spears run across the field.

Heph quickly adjusts the spring of the catapult for a shorter throw. "Launch!" he cries. Now the amphorae are landing and cracking open among the men. Snakes strike their legs with fangs as they run by. Scorpions, their segmented tails curling over their bodies, rattle their poisonous stingers, jabbing the men with stingers. When the men scream and try to pry them away, the creatures bite their hands.

The Aesarian assault is foundering in chaos as amphora after amphora crashes, releasing its deadly cargo. They are retreating, the Macedonians pushing them back.

"Don't launch any more," Heph says. "They would hurt our men as well. Go. Ride to safety."

"No. Take me to the middle of the fighting," Kat says.

"I have the hellion here. I can't really control him—he's too fierce—but I can summon."

"What?" Heph's head is pounding again. But Kat just stares at him with a look of impatience, a look that says *believe me*. And although Alex's men aren't losing any more ground, they aren't advancing, either. The battle could still go either way. Victory might depend on the hellion, if Kat really can call him to fight the enemy. Heph closes his eyes and opens them again. "All right. But stay behind me."

"Not on your life." Kat unsheathes her sword and picks up a shield. Side by side they enter the fray. An arrow comes whistling out of nowhere, and before he can throw Kat out of the way, her shield has blocked it. When a seemingly dead Aesarian springs up with a sword, she knocks it out of his hand before he is halfway up, then impales him with her own. Heph is amazed and realizes he doesn't need to concentrate fully on protecting her; somehow she's doing a good job of it herself. When a Lord jumps out from behind a lame horse, Heph dispatches him quickly.

Then they are in the middle of the battle. Dozens of small groups of men are fighting to the death all around them.

As Heph guards her, she raises her head, eyes closed, lips moving. Heph sees a black shadow circling the battlefield and hears a roar of primeval hunger and rage.

Its cry is so unearthly, so demoniac, that all the men stop fighting and look up. Swords raised in the air don't slice down. Notched arrows aren't set flying. Spears are poised in midair.

The hellion dives down onto a knot of four Aesarians fighting two Macedonians. Its claws shred thick padded leather like parchment. Its fangs sink deep into the exposed flesh of necks and legs, hands and armpits. It's a flash of gleaming black fur and spurting blood. All four Aesarians are dead before they are able to stab the creature.

The two Macedonians shrink back in terror, their swords raised. The beast leaps into battle howling for more Aesarian blood.

Two riderless horses race toward Heph, their eyes rolling in terror. He steps to the right, and they veer right into him, knocking him to the ground. He feels hooves on his arms and legs, but in a second they are gone, running as far from the hellion as they can. He stands up bruised and a bit disoriented, but nothing is broken.

Kat is gone. He sees Telekles wrestling a Lord on the ground, both mud-covered, both holding daggers. He races over and stabs the Lord in the neck. Together he and Telekles traverse the field, coming to their comrades' rescue and, after each fight is won, look for the next one. Once he thinks he sees Kat fighting next to Phrixos, but when he makes his way to them, they are gone.

An Aesarian trumpet blows a haunting call, and those Lords still fighting turn and race back toward their camp. The Lords' withdrawal is like the ebbing of a violent storm surge, a slow retreat of froth and roar that leaves broken corpses and broken weapons littering the blood-soaked shore.

Telekles stops to help a friend of his with a broken leg, strapping a spear to it as a makeshift splint. On the other side of the field, Heph sees Alex on Bucephalus, issuing orders to a group of men. He should go to Alex, he knows. That's his place beside the victorious general. That's where he wants to be. With his friend, basking in victory for Macedon. This is the moment he has been waiting for all his life.

But where is Kat?

He steps over the bloody bodies of soldiers, and weaves among the corpses of horses. Then he spots an Aesarian Lord holding a sword, crouching down. Heph runs up, sword raised, and sees that it's Jacob. The village boy who stole victory from him at the Blood Tournament and was invited to join the king's army, before the Lords recruited him instead.

Now he's bending over Kat. Her eyes are closed, and she's lying in a pool of blood seeping from her crushed breastplate.

"No!" Heph cries, running toward them. Jacob, white-faced and haggard, stands and raises his sword and shield. Their swords clash again and again as they circle. This is what should have happened at the tournament, Heph realizes. A test of battle skills, not nets in trees and tricks. He focuses all his suppressed anger at losing the tournament on this upstart country boy who so quickly became the enemy. And hurt Kat.

Across the field, an Aesarian trumpet blows another haunting call. Jacob casts a last look at Kat and backs away, then turns and runs as fast as he can to join the retreating Aesarians. Heph wants to chase after him, to kill him for what he did to Kat. But he needs to stay with her.

He removes her breastplate. The bloodstain is spreading ever wider over her tunic. He reaches into his pouch and unrolls the thick wad of bandages every soldier is given. Then he rips open her tunic and sees the ugly wound, like a red, jagged oozing mouth. He wraps the bandage under the small of her back, around and over the wound, again and again, and ties it. He has seen such wounds before. She is probably bleeding as much inside as outside. There is nothing any doctor can do. She will die gently in the next six hours or so, after falling asleep.

He cradles her head in his lap and suddenly realizes how much she looks like Alex. Her features are softer, of course, smaller, but they both have the same set of eyes—though Kat's are not mismatched as Alex's are—the broad forehead, straight nose, and pointed chin.

When he looks back at the battlefield, he sees no horned helmets, only the red capes of Macedonians searching for wounded or dead friends and comrades and carrying them off the field on their shields.

"Kat, you're going to be all right," he lies. She doesn't answer. She's looking in wonder at the sky, moving her pale lips.

He turns to see what it is that so fascinates her. It's the hellion, flying in wide lazy circles over the battlefield, howling as it rises higher and higher, and is gone.

CHAPTER THIRTY-ONE

PURE, RAW RAGE THROBS THROUGH OLYMPIAS as she trots down the road toward the house of Cleon the potter.

Still alive.

Her daughter, Alexander's twin, is still alive. That is why the ritual to free Riel from the curse failed. The bones in the ivory box weren't those of her own child. They were the bones of someone else's child. Helen was a lying, deceitful bitch. If Olympias could, she would kill her all over again, though much more slowly this time.

This would all be so much easier if she, herself, possessed blood magic, instead of having to wait upon a man with all the power—even a man she loves. Even a man trapped by a curse.

She still can't believe that her own daughter, alive and well, has dwelled less than a day's ride from Pella, hiding all those years practically in her own backyard. The knowledge that Helen made a fool of her rankles in Olympias's veins.

And then the greater insult—the girl's arrival in her own palace, along with that peasant boy, the one who triumphed in the Blood Tournament. There are no coincidences. Olympias has long learned that. No, the girl, Katerina, was the right age. And her eyes... Olympias should have known.

She'd been looking her own daughter in the eyes this whole time. The thought sickens her.

Olympias had always despised the peasant girl's closeness to Alexander, had simmered with resentment watching her walk beside him, smiling at him, all dressed up like a noblewoman. The feeling was mutual, she knew. Olympias could feel Katerina's hatred hanging in the air between them like an overpowering incense.

When Olympias found the knife on her balcony, she didn't know why this stupid girl wanted to kill her, and she didn't need to know. She just needed to get rid of her.

Olympias thought she had found the perfect solution to arrest Kat without risking her son's hatred. When she caught Lord Bastian trying to poison her, she easily turned the tables on him and made him change sides. Do her bidding. Follow Kat around. When Bastian told her Kat had broken into the secret archives through the window, Olympias had given him the key to the door, instructing him to slip poison in her pouch, then make enough of a scene to be sure the guards knew about it. How elated she was to learn that Kat was her prisoner, in a cell so foul it would surely kill her.

Then, upon hearing the news of Kat's arrest, Iris came to Olympias's chamber, head bowed, plump hands clenching and unclenching. "My lady," she said, "I had no idea Katerina was dangerous. I should have told you immediately—now I see that clearly—and I am so sorry. But I really didn't think it was important so I—"

"By Artemis and Athena, what is it already?" Olympias had cried, tempted to throw the silver hairbrush in her hand at the blabbering woman.

Iris flushed scarlet and took a deep breath. "The day she first came here, the girl was asking a lot of questions about the night of the prince's birth. About her mother and why she disappeared."

"Her *mother*?" Olympias asked, the hairs on the back of her neck rising.

"Helen, my lady. Katerina said her mother was Helen, your favorite handmaiden who vanished the night of Prince Alexander's birth. The one you said was a thief."

Ah.

Olympias stumbled to a chair and sat heavily, thoughts and memories whirling in her head. When her mind calmed, suddenly everything was crystal-clear.

Katerina wanted revenge for Helen's death.

Katerina believed *Helen* was her mother.

Katerina didn't know her own identity.

And Katerina was in a locked cell below the palace.

Olympias dismissed her foolish maid, grabbed Katerina's knife, and marched down to the dungeon. She would enjoy killing her with her own weapon, would enjoy even more using what was left of her in the ritual. Then she could relax knowing that the oracle's prophecy would never come true. That is, if Helen's words all those years ago were to be trusted.

But when the guard opened the door, the cell was empty. The girl had escaped.

Fury causes Olympias's entire body to shiver as she rides, her hands clenched around the reins, feeling the leather rub roughly against the soft skin of her palms, feeling the heat and energy of the beast below her, its hooves pounding into the thick dirt.

There's still a chance to find the girl. After talking to people in the Erissa marketplace, she easily discovered who took

Katerina in after Helen's death. Where would a peasant girl go if she escaped from prison?

Home.

One of the guards she sent on ahead gallops toward her and pulls up his horse. "My lady," says one, "we've found the potter's home. Elias has the family tied up, awaiting you."

"And the girl?" she asks, her heart beating loudly.

He shakes his head. "They say their son sent word she was in Pella, but that was some time ago. They haven't heard anything since."

"We'll see about that," she says through gritted teeth. She kicks the horse in his sides with both heels and it stumbles ahead. Alexander's army took all the good horses into battle.

No matter. Olympias will torture and burn her way through all of Erissa until she finds the answers—and the girl—she's looking for.

Dead or alive.

CHAPTER THIRTY-TWO

BIRDS—CIRCLING. SWOOPING. HUNDREDS, MAYBE thousands of them.

And Ada, tall and dark and feathered herself, arms raised high at her sides at the center of it all.

"Now you," she says, bending her burning gaze on Kat. Those dark eyes that could devour her.

Kat calls silently to the birds, feeling their alertness. Fly, fly. With a whoosh of feathers and caws, they wheel into the air, circling again. She has stray images of hidden nests and scurrying prey, of eggs that hatched and those that will rot from the inside, stinking of loss and yolk. She feels warm sun and bitter wind and cleansing rain. She feels the love of flight racing through her veins as she wheels into the air, as she circles and swoops.

And then, she's no longer flying but falling, falling, and the birds that swirl around her become human faces.

She's back at the palace, but a very different palace than the one she left. Now it's crammed with frightened refugees and their animals. The library is roofless, its facade sooty and cracked from fire. Timandra tells her the men are at battle, and that the women have been asked to remain within the safety of the palace walls. But Kat can see that this order doesn't sit well with her. Good. She can use Timandra's help.

What she's most surprised by, though, is the dark beauty who steps forward from Arrhidaeus's side. Sarina, his young maid. "Let me join you," she says.

Kat tosses on her cot, sweat clinging to her forehead and back. She blinks, then falls again, back into the delirium, the morning light creeping through the flaps of the tent becoming flashes of silver.

No, it's the river behind the palace of Pella, winking at her, gleaming like liquid gold in the rising sun. Her hands are raised and she is calling, calling with all her might. But not birds. The old amphorae from the storage room are spread out across the field, their wide mouths yawning open. White-faced guards and wide-eyed handmaidens step back as hundreds of creatures crawl and slither forward, an incoming tide of snakes and scorpions, and obediently enter the dark cocoon of the amphorae.

A slicing pain makes the world go black.

But in that darkness, arms wrap around her. She gazes into the face...of Hephaestion. Stern. Angry. Relieved. He kisses her, tenderly, lightly, as though she might turn to dust upon touch. And now her whole body feels like it's filled with glowing, pulsating light and all pain vanishes and she shivers with relief and pleasure and joy. And it's no longer Heph's face above hers, hovering in the light, but Jacob's. She has never felt so loved. She doesn't mind now, doesn't mind sinking into darkness...as long as the love stays with her.

Kat sits up with a start. She's on a narrow camp bed in a tent. It's morning, she can tell: the front flaps are pinned up and the good smell of campfires tickles her nose. Outside she hears the crunch of boots and the low rumble of men's voices.

Sitting in a little chair next to her is Ariadne, her head lolling and mouth open, a comical sight. Kat laughs and Ariadne sits up, eyes wide.

"My lady!" she cries. "How do you feel?"

Kat isn't sure how she feels and struggles to remember what happened. Did Jacob really kiss her? No, he was on the enemy side. He couldn't have come to her. Wouldn't have. It must have been a dream.

Or...could it have been Hephaestion?

The wound—she has to see the wound that gushed so much blood she knew she was going to die. She pulls her tunic up—the handmaidens must have put a clean one on her—and sees only the faintest bruise where the spear ripped open the left side of her abdomen. She has the strangest feeling that the kiss—whoever it came from—healed her.

"Are you hungry, my lady?" Ariadne asks.

Kat realizes then that she's ravenous. "Yes," she says. "Starved."

Ariadne nods in approval. "I'll see what I can rustle up from the latest provisions."

She ducks under the tent flaps just as Heph comes in. His face lights up when he sees Kat sitting up in bed. He has round purple-blue bruises around his neck like an amethyst-studded torque, a bandage on his right arm, and a large gray bruise covering the middle of his forehead. There's a long scratch on his cheek, smeared with an oily healing salve. But otherwise he's bursting with health.

She can't help but think again of the dream kiss.

"Kat!" He crosses the space in two long strides and sits down on the edge of the cot. Then he picks up her hand and holds it in his. "Last night I thought I... I thought *we* had lost you."

"Well," she says, "looks like you're not going to get rid of me that easily." She takes her hand back, needing to say something else fast. "I remember… Jacob standing over me with a sword. Was that a dream, Heph, or did that really happen?"

"It happened," he says, and she knows—she knows from his tone of voice. Jacob tried to kill her.

But no. Jacob wouldn't. Jacob *couldn't*.

Of course, he is an enemy of Macedon now. He's fighting for the other side.

And yet, the idea shakes through her like a poison, making her feel suddenly weak and dizzy. She refuses to believe it.

There's a commotion outside, and Heph's eyes go alert. "I must step out. But I will check on you later."

Then Alexander himself enters, passing Heph on his way out with no eye contact, and kneels beside her. He puts his hand to her forehead and pulls it back in surprise.

"You're…you're…"

"Better." Kat smiles.

Alex shakes his head in wonder. "You turned the battle for us," he says. "Without those amphorae, without the hellion, we would have lost. Where have you been since you escaped the dungeon? How did you do that?"

"I was in Caria," she says, "where I learned many things."

She stares at Alex. Brother. Twin. She knows the secret, and he doesn't. What will he say when she tells him?

A man's bloodcurdling scream rends the air.

"We've set up the doctor's tent nearby," Alex says, a wave of sadness passing over his face. "That's probably an amputation. Many have lost arms or legs. Three suffered sword slashes across both eyes and are blind. Anyway, I've promised them I will personally ensure pensions adequate to support their families."

"Are there many dead?" she asks.

"More than eighty." He lets out a long, slow breath. "Can you stand? I would like to show you something."

She nods, pushes away the blanket, and stands a bit unsteadily. Alex is at her side in a moment and takes her arm.

Outside she sees that a small tent city has sprung up overnight. Steam rises from cauldrons as some soldiers stir bandages with wooden paddles while others make stew. Kat sees a guard taking loaves of bread from a portable army oven and her stomach rumbles in envy.

Several men load carts with broken spears and arrows, unstrung bows, cracked swords, and helmets and dented breastplates to be taken back to Pella and repaired.

Beyond them, on the side of the battlefield is a high pile of dead men and horses in their armor, the horses' legs sticking up stiff and straight. Soldiers are dousing them with pitchers of oil and libations of wine for their thirsty souls. The pyre will be set alight at sunset with the entire Macedonian army encircling it, singing hymns. In the morning they will heap earth over it, creating a new hill, an eternal memorial of the battle.

Kat notices Aesarians picking up the stiff bodies of dead comrades on the back of shields and walking to the other end of the field where they are building their own pyre.

Jacob. Is one of those men retrieving the dead Jacob? She resists the urge to race over the battlefield calling his name. Could he really have betrayed her? Could he have tried to kill her?

In that moment she knows that he might as well be dead. They are forever on different sides.

Four men hold down a horse whinnying in protest while a doctor treats an arrow wound on its flank. Kat makes a mental note to go back to it—and all the wounded horses—as soon as she can.

"You can tend to him in a moment," Alex says, one eyebrow raised. "Look over there."

A cart dragging a dead horse by its legs pulls slowly away,

revealing what Alex wants her to see. It's a tree trunk with a branch on either side like wide shoulders, sunk deep into the ground. On its crown sits a helmet with bronze horns. Bound around its middle is a black leather cape over a silver breastplate and leather pants, on each of its branches several Aesarian shields hanging by leather arm straps. At its feet is a pile of enemy swords, spears, arrows, helmets, and five black Aesarian battle standards, ripped and stained with blood.

The battle trophy.

She's heard of them, of course, read about them in Homer, and listened around winter braziers in Erissa to old veterans' tales of war. But she's never seen one.

She approaches it cautiously, as if it's something sacred. And in a way it is. It's Alex's first trophy.

"Victory," she says, savoring the sound of the word.

"A victorious *battle*," Alex corrects her. "We're still going to be fighting the war. When the Lords return they will have thousands of men, not hundreds, and we will need to have as many if not more. I've sent news of the battle to Philip, requesting he send home more men to protect Macedon. I've also requested men from military forts throughout Macedon and the allied territories."

He runs a hand through his hair. "With Philip and his army gone, and the Lords' attack, I fear that other enemies and even so-called allies will seize this opportunity to invade. Thrace is always on the brink of rebellion. Athens speaks out of both sides of her mouth. Persia would love nothing more than to conquer Macedon."

Two scraggly-necked vultures with bald red heads alight on the Macedonian pyre as the men pouring oil wave their arms and yell, causing them to take flight again.

"Our immediate concern," Alex continues, "is a device the Lords have created that breathes fire like a dragon and can incinerate city gates. Macedonian merchants have reported seeing it being tested on the island of Sfacteria and loaded onto a ship headed here. We will have troops dressed as sailors and dock workers looking for it. We have to intercept it. We have a long way to go, Kat."

Now. She has to tell him now. "Alex, there's something you must know. Especially if we might all die soon."

He gives her a quizzical look.

"When I was in Caria, I learned about natural abilities I've had since birth. Abilities to understand animals, for one thing. I learned how to strengthen that understanding...and not just of animals, but of...of people. And there's more. I also learned that you...that you are..." She can hardly say the word, her heart is fluttering so fast.

"Alex," she says, throwing her shoulders back and lifting her chin, "you are my brother. You are my *twin*."

"What?" His eyes grow wide and he just stares dumbly at her for what seems like an eternity. When he speaks again it's as though he has forgotten his own voice. It comes out as a whisper: "Is it true?"

She nods. "You and I have a destiny to fulfill. I don't know what it is yet, only that we must do it together. Your mother— our mother—" how she hates using that word to describe Olympias "—wanted me killed. It was because of me that your leg is injured..." She gestures and he grimaces. "Because of the birth. She wanted to punish me." She doesn't mention the ritual of blood and bones yet. She won't, until she understands more.

"But how did you survive?" he asks in a low voice.

"Helen, your mother's lady-in-waiting, promised Olympias to kill me in the country, where she might avoid the wrath of the Furies, and bring her my bones as proof. But Helen hid with me in Erissa instead, raised me as her own, and told me she was my mother. And then, one day when I was six, your mother found us and came with guards to our cottage." Here, Kat can feel her voice shake, but she plunges on. "She called Helen a thief. All this time, I had no idea what she'd stolen. I thought it must be an object of great value. I had no idea what she'd stolen was…*me*." She takes a deep breath. "Helen gave Olympias a box of baby's bones but they killed her anyway. I was hiding in the wool box and saw it."

A low moan escapes Alex. "I am sorry, Katerina."

"I believe she has finally figured out that the bones weren't mine," she says, "and will be looking for her real daughter. When she finds me, she will kill me."

He stares deeply into her eyes in his probing way, and she wonders if he, too, shares her powers, or some version of them. They have so much yet to learn about each other, and about themselves.

For a long time, he says nothing. "You and I have many enemies between us," he says at last. "I guess we'd better not die anytime soon. It would be a great waste of a legacy."

"I couldn't agree more," she replies as she looks into his eyes—so different from her own, and yet, she realizes, so similar. She puts her hand in his. "The war has only just begun."

★ ★ ★ ★ ★

ACKNOWLEDGMENTS

THOUGH MOST BOOKS BEAR THE NAME OF ONE individual on the cover, I have always found them to be a team effort, particularly this one. It's no easy feat shifting from hammering out adult historical nonfiction to writing a young adult novel.

In my previous books, I dug up fascinating facts and strung them together in an amusing way. It was really very easy, sort of like knitting. In this novel, I had to craft an entire vibrant world, with sights, sounds, and smells, as historically accurate as possible despite the fantasy elements, and show that world from the perspectives of seven very different individuals, six of them teens. I had to create realistic dialogue and keep up a brisk pace.

The most cunningly crafted novels are an easy read, which can lead to the mistaken belief that very little skill is required. Now I know that writing a good novel is like an ice skater doing a triple axel. Spectators take it for granted because it looks so graceful and easy. They don't see all the work that went on before the performance, including the countless times the skater fell hard on her butt.

To my teachers at Paper Lantern Lit, Lexa Hillyer and Kamilla Benko, thank you so much for having faith in me that I would be able to get this right. Thank you for your advice and encouragement and the laughter we shared, much of it in the margins of Track Changes. In today's highly competitive literary world, many agents and editors no longer take the time to develop talent. You have taught me so much about this exciting new field, and I will be eternally grateful.

My gratitude goes to Alexa Wejko, Paper Lantern's star editorial intern, who has put in countless hours of behind-the-scenes work in supporting the development of this project. And thanks to Tara Sonin, Paper Lantern's marketing associate, for all her effort, including coaching me in social media.

Kudos to Stephen Barbara for making the deal with Harlequin TEEN and his continued support over the past year. And many thanks to Jessica Regel of Foundry Literary and Media, who has sold—and is continuing to sell—foreign rights.

At Harlequin TEEN, my thanks go to Natashya Wilson, executive editor, and to Amy Jones, Mary Sheldon, and all the incredible marketing, publicity, and design people who are working so hard to make *Legacy of Kings* a success.

I also want to thank my fabulous cousin, Emily Heddleson, who never outgrew YA literature, adores working in the industry and shoved me hard in this direction. When she was a tiny little thing living three thousand miles away from me, I wrote her stories of mermaids and princesses and magical forest spirits. Perhaps these stories sowed the first seeds of her love of YA fiction. If so, she has amply repaid me by connecting me with her friend, Lauren Oliver, co-founder of Paper Lantern Lit. Thank you, Lauren, for pushing Lexa to contact me and for your work on the manuscript.

Last but certainly not least, I want to thank my husband, Michael Dyment, for putting up with an eccentric wife who has her head stuck firmly in the past and four fat cats glued to her desk.

READER'S GUIDE

AUTHOR'S NOTE

THE EXPLOITS OF ALEXANDER THE GREAT DAZ-
zled the ancient world. He was the most successful military
leader of all time, achieving his first victory at the age of sixteen. His empire stretched from the Balkans to India, and
included modern-day Turkey, Egypt, the Levant, Iran, Iraq,
Afghanistan, and Pakistan—some two million square miles of
territory, throughout which he founded twenty cities named
after himself, including Alexandria, Egypt.

Alexander's conquests greatly expanded trade and cultural
diffusion between East and West. Greeks, who had been some-
what isolated on their rocky islands and in their fortified cities,
suddenly belonged to a much larger, far more exciting world.
Luxury items such as spices and silk—which had been as rare
and costly as jewels—flooded Greek marketplaces at more
reasonable prices. New foods, such as peaches from China,
were introduced throughout the Greek world while Indian
statues of Buddha took on an uncanny resemblance to the
Greek god Apollo.

Alexander was known for his daring battlefield tactics—

which are still taught at military academies today—his utter fearlessness in combat, and, unusual for his time, his generosity to vanquished enemies rather than the wholesale slaughter and enslavement most other victorious generals would have imposed on a defeated enemy. Today we might question what *right* Alexander had to march into other people's countries, wage war, and cause suffering before things settled down under his humane and prosperous rule, but no one in the ancient world would have. War was what kings *did*.

Though this is a work of fantasy with some fictional main characters—Katerina, Jacob, and Zofia—I wanted to make their world of 340 BC as historically accurate as possible. I carefully researched the clothing, weapons, and food, the heating (braziers, not fireplaces), horse accoutrements (stirrups and horseshoes weren't invented until a thousand years later), bathing (scented oils, no soap or shampoo), and lighting (oil lamps, not candles). Lighting is my particular pet peeve with historical fiction set in eras before the invention of electricity. A character can't just wake up in a dark room at night and get involved in some action without a mention of how he lit his way. Nor would people leave lights untended—they could catch the house on fire, which could catch an entire city ablaze in a time when the fire brigade consisted of people throwing buckets of water on a raging inferno. Getting light in a dark place was always a bit of an issue back then, and it's important to show that in fiction to get a correct sense of the period.

While Alexander's half sister, Cynane, might feel too modern, she really did model herself on the Amazons and was known for her military prowess. True, most upper-class Greek women stayed in the house and worked with wool, but Illyria, home of Cynane's mother, Audata, was famous for its physically fit women who ran, wrestled, and practiced archery on horseback. Macedon's northern neighbor, Thrace, was known for its warrior women, as were the Scythian lands north of the Black Sea where Greeks had founded numerous trading colonies and brought back tales of sexy, wild Amazons. In fact, archeologists now know that some 25 percent of the "warrior kings" found decades ago in Ukrainian burial mounds—with skulls cleaved in by battle-axes, arrows lodged in ribs, and surrounded by weapons and sacrificed war horses—were, in fact, women.

The people of the ancient world saw everything around them with the potential for intelligent life and the ability to bestow blessings or ooze malevolence. A tree, a spring, a sword, or shrine could infuse the owner or passerby with spiritual power and good luck, or madness and death. Birds and animals could be gods or magical people in a shape-shifting disguise. The ancients used curses, amulets, and spells to protect themselves from the bad and try to harness the good. Ancient magical recipe books have come down to us, and I have used some of their spells in this novel.

The Greeks of Alexander's time believed that hundreds of years earlier—before and during the Trojan War—Zeus and Hera, Apollo and Aphrodite swooped down frequently from Mount Olympus to meddle in human affairs, marching across battlefields to assist their favorite warriors and taking human lovers. But by the fourth century BC, though Greeks still worshipped the gods in gorgeous temples, no one had seen them in a long time. Where had they gone? Had they fallen asleep? Could even immortals die? Or had they simply lost interest in the exasperating human race? Over the course of the next three novels in this series, I will offer a possible explanation of what happened to the vanished Greek gods.

Ancient warfare abounded with subterfuge and deception. Soldiers entered the open gates of an enemy city dressed as merchants or women. Armies staged their battle camps to make their forces look smaller—or larger—than they actually were. Troops deserted their camps to stage an ambush but left bonfires burning brightly and wandering oxen with burning straw on their horns. They set up dummy soldiers on sticks, hid fresh troops behind hills and released vicious wild animals at the crucial moment of a conflict. The stratagems in the battle between Alexander's men and the Aesarian Lords are taken from reports of real ancient battles.

Even Katerina's snake-and-scorpion bombs were used in antiquity as a kind of early biological warfare which gave new meaning to the term "live ammunition." The great Carthaginian general Hannibal in about 190 BC lobbed amphorae filled with venomous snakes onto the ships of King Eumenes of Pergamum, sending the soldiers on board the king's superior fleet diving into the water. And in the late second century AD when the Roman emperor Septimius Severus besieged a desert fortress, his army was met with a hailstorm of clay pots brimful of fatally poisonous creatures—probably scorpions. The emperor called off the siege.

Macedon was a hardy, rugged country, borrowing a healthy slathering of sophistication from its more civilized Greek neighbors to the south. But the most sleekly refined country of all was a multicultural amalgamation of nations called the Persian Empire. Justifiably proud of their vibrant economy, advanced science, lofty art, victorious armies, complex political systems, and sixteen-hundred-mile-long Royal Road (the model of the US postal system), Persian subjects sneered at the gruff, ill-smelling Greeks from countless tiny, quarrelsome nations. Persians were particularly struck by the fact that Greeks refused to wear pants when riding or in the cold, thereby risking blisters and frostbite, clear proof of Greek stupidity.

Greeks, on the other hand, looked with jaundiced eyes at the silken, perfumed Empire where, they believed, effeminate bejeweled men lolled about in a haze of perfumed decadence, their legs encased in strange cloth tubes. In tracing Princess Zofia's journey from palace to slave cart to traveling on the Royal Road, I hope I have evoked the gulf of cultural differences between the Greek mainland and the Persian Empire, a gulf that would become a jarring culture clash when Alexander conquered Persia.

Alexander's exploits of conquest, begun when he became king of Macedon at the age of twenty, were well documented both during his life and after his death, but stories of his youth were not, other than the popular tale of how he tamed his horse, Bucephalus. The teen years are the time when we figure out who we are and who we are going to be, or at least who we want to be. One thing that binds all humans together as teens and former teens is that we have issues with our family members, except for a lucky minority of people, and they are lying. It's safe to say, though, that Alexander had more challenges than most of us. His father, the king, was distant and harsh; his manipulative, ambitious mother was devoted to her snakes and widely regarded as a witch; his older half sister, Cynane, was a jealous, competitive Amazon; his younger half brother, Arrhideus, was mentally handicapped; and his tutor, Leonidas, employed educational methods that would today land him in jail for child abuse.

We can only imagine Alexander at sixteen, surrounded by irritating family members, smarter than everyone around him but still young enough to be ignored. He must have been like a magnificent thoroughbred colt pacing its pen in frustration, yearning to gallop headlong into the wind if only someone would unlatch the gate.

Knowing what Alexander did later in life, we can extrapolate backward into a time of dark forces, magic, mythical creatures, and bloody battles peppered with trickery. We can imagine Alexander and Hephaestion, Jacob and Katerina, Cynane and Zofia jockeying to forge a path in life, to right old wrongs and find love in a world trembling on the cusp of great change.

Because when Alexander breaks out of his pen, it will never be the same.

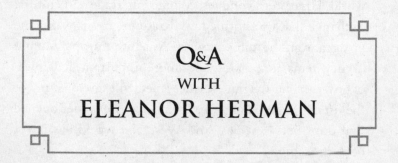

Q&A
WITH
ELEANOR HERMAN

Q) What five words would you use to describe *Legacy of Kings*?

A) Magical
Mysterious
Gripping
Sophisticated
Unputdownable

Q) What inspires you to write?

A) Life to me is a series of stories: my life, your life, the lives of everyone who has ever lived. These stories—these *lives*—overflow with beauty, tragedy, and courage, and teach us lessons about how to live. How to love. Stories give meaning to life, and without them, life would just be a series of random, meaningless events. The fact that I get to write other people's stories thrills and amazes me.

Q) You are a historian with a background in many eras. What drew you to the story of Alexander the Great?

A) Alexander was the pivotal male character of the ancient world. His eastern conquests opened up trade and cultural exchange that transformed civilizations. In his wake, the great caravans heading between Asia into Europe brought luxury items, new foods, and, more important, new ideas of government, religion, science, medicine, architecture— the list could go on and on. Ever since Alexander opened that door between East and West, the world has never been the same.

With regards to his character, Alexander was known for unflinching courage, strategic brilliance, and overpowering charisma. In some ways, he was very modern. For instance, he showed extraordinary kindness to enemies who fought fairly and showed bravery, something practically unknown at the time when slaughter and enslavement ruled the day. He promoted diversity in his army, welcoming troops of non-Greek soldiers and often adopting their weapons, tactics, and clothing, which caused much grumbling among the Greeks.

Like many of us, Alexander had a troubled home life. His mother was considered a witch. His father was gruff and often away. His sister wanted to be an Amazon, and his brother was mentally handicapped. Until his father's death, he had no power, and because he was a teenager King Philip and the council didn't listen to him. It's fascinating to picture what he was like at sixteen, with all his problems, on the cusp of becoming the man who would change the world forever.

Q) Is the magic in the world of *Legacy of Kings* drawn from the beliefs that people had in 340 BC?

A) Yes, to a large extent. It was a world where everything, even streams and trees, was, quite possibly, alive with some sprite or god or ghost that might agree—for a price—to do what you want. I've studied religions and beliefs of the ancient world for many years, have visited the great temples and oracles and spent time in African villages where these beliefs still reign. It's a beautiful, magical, multi-faceted world, if just a little scary. The spells, rituals, and curses in the book are taken from actual ones I found in books on ancient magic.

Q) You've written several nonfiction books for adult readers. What made you decide to write a YA novel?

A) There's a reason that YA novels are the hottest thing in publishing. Compared to adult fiction, they are often faster, edgier, more compelling. I love that so many of them cross over to older readers. Because no matter how old we are, we all want to know *who* we are, how our relationships with our parents shaped us, if our friends really care about us, and where we belong in the world. When you're older you might think you know all the answers, and you sure do a better job pretending to, but psychologically the teenage part of us is always there. The best YA fiction slices through our pretenses like a relentless knife and challenges us to face important, sometimes uncomfortable questions. Every book we read should help us learn something about ourselves—our pain, our anger, our kindness, our love and fear and loneliness. When we finish every story, we should always be a little bit smarter, deeper, and emotionally richer than when we began.

Q) Tell us a little more about yourself. Where did you grow up? What kinds of books did you read as a teen?

A) Growing up in Baltimore, Maryland, I was known as "Book-a-Day Eleanor" because I wrecked my eyes reading a book a day during summer vacation. When my mother sent me to bed, I read with a flashlight under my sheets so she wouldn't see the light. She would come in and check on me and take the flashlight away, scolding me to get some sleep. Then I would slip the book into my pajamas and go to the bathroom, which I would lock, pretending I was constipated so I could keep reading. She would bang on the door and warn me the toilet rim would make indelible marks on the backs of my thighs if I stayed there too long. She was right. I still have those marks.

We didn't have the amazing teen fiction we do now. If I were a teen now, I probably would have been "Two-Books-a-Day Eleanor," I would be totally rather than partially blind, and the marks on my thighs would be much worse. But I loved *Jane Eyre, Wuthering Heights,* the novels of Jules Verne, and novels and biographies of Henry VIII's six wives and other royal women. I always asked myself—and still do—if I had lived in another time, when human nature was the same but so much else was different, who would I have been? What would I have believed? What kind of life would I have had?

Q) What is your research process like?

A) I do two kinds of research. One is quite orderly and well planned. I read everything I can find about different aspects of life in the ancient world: magic, religion, travel, warfare, medicine, warrior women, etc. Many writings of the ancients have come down to us, and I have read them all. I also read books by modern scholars about the latest historical interpretations and excavations.

The other kind of research is spastic, totally unplanned, and distracting, though a great deal of fun. For instance, let's say I am writing a scene where a character carries a shield. What did ancient shields look like? What were they made of? I start to Google, moving from site to site, printing out pictures, and getting really sidetracked from my writing. But by the time I'm done, I know all about shields and have a big file on them printed out. And then I have to remember where I was with my writing.

QUESTIONS
FOR
DISCUSSION

1. Many of the villains in *Legacy of Kings* have complex reasons for their actions. How did finding out about Olympias's traumatic past, for instance, help you understand her character?

2. Both Kat and Alex have a gift for understanding other people or animals on a deep level within moments of seeing them. How does this ability make them the powerful characters that they are? Defend your answer with specific scenes from the book.

3. What did you know about Alexander the Great before reading *Legacy of Kings*? How has your view of him changed? In what ways do you see Alex becoming Alexander the Great? Which decisions and events are shaping him to become one of history's most powerful leaders?

4. Do you agree with Kat's overwhelming need to avenge

her mother's death, even at the possible cost of her relationships with Alex and Jacob? Why or why not?

5. Alex and Heph are friends, but their relationship is unbalanced in terms of power. Do you think Alex and Heph really care for each other, or is their friendship just mutually beneficial? Are there specific scenes in which Alex and Heph truly connect with each other?

6. After winning the tournament, Jacob decides to join the Aesarian Lords, and stays on with them even after finding out that they are plotting to invade Pella. What makes the Aesarian Lords appealing to someone like Jacob? Do you agree with his decision?

7. One of the major themes in *Legacy of Kings* has to do with sibling dynamics, both good and bad. How do you see this theme explored in the relationships between Kat and Alex, Zofia and Roxana, or even Alex and Cyn?

8. Many of the female characters in *Legacy of Kings* hold great power despite being restricted by gender roles. How do characters like Kat, Cyn, and Zofia influence people without overstepping certain boundaries? What about secondary characters like Daphne or Kat's mother? Cite specific examples from the text.

9. Magic exists in the world of *Legacy of Kings*, but not always in an obvious way. How does Eleanor Herman integrate magical themes into a largely historical/realistic novel? What parts of the text inform your analysis?

10. Zofia escapes a regimented but comfortable life to be with Cosmas. What are the consequences of her decision, and how do they change her outlook on the world?

BLOOD. ROYALTY.
FORBIDDEN LOVE. DANGER.

Turn the page to read an excerpt from

EMPIRE OF DUST

the second book in the

BLOOD OF GODS AND ROYALS

series by *New York Times* bestselling author

ELEANOR HERMAN

Only from Harlequin TEEN!

Katerina clings tightly to the brown mare as she races across the wide fields behind the palace walls. She has never ridden like this before, as if she is astride a lightning bolt. Back in Erissa, before she knew she was a princess stolen at birth—back when she was an innocent child—she and Jacob used to play around on the family donkey. But that was a far cry from sleek Kokkymo, who tears through the grass with the speed of a lion and the grace of a doe. Despite her lack of formal riding training, it's as if Kat has become one with the horse, an unstoppable force of nature in perfect harmony with air and sky, earth and water.

A part of Kat's mind slides beneath the tickling mane and smooth, sweat-slick hide, and she inhales the smells of green summer grass and the rich earth of the riverbanks. Soon, it is Kat herself who switches her tail and gallops ahead, stretching her four long legs and pounding the ground hard. If only she could keep going, never return to the palace with its confusing dark-haired boys, its baffling mysteries and all its dangers.

She wants to eat sweet grass and drink cool river water and smell a thousand subtle scents on the wind.

She's always known she has a way with animals, that she can communicate with them in a manner that others cannot. It was a gift that Helen—the woman she thought was her mother—warned her to keep hidden. But she assumed her ability to understand animals came from the fact that she paid attention to them, that she took the time to listen to them while most humans didn't.

Then she met the great sorceress Ada of Caria and everything changed.

Ada told her of the magic flowing in her veins—Snake Blood, one of the two ancient Blood Magics—and trained her to use her abilities. Kat learned to fall into trances, experiencing what it was like to be a bird soaring through the air, a worm pushing through moist earth and a fish darting through cold, deep water. But Snake Blood, she learned, is far more than just a connection with the minds of animals—it is a connection to the power of human thought, too.

In her last trance at Ada's palace, Kat sank into forgotten memories of her own life, all the way back to her birth. These lost memories are what led her to realize that she is Prince Alexander's sister, and that Queen Olympias, the coldhearted murderess, is her real mother. Kat can't shake the details of that memory from her mind.

Kill the girl, Olympias had said as she held her newborn twins, thrusting baby Kat toward her handmaiden, Helen. But Helen didn't kill the baby. She started a new life in a little village called Erissa and raised Kat as her own.

Suddenly, the horse stumbles, and Kat's mind is jolted from the horse's body as she flies through the air and lands hard on her side. She's aware of dirt in her mouth and the gilded sword Ada gave her pressing into her leg. When she finally catches her breath, she stands up shakily and sees her mount galloping away, truly free now, whinnying in delight.

She rubs her arm and notices something glint in the grass: her Flower of Life pendant, a silver lotus blossom on a leather thong she always wears around her neck.

Kat picks it up and holds it to her heart. This belonged to Helen, whom Kat will always consider her real mother. She ties the thong behind her neck and feels the cool slippery metal just below the base of her throat. She remembers Helen's smile, her beauty, the sweet scent of her skin as if it were yesterday she last saw her. But it has been ten years since Kat, hiding in the wool box, witnessed Olympias ordering her soldiers to kill Helen.

Kat never told anyone who killed her mother, not even Jacob's family, who took her in and promised to care for her until she was of age to marry. But vengeance has long since become the blood that pumps through her heart and the air that fills her lungs. It was the reason she came to Pella with Jacob, hoping for an opportunity to get near the queen. It was also the obstacle to marrying Jacob—a quest she had to accomplish before her heart would be free to love.

But now she knows that her sworn enemy is in fact her real mother, that she had, unknowingly, plotted for years to kill the very woman who gave her life. *And* that for some unknown reason, Olympias wants her dead. In the beat of a dragonfly's wings, Kat has gone from predator to prey.

Kat looks for Kokkymo—it's unlike the mare to startle, and now she is nowhere in sight. Stiffly, Kat begins her walk home. The tall grass waves eerily, and a scent she can't name causes her to shiver. The sky has taken on a sickening gray-green color.

A surge of foreboding sweeps through her chest with the suddenness of a spear thrust, knocking the breath out of her.

Something terrible, she knows, has happened.

There's movement in the trees ahead. The strange sorrow that beats in her heart has turned Kat's legs to lead.

The pebbles on the ground jump, and she hears a strange buzz in the air.

A herd of gazelles breaks from the forest, all of them kicking up their hind legs in panic.

Stampede.

They race toward her like a surging tide, and Kat can do nothing to outpace them. Instead she stands, bracing for the impact of fur against her flesh. But it never comes. They veer slightly away from her at the last moment and wash around her, spraying her with clods of dirt.

She sucks in a sharp breath as one of the gazelles skids to a stop directly in front of her, its flanks heaving, its straight black horns trembling.

What? she asks silently, feeling the animal's terror so keenly that now she is trembling, too. *What has happened?*

She stares into the gazelle's dark liquid eyes…and then she sees it.

A house in flames. Smoke. Murder. Screams. She sees bodies in the courtyard.

It's Sotiria, lying next to the well, her dark hair streaming into a widening puddle of blood. Jacob's mother. For many years, practically Kat's own.

She can't breathe. In the gazelle's eyes she sees Cleon, too, next to the gate, an ax head in his broad back.

Jacob's younger brothers, broken and lifeless, lie in the dirt.

And in front of the flames is a flash of white-gold against burning red. Silvery hair. A slender, petite figure: Olympias.

Kat's knees buckle and she sinks slowly into the grass.

So that is where the queen has been these past few days:

looking for Kat. And when she couldn't find her, she killed the closest thing Kat has to a family—Jacob's.

Her chest seizes and she can't breathe.

This is all her fault.

If Jacob's parents hadn't taken her in, raised her as their own, the queen would have had no reason to hurt them.

The children...

She clutches at thick tufts of grass with her hands, holding on because around her the world is reeling. Just like that day when she was six and the queen's men murdered her mother and then came looking for her. She climbed out the upstairs window and clung mutely to the thatched roof.

Kat's lungs don't seem to be working, and golden spots dance in the blackness forming around her. Maybe she will pass out, die here, even, in the sweet summer grass... She gasps and air floods her chest.

More hooves race toward her, but she doesn't look up, not until she feels strong hands on her back. "Are you all right?" She hears Heph's voice, and then she's aware that he's knelt down beside her and is holding her hands. "Were you thrown? I was looking for you. The stable hand said..."

She stares at him, speechless, unblinking, barely understanding the words tumbling from his lips.

"Here, stand up so I can see you," Heph says, pulling her up. He brushes dirt off her head, rubs both thumbs over her cheeks and looks at her ripped tunic. "What is it?" he asks urgently. "For godsakes, Katerina, what has happened?"

Kat tilts her head back and closes her eyes. The sun feels warm on her face, the same sun that Cleon, Sotiria and the children will never feel again. "They're all dead." The words slide out more like an animal howl of pain than a sentence.

"Who?" Heph asks, taking her by the shoulders, gently rubbing the top of her arms. "Who is dead?"

"My family. Jacob's parents and his little brothers. The people who raised me." Kat grabs her stomach, rocking herself back and forth, wishing they were Sotiria's arms rocking her back and forth, comforting her after she'd skinned a knee or missed Helen too much to sleep. "Olympias killed them all. She couldn't find me, so she killed them."

Heph looks around the field in puzzlement. "Did a messenger just come—"

Kat inhales sharply and rubs her eyes. "The gazelles saw it," she says simply.

Heph frowns, but understanding quickly comes to his eyes. Kat can almost see him come to accept again, as he had in battle, that she is something more than just an average potter's daughter.

"After what I saw on the battlefield, Kat, I would believe anything you say."

At the kind words, Kat begins to cry, her body shuddering. "I know she wants me dead—has always wanted me dead since the moment I was born," she says between aching sobs. "I just don't…know…why."

Heph's arms tighten around her, and she leans against his hard chest. "Because of reasons known only to the queen and the gods," Heph murmurs into her hair. He gives her another squeeze, and Kat stays there, tucked against him.

How can she live with herself, knowing she shares the blood of that evil woman? She wants to take a knife and drain every drop of Olympias's blood from inside her. She sees again the pitiful bodies of the children. She hears the queen's cruel laughter and smells the acrid smoke. She needs to cry until she empties herself completely, until there is nothing left except a shell made of cold, hard revenge.

Another sob tears through her body. Her thirst for vengeance—did she inherit that, too, from the queen, along with her green eyes?

She aches for Jacob. For the sight of his wide grin, his broad, friendly face. For his goodness and undying belief in her. Jacob was always there for her when she was sad or lonely. He didn't even need to say a word, just put a strong arm around her. But Jacob is lost forever now—an Aesarian Lord. Her brother's enemy.

And, if she believes Heph's report from the battle, her own enemy now, too. Heph claims Jacob tried to kill her, but Kat doesn't believe it. Can't believe it. He doesn't even *know* that the prince is Katerina's brother. There's so much Jacob doesn't know. But he can't hate her. If he did, she wouldn't be able to live with herself.

Heph holds her tightly, and she feels his beating heart against her back, his chin stubble rubbing slightly against her cheek, and for a moment she pretends he's Jacob. She inhales deeply and smells an expensive citrus cologne, a tunic fresh from the palace laundry, and a whiff of horse and leather. Jacob smelled like wood smoke and clay dust.

It's Hephaestion she's clinging to now—the impolite, vain boy she disliked at first sight when he tried to have her arrested for cheating on bets at the Blood Tournament. The brave, clever boy who got her out of the deepest, foulest dungeon in the palace when she had been imprisoned on false charges.

The boy whose kiss may have saved her life on the battlefield.

Or was the kiss only a dream, and her miraculous recovery just an effect of Snake Blood? For a moment, the face hovering above hers seemed to belong to Jacob, but then it had morphed into Heph, and she passed out. She's been trying to ask Hephaestion about it, but he has been busy after the battle, helping Alex with the refugees and rebuilding the library.

And now, well, it doesn't seem to matter so much anymore if she'd died out there. Maybe none of this would have happened. Maybe Jacob's family would still be alive.

"Kat," Heph says gently. He brushes the hair out of her face. "If Olympias has done what you say, then she must know who you are. And if she finds you here when she returns to the palace, even Alex and I won't be able to keep you safe every moment of the day and night. We must get you out of here. Far away from the queen. She will return."

Kat nods, but she doesn't move from his arms—not yet. Tomorrow, she can plan. Tomorrow, she can be brave. Her tear-stained cheeks are cold as the wind brushes them, its touch as light as a ghost's caress. She shivers and stares out over the swaying grass.

Silently, she says: *Goodbye.*

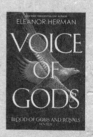

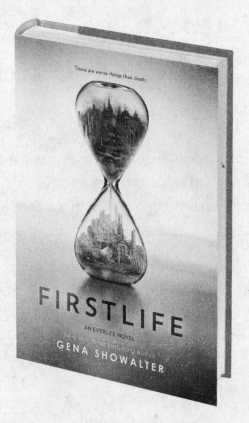

From the limitless imagination of
Julie Kagawa comes the next thrilling
novel in *The Talon Saga*.

THE PRICE OF FREEDOM IS EVERYTHING

 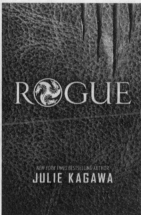 

Read books 1-3 of the epic *Talon Saga!*

Available Now.

Love Harlequin romance?

DISCOVER.

Be the first to find out about promotions, news and exclusive content!

Facebook.com/HarlequinBooks

Twitter.com/HarlequinBooks

Instagram.com/HarlequinBooks

Pinterest.com/HarlequinBooks

YouTube.com/HarlequinBooks

ReaderService.com

EXPLORE.

Sign up for the Harlequin e-newsletter and download a free book from any series at **TryHarlequin.com**

CONNECT.

Join our Harlequin community to share your thoughts and connect with other romance readers!
Facebook.com/groups/HarlequinConnection

♦ HARLEQUIN
SPECIAL EDITION

Believe in love. Overcome obstacles.
Find happiness.

Save **$1.00**

off the purchase of ANY
Harlequin Special Edition book.

Available wherever books are sold,
including most bookstores, supermarkets,
drugstores and discount stores.

Save **$1.00**

off the purchase of ANY Harlequin Special Edition book.

Coupon valid until September 30, 2022.
Redeemable at participating outlets in the U.S. and Canada only. Limit one coupon per customer.

52617195

DPCOUP1021MAX